Praise for Irene Hannon's Novels

Heroes of Quantico Series

"I found someone who writes romantic suspense better than I do."

Dee Henderson on Against All Odds

"Characters that are engrossing, a plot filled with unexpected twists, and a love story that will melt your heart."

RT Book Reviews on An Eye for an Eye

"An ever-climactic mystery . . . engagingly sure-footed."

Publishers Weekly on In Harm's Way

Guardians of Justice Series

"Excellent character development and intriguing suspense."

Relz Reviewz on Fatal Judgment

"Compelling characters and an emotionally engaging plot powered by a surfeit of nail-biting suspense."

Booklist on Deadly Pursuit

"If you're looking for a keeper, this is it!'"

Suspense Magazine on Lethal Legacy

Private Justice Series

"A riveting storyline . . . one of those addictive books that, once started, compels you to shut out the world till you reach the very last page."

New York Journal of Books on Vanished

"The queen of inspirational romantic suspense hits a home run."

Library Journal on Trapped

"An intriguing thrill ride from start to finish."

RT Book Reviews on Deceived

BURIED SECRETS

Books by Irene Hannon

HEROES OF QUANTICO

Against All Odds
An Eye for an Eye
In Harm's Way

GUARDIANS OF JUSTICE

Fatal Judgment
Deadly Pursuit
Lethal Legacy

PRIVATE JUSTICE

Vanished
Trapped
Deceived

MEN OF VALOR

Buried Secrets

That Certain Summer
One Perfect Spring

MEN OF VALOR · 1

BURIED SECRETS

A NOVEL

IRENE HANNON

Revell

a division of Baker Publishing Group
Grand Rapids, Michigan

© 2015 by Irene Hannon

Published by Revell
a division of Baker Publishing Group
P.O. Box 6287, Grand Rapids, MI 49516-6287
www.revellbooks.com

Printed in the United States of America

Library of Congress Cataloging-in-Publication Data is on file at the Library of Congress, Washington, DC.

ISBN 978-0-8007-2126-8

This book is a work of fiction. Names, characters, places, and incidents are the product of the author's imagination or are used fictitiously.

15   16   17   18   19   20   21   7   6   5   4   3   2   1

To Kay Schumert and Martha Roux,
with happy memories of our days at the BPL.
Thank you for the gift of your friendship.
It is one of my treasures.

Prologue

It was meant to be a joyride.

No one was supposed to die.

"She's not breathing!" Erika's shrill, hysteria-laced whisper pierced the humidity-laden air.

Heart pounding, I fisted my hands. "I can see that."

The clammy smell of panic overpowered the scent of fresh-cut hay in the adjacent field as we huddled on our knees over the motionless figure in the ditch.

"What should we do?" Joe's voice cracked on the last word.

They both looked at me like I had the answer. Like I knew how to make this nightmare go away.

I didn't.

Not yet, anyway.

I was still trying to wrap my mind around what had happened. To figure out how my well-planned life could career out of control in the space of a few heartbeats.

The answer eluded me.

But I did know one thing. Any whiff of scandal could deep-six the coveted job I was a breath away from getting after acing the final interview.

I couldn't let that happen.

When I didn't respond, Joe leaned across the crumpled body and grasped my shoulders, his fingers digging into my flesh like talons. "What should we do?"

I shook him off. "I heard you the first time! Give me a minute!"

I straightened up and checked out the rural Missouri road, with its undulating dips that provided high-speed thrills.

Empty.

But headlights could appear at any moment, illuminating us in twin spotlights.

If they did, we were hosed.

My fingers began to prickle.

We had to make a decision.

Fast.

"Should we try CPR?" Joe's voice was shaking now.

I surveyed the broken body. Every twisted angle said it was too late for lifesaving measures, but I pressed my fingers to her carotid artery anyway. Just in case.

Nothing.

"She's dead."

"Oh, God!" Erika began to hyperventilate, her breath coming in ragged, shallow gasps.

I gave her a hard shake. "Stop it! If you keep that up, you're going to pass out!"

"But w-what are we going to do?" Her question came out in a whimpering blubber.

Disgust soured my mouth.

I hate weak women.

If Erika's father hadn't had the kind of connections I needed, I would never have befriended her—and I wouldn't be in the middle of this mess.

Anger began to churn in my gut.

"We need to do *something*. Now!" Joe gave the deserted rural highway a spastic sweep.

"I know that! Shut up and let me think."

I glared down at the contorted figure at my knees. I should never have let Erika invite her tonight. So what if they were roommates? So what if the girl didn't have a lot of friends? So what if she was feeling depressed?

Those were her problems.

Except now she was *my* problem.

Despite the fury nipping at my composure, the left side of my brain began to click into gear. Logic under duress had been my father's strong suit too—on his few good days.

But I wasn't like my old man. There were better things in store for me. I had plans. And nothing—nothing—was going to disrupt them.

Including a dead girl.

I held the keys out to Joe. "Open the trunk."

"What?" He stared at me, the whites of his eyes glimmering in the darkness.

"Just do it."

"But . . . shouldn't we call 911 or something?"

"Yeah, that's a good idea," Erika seconded.

What idiots.

Speaking slowly to give my words a chance to sink into their thick skulls, I explained the problem. "We're all high as kites. Don't think the cops won't notice that." I locked onto Joe. "You were driving. What do you think a charge of vehicular manslaughter would do to your Rhodes Scholarship?"

I let him mull that over while I turned to Erika. "And a squeaky-clean state senator who's built his political career on an antidrug platform might very well disown a daughter who generates bad press that could cost him the U.S. Senate nomination. So much for that grand graduation tour of Europe you had planned for this summer, and your fancy car." On the shoulder above us, the hot engine of the Mercedes convertible was still pinging.

Only the sound of harsh, erratic breathing and the distant wail of a train whistle broke the silence as they digested my rationale.

I gave them ten seconds to think through the ramifications.

Then I held out the keys again.

This time Joe took them.

Since Erika had collapsed into a useless, quivering lump, I waited for Joe to return to deal with the body. "I'll take her arms. You get her feet."

We moved into position.

"On three. One, two, three."

We lifted together. Erika scrabbled backward as the dead girl's head lolled forward.

I paid no attention—to either of them. I was too angry . . . at myself now as much as them.

What had possessed me to go along with their stupid joyriding scheme, anyway? I didn't do foolish and reckless. I didn't do *anything* that could interfere with my plans, with the future I'd mapped out for myself.

Tonight was the biggest mistake of my life.

And I never intended to make another one.

Joe and I hefted the girl into the trunk. The liner would have to be replaced—but we could deal with that tomorrow.

I closed the lid and retrieved a flashlight from the glove compartment. "We need to make sure nothing incriminating is left behind. Help me look around. And hurry."

As I swept the light back and forth in a wide arc over the pavement and ground, they hovered at my shoulders like overzealous prison guards.

Talk about a distasteful image.

I shoved it from my mind.

Three minutes later, once I was confident that mashed-down grass was the only evidence of our unplanned stop, we piled back into Erika's convertible.

This time, I took the wheel.

"Now what?" Joe spoke from the backseat as I pulled onto the pavement, gravel crunching beneath the tires.

I'd been thinking about that, my mind working through various scenarios as we'd silently searched the roadside.

"Yeah. Now what?" Erika cowered into the corner of the seat beside me, her voice small. Scared. Tear-laced.

What a loser.

"If someone finds out . . ." Joe's words trailed off.

I clenched the wheel.

Not going to happen.

Ever.

"No one will. I'm working on a plan."

As the minutes ticked by, a strategy began to coalesce in my brain, the pieces clicking into place one by one.

It wasn't bad.

Not bad at all.

And we were lucky in one regard.

Making the girl in the trunk disappear would be far easier than disposing of anyone else we knew.

"Do you still have that state map in your glove compartment?" I checked the rearview mirror as I directed the question to Erika. The road stretched dark and deserted behind us. Perfect.

"Y-yes." Her response came out in a choked whisper.

"Get it out."

I heard her fumbling with the latch.

"Do you have an idea?" Joe leaned forward and spoke behind my ear.

Of course I did. I always had ideas. I was the only one in

13

this bunch who ever did. Erika was a twit, and while Joe might be smart with numbers, he didn't have one imaginative bone in his body.

"Yeah, I have an idea."

And as the miles rolled by, I laid out my plan.

They listened in silence for the most part, especially when I reemphasized the stakes. None of us wanted to deal with the ramifications of this disaster. On that much, at least, we were in agreement.

When I finished, neither spoke.

I waited them out.

"It might work." This from Joe, though he sounded uncertain.

"It *will* work—as long as we stick together. And there's no going back once we start down this road. Understood?"

Not that we had much choice at this point. We'd already started down the road by moving the body. But I wanted their verbal buy in.

"Yeah. I'm in." Resignation flattened Joe's words.

"Me too . . . I guess." Erika sniffled.

"There's no guessing, Erika." I used my harshest tone. These two needed to get with the program. "We're either all in or it's a no-go—and we face the not-so-pleasant consequences."

"Okay, okay. I'm in."

"Good. You do remember how to get there, don't you?"

"Yeah. I can find it with the m-map. Mom and Dad have dragged me there every year s-since I was a kid."

Like I didn't know that. I'd been listening to her complain about the annual summer command performance since freshman year.

A gust of wind whipped past, and a splatter of rain stung my cheek. For once the weather people had been right. A storm was brewing.

"We need to put up the top." The road in front and behind remained dark and empty, so I pulled to the side. "Don't dawdle."

They didn't—but by the time the three of us got back in the car, my clothes were damp and sticking to me uncomfortably.

Before this night was over, though, they'd be in far worse shape.

Still, if things went according to plan, both the clothes and the incident would soon be history.

And things *would* go according to plan.

I'd make sure of that.

Whatever it took.

Present Day

Mac McGregor had no trouble finding the site, even if St. Louis was new turf for him. You didn't have to be a detective to figure out that a police cruiser, yellow crime scene tape, and a media van marked the spot.

Pulling up beside the squad car, he scanned the construction site for the police chief of the small municipality who'd put in the call to County for assistance.

An officer stood in the distance, talking to a woman and a guy in a hard hat. He seemed on the young side, based on a quick glimpse of his profile, but he was the only uniformed presence on the scene. Since Carson was more village than town, maybe they'd had to take what they could get for the chief job when they'd established the department last year.

Mac set the brake, grabbed the notebook and sport coat in the passenger seat, and slid out from behind the wheel. Once he'd slipped the jacket on, he ducked under the yellow tape and wove through the idle construction equipment.

The trio was facing away from him now, toward a slight

depression in the ground, and he stopped about four feet away. "Chief Grant?"

All three of them turned.

He stuck out his hand toward the officer in the middle. "I'm Chief Grant."

The woman to the man's right spoke, her voice brisk, businesslike—and a touch irritated.

He checked out the nameplate above the guy's left pocket.

Officer Craig Shelton.

Whoops.

So much for making a good first impression.

He shifted his attention to the woman—and gave silent thanks for the sunglasses that hid the slight widening of his eyes.

Chief Grant was drop-dead gorgeous.

But he had a feeling she would *not* appreciate his appreciative perusal.

Too bad his so-called buddy Mitch hadn't warned him she was smoking hot when they'd run into each other earlier in the headquarters parking lot. It was the least SEALs—or ex-SEALs—could do for each other.

"May I help you?" Chief Grant's chilly prompt refocused him.

Clearing his throat, he moved his hand to the left. "Detective Mac McGregor. Your reinforcement from County."

She waited just long enough to make him squirm before she grasped his fingers with a surprisingly strong grip. "Lisa Grant."

"Nice to meet you." He shook hands with the officer too. Like his chief's, the man's eyes were masked by dark glasses. "Sorry about the mistake. I assumed you'd be in uniform."

"Or maybe you assumed I'd be a man." Her tone was conversational, but he heard the steel underneath.

A spurt of irritation spiked his blood pressure—but he tamped it down. No doubt she'd faced her share of bias in a field long dominated by men. And he'd added to it . . . in her mind, anyway.

All at once it felt a lot hotter than it should for a first-week-of-June morning, and the temptation to loosen his tie was strong.

He resisted.

"It's dangerous to make assumptions in this business."

"Yeah." She let a beat pass. "It is."

The air temperature seemed to edge up another degree or two.

Best to get down to business.

"I understand you have some bones that may be human."

"We have some bones that *are* human." She angled toward the ground behind her.

He stepped closer and looked down.

The empty eye sockets of a partially unearthed skull stared back at him.

She was right.

The bones were human.

He straightened up. "You want to brief me?"

"This land is being cleared for home sites. According to Mr. Phillips, the foreman"—she indicated the guy in the hard hat—"one of his crew noticed the skull after he toppled a tree with the excavator. That yellow piece of equipment." She pointed it out. As if he'd never seen an excavator.

He frowned as a second spurt of irritation elevated his blood pressure another notch.

The subtle tilt of her lips told him that had been her intent. "When the roots came up, they disturbed the surrounding ground. The operator spotted the edge of the skull peeking through and went to investigate. Now you know as much as I do."

He surveyed the police tape again. "Looks like you've secured the site."

"First thing. We also documented with photos and video. I got an A in Crime Scene 101."

Man, he was putting his foot in it big time today—and she wasn't cutting him any slack.

The uniformed officer's radio crackled to life. Perfect timing. The static and back-and-forth conversation about a fender bender with possible injuries saved him from having to come up with a PC response.

"Go." Chief Grant rubbed at the faint parallel creases in her brow. "Dave's tied up with that DWI. By the time he finishes all the paperwork, his shift will be almost over. Call if you need me to cover anything else before you wrap this up."

The younger cop signed off, slid the radio back on his belt, and nodded toward him. "Nice to meet you."

"Likewise." He tucked the card the guy handed him in his pocket.

"What do you want to do about them?" Craig studied the media van. "They'll be all over me once I get past the tape."

The creases on her forehead deepened.

Nervousness or annoyance?

"They must have burned rubber getting here. You'd think they'd have more important things to cover than a couple of police cars at a construction site." She blew out a breath.

Annoyance—no question about it.

She planted her fists on her hips. "Tell them I'll be over to give a statement in a few minutes. Stick with no comment if they ask any questions. I'll handle them."

Yeah, she would. Lisa Grant didn't look much over thirty, but her seasoned manner spelled experience in capital letters.

So where had she acquired it?

"I don't mean to be disrespectful to the dead." The site foreman moved closer as the officer departed. "But I've got deadlines to meet and payrolls to make. I can't have my people stand around all day doing nothing. Can we work anywhere in the area, or do I need to reassign them?"

Chief Grant adjusted her shades. "How large is the site?"

"Twenty acres."

"If you stay clear of the couple of acres around the skull, you should be fine. We can't have this area contaminated. My guess is the forensic anthropologist County will send won't finish here until midday tomorrow at the earliest." Only then did she defer to him. "Of course, Detective McGregor may have a few thoughts on that."

He bit back the retort on the tip of his tongue.

What was with this woman, anyway? So he'd made a mistake. Big deal. How had she expected him to peg her as the chief in those khaki slacks and that soft-looking sky-blue sport shirt? She could have been on the construction crew, for all he knew. Besides, none of the police chiefs he'd ever met had killer curves or a mane of dark hair shot through with fiery sparks that glinted in the sun.

"Detective McGregor?"

At her impatient prod, he refocused. "I agree on the timing—and the need for a forensic anthropologist. I'll put in a call to the medical examiner's office now. If you'll excuse me."

He escaped before she could lob another volley at him, turning his back as he pulled his phone off his belt and speed-dialed the ME.

Once he was a safe distance away, he angled toward her again. She was still talking to the foreman. The sun was rising in the sky now, warming the air—and putting a sheen on her complexion. Interesting. With her dark hair, he'd have expected darker skin. But hers was creamy and fair. Almost too fair.

The ME's office picked up, and while he passed on the pertinent information, he continued to watch the slender woman standing sentinel over the skull. No matter what she thought, he wasn't a chauvinist. Not by a long shot. His mother had seen to that, with her frequent lectures to her three sons on the merits of female intelligence, spunk, and strength. And she'd modeled those qualities in spades as she'd shepherded their clan from one corner of the globe to the next, never missing a beat as a wife, mother, and commercial artist, despite his father's frequent reassignments.

He had a feeling Mom would like Lisa Grant—even if the chief hadn't been all that cordial to her oldest son.

After wrapping up his call, he planned his strategy while checking messages. If he and Lisa Grant ended up working together, they needed to be able to communicate, not snipe. He was a pro, and his gut told him she was too. They should be able to smooth out their rocky start. Maybe they could agree he'd been less than tactful and she'd been a tad too sensitive, then kiss and make up.

A decidedly unprofessional image popped into his brain, which he suppressed at once.

Bad metaphor.

Besides, thirty-five was too old for such adolescent reactions— especially in a serious situation like this. The skull of someone who had been buried in a shallow, unmarked grave in a wooded area lay steps away.

And while he'd wait for the anthropologist and ME to weigh in, based on circumstantial evidence, the whole thing reeked of foul play.

Murder, even.

His mouth settled into a grim line, his perspective restored.

Death had a way of doing that.

Fast.

◆

Standing guard over the construction guy's grisly discovery, Lisa kept one eye on the site and the other on the tall, broad-shouldered detective a dozen yards away. He was done with his call and fiddling with his phone. A delay tactic, perhaps? Buying himself a few more minutes before he had to face the dragon lady?

She blew out a breath.

Why on earth had she jumped all over him for a simple mistake? The man was right. She wasn't exactly dressed the part of a police chief. If she'd been in his place, she'd have headed for the one uniformed person too. Not every guy was a chauvinist—even if she'd crossed paths with more than her share.

She owed him an apology.

As he started back toward her, she rubbed her palms on her slacks and turned to meet him.

"The anthropologist should be here by eleven." He slid the phone back onto his belt.

"Okay. Thanks." She flexed her fingers and tipped her head back. At five-seven, she wasn't short, but the man topped her by half a foot. "Look . . . I'm sorry if I sounded a little . . ." She broke eye contact as she searched for the best word.

"Defensive?"

Her gaze jerked back to his. Unlike her closed-in stance, his posture was open and approachable. A tiny smile flirted at his lips, and his tone was relaxed—as if they were talking about the weather. If she'd offended him, he seemed to have dealt with it and moved on. In fact, she got the distinct feeling he was trying to initiate a warmer, more amiable atmosphere.

As if to verify that, he took off his concealing sunglasses.

Oh.

My.

Word.

The guy had amazing eyes. Dark brown, like his hair. Intelligent. Intent. Perceptive. And fixed on her.

She transferred her weight from one foot to the other. "That's a fair description."

"You're not in the most female-friendly business. I expect you have reasons for reacting the way you did."

He was empathetic too.

"That's no excuse for rudeness. But I tend to get touchy when I'm tired." She exhaled, then removed her own glasses and looked up at him.

For less than a millisecond, an expression she couldn't identify flashed through his eyes. And was that a faint hitch in his breathing?

Even if exhaustion wasn't dulling her instincts, the moment passed too fast for her to get a read on his reaction.

"Kind of early in the day to be tired, isn't it?"

She combed her hair back with her fingers. "Not when you've been up most of the night working a burglary."

And with a skull of unknown origin at her feet, catching up on shut-eye would have to wait.

"I thought you were the chief."

She sent him a wry look. "Being chief in Carson isn't like being chief in a big city. My boss in Chicago—let alone the chief up there—never got his hands dirty."

"You were with the Chicago PD?"

Her spine stiffened at the hint of surprise in his voice—but she was *not* going to overreact again.

"Yes. For ten years. There, the roles were defined. Here . . . not so much. We wear many hats. I'm not only chief of police, but chief detective—though I'm teaching the other officers the ropes, so at some point I won't have to take every midnight call that requires detective work."

"Do you get a lot of those?"

"Very few—but last night happened to be one of them." A yawn snuck up on her. "Sorry."

"Hey, Chief! Can we get a statement?"

At the summons from the reporter, she grimaced. "This is the one part of the job I could do without. In Chicago I always passed the media off to someone higher up." Shifting her weight to look past the broad shoulders and powerful chest blocking her view of the news crew, she studied the reporter. It was the same guy who'd hounded her three weeks ago about an attempted break-in at the local hardware store. Must be low man on the totem pole if they'd assigned him to her quiet rural territory.

"I'll be with you in a minute, Rick."

He acknowledged her response with a salute.

"How did they get wind of this already, anyway?" The County detective inspected the media contingent.

"The traffic copter flew over earlier and hovered around a while. I'm guessing they passed the tip along."

"Too bad."

"It would have gotten out sooner or later. I can deal with it. That's another one of my titles, by the way—media relations coordinator. No one else in Carson has any experience with the press."

"How large is your department?"

"Me, plus five officers, an office manager, and Tally." At his raised eyebrows, she answered his unspoken question. "A stray I found hiding under my car in the office parking lot my first week on the job. He just kept hanging around. I suppose it didn't help that I gave him half of my turkey sandwich. Now he's the department mascot. He even rode in one of the squad cars during the Fourth of July parade last year, head hanging out the window, eating up all the attention. Which he gets plenty of at the station." She gave a soft laugh.

His focus dropped to her mouth, and her heart did an odd skip.

What on earth was that all about?

She flattened her smile. "Anyway, we may be small, but we try to be full service." She gestured to the skull in the ground beside them. "This, however, pushes our limits."

"County is glad to help. I'm told we're always at the disposal of smaller police departments within our jurisdiction."

"You're told." She cocked her head. "Does that mean you're new?"

"To St. Louis. Not to the business."

"How long have you been here?"

"A month."

"That *is* new. Where were you before?"

"Norfolk." He continued without giving her a chance to ask any follow-up questions. "Since the anthropologist won't be here for a while and you haven't had any sleep, why don't you go catch a few z's while I keep an eye on things?"

She was shaking her head before he even finished. "This scene is my responsibility. I need to make sure it stays secure."

"I got an A in Crime Scene 101 too."

Warmth crept across her cheeks as he parroted her snotty words back to her. "Sorry about that. I didn't mean to imply you weren't capable."

"Apology accepted."

He waited, watching her. Not pushing. Just letting his offer stand.

And she was tempted.

Very tempted.

If McGregor had been hired by County, he was more than competent. Every person she'd come into contact with there over the past year was a pro. The scene was safe in his hands—at least long enough for her to run home for a quick shower, change of clothes, and catnap.

Food first, though. The buzz in her nerve endings told her that needed to be top priority.

"Okay." She fished her creds out of a pocket, extracted a card, and handed it over. "I'll only be gone a couple of hours, but call me if anything comes up. I always have my cell with me—or within reach."

"Let me give you my card too."

As he reached for it, she bent down to tie her shoelace. All at once her vision blurred and she lost her balance.

A firm, steadying hand grasped her arm. "Careful."

She took a deep breath and straightened up. "Thanks. The ground's pretty uneven here."

Not that uneven.

He didn't say the words, but she could read them in his probing gaze.

Once more her fingers began to tingle.

It was time to go.

"I'll give the media a topline and head home. Don't forget to call if anything comes up."

"Got it."

Smoothing her slacks, she walked toward the waiting news contingent. In less than five minutes, she'd be on her way. And in two hours, she'd be rested, fed, and back on the job. Getting to the bottom of the mystery bones. Digging into this case—or watching the forensic anthropologist dig in, anyway.

And it was a case. Every instinct she'd honed over the past ten years told her that—and she trusted her instincts. They'd saved her too many times to count.

Only at the end had they failed her . . . for good reason.

But those days were over. Things were better now. The job of Carson police chief might not have been in her plans eighteen months ago, but God had planted her here for a reason.

Joining the news crew, she stole a quick glance back at Detective Mac McGregor. He was standing where she'd left him, arms folded, looking very much the formidable sentry.

And all at once she had the strangest feeling he might be part of that reason.

2

By the time Chief Grant returned to the construction site, the forensic anthropologist was hammering in the final stake for the canopy she'd erected over the remains. Barbara Romano had wasted no time getting to work, moving with smooth, practiced efficiency to ready the site for excavation.

Mac checked his watch as the dark gray Impala nosed in behind his Taurus. Two hours on the dot.

A lady who meant what she said.

The car door opened, and the Carson police chief emerged—in uniform. Navy slacks hugged her trim hips. A navy short-sleeved shirt, loose enough to be professional and tight enough to leave no doubt she was a woman, was adorned with badge, nameplate, and Carson PD sleeve patches. A wide belt complete with gun, phone, radio, and other cop accoutrements circled what appeared to be a hand-span waist.

Nice.

"What did I miss?" She did a sweep of the area, brisk and businesslike as she strode over, her attention homing in on the area under the canopy.

"Just setup, initial photography, and grid-making. The dirty work hasn't started yet."

As she watched Barbara secure the final stake, he inspected her profile. Her face had a little more color now, and her energy was almost palpable.

"You seem fully charged."

"Amazing what forty-five minutes of shut-eye can do, isn't it?"

"A short-term fix. Not enough to make up for a sleepless night."

"It'll get me through the day."

With one last tap on the stake, the jeans-clad anthropologist rose, tugged down the baseball cap that covered her close-cropped, graying brunette hair, and circled around the perimeter toward them.

As he did the introductions, the two women shook hands.

"I guess it's too soon to ask if you've learned anything." The chief rested her hand on her hip, near her holster.

Barbara grinned. "I'm good, but not that good. Ask me again in a few hours." She pulled a pair of heavy-duty latex gloves from a tool chest resting on the ground near one corner of the canopy. "You staying around?"

"Yes. Or someone from my department will be. I need to pay the previous owners of this property a visit this afternoon."

"I doubt I'll wrap up today. We'll need security here this evening and overnight."

"I'll assign two people."

Mac frowned. Why did he have a feeling she'd be one of them—and miss yet another night's sleep?

Keeping his tone casual, he joined the conversation. "I don't think it would be a problem for County to send some reinforcements to help cover the night shift."

For the first time since her return, she looked at him. "I appreciate the offer, but we should be fine. I have great officers, and they're always willing to put in extra hours in emergencies. I'd rather save my County chits for when I need a real favor."

"We don't run a tab."

"Maybe not officially. But I don't want to wear out my welcome."

He prepared to argue the point—only to have his phone vibrate. His boss, according to caller ID. "Excuse me a minute." Putting the phone to his ear, he moved a few feet away. "McGregor."

"What's happening out there?"

Typical cut-to-the-chase Sarge.

He filled him in, leaving out his conversation with the chief about reinforcements.

"Sounds like everything's under control. Good. I need you to respond to an armed robbery in a residence. High-profile citizens. Mitch is on the way too."

While Sarge gave him the particulars, he fished his notebook out of his pocket and jotted down the victim's name and address.

"It's not far from your location. You'll probably beat Mitch."

"I'm on my way." He flipped the notebook closed.

"Chief Grant need any more help today?"

He hesitated. Should he mention night-shift reinforcements? No.

Lisa Grant had been clear she wanted to handle this on her own. Interfering would *not* win him any brownie points—and he didn't intend to make another faux pas today.

"She says she has it covered."

"Okay. Give me an update on the robbery once you check it out."

"Will do." He slid the phone back into its holster.

The chief looked his way, then strolled over. "I wasn't eavesdropping . . . but sound carries in open country. I take it you're heading out."

"Yeah. A robbery. I'll swing by again after I finish there."

"No need to make a special trip back. We're fine." Her voice was cool. Professional. Dismissive. "I'm sure you have a lot of other cases that need your attention."

30

He couldn't dispute her comment—there weren't enough hours in the day as it was to deal with everything on his desk.

Still . . . he found himself wishing he could find an excuse to return.

How nuts was that?

Instead of responding, he walked over to a Bobcat and grabbed the jacket he'd ditched as the sun rose.

"Listen . . . I appreciate the offer, Detective McGregor."

He turned back to her. She'd removed her shades, revealing those clear hazel eyes that had captured him earlier when she'd shed the glasses the first time. They held a touch of contrition.

Extracting the card he'd meant to hand over earlier, before she'd lost her balance, he walked back to her and held it out. "Not a problem. If you change your mind, or need anything before I touch base again, don't hesitate to call."

She accepted the card, holding it up as she gave it a quick read. She had pretty hands. Graceful, with slender fingers.

Strange.

He couldn't remember ever noticing a woman's hands.

"Lisa . . . would you mind dropping the flap on the other side of the canopy? The sun's hitting me in the eye."

"Sure."

Huh. She and the anthropologist were on a first-name basis? Must have happened while he was on the phone.

Maybe he could join that cozy club.

"I'll be in touch, Chief Grant." He reached up to tighten the tie he'd loosened as the temperature climbed. "And just call me Mac from now on. I'm not into formalities."

"Okay."

No reciprocal sentiment.

Swallowing past his surprisingly strong disappointment, he secured the knot at his throat. Then, with a dip of his head, he turned and trekked toward his car.

Once behind the wheel, he started the engine and cranked up the air. The tinted windows gave him a chance to study Lisa Grant unobserved, and he took full advantage of the opportunity.

She'd moved to the shade of a nearby tree, but her attention remained fixed on the ground under the canopy as she paced and talked on the phone. Was she trying to line up reinforcements for the late shift? If so, would she succeed—or would she take one of the spots herself, forgoing sleep for another night and losing the color she'd regained after her nap?

More to the point—why should he care?

He didn't have a clue.

Shifting the car into drive, he eased down the bumpy construction road. He ought to put the independent police chief out of his mind and worry more about the job at hand. An armed robbery deserved his full attention, no matter the victim's status in the community.

Nevertheless, he found himself stealing a final glance at the slender woman in the distance.

And looking forward to seeing her again—sooner rather than later.

◆

"I think we may have a full skeleton here."

As Barbara called out that update, Lisa left the shade of a towering oak tree and approached the edge of the excavation area. The anthropologist had been hard at work since Mac McGregor left four hours ago, and given that she seemed to prefer the feed coming through her ear buds to conversation, Lisa had kept her distance. Having people watch over your shoulder as you worked was no fun. Been there, done that.

She'd passed that same instruction on to Craig when he'd come to relieve her while she interviewed the previous owners of the property.

Besides, the woman was a pro, moving back and forth between excavation and photography, documenting every step she was taking. No reason to get in her way.

Barbara rose from her kneeling position and arched her back as Lisa peered at the ground under the canopy. The woman had rearranged a fair amount of dirt—but it all looked like plain dirt to her.

"You're obviously seeing something I'm not."

"That's why they pay me the big bucks." The woman flashed her a smile, then lowered herself back to her knees and pointed a gloved finger at an area about eighteen inches below the skull. "That's a rib poking up through the tree roots."

If she squinted, Lisa could make out an arched, dirt-darkened object protruding above a fibrous root. Sort of.

"Yeah. I see it—I think."

"It's there. Trust me. Even though the skull is out of position, the relationship is close enough to suggest we may have an intact skeleton. I don't usually get this lucky."

"Can you tell anything else yet?"

Barbara lifted her arm and wiped her forehead on the sleeve of her T-shirt. "I don't like to make conjectures in the field; lab and X-ray results are much more reliable."

"I won't hold you to anything."

The woman considered her. "And I'll hold *you* to that." She stood again, once more stretching her back and swiveling her head. "First observation: based on cranial development and rib morphology, you have an adult. Second observation: as I was working around the skull I noticed a depressed area in the right parietal bone."

"Blunt force trauma."

"Yes."

Adding blunt force trauma to the wooded location and shallow grave gave credence to her earlier conclusion.

This was a crime scene.

"I had a feeling you'd find something like that."

"There could be more once I get into the lab and give these bones a thorough cleaning." Barbara stepped back from her work site and motioned toward a small cooler as she removed her surgical mask. "I'm going to break for a soda. Can I offer you one?"

Lisa hefted her bottle of water. "I'll stick with this, thanks. But I'll keep you company, if you like." And maybe ask a few questions about a certain detective named McGregor. The one with the bare ring finger.

Yeah, yeah, she'd noticed.

But a ring-check was standard operating procedure for most single women when they met a good-looking guy, after all. And McGregor was more than good-looking.

How had a man who appeared to be in his thirties, with all his obvious assets, managed to escape a walk down the aisle?

There had to be a story there, and the detective in her wanted to know—as did the woman, much as she hated to admit it. Mixing business and pleasure had always been a no-no. Still was.

But what could it hurt to ask a few questions?

"Some company would be nice. I prefer music while I work unless I've got an intern with me, but I like to exercise my vocal cords on breaks since my clients don't talk much."

Lisa's lips flexed. Cute. No doubt it paid to have a sense of humor in the type of work Barbara did. "There are days I wish I had that problem."

"I'll bet." Barbara extracted a Coke from the cooler.

"So what kind of music do you listen to?"

"Would you believe Grateful Dead?"

Lisa eyed her. Was that a joke?

"I'm not kidding. Weird, isn't it? Kind of like an exterminator listening to the Beatles or a carpenter listening to—who else?—the Carpenters. What can I say? But I also throw in a little Garth Brooks to mix things up. Here's to the oldies but goodies." She lifted her can in salute, then motioned toward the shady base of the oak tree where Lisa had spent the past couple of hours. "That spot has my name on it."

Lisa followed her over, propping a shoulder against an idle Bobcat while Barbara sat with her back braced against the trunk of the tree and downed half the soda in several long gulps.

"Mmm. That hit the spot." She stretched out her legs and crossed her ankles. "I love my job, but summer fieldwork in St. Louis can be brutal—as I'm sure you know."

"I grew up here. I'm used to the heat. But I'll admit it took me a while to readjust after a decade in Chicago."

"Nice town, Chicago."

"It has its good points—not that I saw many of them in my work."

"Mac said the same about Norfolk."

The perfect opening.

"He mentioned earlier that's where he's from." She tried for a shoot-the-breeze tone.

"I don't know about from, as in born there, but that's where he spent the past two years."

A short-termer with the Norfolk PD. Interesting. Once cops landed a spot in a big-city department, they tended to stay put and move up through the ranks.

Of course, she'd been the exception to that rule too.

"I didn't realize he was there such a short time." She swiped at a bead of sweat on her temple.

"Apparently one of his SEAL buddies on the force here convinced him to jump ship and relocate to our fair city last month."

Mac was an ex–Navy SEAL?

Impressive.

"He seems like a good guy." Barbara took another swig of soda, watching her.

Was that an amused glint in her eyes?

Lisa slipped her sunglasses back on. "That wouldn't surprise me. From what I've seen, County hires the best. I can't comment on McGregor, though. We just met today."

"Same here. But I got positive vibes."

Plus a whole lot more information than she had.

Then again, she hadn't exactly been Miss Congeniality.

"Well, back to work for me." Barbara drained the can and stood. "I'm going to take advantage of the dry weather and stick with this until about seven. The forecast calls for rain tomorrow afternoon, so I'd like to wrap up by noon."

"Let me know if I can assist in any way."

"I've got an intern coming tomorrow to help remove and package the bones, and that will speed things up. As long as you keep this spot secure, I'll be happy."

"My number one priority."

With a nod, Barbara returned to the canopy. After slipping the mask back on, she popped the buds in her ears and retook her place next to the emerging skeleton with her trowel and brushes and the other tools of her trade.

Lisa's cell began to vibrate, and she shifted into a more comfortable position against the Bobcat, reading the display before putting the phone to her ear. "Hi, Mom."

"Hi to you too. Guess who I saw on the noon news?"

Great.

"We had a bit of excitement out here."

"Sounds like it. You looked pale."

Her mother wanted to talk about her, not the bones—surprise, surprise.

Not.

"I'm fine. Just a little shy on sleep."

"You need to take care of yourself."

"I do." Usually.

"Did you eat lunch?"

"Next on my agenda." The minute Craig got here to relieve her.

"Don't skip meals."

"I know the drill."

"You work too hard."

"Not as hard as I used to."

"Considering the hours you put in now, I don't even want to think about your schedule in Chicago." A sigh came over the line. "I worry about you, you know."

"I know. But there's no need. Spend your worry on those darling babies in the neonatal ward."

"They get lots of TLC—but I always have enough to spare for you and your sister."

Lisa watched a robin swoop onto the branch of a nearby pine tree as several hatchlings craned their necks for lunch.

"I appreciate that, Mom. Why do you think I came home instead of taking that job in Kentucky?"

"Trust me, I love having you close at hand—even though I still don't see all that much of you. I wouldn't mind if I thought you spent a few hours each week socializing with people your own age, but near as I can tell, that's not happening. How do you ever expect to find Mr. Right if you don't look?"

An image of Mac McGregor flashed through her mind. Frowning, she erased it.

"I lead a busy life, and finding the right guy takes time. It'll happen if it's supposed to. I've put it in God's hands."

"You can't expect him to do all the work, honey. God helps those who help themselves and all that."

"I think I've heard that once or twice."

"Then I won't repeat it again—at least not today. So what's happening with these bones you found? Sounds macabre."

"Not really." She glanced toward Barbara, who was once more bent over her task. "They've been in the ground a while, as far as I can tell. It's definitely not a body that's only a week or two old."

"I am *not* going to visualize what that would look like."

"Smart move."

"Have you been there all day?"

"Except for a couple of hours. It's a crime scene until we rule out foul play." Which wasn't going to happen, based on the facts so far.

"Are you still coming over Wednesday?"

Right. Their standing dinner date.

"Shouldn't be a problem. The anthropologist hopes to finish by tomorrow."

"I'll let you get back to work then. Do you think you'll be able to identify that poor soul you found?"

"Depends on what kind of clues the anthropologist unearths and the insights the ME offers. But I intend to give it my best shot."

"That means more twelve hour days, I bet."

"Nope. That was in my workaholic days."

"Past tense?"

"Hey, I'm getting there. Now that I've settled into the job, I do have a life away from the office."

"A solo one."

They were back to that.

"I hate to run, but work is calling. We'll talk Wednesday."

"Not about this, I bet."

"There's nothing to talk about at the moment—but when there is, I promise you'll be the first to know. Gotta run."

Ending the call, Lisa let out a slow breath. She loved her mother. Stephanie Grant was a kind, caring, nurturing woman who'd always put the welfare of her family above her own needs. Who'd waited until her children had grown and her husband had passed away to go back to the nursing career she loved. She was selflessness incarnate.

And that was the problem. No matter how hard she tried, Lisa knew she could never live up to that example. She wasn't wired the same as her mother. The homemaker-supreme gene had gone to her sister, with her perfect husband, perfect son and daughter, and home-based sewing business. Like their mother, she'd arranged her life to put family first.

But how did you do that when you had a career in law enforcement? Crime didn't stop just because it was someone's birthday or dance recital or soccer tournament. Her sister could defer a sewing project; she couldn't defer a robbery or assault investigation.

Lisa sighed. Someday, if fate was kind, perhaps her juggling act would include a husband and children. But finding a man who was willing to work with her to create a life that encompassed both the demanding career she'd chosen and a family was a challenge.

As the phone vibrated again and Craig's name popped up on the screen, her thoughts once more strayed to Mac McGregor. If anyone could figure out how to deal with multiple priorities, it was a Navy SEAL.

And what in the world did that have to do with anything?

You know what it has to do with, Lisa. The guy's attractive, appealing . . . and single.

She blew out a breath and jabbed at the talk button. Fine. But even if the idea of getting to know him did hold some appeal, he was a colleague. Off-limits.

Yet as she greeted Craig, she couldn't quell the surge of longing that swept over her—nor the wish that she'd met the tall detective under different circumstances.

Because Barbara was right.

He seemed like a good guy.

3

I t's about time you got here." Mac shot Mitch Morgan a disgruntled look as his fellow detective joined him in the backyard of the upscale house where the armed robbery had occurred.

"Sorry. I got redirected to a possible kidnapping while I was on my way here. All ended well, though. The kid just wandered off." He surveyed the impeccably landscaped yard that featured a slate terrace, swimming pool, and waterfall. "This cost some big bucks."

"And big bucks were what our guy was after."

"What happened?"

"The owner was sunbathing over there." Mac pointed toward a lounge chair. "A masked guy came out of nowhere, aimed a gun at her, forced her inside, made her open the safe, and took off with an estimated quarter of a million dollars in jewelry."

Mitch let out a low whistle. "Big bucks is right. Was there an assault?"

"No."

"One plus, at least." He inspected the corners of the house and yard. Zeroed in on a security camera attached to a tree.

"I already asked." Mac spoke before his colleague could voice the question. "She turned it off before she came outside. Didn't want anyone watching her sunbathe."

"Too bad. That would have made our job a whole lot easier. I assume you already spoke to the victim?"

"I had plenty of time while I waited for you."

"Hey—I just follow orders. What did she have to say?"

Mac filled him in, using the rapid-fire briefing style they'd both perfected as SEALs. Once he finished and they'd divvied up next steps, he closed his notebook and moved to the next item on his agenda. "I had an interesting experience earlier today."

"Yeah?" Mitch was giving the yard another once-over.

"When I mentioned my assignment after I ran into you in the parking lot this morning, you neglected to offer a few pertinent details. One in particular."

Mitch smirked at him. "You met Chief Grant."

"Yes. Chief *Lisa* Grant. Might have been nice to be prepared for that."

"You have a bias against women police chiefs?"

"That's not what I meant, and you know it."

"Then what's the problem?"

Mac folded his arms. "Can the innocent act. It doesn't suit you."

"Let's see . . ." Mitch pretended to consider. "Could you be referring to the fact that she's hot?"

"That's one way to put it."

"Can you think of a better way?"

At his colleague's unrepentant grin, Mac narrowed his eyes. "I bet Alison wouldn't appreciate that assessment. She's practically still a bride."

"Chief Grant is hot; Alison sizzles. Trust me, my wife knows that her place in my life—and my heart—is secure. But a guy would have to be blind not to notice Lisa Grant's assets. A normal guy, anyway. Congratulations. You passed the test."

"Thanks for the vote of confidence." Mac fiddled with the cell on his belt, preparing to fish. "She seems capable."

"That would be my take from the couple of times I've seen her in action."

"On the prickly side, though."

Mitch arched an eyebrow. "How so?"

He shifted his weight. *Careful, McGregor.* "Sensitive might be a better word."

"Sensitive." His buddy considered that. "Nope. Doesn't fit. Don't get me wrong, I'm sure she has a softer side, but in my professional encounters with her, she came across as cool, composed, and thick-skinned. I was at County jail when she hauled in a meth tweaker. Guy had a lab in his basement and was not thrilled to be busted in the middle of a cook. He called her every name in the book, and she never flinched." Mitch cocked his head. "What did she get prickly—excuse me—sensitive about?"

He was in too deep to change course now.

"I, uh, mistook the male officer on the scene for the chief."

Mitch winced. "Ouch."

"Then she took offense at a comment I made about crime scene protocol."

"Let's see. You assumed the chief was a man and questioned her professionalism." He shook his head. "Buddy, you have a lot of ground to make up."

Mac's neck warmed. "Look, the officer was uniformed. She wasn't. The crime scene comment was nothing more than that—a comment, not a criticism. I don't know why she got bent out of shape."

"Maybe she was having a bad day." Mitch lifted one shoulder. "Besides, what does it matter? You won't be crossing paths with her much once this situation is resolved."

True . . . professionally speaking. On the personal side, however . . . could be a different story. And he wanted more info, just in case.

42

"In the meantime, though, we have to work together. What do you know about her background?"

"Only what I've heard through the grapevine. She's been here about a year. Came from Chicago when Carson started its own PD."

"Yeah, yeah, I already know all that."

"So you two did talk."

"Not much. What did she do in Chicago?"

"Started out as a cop, worked her way into the detective ranks."

"Why did she leave?"

"I have no idea. I heard she has family here. That might have been part of the reason."

"But why didn't she get a job in a bigger municipality? Or even County?"

"How should I know?" Mitch gave him a speculative look. "And why are you interested, anyway?"

Time to back off.

He shrugged. "I like to be fully briefed on the players—especially when I may be dealing with them for a while. My guess is we're looking at a crime scene out there. A shallow, unmarked grave in a wooded area? More than suspicious."

"How recent is the grave?"

"That's for Barbara and the ME's office to estimate. I'd say it's a year old, minimum. Maybe a lot older than that. The part of the skull I saw was completely skeletonized."

"The ID could be a challenge."

"No kidding."

Mitch propped a shoulder against the stone retaining wall behind him. "Any other questions about Chief Grant?"

"No."

"I'll give you the answer, anyway. No, she's not married."

Since her ring finger was bare, he'd already guessed that—but it was nice to have it confirmed.

Not that he intended to share that with his buddy.

"I didn't ask about her marital status."

"You wanted to." Mitch's smirk was back.

"I don't date colleagues."

"She works for a different municipality—and this case won't last forever."

"For an ace detective, you're jumping to a lot of shaky conclusions."

"Yeah? Are you saying you're not interested in getting to know her better?"

He would ask that.

Mac turned away. "Let's work this burglary."

His buddy's chuckle followed him. "That's what I thought."

Beating back the impulse to refute Mitch's conclusion, he kept walking. Better not protest too much, as Shakespeare once noted.

Besides, he didn't lie.

And even if he did, Mitch would see right through it.

◆

"Looks like Barbara's made a lot of progress in the past twenty-four hours."

As the baritone voice spoke behind her, Lisa jerked around.

Mac McGregor stood less than three feet away.

How had he done that? She might once again be operating on too few hours of sleep, but her ears worked fine.

On the other hand, the man was a former Navy SEAL. Trained in stealth. Approaching undetected was his stock-in-trade. And he'd parked quite a distance away too, masking the sound of his tires.

"Sorry." Remorse softened his eyes. "I didn't mean to startle you."

"No problem." She put the brakes on her pulse and stepped aside. "Take a look."

44

He moved closer. Close enough to tease her nostrils with a faint whiff of some rugged, masculine—and oh-so-appealing—aftershave.

Her pulse surged again . . . and this time it was a lot harder to rein in.

"Hi, Barbara."

The anthropologist didn't respond to his greeting.

"She likes to listen to music while she works. Grateful Dead." At Mac's double take, Lisa smiled. "I had the same reaction when she told me yesterday."

A chuckle rumbled in his chest, deep and pleasing, and faint crinkles appeared at the corners of his eyes. "You couldn't make that one up."

The guy was dangerously handsome when he was serious, but that smile—not to mention a killer dimple—whoa!

How many women had melted into a little puddle at his feet once he'd turned those weapons on them?

Probably too many to count.

"I agree." She swallowed, transferring her attention back to the depression and the intact skeleton that had emerged from the ground. "She's getting ready to do one more set of photos before she removes and packages the bones." She indicated the bags and acid-free boxes waiting off to the side. "One of the graduate interns she works with should be arriving any minute to help with that job."

Mac squinted at the western horizon, where dark clouds were massing. "I hope so. This could be a race to the finish."

"She seems confident she'll beat the storm. The only other thing she wants to do is take some soil samples."

"Did she find any clothing remnants that might help date the grave?"

"Not yet. Based on the intrusion of tree roots into the skeleton, though, she's guessing the body's been there a while. I've got a call into the Botanical Garden—they're sending out a tree specialist to take a look at the roots. That was Barbara's idea, actually. She thought a horticulturist might be able to give us a potential window of time on burial based on root growth."

"Ingenious."

"I thought so."

"If that doesn't work, though, making an ID will be hard, if not impossible."

"Tell me something I don't know."

He sent her a cautious look. "I didn't mean to suggest you—"

"Wait." She put up a hand. "That wasn't a smart-aleck response." She met his careful gaze, her own steady. "It was just a comment. I overreacted yesterday, and I'm sorry. People don't usually have to walk on eggshells around me. Okay?"

As he appraised her, she resisted the urge to break eye contact. "Okay."

"Good." She eased a few inches back from that appealing aftershave. "For the record, I was agreeing with you. There are more than 85,000 missing persons listed with the National Crime Information Center."

"Except most people who go missing locally get found locally."

"True. But according to the FBI database, there are 2,200 listed in Missouri and Illinois. Even after narrowing that number down based on whatever identifying criteria Barbara finds, it will still be like looking for a needle in a haystack." She sighed and pushed back the hair sticking to her damp forehead. "We can try to find a match in the National Missing Persons DNA Database, but that won't help if the bones predate that."

"The database goes back to . . . what? 2000, 2001?"

"2000. We'll have to cross our fingers and hope Barbara or the ME or the tree expert comes up with some clues that narrow the window."

"Prayer might be a better option."

At Barbara's comment, Lisa turned toward her. The anthropologist had removed the buds from her ears and was sitting back on her heels.

"I'm not liking the sound of that." Lisa rested one hand on her holster.

"I don't want to be pessimistic, but I'm not seeing a thing here other than bones. No jewelry, no buttons, no shoe buckles or synthetic soles. I'm going to sift through the dirt under and around the body, but this appears to be clean."

"I wonder if the body was stripped before it was buried." Mac voiced the very thing she was thinking.

"That's possible." Barbara swiped a bead of sweat off her temple and readjusted her surgical mask. "Or it may have been here for a very long time. The tree expert might offer some insights on that. Here's something a bit strange, though." She scooted down the length of the right arm, which was lying flat, and pointed to the hand. "Notice that the fourth finger is missing above the metacarpal joint."

"Sorry . . . can you say that in plain English? I need to bone up on my anatomy." A flash of humor twinkled in Mac's brown irises. "Pardon the pun."

A man who wasn't afraid to admit what he didn't know. Admirable.

Barbara rolled her eyes. "I've heard all the jokes, believe me. In plain English, it's the joint that attaches the finger to the hand. And it's not really missing. I've already bagged it. But I found it here, on the ground, between these ribs." She indicated the spot.

"That's weird." Lisa frowned. "Could the finger have been broken when the body was put in the grave?"

"Yes, but in that case it should still be in the correct anatomical position."

Right. That was a dumb question. The lack of sleep two nights in a row was taking a toll.

She peeked at Mac. If he noticed her gaffe, he was kind enough to keep it to himself.

"Do you want my take?"

Lisa looked back at Barbara. "Yes."

"I suspect this finger was severed and thrown in before or after the body was put in the ground. If it was tossed on the chest afterward, it would have fallen through the rib cage once the body decomposed."

"Hmm." Mac inspected the skeleton. "Assuming the perpetrator did strip the body to eliminate clues, what would he do about jewelry that wouldn't come off?"

Of course.

"You're thinking this person was wearing a ring." Lisa angled toward him, shading her eyes from the sun.

"That crossed my mind too," Barbara said. "And now that the bones are fully exposed, I think it's safe to conclude this was a woman. The wide pelvic girdle and gracile appearance of the skull—brow ridges that aren't robust and muscle-attachment sites that aren't pronounced—are obvious indicators. I'll verify that in the lab, but it fits with the ring theory, since women are more likely than men to wear rings." She glanced at the ominous sky. "My assistant has arrived just in time." She gestured toward a blue car that had turned off the main drag and was bumping along the dirt construction road.

"We'll get out of your hair and sign him in." Lisa headed for the shade of the oak tree to retrieve the scene log.

"Sorry I didn't get back last night or earlier today." Mac fell into step beside her. "The robbery had us scrambling."

"No problem. Maintaining security here wasn't that difficult—except when my favorite reporter showed up earlier."

"Did you give him anything?"

"No—and he was not a happy camper. Until I get the official

48

report from Barbara and the ME, though, I'm going to stick with my no-further-developments script."

"Makes sense. Did you manage to track down the previous owners of this land?"

"Yes. Ron and Marjorie Wright. Ron died three years ago and Marjorie is in a nursing home, in declining health. She and her first husband bought the property years ago as an investment, and with her rising medical bills she thought this was a prudent time to sell. They never used the property, or even visited it much beyond an annual summer picnic they always hosted for friends and neighbors. She was beyond shocked to hear the construction crew had unearthed a skeleton."

"Any family who might be able to offer a few more insights?"

"No children, and all the other relatives are distant and living in other parts of the country. Their estate is earmarked for charity."

"In other words, a dead end—pardon the second pun—in terms of IDing our victim."

"That's my conclusion." Lisa retrieved a clipboard off the Bobcat. "Any idea how long it will take to get Barbara's report? I haven't had to use the County forensic anthropologist until now."

"We should have a preliminary analysis back in a day or two. The full report takes about a week. If we need to extract DNA from the bones, we'll have to send samples to the University of North Texas. They're the best on skeletal remains."

"I know. We used them in Chicago on occasion. Never on one of my cases, though." A yawn crept up on her. "Sorry."

"Another long night?"

Did she detect a nuance that was more personal than polite—or was her overtired mind playing tricks on her?

Must be the latter. Why should he care how many hours she put in on the job?

"Not as long as two nights ago, when I was dealing with the

burglary. But one of the guys on security here last night is an expectant father—or was. His wife called him while he was on duty, and I relieved him so he could take her to the hospital. I'm happy to report mother, father, and daughter are all doing well."

"How long were you here?"

"Does it matter?" The question was out before she could stop it.

For a moment, he seemed taken aback, but he recovered fast. "I was wondering if I should send out for coffee."

"I appreciate the thought." She dredged up a weary smile. "But I can last until Barbara and her assistant finish. Speaking of that . . ." She motioned toward the young man approaching the police tape. "Let me log him in."

"I need to log in too. Leave a line for me."

"That was my plan."

She dispensed with the protocol quickly for the new visitor, and as soon as she rejoined Mac, he took the clipboard from her and checked his watch.

"I can't believe it's already time for lunch." He scribbled his signature.

"I can. The hours have been dragging by out here. Carson may be a lot quieter than Chicago, but I'm used to more action than guard duty." She took the clipboard when he held it out. "It's hardly worth signing in for such a short visit if lunch is on your agenda."

"I like to follow procedures, and I suspect you do too."

"Always." She tucked the clipboard back into a nook of the Bobcat.

Silence fell between them, and she snuck a peek at his strong profile as he watched the new arrival pull on a pair of gloves. He'd inferred he was hungry, yet he was lingering.

Why?

"You know, I appreciate you stopping by, but you don't have

to hang around. I'm sure you have more interesting things to do on your lunch break than watch Barbara disassemble a skeleton."

He regarded her for a moment, as if he was waging an internal debate. "Nope. I'm too new in town to have any friends to meet up with for lunch, other than a fellow detective I've known for years. But he always meets his wife if they can coordinate their schedules." He gestured toward his car. "I picked up some food on my way here, so lunch is at hand. In fact, there's enough to share if you're interested. Consider it a peace offering after my foot-in-the-mouth performance yesterday."

Despite her best effort to suppress it, a tiny shiver of pleasure rippled through her.

He wanted to have lunch with her.

What a perfect way to spice up her otherwise dull day.

Still . . . mixing business and pleasure wasn't smart.

Wasn't this business, though . . . sort of? It certainly wasn't a date. Besides, what harm could come from enjoying the man's company for twenty or thirty minutes?

Without giving herself a chance to reconsider, she took the plunge. "I'll tell you what—I brought some lunch stuff too. Why don't we pool our resources? We can spread everything out on the hood of my car and have a buffet."

"I like that idea. I'll grab my food and meet you there."

As they moved toward their respective cars, Lisa's exhaustion evaporated but her renewed vigor had nothing to do with the anticipation of an energy-boosting meal. The explanation was much simpler: a handsome man had dropped in for lunch.

Pulling her small cooler from the trunk of the car, she regarded the hot, dusty terrain.

The setting wasn't ideal.

The ambiance wasn't perfect.

The table wouldn't be set with fine china or crystal.

But on this sunny June day, she'd rather eat sandwiches from the hood of a car with Mac McGregor than dine at the finest restaurant in the city with any other man she'd ever met.

As for what that said about her—or him—she'd leave that analysis for another day.

Because for once, she was just going to enjoy the moment.

4

She'd agreed to share lunch with him.

As Mac opened the back door of his car, shed his jacket, and loosened his tie, he couldn't rein in his smile.

In town barely a month, and already he'd met an interesting woman.

An interesting, *appealing* woman.

Of course, if he did get serious about someone in St. Louis, Mitch would claim a lion's share of the credit for nudging him to relocate.

But for the right woman, he could put up with a healthy dose of ribbing.

He tossed his jacket into the backseat and snagged the Panera bag. While it was much too soon to be linking the word *serious* with the Carson police chief, one thing was clear. Despite their rocky start, there was a spark between them that had far more to do with attraction than antagonism. On his side, anyway.

Did she feel it too?

Closing his door, he checked her out. She was pulling stuff out of a small cooler and arranging it on the hood, but she looked over at him, as if sensing his perusal.

He smiled.

She smiled back.

And all at once, the atmosphere between them morphed from friendly to electric.

The attraction wasn't one-sided.

Only when he started toward her did she jerk her gaze away and go back to pulling items from her cooler.

He slowed his pace, buying them both a few extra moments to regroup—yet when he moved beside her and set the bag on the hood, she fumbled a plastic container. They both grabbed for it, bringing them even closer together.

"Got it." His fingers closed over the small lidded drum, brushing hers.

She stared at their hands, then up at him—and eased back a few inches. "Thanks."

He set the container on the hood of the Impala. Sparks were pinging all over the place . . . and she was getting nervous. He needed to lighten up the atmosphere with an innocuous comment.

"You know, the detective buddy I mentioned has a car very similar to this." He tried for a casual tone—and almost succeeded. Only a slight huskiness roughened his words.

"I'm not surprised." Her reply came out breathy, but she followed his lead and stuck to a safe subject. "Carson picked up some older vehicles from County when you upgraded your fleet. This was a detective car."

He peered through the windshield. Yep. Light bars front and back. That meant she'd have a siren too.

"No wonder it looked familiar."

"It's a solid vehicle." She wiped her palms on her slacks and motioned toward the Panera sack. "So what's in that giant bag?"

He ticked off the menu as he removed the items. "Chicken salad sandwich. Chicken cobb salad. Turkey and avocado BLT. Plus chips and some cookies."

After he set the last item on the hood, he turned to find her gaping at the food.

"You bought all this stuff for lunch?"

He gave the repast a quick perusal—and ran a finger around the edge of his collar. Overkill with a capital *over*.

"Possibly dinner too. I'm not much of a cook, so I tend to stock up when I get takeout." True . . . but not to this extent.

She gave the spread a skeptical inspection. "A lot of this stuff won't be too appetizing by tonight."

After one too many soggy tuna salad sandwiches and wilted salads, he knew that as well as she did.

"Then I'm glad you're going to help me eat it, Chief Grant." He inhaled, slow and steady. Might as well lay his cards on the table. "To be honest, that's what I was hoping for all along. Solitary meals are getting old."

She shot him a startled glance, as if his candid confession surprised her, then focused on prying off the lid of the container they'd rescued. "Just make it Lisa. And I'm kind of tired of eating alone too." She set the selection of fresh fruit on the hood and opened the lid of another container to reveal vegetables and dip.

The first-name club had been expanded to include him—and if she typically ate alone, she must not be involved in a serious relationship.

That was the best news he'd had all day.

He pulled two large, clear plastic lids out of the Panera bag. "I asked the clerk for disposable plates, but they didn't have any—so I sweet-talked her out of these."

"Mmm." She gave him a quick head-to-toe. "I bet that wasn't hard."

Was that a compliment—or a criticism?

Impossible to tell from her inflection . . . and she offered no further clue as she reached for one of the lids.

He relinquished it, surveying the food she'd brought. Besides the fruit and vegetables, she had nuts, a halved hard-boiled egg, a few thin slices of what looked like pork tenderloin, and whole wheat crackers.

No wonder she was so thin.

"Kind of a lean lunch, isn't it?"

"You don't expend many calories standing around all day." She regarded the Panera spread. "But I'm not exactly making an equal contribution to this meal, am I?"

As far as he was concerned, her presence was contribution enough—though better to keep that to himself.

"Let's just say we have plenty and leave it at that. After all, you weren't expecting guests. So what looks good to you from my cache?"

"I'd love to try the chicken cobb."

"It's yours." He handed her the container.

Her eyes widened, and she held up a hand. "I could never eat that whole thing unless that was *all* I ate. Why don't we each take some?"

"Deal . . . if you'll sample the sandwiches too."

She considered the other two offerings. "I'll take a fourth of each—fair enough?"

"Fair enough. I'll let you divvy them up."

He helped himself to some fruit, veggies, and salad while she cut up the sandwiches.

After they'd filled their plates, he grabbed the bags of chips, cookies, and . . .

Uh-oh.

At his grimace, she gave him a quizzical look. "What's wrong?"

"I forgot the drinks."

"Will you be satisfied with water? I have a coolerful in the backseat."

"That'll do." He took her makeshift plate and hefted it toward the shade. "I'll meet you over there."

"Okay. Let me get the rest of the food out of the heat."

By the time she joined him, he'd managed to find a reasonably clean, shady spot atop a large boulder unearthed during construction.

"It's not the Ritz, but I've eaten in worse places—and in far less pleasant company."

Keeping a respectable distance between them, she scooted onto the boulder. "Considering the kinds of conditions SEALs have to deal with, I'm not going to let that pseudo compliment go to my head."

She knew he'd been a SEAL?

As if reading his mind, she spoke again. "Barbara mentioned your background yesterday."

He was going to have to work on his poker face if she could read his thoughts that easily.

Lisa set her lunch in her lap and forked a piece of fruit as she continued. "If that's an off-limits topic, just say so. I know a lot of guys who've been to the Middle East don't like to talk about it."

"It's not that I mind talking about it, but there isn't much I can say. All of my missions were classified."

"Understood. So how long were you in the navy?"

"Ten years. I signed on right out of college. I was a SEAL for the last five."

"That's a long time to spend in a very high-risk job." She peeled the top half of the croissant off her chicken salad sandwich and scooped up a forkful of the filling. "Why did you leave?"

"Because it was a long time to spend in a very high-risk job."

She studied him. "Meaning?"

"Meaning if you stay in a job like that long enough, you'll likely die doing it. I wasn't ready to meet my maker—and I came close to cashing in my chips once too often. I figured my luck was about to run out."

"Sounds reasonable."

"Not to hear my younger brothers talk. They're always giving me grief for bailing."

"It's easy for people who aren't in risky jobs to pass judgment—and come to a lot of wrong conclusions—when someone pulls back."

He watched as she plucked the yolk out of the egg, set it aside, and bit into the white. She'd scaled down the danger meter in her job too. What were her reasons—and had she also gotten flack for it?

Maybe if he shared some of his story, she'd reciprocate.

"Actually, they're both in risky jobs too. Lance is a Delta Force operator and Finn is an Army Ranger."

Her forkful of chicken salad froze in midair. "Are you serious?"

"Yeah."

"Talk about high achievers. Does the danger gene run in your family, or what?"

He popped a grape into his mouth and shrugged. "I don't know about danger genes, but we do come from solid law enforcement stock. My grandfather was a police officer, and my dad was with the State Department's Bureau of Diplomatic Security. Both of them saw a fair amount of on-the-job action—especially my dad. We lived in some hot spots while I was growing up."

"Such as?" She extracted the bacon from the turkey BLT.

Huh. He wouldn't have pegged her as the picky-eater type.

But everyone had quirks.

"Cameroon, Pakistan, Qatar. And a few tamer places like London and Washington, DC."

"You *have* been around." She nibbled on the edge of the sandwich. "Is your dad still with the State Department?"

"No. He retired from his government job five years ago and

opened a private security firm in Atlanta—my mom's hometown."

"Did you think about joining him after you left the service?"

He grinned. "I may be tired of dodging bullets, but I'm not ready to babysit celebrities. Maybe someday."

"Is your mom living?"

"And how. She's a commercial artist—a career she nurtured despite all our years of globe-trotting once email and the internet simplified global communication."

"Sounds like you come from a remarkable family."

"I don't know about remarkable—but interesting. And close-knit."

"Do you all see each other much?"

His smile faded as he shoved his remaining fruit around with his fork. "Not enough. I've made a few trips down to Atlanta since I left the service, but Lance and Finn are both stationed in the Middle East. They don't get home often, and rarely at the same time."

"You must worry about them a lot." Her voice softened—and warmed.

"Yeah." The word came out scratchy, and he took another swig of water, buying himself a few moments. Strange. He'd already told Lisa more about himself than he typically shared with people he'd known a whole lot longer than two days. Too much, perhaps.

Time to shift the spotlight.

"What about you? Are your parents still living? Any brothers and sisters?"

She shook her head when he held out the bag of chips. "One sister, Sherry, happily married in Houston, who gave me a darling niece and nephew. My mom is a neonatal nurse here. Unlike your globe-trotting family, we were all born and raised in St. Louis. Dad owned three franchise restaurants and was an inventor on the side, with five patents to his credit. There weren't enough hours in the day to accomplish everything on his to-do list . . . yet he always made time for the family." Her expression grew melancholy. "He died of a stroke six years ago—here one day, gone the next. It was hard."

Based on the sudden sheen in her eyes before she dipped her head, it still was.

"Sounds like your family is close too."

She blinked and stabbed at some lettuce. "Yeah. So . . . Barbara mentioned that a SEAL buddy on the force here is the reason you relocated to St. Louis."

The lady wasn't ready to share more about her family.

Message received.

"That's right. Mitch Morgan."

"Mitch Morgan and Mac McGregor. Hmm. That's a lot of Ms."

"Trust me, our SEAL mates noticed that too. They used to call us the two M&Ms."

A glint of humor sparked in her irises. "Did that bother you?"

He hitched up one shoulder. "We all had nicknames—and it was better than being called Porker or Geeky. Besides, as we never failed to remind our team, M&Ms don't melt when things get hot."

"Cute. So how did Mitch convince you to leave Norfolk?"

Careful, McGregor. Don't spook her.

"Let's just say he did a persuasive sell job."

"Yeah?" She broke off a tiny piece of crust. "How so?"

He hesitated again. How much could he share about his motives for relocating without scaring her off?

On the other hand, he had a feeling she'd appreciate a man who was honest and forthright.

"You don't have to answer that if you don't want to. Sometimes I slip into interrogation mode in my personal life. One of the hazards of the job, I guess." She offered him a wry smile. "To tell the truth, I've scared more than a few guys off that way."

"You don't scare me." He let a beat pass to emphasize his statement. "But here's an odd coincidence. I was holding back because I don't want to scare *you*."

She arched an eyebrow. "Now you've piqued my interest. And I don't scare easily, either."

"I wonder if I should test that theory?"

"I dare you."

He liked the flash of spirit—and impish humor—in her eyes . . . and he wasn't the type to back down from a dare.

"You're on." He set down his fork and gave her his full attention. "I liked Norfolk—but I knew the town too well. I was stationed nearby when I wasn't overseas."

"Where?"

"Virginia Beach."

He could almost hear the gears in her brain clicking as she scrutinized him. "You were on SEAL Team Six, weren't you? The elite of the elite."

"All SEALs are equal." It might be his standard response—but it was also true.

"Got it. So tell me what you mean by too well." She dipped a carrot stick into the cottage-cheesy dip she'd brought and swirled it around. "I wouldn't think a cop—or a detective—could ever know a city too well."

"On a professional level, it was a definite advantage. I'd probably have stayed if Mitch hadn't cornered me when I came to St. Louis for his wedding and convinced me I needed a change of scene. Social scene, that is."

She chomped on the carrot, watching him in silence.

He could still make a joke, back off, and change the tenor of this conversation.

But he didn't.

Because he believed Lisa's assertion that she didn't scare easily—and he was too old for games.

"Here's the bottom line. I'm thirty-five. I spent a lot of years giving everything to my job, until there was nothing left for anything else—including a relationship. And that was fine for a long time. I have no regrets about my choices."

He paused and looked toward the excavation site a dozen yards away. "But one night in Afghanistan, all of that changed. We were out on patrol. One of my buddies, who was planning to head home for good in two weeks and get married, stepped on an IED. In an instant, the future he'd planned vanished."

Lifting his bottle of water, he took a long drink. When the plastic crinkled, he loosened his grip. "The thing is, that could have been me. I was next in line. So I began praying for guidance, asking if it was time for me to move on and start building the future I'd always assumed was waiting for me—a future that included a less dangerous life and a wife and family."

Lisa leaned toward him, intent. "And you got an answer?"

"Yes, but not in any kind of dramatic way. There was no blinding flash of insight, no writing across the sky, no message in a dream, no supernatural sign. But over the next few weeks, I felt myself moving this direction. And one day I woke up and knew with absolute certainty my life as a SEAL was winding down."

"So you switched from fighting terrorism in Afghanistan to fighting crime in Norfolk."

"That about sums it up."

"Police work is dangerous too—especially in big cities."

Her words were straightforward, but a subtle tautness in her inflection blipped on his radar. There was a story there—and he wanted to hear it.

"Yes, it is. I'm sure you saw your share of danger in Chicago."

"More than I've seen in Carson." He held his breath, but she didn't take his opening. "I suppose from your perspective, though, police work was a significant improvement on the risk scale."

"Yeah. So I went to the police academy, spent a year as a street cop, then fast-tracked into the detective ranks. And now here I am."

"So why do you think St. Louis will be better socially?"

He finished off his remaining BLT—including the bacon—while he composed his answer. "My buddy met his wife after he moved here, and since I'd exhausted most of the usual avenues for meeting interesting women in Norfolk, I thought some of his luck might rub off on me if I followed him to St. Louis."

She made a project out of scraping up the last of her cottage cheese with a carrot stick. "Has it?"

"Maybe."

The only response he got to that comment was a momentary freeze-frame before she went back to her food.

Okay. Enough soul-baring for one day. Now it was her turn. He hoped.

"So what about you? Why did you leave Chicago and come back here?"

She examined the remains of her lunch. "For a lot of the same reasons you did—including an eye-opening incident, followed by much prayer."

"What happened?"

Even if she'd been inclined to answer that question, the sudden crunch of gravel announcing the arrival of the horticulturist broke the private mood.

"Duty calls." She set her plate down and stood.

He stifled his disappointment. "No problem. If you're done, I'll gather up all this stuff."

"Yes. Thanks."

As she walked over to log in the new arrival, he rose too. His plate was empty. Hers was picked over. He took a quick inventory. The chicken salad from her quarter portion of that sandwich was gone, but the croissant had been left behind. The bottom piece of bread and the contents of her quarter of the turkey BLT were gone . . . except for the bacon she'd extracted. She'd eaten about half of the small serving of salad she'd taken, again picking out the bacon and egg yolks. And the fruit, veggies, single slice of pork tenderloin, and half dozen nuts she'd taken from her own cache had been consumed.

Finicky eater, no question about it.

After discarding the remnants of their lunch in a trash container the construction company had installed, he looked over at her. She was deep in conversation with a middle-aged man as she led him over to the excavation site. While he watched, a gust of wind whipped past, ruffling her hair.

She had nice hair. Full, soft-looking, a slight wave in the ends that brushed her shoulders. It was the kind of hair that called out to be touched and . . .

Suppressing those inappropriate thoughts, he turned away.

Get a grip, McGregor. You hardly know the woman. You've laid the groundwork, given her hints you're interested. The ball's in her court now. Let her have some space, or despite what she said, you might scare her off.

Not a risk he wanted to take.

So he'd follow his advice—and hope someday in the not-too-distant future she'd explain how her reasons for making a dramatic change in lifestyle were similar to his. Did they include wanting time for a relationship? What was the incident she'd referenced that had triggered her return home? And why take a small-town police chief job when she was clearly qualified to do more?

His cell began to vibrate, also calling him back to duty after their impromptu lunch.

As he talked to Mitch about a follow-up interview for yesterday's robbery, however, his attention was focused more on questions about a certain female police chief than on the conversation with his colleague.

He had no answers—yet.

But one thing was clear.

Buried bones weren't the only mystery on this construction site.

◆

In her peripheral vision, Lisa kept tabs on Mac while she explained the scenario to Dave Brennan, the tree expert from Missouri Botanical Garden. He asked a few questions, then joined Barbara in the excavation trench. With her assistance, he sawed off a section of root, stood, and moved aside to examine it.

As he wandered off a couple of minutes later to look at some nearby trees, Mac rejoined her. He shaded his eyes and glanced at Dave, who was now getting up close and personal with an evergreen-type tree. "Did you get any kind of reading from him yet?"

"No . . . but he didn't say the task was impossible. I'm deeming that a hopeful sign."

"Did he give any indication how long this might take? I wouldn't mind hanging around a few minutes to hear his thoughts, but that's about as long as I can push it."

Even as Mac asked the question, the man was circling back toward them.

"Uh-oh. That was fast." Lisa squinted at him as he approached, her stomach kinking. If her tree expert didn't come through for them with a time frame, the odds of making an ID were going to nose-dive.

When the horticulturist joined them, she did a quick introduction.

The man shook Mac's hand. "As I was telling the chief here, this is the most unusual call I've ever had. Mostly I deal with dead trees, not dead bodies." The man darted them a nervous smile, then flicked a quick look at the bones Barbara and her intern continued to extract from the tentacle-like roots.

"I realize we could be grasping at straws, but as I explained, the anthropologist isn't finding much, if anything, that will help us determine how long these bones have been here." A shaft of sunlight peeked through the dark clouds, and Lisa shaded her eyes. "We're hoping you can give us more to go on. Otherwise, this person could remain a Jane Doe."

"I can try—but keep in mind this isn't an exact science."

"Understood." The breeze kicked up, ruffling her hair, and she tucked it out of the way behind her ear.

"Let's start with what I can tell you for sure. These roots belong to an eastern red cedar tree." He held up the section of root he'd removed. "Those are the evergreens you see growing haphazardly in this area among the smaller deciduous saplings. I'd guess this piece of land was once more open and surrounded by those hardwoods and pines." He swept his hand toward the tall perimeter trees around the newer-growth area.

"So how did these cedars get here?"

"Birds. They eat the cedar berries and leave calling cards everywhere. That's one of the reasons cedars can become invasive. They're often the first species to populate cleared land. They also like open rocky woods—and with the limestone in evidence here"—he indicated some outcroppings of rock—"they'd be very much at home in this spot."

Lisa studied the root in his hand. "How can you be certain that belongs to a cedar?"

"Their roots are shallow and fibrous. And in this kind of rocky terrain, they tend to spread widely. Plus, the smell is an excellent clue."

He held it out, and she took a whiff. "I see what you mean. Reminds me of my grandmother's cedar closet."

"Right. As for how long ago this body was buried, I can't give you a precise answer. But I can tell you, based on the growth rings in this root, that these bones have been undisturbed for at least fifteen years. It's possible they've been here a lot longer, of course, since we have no way of knowing when the roots started to grow into the bones."

No matter. They had a time frame. Rough, perhaps, but more than they'd had before.

"So you're saying there's no chance the burial could have happened less than fifteen years ago?"

"Not unless someone dug under existing roots to try to fool a horticulturist who might count rings."

The chance of that was zero to none.

Lisa exhaled. "That's a tremendous help. Thank you."

"Glad to be of service." He extracted a card from his pocket and handed it to her. "If any other questions come up, don't hesitate to call. Nice to meet you both." After shaking hands with the two of them, he returned to his car.

Mac turned to her. "That may be the best lead yet."

"I agree."

"You'll keep me in the loop?"

"Absolutely."

"Okay. Talk to you soon."

She watched him walk away, lifting her hand in farewell when he reached his car. Then she shifted her attention back to the excavation site. Barbara and her assistant had made remarkable progress in freeing the skeleton from the earthen tomb that had concealed its dark secrets for too many years.

But things were looking up. She had a window of time now—which translated into a window of opportunity.

One she intended to maximize.

Whatever secrets had been buried in this grave were already being exposed to the light. Pieces of the puzzle were starting to appear. Not enough yet to get a handle on what had happened in this lonely field long ago, but she'd find more. Enough to begin fitting them together until a picture emerged.

And in the end, she'd solve this case.

Whatever it took.

5

Y ou're going to spoil that mangy mutt if you keep giving him snacks."

Lisa stroked Tally's head and fed him another biscuit from the stash she kept in her bottom desk drawer. "Now, Florence, everyone needs a little spoiling once in a while. And this is much healthier for him than those slices of summer sausage you slip him when you think I'm not looking."

Florence Kelly straightened up to her full five-foot-three height, wiry form taut, spiky white hair quivering. "I'll have you know I've only done that a time or two. Maybe three. And just for special occasions."

As near as Lisa could remember, May 29 wasn't an occasion of any sort, special or otherwise, but she let the transgression she'd witnessed last week pass. Could Tally help it if he was a loveable charmer?

After giving her canine companion a final pat, she leaned back in her chair. "So what's been going on while I've been occupied with old bones and catching up on sleep?"

"Nothing the boys and I couldn't handle."

Lisa had no doubt of that. All the officers she'd hired were dedicated and smart, and as for their office manager—the woman might be Social-Security eligible, but she was one sharp cookie. Her white hair may have fooled a few people who'd shown up at the station all bluster and indignation about one thing or another and assumed the octogenarian gatekeeper was a pushover . . . but no one made that mistake twice. Florence could put people in their place faster than Tally could snatch a dog biscuit from outstretched fingers.

"I always know the station is in capable hands when I'm not here. To be honest, I sometimes feel like I'm taking my salary under false pretenses."

Florence adjusted the collar of her crisp blue shirt. Smoothed a hand down the hip of her knife-creased navy slacks. Sniffed. "Hardly. You've taught this crew a thing or two in the past few months. And some of the cases you've handled—that meth dealer, and the gang member who assaulted poor Mrs. Jenkins in the garden shop parking lot while she was buying her pansies, and those young punks who were spraying nasty graffiti all over town—those took some serious, big-city-detective smarts. You've more than earned your pay."

High praise coming from the taciturn Florence.

"I appreciate that. Now tell me about the new papa and family."

"They're all doing fine. We rearranged the work schedule so he could spend some time with them for the first few days and see that his wife gets enough rest. Speaking of rest—did you really sleep in today?"

"Yes. Why else would I be strolling in at noon?"

"Good point, seeing as how you usually beat me here—not an easy feat, given my early-bird habits. Anything new on those bones?"

"Not yet. The anthropologist said she'd call with her preliminary findings as soon as possible, but it could take a . . ."

Her phone began to vibrate, and as she pulled it off her belt, Barbara's name flashed on the display.

"As a matter of fact"—she held up the cell—"this is her."

"I'll leave you to it, then."

As Florence exited, Lisa put the phone to her ear. "Barbara? It's Lisa. I didn't expect to hear from you this soon. You only finished excavating yesterday."

"Having a whole skeleton to work with is making my job much easier—and faster. I won't have the official report finished until early next week, but I can give you a few preliminaries based on measurements and X-rays."

"I'll take whatever you have." She picked up a pen and pulled a pad of paper toward her.

"We've got a Caucasian female, age eighteen to twenty-five. Height, five-three to five-five. The depressed area in the right parietal bone is much more pronounced now that we've cleaned it up. There's also a pattern of radiating fractures around the point of impact, and all three layers of the skull are shattered."

"The lady got hit very hard."

"That would be a safe conclusion."

"Any other obvious injuries?"

"Fractures of the tibia and radius—that's leg and arm for the layperson. The bones are completely healed, so they're old injuries. I'm bringing in an odontologist to examine the teeth too. And I have quite a few more tests to run. We're also going to send some samples to the lab in Texas. Given the condition of the remains, we'll have to settle for mitochondrial rather than nuclear DNA. It's a lot more resistant to destruction and can provide just as definitive a match on the maternal side."

It took Lisa a few moments to catch up, even though she was scribbling as fast as she could. "Any better idea how long the woman's been buried beyond what the horticulturist told us?"

"Unfortunately, no."

Lisa sighed. "That's what I was afraid you'd say."

Tally looked her way, rose from the corner of the office he'd claimed for his own, and trotted over, resting his head on her knee as he sent her a soulful look.

Lisa gave him a pat. Amazing how the golden-haired pooch could pick up on moods.

"I'll get my final report to you as soon as I finish my tests and the medical examiner weighs in on cause of death."

"Thanks, Barbara."

"Mac asked for a report as soon as I had anything too. Do you want to brief him, or shall I?"

A perfect excuse to call the handsome detective!

"I'll fill him in."

"That's what I figured."

Lisa let the woman's amused observation pass without comment. "I'll be watching for the final report."

"I'm not certain it will give you a whole lot more to go on, but there are a few things I still need to sort through. Good luck with this."

"Thanks. I think I'm going to need it."

As Lisa ended the call, she pulled Mac's card out of her pocket. It wasn't as if there was any need for him to play an ongoing role in the case, despite the offer he'd made before they parted at the excavation site. She could have let Barbara handle what might turn out to be nothing more than a wrap-up call.

But if his willingness to assist was sincere rather than just polite, why not take advantage of it? On a case like this, a fresh perspective from a fellow detective could come in handy.

Besides, professional rationale aside, she liked talking to Mac.

In fact, she liked Mac.

Odd how a set of old bones had hooked her up with the most interesting man she'd met in quite a while.

Maybe ever.

Easing back in her chair, she tapped in his cell number.

He answered on the first ring with a curt, clipped command. "Hold."

Not the most auspicious beginning for their conversation.

Though he continued to talk, his voice muffled as he barked out commands, she could distinguish only tone, not words—and it was focused and serious.

When he finally got back to her, his deep baritone remained no-nonsense and professional. "McGregor."

"Mac . . . it's Lisa Grant from Carson. Sounds like I caught you at a bad time."

"Lisa." A couple of seconds ticked by, and when he spoke again, he sounded much warmer—and welcoming. "Busy, not bad."

She let out the breath she'd been holding.

"I heard from Barbara. She said you'd asked for an update too, so I offered to call you. We can catch up later."

He hesitated. "That might be better. We just arrived at the scene of a homicide."

"My victim has waited years for justice; she can wait until you have a free minute."

"I'll call you as soon as that happens. It could be a while."

"I always have my cell. In the meantime, I'll touch base with my favorite reporter, who's been hounding me for an update."

"Have fun."

"Yeah. It'll be the highlight of my day. Talk to you later."

As she slowly slid the phone back on her belt, Tally looked up at her as if to say, "Everything okay now?"

She stroked his head and ruffled his ears. "The day just got brighter, my friend. Or it will, as soon as I deal with the press. Because I get to talk to Mac again later. Isn't that great?"

Tally thumped his tail, swiped his tongue over her knuckles, and trotted back to curl up on his rug in the corner, happy and content.

Lisa grinned.

She could relate.

———◆———

At the sudden vibration on his hip, Mac bit back a word he rarely used. What was with his phone today, anyway? It had been ringing all afternoon.

Maybe he could let this one roll.

Yanking the cell off his belt, he checked caller ID.

Blocked.

He weighed the phone in his hand. It could be a source for one of his cases who didn't want to be identified.

Better take it.

After punching the talk button, he put the phone to his ear and turned away from the homicide scene. "McGregor."

"Ditto."

Mac frowned and cocked his head. It was hard to tell from that one-word greeting, but the guy on the other end of the line sure sounded like the middle McGregor brother.

"Lance?"

"Bingo."

His adrenaline spiked. "Where are you? Is everything okay?"

"Man, you are so predictable. Do you realize you follow the exact same script every time I call?"

"You didn't answer the question."

"In reverse order . . . I'm fine and I'm stateside."

Mac's lungs kicked back in and he loosened his grip on the cell. "Where stateside?"

"Where I usually am when I'm in the good old U.S. of A."

That meant Fort Bragg, North Carolina . . . home of Delta Force.

"How long will you be here?"

"Hard to say." Typical Delta Force answer. "But I have two

weeks' leave—and I'm free as a bird for the next seven days. Want some company? I've never been to St. Louis, and I wouldn't mind scoping it out."

A rare chance to hang out with his brother? Was he kidding?

"You know you're always welcome."

"Does this weekend work? I'm going to run over and see the folks first, then I could swing your way."

"That'd be great. The apartment isn't much to look at, and I still haven't unpacked half my boxes, but you can crash on the couch."

"Do you have room for one more?"

Mac blinked.

That was a first.

"You're bringing a . . . friend?"

"I don't know if I'd go that far. His name is Finn."

Mac squinted at the ME's van as it pulled away from the crime scene. "Finn's with you?"

"Not yet, but he'll be stateside by tomorrow. He's looking for a change of scene too, after we pay a visit to the folks."

All three McGregor brothers in the same place at the same time? When had that last occurred?

Too long ago to remember.

"Sounds like we're about to have a long overdue reunion."

"Except we get to loaf while you work." Lance snickered.

"I'll take it anyway. You're flying in, right? You need me to pick you up?"

"Nah. We'll grab a rental. Look for us around noon on Saturday."

"I should be at home, but if I'm not, I'll leave a key with my neighbor on the right."

"Man or woman?"

"Woman."

"Single?"

Leave it to Lance to ask that.

Mac grinned. "Uh-huh."

"Cute?"

"Very."

"What's her name?"

"Adele."

"Can't say I've heard that name much. It's kind of old-fashioned."

"Not when she was born."

Silence.

"Okay, you got me. How old is she?"

"Eighty-two in April. And cute as a button."

Lance muttered some comment he couldn't make out. "I hope there are some better prospects around."

"I thought you were coming to visit me, not pick up women."

"Anything wrong with doing both?"

Vintage Lance.

"Nope. But don't expect me to introduce you to anyone. I'm too new in town."

"You've been there a whole month. Are you telling me you haven't met any hot chicks?"

An image of Lisa Grant flashed through his mind—not that she'd appreciate either of those labels.

"I'm still learning the new job. No time yet to play."

"Yeah?" Lance sounded skeptical. "Since when haven't you made time to play?"

"Since I left the military and joined the nine-to-five crowd."

"You're not turning into a stick-in-the-mud, are you?"

"No, but the quieter life has its advantages."

"Well, Finn and I will liven things up for you once we get there."

"I have no doubt of that. Give Mom and Dad my best."

"Will do. See you in three days."

As Mac holstered the phone and turned back to the crime scene, he did his best to switch gears.

But he couldn't quite shake the feeling that the upcoming reunion was more than a simple, friendly visit from his brothers. Lance hadn't hinted at an ulterior motive, but his voice had held an undertone of . . . tension? Excitement? Trepidation?

Whatever it was, something was up. He could feel it in his bones.

Still, as long as his brothers were on his turf for a few days, he wouldn't have to worry about them being in the line of fire—and that was worth celebrating.

Even if he had to wait until they showed up to satisfy his curiosity about the real reason for this visit.

◆

"That was great, Mom. Sorry again about getting hung up at the office and delaying dinner." Lisa speared the last piece of chicken in her Caesar salad and leaned back in the patio chair as she munched.

"No problem. I'm just glad it cooled off enough to eat outside. Though maybe this wasn't such a smart idea. You look like you've gotten a fair amount of sun since I saw you last week. Shall I tilt the umbrella to give you a little more shade?"

"I'm fine, thanks. Besides, the sun will be below the trees in a few minutes." She waved toward the golden orb dipping low in the sky. "I did spend a lot of hours outside at the excavation site this week. I guess I should have used more sunscreen." She smoothed a finger over the sensitive tip of her nose.

"I wasn't going to bring that up in case you were trying to disconnect from work for the evening, but as long as you mentioned it . . . I saw a short item about the discovery on the evening news."

Her friendly reporter hadn't wasted any time publicizing the latest update.

"What did he have to say?"

"Not much more than the first story. He said the bones appear to be female and are quite old. He showed the same video as the first story, along with some shots from the traffic cam and from behind the police tape at the site. There was one new piece of footage, though. You were talking to a tall, nice-looking man near a canopy. He had on a sport jacket."

Lisa picked up her plate and her mother's and stood. "That's the County detective who came out to assist."

"You two seemed to be having a very intent conversation."

"When you discover a skeleton, things can get serious fast. Stay put. I'll clear the table and load the dishwasher."

"I'll help. Many hands and all that." Her mother picked up the pepper mill and basket of crackers and followed her inside. "What's this detective's name?"

So much for her evasive maneuvers.

"Mac McGregor." Best to get the third degree out of the way ASAP.

"Is he nice?"

"Personable."

"Married?"

"No."

Her mother stowed the pepper mill in the cabinet and tucked the uneaten crackers back into their box. "Is he going to stay involved in the case?"

"I don't know. He's a busy man. What's for dessert?"

"Strawberries and whipped cream."

"Yum. My favorite. So what's on your agenda for tomorrow?"

"Changing the subject, hmm?" Her mom put the crackers away and closed the cabinet. "Why don't you want to talk about this detective?"

Turning aside, Lisa reached into the cabinet for two dessert bowls. "We can talk about him if you want to, but I just met the man two days ago and I've only spent a couple of hours with him. There isn't much to say."

"I don't know . . . you had an interesting expression on your face in that news clip when the two of you were deep in conversation."

Oh, for goodness' sake!

She retrieved the bowls and swiveled back to her mom. "I couldn't have been on camera more than five or ten seconds, max."

"It was long enough. I know that look. I had it once myself, years ago when I met your dad." A gentle smile softened her features. "A woman never forgets what that feels like."

"What *what* feels like?"

"The sense that maybe, just maybe, he could be the one."

This was getting way out of hand.

"Mom, listen to me." She fixed the older woman with an intent look. "I don't even know this man."

Her mother winked. "You'd like to."

The bare truth nailed in three words.

How did her mother do that? Since her older daughter's second-grade crush on Timmy Maloney, Stephanie Grant had been able to delve with the precision of a neurosurgeon into the romantic crannies of her brain. It had been kind of entertaining, in a comical sort of way.

Tonight, however, she was not amused

This might be a short evening.

"You know, it's silly to jump to a lot of conclusions when . . ." Her phone began to vibrate. *Yes!* She handed her mother the dessert bowls. "I need to take this."

"Saved by the bell—for now." After tacking on that caveat, her mom took the bowls and began preparing the dessert.

Huffing out a breath, Lisa pulled the phone off her belt—and froze as the name on the caller ID panel registered.

It was Mac.

Talk about bad timing.

Of course she'd expected him to call her back. He'd said he would, and he struck her as a man of his word.

But did it have to be right this minute?

"I thought you had to answer that?" Her mother arched an eyebrow.

"I do. I'll meet you outside." She headed toward the back door and the privacy of the patio, phone to her ear. "Lisa Grant."

"Lisa, it's Mac. Sorry to call so late, but I got hung up with the homicide. Did I catch you in the middle of dinner?"

"No. We just finished."

Silence. "Look, if I'm interrupting anything . . ."

"No." Her reassurance was fast—and firm—as she pushed through the door. No way did she intend to leave the impression she was on a date. "I have dinner with my mom every Wednesday. We're at the clearing-the-table stage."

"Oh. Good." The relief in his voice was obvious—and encouraging. "I'm getting ready to nuke a dinner myself. Can you fill me in on the bones while I work? I'm starving."

"Sure." Keeping her mother in view through the sliding door, she retook her seat at the table while she briefed him on the latest news.

"Not much to go on, is it?" As he spoke, she heard the familiar sound of a microwave door being opened, then closed in the background . . . followed by several beeps.

"No. Barbara said she was checking out a few things, but I'm not optimistic there'll be a breakthrough."

"So what's your plan?"

Excellent question.

"It's still in the development stage. If there's no obvious lead in Barbara's report, I'll go over it with a fine-tooth comb and try to connect some dots. If I can do that, I'll move on to a review of missing persons files fifteen years and older from within a hundred-mile radius of the excavation site. What you said earlier in the week is true—most people who go missing locally get found locally."

"That kind of review could take a while, even narrowing it down by the age, gender, and race criteria you have."

"It will give me something to do in my free time." Her mother sent her a curious look through the glass door, and she averted her head. She'd had enough mind-reading for one day, thank you very much.

"Do you have a lot of that?"

She tried to recall what they'd been talking about. Free time. Right.

"More than I had in Chicago."

"I have a feeling that's not saying much."

"You sound like my mother." She peeked back toward the kitchen. Her mom was still watching her.

"Is that a bad thing?"

"Not necessarily." In truth, it was kind of nice to think the man on the other end of the line might care how many excess hours she worked. "But I'll have less free time if I have to dive into this case."

"Remember, if you want any help, all you have to do is pick up the phone."

She used a finger to gather up the cracker crumbs on the glass-topped table, brushing them into a nice, neat pile. "To tell you the truth, I wouldn't mind having someone to bounce ideas off of as the investigation progresses—assuming it does. I did a lot of brainstorming in Chicago with the other detectives, and even though I'm training the Carson officers, they're not at the level yet where they can contribute much to a case like this."

"I'd be happy to be your bouncer." She could hear the smile

in his voice. "Why don't you send me a copy of Barbara's report and we can touch base after we both have a chance to review it?"

"That would be great. Considering how busy you are, I expect I'll finish my review first. Do you want to call me once you look it over?"

"Sounds like a plan." The muffled clunk of ice from an ice maker came over the line.

Much as she was tempted to prolong their conversation, the man needed to eat dinner.

"I'll let you go, then. Enjoy your meal."

"Not likely. The package said this was pork, but it looks more like the mystery meat in an MRE . . . also known as a ready-to-eat military ration."

"I hear you." She let her eyelids drift closed and lifted her face to catch the last rays of the sun. "What about the leftovers from our Panera lunch?"

"I finished them off for dinner last night—but you were right about a lot of that stuff not holding up very well. The limp lettuce and soggy chicken salad would have made Julia Child cringe."

"At least your dinner will be better than that."

"I'm not placing any bets on that."

"So . . . I guess I'll talk to you early next week?"

"Count on it. Enjoy the rest of your evening."

As he ended the call, Lisa gave a soft sigh, opened her eyes—and found her mother standing on the other side of the table, bowls of strawberries in hand, beaming like she'd won the lottery.

How long had she been there?

"You had lunch at Panera with that handsome detective?"

Too long.

She sat up straighter, scattering the crumbs she'd gathered. "He brought some takeout food to the excavation site. It was a working lunch, not a date."

"Uh-huh." Her mother set the strawberries down and took her seat.

Lisa braced for the next question.

It didn't come.

Weird.

Shooting a wary glance across the table, Lisa picked up her spoon. "Aren't you going to ask me a bunch of other questions?"

"Why, when I already know the answers?" Her mother gave her a smug smile and kept eating.

"What's that supposed to mean?"

Her mom began to hum "Some Enchanted Evening."

Oh, for crying out loud.

"That's crazy."

"Is it? We'll see. Eat your dessert before the topping deflates."

Lisa looked down. Too late. It had already collapsed—sort of like the arguments she was trying to dredge up to counter her mother's assumptions. Not that any protest she might make would matter. Once Stephanie Grant made up her mind about anything, getting her to budge was harder than convincing Tally to give up his spot in the corner of her office.

Better to let it ride.

Besides . . . even if her mother was rushing things . . . even if logic told her it was much too soon to be thinking about enchanted evenings . . . even if she'd never believed in that love at first sight nonsense . . . she couldn't help but hope that she and Mac might, indeed, find they had more in common than a case involving old bones.

6

As the wheels of the Boeing 747 clicked into position for landing at LaGuardia Airport, Jessica Lee looked across the first-class aisle at Robert Bradshaw. The younger founding partner of Peterson-Bradshaw was out cold, as he'd been for most of the London to New York flight. Yet several hours of sleep hadn't erased the lines of fatigue on his face. He might have laughed earlier today about getting too old for all the jet-setting required of the CEO of an international PR firm, but at sixty-five, her mentor was, indeed, showing the strain.

How fortunate for him he had her waiting in the wings when he retired, now that Drake Peterson was sidelined by Alzheimer's.

Such a sad end for the senior partner.

The corners of her mouth lifted as she reached into the Louis Vuitton shoulder purse at her feet and removed her makeup bag. Which lip color to apply—Dior's Rouge Blossom or Chanel's understated Peregrina? She examined her reflection in the mirror of her compact. The red might be too much after such a long, tiring flight, even with a retouch of blush. Better to go with the more demure Chanel.

After freshening her makeup and spritzing her hair, she peered again into the mirror. Was that a *gray hair* among the ash-blonde strands?

Yes.

She snapped the compact closed. Considering Kenneth's exorbitant fees, mistakes like this were unacceptable. In her business, image was everything—especially when one was being groomed for the top slot.

An attendant smiled at her as she passed by for a seat-belt check, but Jessica averted her head. If she had to conjure up one more pleasant expression, her face would crack. Being the point person for every major client meeting on both sides of the Atlantic was getting old. Once she took over the firm, she'd delegate the bulk of those duties to her replacement. The next Senior VP of Client Services and New Client Development could handle chores like that, just as she had since her promotion five years ago.

Until that day, though, she'd continue to perform at the stellar level that had impressed her mentor. All she had to do was hold out another few months, and the prize she'd had her eye on for the past fifteen years would be hers. Maybe Robert hadn't yet announced his retirement, but why else would he have bought a place in Florida? Why else would he be letting his many board memberships lapse? Why else would he have secured her a place on the strategic planning committee last year, if not to groom her for his position?

As the plane banked and began its final descent, she exhaled. One more flight, and she'd be back in St. Louis, insulated from the world in her high-rise condo. Best of all, the whole weekend stretched ahead. Robert had insisted they needed a couple of days to decompress after the rigorous round of meetings that had kept them on the go late into the evening every day of their weeklong visit, and for once she hadn't demurred. Long hours and weekend appearances at the office were important—and rewarded—but she'd take at least Saturday off.

She rested her elbows on the arms of her seat, planning her Saturday. A stop at Starbucks. A circuit through Saks to check out new merchandise. A swing by Gourmet to Go for a takeout dinner. And if she didn't talk to a single soul—heaven.

Returning her purse to the floor, she leaned closer to the window and watched the runway approach as the plane returned to earth.

A successful European trip, a CEO job on the horizon, and a quiet weekend.

What could be more perfect?

◆

At the impatient, staccato buzz of his doorbell early Saturday afternoon, followed by vigorous knocking, Mac grinned.

His siblings had arrived.

Leaving his laptop humming on the kitchen table, he crossed the living room and pulled open the door.

Lance and Finn, duffels over their shoulders, grinned back at him—lean, fit, tanned . . . and best of all, safe.

"About time you answered. We were just getting ready to bother Adele. Finn wants to meet her." Lance winked at him—meaning he hadn't let their youngest sibling in on the joke.

"It can wait." Finn moved into the room, dumped his bag on the floor, and sniffed. "You have any food in this joint?"

"Good to see you too, bro." Mac stepped back to allow Lance to enter, sizing up his middle brother. "Did you have a growth spurt, or what?"

"Still six-two—but these boots give me an inch on you." He motioned to his feet, then directed his attention to Finn. "Hey, runt—you want to say hello before you stuff your face?"

Color surged on Finn's cheeks, and Mac reined in a snigger. That auburn hair had always been the bane of his baby brother's existence. "Don't call me runt, old man. You're only two inches taller than me. Besides, you're two years older—and weaker."

"I could take you any day."

"Yeah? You want to prove that?"

"Hey!" Mac held up his hand. "Rule number one in this house—civility."

Lance dumped his duffel next to Finn's. "You always were the peacekeeper."

"Somebody had to be, with two knuckleheads like you guys for brothers." He pulled Lance into a bear hug, then did the same with Finn. "It's great to see you both."

"Yeah." Finn clapped him on the back. "Like old times, you know?" His voice grated, and he swallowed.

"Real old. I can't remember the last time the three of us were together."

"Christmas, eight years ago, London," Lance supplied. "We all converged on Mom and Dad."

"That's right." Mac folded his arms. "How are they?"

"Same as always. There's no energy shortage in that house. They send their love, by the way." He surveyed the couch, an end table empty except for a family photo, floor lamp, and treadmill in the living room. "You need to hire an interior decorator."

"I'll get around to fixing the place up once I settle in. The sofa's a queen sleeper, by the way—if you guys don't mind sharing."

Finn shrugged. "I've bunked with worse. So is there any food in the place?"

"Same old Finn. Always hungry." Lance elbowed his brother and rolled his eyes.

"A growing boy needs nourishment."

"I stocked up on sandwich stuff, chips, pretzels, and drinks yesterday. I take it you guys haven't had lunch."

"Nope." Finn headed for the kitchen. "I asked Lance to stop, but he said we should come straight here in case you had food for us."

Finn disappeared, and a moment later the sounds of drawers sliding and a fridge opening echoed through the apartment.

"Make yourself at home." As Mac called the wry comment to Finn, he smiled at Lance. "Some things never change."

"Yeah." Lance threw him a quick glance. Then, instead of coming back with some sarcastic remark, he knelt down and busied himself with a clasp on the duffel.

Not his usual style.

"Hey . . ." Mac rested his hand on Lance's shoulder.

Lance hesitated. Looked up.

"Everything okay?"

"Sure. Everything's good. You worry too much, you know?"

"The lot of the oldest brother."

"Well, save your worry for the youngest McGregor. He needs it more than I do."

"Meaning?"

At Mac's frown, Lance stood and raked his fingers through his hair. "Meaning nothing. Seriously, Mac—stop reading so much into everything. I've got things under control; Finn is . . . Finn. He takes too many chances, like always."

"And you don't?"

"No more than you did when you were a SEAL."

"Oh, that makes me feel a whole lot better."

Lance punched him in the arm, one corner of his mouth hitching up. "Look at it this way. I'm as careful as you are, and you survived just fine."

He almost hadn't—but only Lisa knew that story.

Strange that he'd tell her but leave his family in the dark.

"You did survive just fine, didn't you?"

At Lance's too-sharp question, he switched gears. "Better than fine. I have a great job in a new city, and I rarely have to worry about dodging bullets."

"There's only one thing missing from that picture-perfect life."

"What?"

"A girl."

"I'll get around to that one of these days."

"You're thirty-five, Mac."

Like he needed to be reminded.

"You're thirty-three." Offense was always better than defense in discussions with his brothers.

Instead of the smart-aleck comeback he expected, Lance shrugged. "I can't argue with that."

"Hey." Finn stuck his head into the living room, one fist buried in a bag of chips. "Have you got any mustard?"

"A whole jar." Mac waved Lance toward the kitchen. "We better join the party or there won't be anything left."

"I'm on it." Lance jogged in the direction of the food.

Mac followed more slowly.

Was he imagining things, or was Finn more wired than usual? And why did Lance seem on edge?

As he dived into the melee in the kitchen and they all resorted to their typical good-natured bantering and teasing, he doubted the opportunity would come up to deal with those questions today.

But he had a whole week in close quarters with his younger brothers.

And before they left, he'd get his answers.

⬦

Glass of chardonnay in hand, Jessica opened the sliding door that led to the balcony of her condo and stepped out. At least the temperature had moderated during her trip to London. The evening was perfect—balmy and cooled by a gentle breeze.

She strolled over to the railing, resting her elbows on the top as the lights of the city twinkled to life below her. She ought to reheat the gourmet dinner she'd picked up earlier . . . but she wasn't hungry yet. Nor did she have to accommodate the needs of a husband or children—highly overrated commodities, even if Peterson-Bradshaw's family-focused clients preferred to deal with companies whose executives favored traditional domestic situations.

Corporate player that she was, however, she'd done her time on that score. Thank goodness those days were over and her life was her own again.

Sipping the wine, she moved to a chaise lounge and pulled her cell out of the pocket of her capris. Not much chance Robert would call her today, but higher-ups always appreciated accessibility—though only he fell into that category these days.

A clear sign all her hard work and sacrifices had paid off.

Smiling, she sat on the side of the cushioned chaise. Of course, if an important client's name popped up, she'd take the call—but that didn't typically happen on Saturday nights . . . and almost never on Sunday.

Funny.

If she'd known Peterson-Bradshaw would morph into a magnet for Christian-based companies with strict, honor-the-Sabbath-type moral standards, she might have aligned herself with a different organization. But by the time that trend had become obvious, she'd invested too many years, built too much political capital in the firm, to switch alliances.

Oh, well. In exchange for a lifestyle that met all the requirements she'd laid out decades ago, she could afford to restrict her moderate alcohol consumption to the privacy of her condo and attend an occasional church service.

Setting the phone on the teak and glass table beside the lounge, she mulled over her plans for tomorrow. As long as she'd played all day today, it might be smart to swing by the office for an hour or two and leave a few things in Robert's in-box. Her place as the heir apparent might be secure . . . but earning a few bonus points by logging some extra hours couldn't hurt.

Just as she started to swing her legs onto the chair, the jarring vibration of her cell intruded on the evening's tranquility.

Reining in her annoyance, she picked it up, checked caller ID—and muttered a word neither her clients nor her boss would approve of.

Why was Erika calling? Hadn't they agreed infrequent contact would be best? They'd just talked . . . when? Last month?

But the woman had always been a loose cannon—more so since her husband's indictment for fraud.

Listening to another one of Erika's sob stories was not on her agenda for the evening, however. Whatever crisis she was dealing with would have to wait a day or two.

She let the phone roll to voice mail, picked up her wine, and took a measured sip. One glass a day, no matter the stresses that might tempt her to make an exception. That was her rule.

And she never broke her rules.

As the minutes ticked by, her pulse slowed and she closed her eyes. The muted sound of the traffic far below was calming, connecting her to the world without intruding.

Distance was a good thing.

And that was the very reason Erika's calls were always jarring. Who wanted to be reminded of their past—especially the one *they* shared? If Erika wasn't always teetering on the brink of a meltdown, she'd have cut ties with her as she'd done with Joe.

But Erika needed to be managed—and kept under control.

The phone began to vibrate again, and her hand jerked, sloshing the wine.

Once again she spat out a word she never uttered in public.

Setting the glass on the table, she picked up the phone.

Erika again.

She waited until the phone stilled in her hand, then punched in her voice mail code. Better see what the twit wanted.

"You have two messages. First message. Saturday, June 6, seven forty-five."

For a long moment, nothing but the sound of ragged breathing came over the line. At last Erika spoke. "Hey, Jess. It's me. Erika. Look . . . I need to talk to you ASAP, okay? Something's . . . happened. Something bad. Call me as soon as you get this."

A click signaled the end of the call.

Jessica reached for her glass and took another sip of wine as she waited for the second message to kick in.

"Saturday, June 6, eight ten."

"Jess, ish me again. You know . . . Erika. Call me, okay? Like right now. Ish really important. I'll wait by the phone. Ish not just about me this time."

The line went dead.

Great.

The woman was getting seriously sloshed.

So what else was new? She'd always gone overboard on alcohol when stressed. And if the news reports were to be believed, her husband was about to be convicted. Translation: big-time stress. She must want a shoulder to cry on, as usual.

Except she'd said this wasn't just about her.

Or was that a ruse to expedite a callback?

Frowning, Jessica tapped a freshly manicured fingernail on the arm of the chaise lounge, weighing the phone in her other hand. She could put the call off until tomorrow—but deferring issues never made them go away. It was always better to fix problems immediately, before they escalated.

Annoyance muting the soothing effects of her wine, she scrolled through her directory and pressed autodial.

Erika answered on the first ring. "Jess?"

"I don't use that nickname anymore, Erika." She tightened her grip on the stem of her wine glass.

"Sorry. I always forget." A soft hiccup came over the line.

"I noticed. What's the problem?"

"We have trouble."

"What do you mean, we?"

"They found her."

A niggle of unease snaked down Jessica's spine. "Her who?"

"You know . . . *her.*"

She set the wine glass on the table, holding it in place by the delicate stem until it stabilized. "Are you talking about who I think you're talking about?"

"Yes. Haven't you been watching the news?"

"I've been in London."

"I missed the first couple of stories too, with the trial and all." She hiccupped again.

"Erika—tell me exactly what you've heard." She could google for info, but establishing any sort of traceable connection to this would be foolish.

"Some construction guys found her. I guesh my parents' neighbors shold the property for a subdivision."

Jessica rose and paced over to the railing. Paced back again.

"Are you shtill there?"

"Yes. Hang on a minute."

She stopped pacing and stood still, giving the analytical side of her brain a chance to engage.

Okay, they'd found the body. So what? There couldn't be much left except some bones. After all, the whole thing had happened twenty-four years ago. And there was nothing else in the grave to give the authorities a clue about the girl's identity. She'd made sure of that.

They were fine—as long as they stayed cool.

"It's not a problem, Erika. Trust me."

"Are you sure? I mean, what if—"

"Erika." She sharpened her tone as she cut the other woman off. "Chill. If you want to talk about this, we can meet for coffee.

But it's not a topic suitable for phone or email. Ever. Are we absolutely clear on that?"

"Yes." A soft sob came over the line.

Erika might be giving her verbal assent, but in light of her shaky emotional state and inebriation, it wasn't all that credible.

Distasteful as it was, she'd have to do some damage control.

"I'll tell you what . . . let's get together for coffee this week. You pick the day."

"I don't know . . . I have to be in court for Jack's trial. But after lishening to all the witnesses, I think he's going to jail." Her voice choked. "How could he do all that s-stuff? And how did I end up in the middle of it?"

Because you were stupid enough to pick a jerk of a husband who sold bogus investments to gullible retirees—and the slimeball is getting exactly what he deserves.

All true—but this might not be the best time to say it.

"You'll have a few free minutes, I'm sure. Why don't you call me? I'll rearrange my schedule to meet you."

"Thanks, Jess. I'm glad we're friends." The clink of ice came over the line.

Friends?

Not even close.

Erika had never been more than a useful tool.

But she'd finished being useful more than two decades ago. Once her doting state-senator father had connected his daughter's best friend with people who could give her a leg up in the corporate world and pave the way for her rise to the executive ranks, Erika had been expendable. If they hadn't been linked by a force far more potent and binding than the friendship Erika thought they shared, she'd have severed all ties with the needy woman on the other end of the line the day her father died.

Secrets could create very odd . . . and unpleasant . . . alliances.

94

"I'll call you, okay?" Erika's words were tear-laced.

Jessica tamped down her annoyance—and impatience. "Fine. Use my cell number. And cut back on the booze."

"Why? Isht's the only thing that makes me happy."

"You need to stay clearheaded until this dies down."

"I get depressed when I'm clearheaded. I feel better after a few scotches."

Understandable, given the mess she'd made of her life.

"Go to bed, Erika. Sleep it off." Reasoning with her tonight would be fruitless.

"Should we tell Joe?"

Her antennas went up. "You don't keep in touch with him, do you? We agreed not to."

Silence.

Not good.

He and Erika had been an item back then; maybe they'd been keeping in touch all along.

"Erika?"

"I send him a card at Christmas."

"Is that it?"

"Mostly."

Jessica tightened her grip on the phone. Another subject to discuss when they met. She might keep tabs on Joe's whereabouts as a precautionary measure, might have his address in Paducah, Kentucky, tucked away in her mental file . . . but having her two companions from that fateful night talk was not wise—and she thought she'd convinced Erika of that.

Apparently not.

"Look . . . promise me you'll keep your mouth shut until we meet. If you feel the need to talk about this before then, call me, not Joe. Got it?"

"Yeah."

Not convincing.

"I'll tell you what. Why don't I stop by your place tomorrow on my way home from the office?"

"Tomorrow's Sunday, isn't it? Why are you going to work?"

Because that's how people get ahead in the business world, you idiot.

Despite the temptation to respond with sarcasm, she did her best to maintain an even tone. "There's a lot to catch up on after being gone for a week."

"Oh. I guess. No, tomorrow's bad. Jack won't want any visitors, not with the trial winding down. I'll call you when I have a free minute during the week."

Not ideal, but it would have to do.

"Fine. In the meantime, zip it."

"Right." The ice clinked in the glass again. "G'night, Jesh."

The line went dead.

Jessica set the phone back on the table and picked up her glass of wine. Why couldn't people be disciplined? Why did they feel the need to indulge in destructive behavior? Between her eating and drinking binges, not to mention her chain smoking, Erika was a mess. Overweight, bombed half the time, already exhibiting early signs of emphysema.

What a wasted existence—even before adding in her marriage to that lowlife.

Sipping her wine, Jessica tried all her usual tricks to restore her earlier placid, I'm-in-control mood.

She took slow, deep breaths.

She conjured up a mental image of her name on the brass plate beside the CEO's office.

She took a stroll through her private domain, stopping to admire the limited edition Ansel Adams print that complemented the monochromatic palette of her living room. Ran a hand over the smooth, enameled lava stone countertop in the kitchen. Trailed a finger down the line of the form-fitting Carolina Herrera cocktail dress in her closet, added to her wardrobe mere hours ago.

But none of the typical stress-reducing techniques worked.

Tossing back the last of her wine, she returned to the kitchen and set the empty glass beside the sink.

Of all the bizarre things to happen after twenty-four years.

Still, what she'd told Erika was true. There was nothing to tie them to the bones at that construction site. They might have been young and scared that night—well, Erika and Joe had been scared—but she'd thought through every contingency, had rehearsed her companions over the weekend until all their stories meshed perfectly. They'd covered their tracks, created alibis, and left no trace of their connection to the tragic disappearance of a fellow student.

There was no reason for alarm—if they all stayed the course and didn't panic.

But therein lay the problem.

Erika couldn't be trusted. Heavy drinking could lead to a loose tongue, which in turn could create a loose end—and loose ends were dangerous.

They needed to be dealt with.

The question was, how?

7

Things were looking up.

Big time.

It seemed Barbara had unearthed far more leads than expected.

With the reports from the anthropologist, medical examiner, and odontologist all opened on her screen, Lisa took a swig from her bottle of water and went through them a second time, highlighting the findings that held promise.

They'd already nailed gender, race, height, and age . . . and the ME had confirmed cause of death as blunt force trauma to the head.

She paused at Barbara's notation that the long bones in the woman's arms and legs appeared stunted.

That deserved a highlight.

So did the section of the report where she described a small, faceted, blood-red stone she'd found while sifting through the dirt around the body. The geologist she'd consulted had identified it as a pyrope garnet. According to him, the stone was not naturally found in Missouri—or anywhere in the Midwest—and it had been cut by a gem cutter.

In other words, it was the kind of stone that might have been in a ring.

A ring that might have been on a severed finger.

Lisa took another drink, adrenaline pinging. An excellent lead.

And there was more.

She continued to read, highlighting Barbara's reference to bilateral periosteal lesions of the lower limb bones—because lesions came up again in the odontologist's report, this time located on the medial surface of the mandible—middle of the lower jawbone, per the English translation he'd provided. Also, for a young woman, the victim had had very poor teeth, with many showing evidence of antemortem decay.

In other words, she had a mouthful of cavities.

Leaning back in her chair, Lisa tapped the water bottle.

All of those clues were useful.

But she also had questions based on the new information. Questions perhaps best addressed by the medical examiner.

"You know, twenty years ago the sages predicted we'd be living in a paperless society." Florence marched in and plopped a stack of files in Lisa's in-box. "So much for the sages. Find anything interesting in the anthropologist's report?"

"Maybe. Do you by chance have the County ME's cell number?"

"Doubtful—but if not, I can get it. You need it right away?"

"Yes. I want to pick his brain about some of these findings."

"Give me ten. And speaking of time . . . aren't you supposed to be at the County courthouse soon to testify against that graffiti gang?"

"Yep. I'm on my way." She began printing out the sheets she might need to reference in her conversation with the ME. "Will you call me with the number as soon as you find it?"

"You'll have it before you get to I-64."

As she pulled the first sheet from the printer, Lisa watched out of the corner of her eye while Florence bent down to give Tally a quick pat on her way out.

The old softie.

Florence stopped at the door. "Do you want me to get you another bottle of water for the road?"

"That would be great, thanks." She swung back toward her printer and smiled at the older woman as she retrieved more sheets. "What would I do without you?"

"Hmph." Florence picked a nonexistent piece of lint off her slacks. "I expect you'd get along fine—but to tell the truth, it's nice to be needed. That whole retirement gig is highly overrated. I was bored out of my mind after three weeks. Nothing feeds the soul like doing work that matters. You get a move on, now."

"I'm on my way." Lisa gathered up her papers, stuck them into a file folder, and stood as Florence exited.

Tally rose too, and sent her a hopeful can-I-go-too look.

"Sorry, boy. Not today. You'd enjoy the ride, but the court-house wouldn't be your cup of tea."

Snorting out a breath that sounded a lot like disgust, he plopped back onto his rug. The one he'd pilfered from the laundry room in her house and insisted on dragging into the office after she'd lost their tug-of-war.

"I'll give you a treat later. How's that?" She slid her uniform jacket off the hanger on the coatrack.

The appeasement attempt earned her a tiny tail swish, though he continued to sulk.

A biscuit on her return, however, would smooth things over—unless Florence beat her to it.

Five minutes later, the station still visible in her rearview mirror, her cell began ringing.

Speaking of their efficient office manager . . .

"So did you have it, or did you have to make some calls and

do some fast-talking?" She eased onto the shoulder and picked up the folder from the seat beside her.

"The latter—and I can fast-talk with the best of them when the need arises. Do you have a pen handy?"

Lisa pulled one out of her shirt pocket. "Ready." She jotted the number on the folder as Florence recited it. "Got it. Thanks a million."

She disconnected that call and punched in the ME's number.

The phone rang several times—but just when she thought it would roll to voice mail, he picked up.

Lisa introduced herself and got straight to business, explaining the case she was working on and the reports she'd received that afternoon.

"Yes, I recall the case. How can I help you?"

"I'm not certain you can, but I thought it would be worth having a conversation. There were a few facts in the different reports that seem as if they could be linked. I hoped, with your medical background, you might be able to connect the dots—or at least offer a theory, off the record."

"I'll give it a try."

Lisa ticked off the information about the lesions, the woman's poor dental history, and the old breaks in her arm and leg. "I wondered if there might be some relationship among all those things."

"An interesting set of circumstances, no question about it. The bone issues, plus the teeth situation, make me wonder if the victim had some sort of dietary deficiency."

"Such as?" She flipped open her notebook and began jotting.

"Inadequate vitamin D and calcium, or perhaps insufficient vitamin C. A person who was lactose intolerant and avoided milk products might develop some of those conditions . . . but the importance of calcium has been well documented for years, and supplements are readily available. Likewise with vitamin C.

Most people even twenty or thirty years ago were savvy about nutritional basics."

"Let's suppose for a minute this person wasn't. What sorts of conditions might those deficiencies cause?"

"In the most severe cases, untreated calcium deficiency can lead to problems like osteoporosis, high blood pressure, and cardiac arrhythmia. Insufficient vitamin C can compromise the immune system and cause dental issues." A couple of beats ticked by. "And here's one that's out in left field—have you ever heard of scurvy?"

Lisa frowned. "Wasn't that associated with sailors?"

"Yes. They were at sea for extended periods without any foods containing vitamin C, and that's what scurvy is—a vitamin C deficiency. It was also a huge problem during the potato famine in Ireland. I read an intriguing article about that in a medical journal just a few weeks ago. But I've never run across a case of it in all my years as an ME."

"What specific conditions make you think my victim might have had this?"

"The lesions of the lower limb bones could reflect the formation of ossified hematomas, which can be an indication of scurvy. So can periodontal disease—and jawbone lesions are a textbook characteristic of the disease. Your victim also broke two bones. That's a lot for a young woman . . . but infants and children with scurvy have thin bones that fracture easily. Then there's her short stature. The undersized long bones in the arms and legs would be a factor in that—and stunted bone growth is another indicator of the disease. When infants or children have scurvy, the growth plates in those bones harden prematurely."

Lisa's frown deepened. "But even if the woman in that grave was born forty or fifty years ago, scurvy wasn't that common, was it?"

"No."

"This is weird."

"I agree. That's why I gave the left-field warning. Scurvy is very difficult to definitively determine based on bones alone. Too many of the individual indicators are also symptomatic of other illnesses. Put them all together, though—it's classic scurvy."

Lisa flicked a glance in the rearview mirror and moved back into traffic. "You've given me a lot to think about."

"Which may go nowhere. If you have any other leads worth pursuing, I'd start with those rather than something this speculative."

"I will . . . but it takes a lot of pieces to complete a puzzle. Yours may fit somewhere. Thanks again for taking the time to talk with me."

"My pleasure—and good luck."

"I'll need all I can get with this one."

As Lisa ended the call and accelerated toward her court date, she did her best to switch gears. She needed to get her head into the testimony she'd be giving in less than an hour.

But the minute she walked out of that courtroom, she'd be back on this—and looking forward to discussing it with Mac. It would be interesting to get his read on the new developments.

One thing for sure—a search through missing persons reports was ahead of her, starting tomorrow. Because even though decades might have passed since the crime, there could still be people who grieved for —and wanted answers about—the girl in that grave. Loved ones who needed closure.

And she intended to do everything in her power to give them both.

⁓

Was that Lisa?

Mac shaded his eyes against the late-afternoon sun and peered at the figure striding away from him down the sidewalk. The uniform didn't make an ID easy—but that dark hair with fiery sparks? Very distinctive.

Hesitating, he surveyed the street in front of headquarters. No sign of his brothers yet—and they weren't due for ten minutes. Meaning they'd likely show in fifteen or twenty. Maybe he could steal a few moments with the Carson police chief before he had to meet them for dinner at their designated rendezvous down the street.

He took off after the retreating woman at a half jog, waiting until he was closer to call out. "Lisa?"

She stopped. Turned. Smiled.

He closed the distance between them. "I thought that was you. What brings you to Clayton?"

"I was testifying in a case." She waved toward the courthouse.

"Fun and games."

"Not." She fanned herself, then slipped her jacket off and draped it over her arm in one lithe movement. "It's a hot one today."

Hot was an appropriate word.

He kept his gaze fixed firmly on her face. "Yeah."

"I don't suppose you've had a chance yet to look over the final reports in the buried bones case."

"No. Sorry. I've been on the run all day. I did see your email in my in-box, but I haven't had one spare minute to open it. Did they offer any new clues?"

Animation sparked in her eyes. "More than I expected."

As she gave him an update, enthusiasm chased the fatigue from her features. It took all his powers of concentration to focus on the words instead of the woman.

When she finished, he folded his arms. "The garnet, coupled with the severed finger, strikes me as the most helpful pieces of information. That whole scurvy thing is an interesting theory, but it seems far-fetched."

"I know. The ME warned me not to put too much stock in that and to check other leads first. But I'm not discounting the notion; it may end up being significant. In any case, I'll be interested to hear your take after you review the reports in detail."

"I'll tell you what . . . why don't I do that tomorrow morning and swing by your office sometime in the afternoon? I'm going to be out that direction anyway." For some reason he'd concoct between now and then. "I can give you an ETA by noon."

"Are you certain that's not too much of an imposition?"

Finding an excuse to trek west so he could spend time with the woman across from him?

Never.

"Not at all."

"All right. That would be great. I plan to stick close to my desk most of the day and dive into missing persons reports."

"That could be a long, boring job."

"Could be. But I decided to start with NamUs. It might not be as comprehensive as NCIC, but it's more manageable. Maybe I'll get lucky."

NamUs . . . NamUs . . . oh, yeah. The National Missing and Unidentified Persons System.

"I've never used that database. We didn't have any unidentified bodies during my tenure in Norfolk."

"We didn't have many in Chicago, either. I've only been on the site once myself. It's a lot newer than NCIC, but the missing persons data is more comprehensive. I think it's worth checking."

"If that doesn't pan out, NCIC may be—"

"Sorry to interrupt . . . but we're parked illegally and we don't want to get a ticket—even if we do have connections."

As Lance spoke behind him, Mac stifled a groan.

For once his brothers had shown up early.

Go figure.

Bracing, he shifted toward them. Their eyes were unreadable behind dark sunglasses, but he had no doubt they were both giving Lisa a thorough once-over under cover of those concealing shades.

He eased slightly between her and them as he checked out their vehicle.

Yep. Illegally parked—right in front of headquarters. And they were minutes . . . if not seconds . . . away from a ticket.

It would serve them right too, for their out-of-character punctuality.

"You're early—and I thought we were going to meet at the restaurant."

"We were trying to find a parking place when we spotted you and decided to join the party." Lance flashed Lisa a smile. "And we're early because Finn's hungry. So . . . aren't you going to introduce us?" He removed his sunglasses and crinkled his baby blues at Lisa.

Her lips rose in response.

So did Mac's blood pressure.

Better to get this over with fast—and get them away from Lisa.

As he did the intros, Finn grinned at the chief and also took off his shades, holding her hand a heartbeat too long . . . by Mac's calculation, anyway.

If Lisa noticed his siblings' less-than-subtle flirting, however, she gave no indication.

"I've heard about you guys. Delta Force and Army Ranger. Talk about a high-octane family." She included him in her quick sweep. "I don't know if I've ever been in the presence of this much testosterone."

She had no idea.

In his peripheral vision, Mac saw a patrol car slow beside his brothers' rented SUV.

Yes!

"I'd move the vehicle if I were you." He nodded toward the officer who was now getting out of his car.

"Finn . . . go take care of that." Lance waved his younger sibling off, his gaze leaving Lisa's only long enough to assess the situation.

"Why don't you go take care of it?"

"Because I'm about to invite this lovely lady to join us for dinner."

Lisa cast a quick glance at Mac as Finn grumbled an unintelligible comment and sprinted toward the SUV.

Now what was he supposed to do? He'd love to have dinner with her . . . but not in the company of his siblings.

As if she'd read his mind, she shook her head. "I appreciate the offer, but I still have a few things to wrap up at the office. Besides, I wouldn't want to intrude on family time. I know you three don't have much of a chance to get together." She slid her sunglasses over her nose and once more focused on him. "I'll look forward to hearing your take on that case. You all enjoy your evening."

She was gone before either of them had a chance to respond.

Mac motioned toward Finn, who was having an intent discussion with the officer. No doubt doing his best to talk himself out of another self-inflicted sticky situation. "Let's go rescue the kid."

Lance fell in beside him. "You've been holding out on us."

Mac picked up his pace.

His middle brother remained silent while he handled the situation with the officer.

As soon as the man started toward his patrol car, Finn looked past his brothers in the direction Lisa had disappeared, disappointment scoring his features. "Is the babe gone?"

Babe?

Mac fisted his hands. "*Chief Grant* had work to do."

"I invited her to dinner, but Mac didn't enthusiastically endorse the idea." Lance smirked at him. "I wonder why?"

Finn was still peering into the distance, as if hoping to catch one final glimpse of Lisa. "I thought you said you weren't dating anyone here yet."

"I'm not. I know her only in a professional capacity. County is helping her out with a case."

"Yeah?" Lance squinted at him. "Then how come I'm picking up some serious—"

"Stop." Mac held up his palms. "I'm not having this discussion on a street corner." Or anywhere else for that matter, if he could help it. "And if I were you two, I'd make this SUV disappear pronto. That officer hasn't moved, and he's giving you the evil eye. I'm not going to bail you out a second time."

"Fine. Where should we park?" Finn fished the keys out of his pocket.

"Where I told you to park when we discussed it this morning."

"That was before I had my coffee. I'm not responsible for any information delivered pre-caffeine."

"Yeah? How does that work for you in the field?"

A flash of—pain?—whipped across Finn's face, replaced so fast by his usual jaunty grin that Mac wondered if he'd imagined it.

Somehow he didn't think so.

What was going on with the youngest McGregor?

"I always have a large supply of java on the job. Now you want to repeat the instructions?"

This time Mac complied. When he finished, he gestured down the street. "I'll meet you guys at the restaurant. They won't hold reservations more than fifteen minutes."

"I'll go with you." Lance clapped his younger brother on the shoulder. "See you after you park the car, kid."

For a moment, Mac thought Finn was going to object. Instead, he jingled the keys and circled the car. "Order me my usual drink. Your treat."

As he slid into the SUV and pulled away from the curb, Mac led the way toward the restaurant. "Does Finn seem on edge to you?"

"He's always been hyper." Lance fell in beside him.

"No, he's always been energized. This is different."

Lance slipped his sunglasses back on. "Yeah . . . I hear you. I noticed it when we met up for the flight here. I tried to ask a few subtle questions, but he's not talking."

Lance, subtle?

An oxymoron if ever there was one.

"How subtle?"

"Hey . . . I know how to be discreet. So tell me about Chief Grant. Man, she is one hot number."

So much for discretion.

The Don't Walk light flashed, and Mac stopped on the edge of the curb. He needed to neutralize this topic or they'd pester him all evening.

"She's a colleague. End of story."

"Sorry. Not buying."

The late spring sun bearing down on them wasn't responsible for the bead of sweat that broke out on his forehead. "What do you mean, not buying? For your information, I just met her a week ago. At a crime scene, not socially."

"Doesn't matter. When electricity flies, it flies—and it was zipping at warp speed back there. As for that proprietary move you pulled after we joined you, edging in between her and us to protect your turf—very smooth. See, I get subtle."

Had he done that?

Maybe.

"Come on, the light's changed." He strode ahead, leaving Lance to catch up.

Weaving through the rush hour crowd on the sidewalks, and maneuvering through the crush of people in the small foyer of the popular restaurant, made conversation impossible. Maybe by the time they were seated, the subject of Lisa Grant would be forgotten.

His luck held until Finn slipped in beside him.

"So let's talk about the babe."

He picked up his drink. "Let's not."

"Why not?" Finn winked at the waitress as she delivered his drink—but his momentary distraction didn't last. "You have something to hide?"

Mac took a gulp of his iced tea. He was going to have to give them a few crumbs or they'd never let this alone.

"No, I have nothing to hide. In fact, I'll share all the pertinent data." He linked his fingers on the polished wood table and gave them a topline of their interactions, throwing in Lisa's marital status for good measure. If he left that out, they'd be sure to get suspicious. Any single guy—let alone a detective—would find a way to confirm that piece of data with someone who looked like Lisa. "So now you know everything." He picked up his drink again.

"Not quite." Lance helped himself to a tortilla chip from the basket the waitress had left.

"What's that supposed to mean?"

"The lady's gotten under your skin." Lance grinned at him and crunched the chip.

Mac lifted the iced tea and took a long, slow swallow as he debated strategy. Deny or admit? The first would earn him snickers; the second, ribbing.

Better to take the ambiguous middle road.

He set the glass back on the table and picked up the menu. "Maybe. Time will tell, I guess. What looks good to you guys?"

"Besides the lady?" Finn grabbed a second handful of chips.

At least they'd moved from chick and babe to lady.

It was a start.

"I have to admit, she's easy on the eyes." He kept his tone light and casual, playing it cool.

"More than." Lance skimmed the menu and set it aside. "I want the loaded burger. With extra fries."

"Me too." Finn finished off his chips and reached for more.

Mac set his menu down. "Doesn't the military feed you guys anymore?"

"Not this kind of grub."

"Keep this up, you'll ruin your girlish figures."

"Hey—we're on vacation. As for girlish figures . . . you worry about *yours*"—Lance waggled his eyebrows—"and we'll worry about ours."

Oh, brother.

Make that *brothers*.

He loved these guys—he really did.

But it was going to be a long evening.

8

Lisa stared at the NamUs screen on her computer.

Could it possibly be this easy?

She homed in on the photo of a black-haired young woman with blunt-cut bangs, a round face, and wide-set brown eyes.

A woman she'd found after culling through the Missouri and Illinois NamUs reports, eliminating those that didn't fit her time frame.

A woman who matched all her basic criteria.

Alena Komisky.

Lisa skimmed the missing person case information again. Age twenty-one. Caucasian. Five-four. No distinctive body features. She'd disappeared from Columbia, Missouri—but she was a Czech Republic national. Alena had last been seen twenty-four years ago in May, eating dinner alone in a Missouri U dorm cafeteria, wearing jeans, an MU sweatshirt—and a ring with red stones.

The ring was the clincher.

A spurt of adrenaline zipped through her.

While it was possible the red stone Barbara had found was coincidental, every investigative instinct she'd fine-tuned over almost a dozen years told her it wasn't.

And a DNA sample from a relative would confirm that.

She was reaching for her phone to touch base with the local FBI office when Florence appeared at her door.

"Your detective is here."

Lisa checked her watch. One-thirty—half an hour sooner than she'd expected, based on Mac's lunchtime call.

And he couldn't have arrived at a more opportune moment.

"His timing is perfect."

"I'd say more than *that* is perfect, if you get my drift." The older woman arched her eyebrows and fanned herself.

Lisa did a double take.

"What? You think I'm too old to notice a good-looking man?" The woman sniffed and patted her hair.

"No. Of course not. I just didn't expect . . . I mean, you've never . . . I didn't think you'd . . ." Stop. No sense digging herself in any deeper.

"Hmph. Maybe because I haven't seen a specimen like this in quite some time. That is one handsome man. And in case you haven't noticed, he isn't wearing a ring."

"Are you interested?" She tried to keep a straight face.

"Only in appreciating from afar. I had one good man, God rest his soul. I'll leave this one for a woman who hasn't yet experienced that blessing." Florence sent her a pointed look.

Their office manager was now becoming a matchmaker? Wonderful.

Maybe Florence and her mother should meet up.

A shudder rippled through her at that scary thought.

"Send him in, okay?" She swung back to her computer screen.

"With pleasure. But you might want to touch up your lipstick. I'll stall him for thirty seconds."

Lisa rolled her eyes—but groped for her shoulder bag as their office manager disappeared. She had an image to uphold as chief of police, after all. This was more about presenting a professional appearance than primping.

Right.

Not even Tally would buy that excuse.

She'd no sooner capped the lipstick, run a comb through her hair, and stashed the bag again than Mac appeared in her doorway. When Florence had said thirty seconds, she hadn't been kidding.

"I'm a little early. Is this convenient?" He stopped on the threshold and turned on that killer smile.

Her heart stuttered.

"Perfect." The word came out in a croak. She took a swig of water and tried again. "I have news."

"And I've been through the reports." He held up a file folder. "May I?" He entered and tapped the chair on the other side of her desk.

"Of course." She should have offered that at once. What was wrong with her, anyway?

Her mother would offer the obvious answer . . . but she wasn't going to consider it at the moment. She needed to focus on this case, not on the tall detective whose subtly patterned sport coat emphasized his broad shoulders.

As Mac took a seat, her canine friend rose and padded over to inspect the new arrival.

"Ah. This must be Tally." Mac scratched the dog behind the ear. "Hey, boy. Nice to meet you."

She opened her drawer and withdrew a dog biscuit. "If you want to make a friend for life, give him this."

As she started to hand it over, he held up a small bag she hadn't noticed before.

Some detective she was.

"I'm ahead of you." He pulled out a box of gourmet dog biscuits. "I stopped and picked these up on my way here. I was

114

hoping to make a better first impression on your friend than I did on you."

The man had taken time out of his busy day to buy a treat for her dog?

Definitely a good guy.

Tally nosed closer, tongue hanging out.

"May I?" Mac held up the treats.

"I guess so—but those are much more posh than the ones I buy. You're showing me up."

"I can put them back in the bag."

"Want to bet on that?" She motioned toward Tally. "Take a look at those eyes."

He glanced down at the dog. "Hmm. I see what you mean. Amazing, the power of eyes, isn't it?"

Though he kept his focus on Tally, she had a feeling he wasn't talking about her dog anymore.

She busied herself arranging papers on her desk while he fed the eager dog two biscuits.

"Sorry, boy. That's it for now. But I'll leave these with your friend and she can dole out the rest as she sees fit." He closed the box and set it on her desk.

After snuffling out a sigh, Tally curled up at Mac's feet instead of returning to his rug.

Huh.

He'd never done that with anyone else.

Of course, none of her previous visitors had come bearing dog gifts—nor over-indexing on the charisma scale.

"Do you want to start, or shall I?" After giving Tally one more pat, Mac leaned back in his chair and lifted the file he'd brought.

"I'll go first so you can factor in the new information."

It didn't take her long to bring him up to speed on her morning's work—and her discovery. He listened in silence until she finished.

"I was just about to contact the local FBI office when you arrived." She folded her hands on the desk. "I think they're my best bet in terms of arranging for a DNA sample from a relative."

"I agree. Their legal attaché in Prague could coordinate with the local police. County could process it for you—and by then you may have a DNA profile from Texas. My gut tells me you're right, that we'll get a match. The whole scurvy thing makes more sense now too. In a country like that, and depending on her background, it's possible she might have grown up on a less-than-ideal diet."

"That occurred to me too."

"Let's see . . . doing the math, she came here not long after the fall of communism in Czechoslovakia."

"Right. I'm thinking it was some sort of student program, maybe opening up learning centers in the West to former Eastern-bloc countries. I'm going to follow up with the Columbia Police Department for details and the original report."

"Was there a photo of Alena in NamUs?"

"Yes." She swiveled back to her computer and pulled up the page, angling the laptop toward Mac.

Instead of leaning forward, however, he rose and circled her desk, stopping behind her to study the screen over her shoulder.

He was so close she could feel the heat radiating from his body—and his warm breath on her temple.

Had the air-conditioning suddenly shut down in here?

"Seeing the photo makes it feel a lot more real, doesn't it?"

At his soft question, she refocused on the girl with the poignant Mona-Lisa smile, who'd died far away from the country of her birth and the people she loved. A girl who'd met an untimely end and lain in an unmarked grave for more than two decades. A girl who deserved justice—and internment in a place where she could rest in peace.

116

Perspective restored, Lisa eased closer to the screen . . . and away from Mac. "Yes, it does."

Perhaps taking the hint, he moved back and returned to his chair. "I guess I didn't need to review this." He held up the file.

"Sorry about that. I only found this a few minutes before you arrived."

"Not a problem. I'm glad the search ended up being easier than expected."

A discreet knock sounded on the open door, and Florence stuck her head in. "I hate to interrupt, Chief, but the mayor just dropped by. He says he needs to speak with you. I told him you were in a meeting, but he promised this would take less than five minutes."

Of all times for the man to show up.

"Tell him I'll join him in the conference room."

As the woman exited, Mac started to rise. "I'll get out of your hair."

"No!"

He halted and sent her a quizzical look.

Real smooth, Lisa. Could you sound any more desperate to buy yourself a few more minutes in his company?

"I mean . . . this won't take long, and there were a couple of other things I wanted to ask you." Or there would be, as soon as she thought up a few. "If you have another fifteen minutes, that is."

He settled back into the chair. "I might even have twenty." He flashed her a grin and patted the dog at his feet. "Don't rush. Tally and I will keep each other company. Right, boy?"

Tally gave him a lopsided doggie grin and eyed the box of treats.

"Why do I have a feeling you're going to succumb to his charms again?" She circled the desk toward the door.

"Because I'm a pushover for expressive eyes?"

Her step faltered.

Was the man flirting with her?

Hard to tell without looking directly at him—and she wasn't about to take that risk. She needed to keep her wits about her for her tête-à-tête with the mayor.

"I'll be back in a few minutes. No more than one or two treats, okay?"

"I promise I'll be good."

I have no doubt of that.

She curbed the temptation to voice that flirty comeback. Talk about inappropriate and unprofessional.

Picking up her pace, she strode toward the door.

It was time to put some distance between herself and the handsome man who'd won over her dog . . . and was fast making inroads with his owner as well.

◆

Once Lisa disappeared through the door, Mac leaned back in his chair and exhaled.

What in creation had possessed him to make all those suggestive comments? That wasn't his style—at least not on the job. In a social setting . . . different story, assuming an attractive female caught his attention. But in those cases, his glib remarks were nothing more than idle flattery. The dialogue of the dating game.

With Lisa, though, flirting felt different. More serious, somehow. Perhaps because what he'd said had been true. Her eyes *were* expressive. They *did* have amazing power.

As for that move he'd pulled by circling around behind her . . . not smart. Invading people's space wasn't wise unless the invasion was welcome—and it was too soon to be sure of that with her. Yes, there was electricity, as his brothers hadn't failed to notice. Yet he got the feeling she wasn't a woman who made rash moves . . . or welcomed them. Her discreet attempt to put a little distance between them confirmed that.

He raked his fingers through his hair, loosened his tie a notch—and put the blame for his reckless behavior squarely where it belonged.

On his brothers.

After their teasing banter about Lisa at dinner pushed his libido into overdrive, he'd spent half the night staring at the ceiling, far too aware of the lack of female companionship in his life.

No wonder he'd let impulsiveness override prudence.

Heaving a sigh, he leaned down and patted the dog again.

"What do you think, Tally? Did I come on too strong? Did I scare her off?"

His new buddy rose, sank back on his haunches, and scrutinized the dog biscuits again, his tongue hanging out.

"Not talking, huh?" He fished another treat out of the box. The biscuit disappeared from his fingers almost before he extracted it from the box.

"Whoa. Let's not take the hand too. And don't turn those baby browns on me again. That's all you're getting for now. I don't want to do anything else to hurt my chances with your office mate."

Giving in to a yawn, Mac closed the box and rose. Hopefully, his brothers had exhausted the subject of Lisa yesterday and would leave him in peace when they all went out for pizza later. He needed a decent night's sleep. Twenty-four-hour stretches of high-intensity action as a SEAL had been fine, but after two years in the civilian world, he was getting used to six or seven hours of shut-eye a night.

Or maybe he was just getting old.

Pushing that possibility aside, he wandered over to the window overlooking the back parking lot and inspected the sky. Blue and cloudless. Perfect for a long run. Could he convince Lance and Finn to accompany him? If he wore them out, they might be less inclined to bring up the subject of Lisa again.

It was worth a try, anyway.

He dropped his gaze to the credenza. Stacks of files were lined up in military precision at one end, with the remnants of what must have been a working lunch closer to Lisa's computer. A cup with a half inch of . . . milk? . . . in the bottom. A small disposable bowl with a few grains of rice and carrots clinging to the sides. Cellophane from a pack of saltines. An untouched apple.

No wonder her eyes had widened when he'd produced all that food from Panera last week. She must be one of those women who had to count every calorie in order to keep her figure.

If so, her regimen was batting a thousand—not that he'd give voice to that.

No more flirting today.

Turning away from the remains of her meal, he caught sight of a small, palm-sized device. A pager?

Who used pagers these days?

As he leaned closer to examine it, her office door swung open.

"I hope Tally kept you comp—" She came to an abrupt halt, her smile fading.

Great. First he flirts, then he gets caught nosing around her office.

His orchestrated trip to West County wasn't going anything like he'd planned.

He straightened up. "I was checking out the view." *Lame, lame, lame.*

"It's just a parking lot." Her tone was cool and flat.

"I noticed." He shoved his hands in his pockets. Might as well give her the whole story. "To tell you the truth, I needed to get the blood moving, so I was wandering around while I waited for you to come back. I didn't get enough sleep last night."

Her rigid stance seemed to soften slightly.

Or was that wishful thinking?

"I expect entertaining your brothers requires a fair amount of energy and stamina. Are they the culprit for your lack of shut-eye?"

"Yeah." But not for the reason she'd suggested.

"I thought SEALs were trained to go without sleep for extended periods."

"I'm not a SEAL anymore."

"Getting soft?" A flicker of amusement sparked in those hazel irises.

"Must be. But don't ever tell Lance or Finn I admitted that."

That earned him a real smile. "My lips are sealed."

He skirted around the edge of her U-shaped desk, and she sidled past him as they exchanged places.

"For the record, I didn't touch any of your files or your computer." He retook his seat beside Tally.

She slid into her chair. "I'm sure you didn't. Sorry for overreacting. Seeing someone hovering over my desk brought back a few . . . unpleasant memories."

"Want to share them?" The question was out before he could stop it.

She gathered up the remains of her lunch and dumped them in the trash can. When she continued, her words were measured and careful. "Let's just say being a female cop isn't always easy. Some men resent women on the force, which can be communicated in a lot of ways—including sabotage. Didn't work with me, though. On the positive side, it's less of a problem now than in my early days in law enforcement." She seized a wayward piece of cellophane and disposed of it too. "Sorry about the mess on my credenza. I usually clean up from lunch right away, but I got too engrossed in the case."

That was all he was going to get about her background.

But it was enough to know his initial assessment of this woman had been spot-on.

She was a smart, savvy, seasoned pro who'd made a success of a career that would have intimidated a lesser person. When it came to guts and determination, Lisa Grant stood second to no one.

So why had she left a coveted, hard-earned detective slot with a big-city PD to be chief of a tiny municipality?

The question hovered on the tip of his tongue—but he bit it back. If she wanted to explain, she wouldn't have changed the subject. Best to follow her lead and stick to safe topics. He was past his pushy allotment for one day.

"If you call that a mess, I hope you never see my apartment—especially while my brothers are inhabiting it. And to tell the truth, I was more interested in that device on your desk than the food. I was leaning down to look at it when you came back." He gestured toward the beige gadget with the LED window. "Does Carson still use pagers?"

She angled away, toward the apparatus, then slowly reached out and picked it up, weighing it in her hand as if debating how to answer his question.

At last she swiveled back to the front and regarded him with an expression that was neutral . . . and unreadable. "It's a glucometer."

He might never have seen a glucometer before, but he'd heard the term—and drew the obvious conclusion.

So much for safe subjects.

"You're diabetic?"

"Yes." The admission came out flat. Resigned. Weary.

He tried to wrap his mind around the fact that the vibrant woman across from him had a serious medical condition.

It wasn't computing.

Yet the device in her hand was real.

He dredged his brain, searching for any stray facts about the disease, but came up blank. No one in his circle of family or friends had it.

So how sick was she? Did people still die from diabetes?

His stomach contracted.

He wanted to press for details—but in the end he listened to the advice coming from the left side of his brain and gave her an opening, leaving the choice about how much to share up to her.

"I'm very sorry to hear that." His words, too, were measured. "Have you always had it?"

"No." She set the glucometer on the desk in front of her. "I was diagnosed a year and a half ago."

About the time she left Chicago.

Had the disease played a role in that decision?

He didn't ask—much as he wanted to.

"That had to be tough."

"Yeah."

"How serious is it?"

In the silence that followed his question, Tally left his side and padded around the desk.

As he laid his head on her knee, she scratched behind his ears. "I have an amazing friend here. He always knows when I need a dose of moral support."

"New friends might be willing to offer that too." Once again, the words were out before he could stop them.

Lisa transferred her attention from Tally to him. He saw speculation in her eyes . . . and something else he couldn't identify.

The silence lengthened.

He waited her out.

At last she leaned back in her chair, keeping one hand on Tally's head. "I appreciate that. And I'd be happy to answer your questions about diabetes, but that could take more time than you have available on a busy Tuesday afternoon."

"I have the time." Not really—but he'd make it.

She opened the box of dog biscuits he'd brought, fished one out, and fed it to Tally. "How much do you know about the disease?"

"Almost nothing."

"Then here's the quick and dirty. Diabetes happens when the pancreas either doesn't produce enough insulin to make glucose, or the body isn't able to recognize and use insulin properly. There are two types. Type 1 is the more serious and requires insulin. Type 2 can often be controlled with diet and exercise, though sometimes medication is needed. I have Type 2, the most common form, and so far I've avoided medication. But I have to monitor my blood sugar every day with this." She tapped the glucometer. "I also have a regular exercise routine and a strict diet."

So she wasn't a picky eater after all. Her food choices were dictated by her disease.

"Is this hereditary?"

"It can be—but not in my case. Type 2 is also most common in people who are overweight, have a low activity level, and eat an unhealthy diet. None of those apply, either . . . except maybe the unhealthy diet part. When I was working a case hard in Chicago, I grabbed whatever was handy. Fast food and vending machines were my friends. But in general I ate healthy. So I wasn't a typical candidate."

"How did you know you had it?"

Her eyes clouded, their usual spark dimming. "This is where the story gets a bit more involved. You sure you have time?"

"Yes."

She picked up her bottle of water and lifted it in his direction. "Would you like some? Or we have coffee. Florence always keeps a pot going."

"No, thanks."

After taking a swig, she set the bottle on her desk. "My diagnosis came the hard way. I'd been working a juvenile homicide. A six-year-old girl who'd been found in a field, beaten to death. Everything pointed to her father as the killer, but we didn't have any hard evidence—and I was determined to find some."

"Did you?"

"Yes."

Why was he not surprised?

She took another drink. "But along the way, I was not being kind to my body. I was subsisting on lots of caffeine, lots of carbs, and too little sleep. I was always hungry and thirsty and tired, which didn't surprise me given the circumstances. I figured the episodes of blurred vision were also related to fatigue, and the weight loss was due to stress. So I kept going. On top of all that, I was watching over my shoulder for a recently released ex-con I'd helped put behind bars, who'd vowed to get revenge."

"Talk about a full plate."

"Yeah." Tally nuzzled closer, and she patted his head. "One night I arrived home very late after following up some leads on the homicide. As I got out of the car in the alley behind my apartment, something didn't feel right. But since I had a mega headache and my hands and legs were shaky, I assumed my instincts were off after another long day without proper food. So I wasn't in fighting form when the knife-wielding ex-con jumped me."

Mac's heart stumbled. Given that Lisa was sitting across from him, she'd clearly survived the attack—but at what cost?

Before he could ask, she continued.

"I managed to kick the knife out of his hand and pull out my gun, but all at once I got dizzy. He was on me in a heartbeat. I held on to the gun, but I knew I wasn't going to win the struggle. He was big, and my strength was ebbing. Then all at once, a miracle happened. A patrol car turned into the alley. He yanked the gun away, backed off—and the last thing I remember is a loud bang."

Shock ricocheted through him. "You were shot?"

"In the shoulder."

Despite all his years of high-risk SEAL ops in war-torn countries, he'd suffered nothing worse than a sprained ankle. Yet Lisa had been shot in the line of duty on a Chicago street.

Somehow that didn't seem right.

Yet she'd made a full recovery—hadn't she?

"You're okay now, though?"

"After months of physical therapy, yes."

He exhaled. "I'm sorry you had to go through all that. It had to be a nightmare."

"Yeah. But you know what? It was also a blessing."

He squinted at her. "Getting shot was a blessing?" That seemed like a stretch, even for a person of faith.

"Yes. The ER docs were the ones who discovered the diabetes after I went into insulin shock. That can be deadly—and I'd ignored my symptoms far too long. So they not only treated my shoulder, they got my insulin situation straightened out. The whole experience also straightened out my head."

"What do you mean?"

With one finger, she traced a trail of condensation down the side of her water bottle, then swiped up the moisture pooling at the base. "The day you told me about your life-changing experience in Afghanistan, I said I'd left Chicago for a lot of the same reasons. I loved what I did, but the job sucked up all my time and energy. While I was recovering, I had a lot of time to think—and to reexamine my priorities."

She paused and took another long swallow of water. "I knew I wanted more in my life than work, but since I can never do anything halfway, I realized the demands of big-city law enforcement weren't going to give me the luxury of doing other things—like falling in love and creating a family. I heard about this job while I was recovering, and it struck me as providential. The rest, as they say, is history."

She was right. Their stories had a lot of parallels.

"Do you ever miss the big-city job?" Because he'd sure missed being a SEAL in the beginning.

"Once in a while." She shrugged. "But there are trade-offs in life for everything. I was willing to ratchet down the job intensity in order to create a life that could accommodate a family."

"Has your new life done that?"

She averted her gaze as she ruffled Tally's ears. "I've only been in Carson a year. I figured it would take that long to get the lay of the land, establish a routine, and make certain I had the diabetes under control. I still have occasional issues with the latter."

Now the incident made sense.

"Like the day you lost your balance at the excavation site?"

"I had a feeling you didn't buy my explanation. Yeah, I was tired and hungry and my blood sugar was off. I carry hard candy around for just such situations. But those don't happen often anymore, and I'm now starting to get around to next steps."

"Such as?"

"Putting more emphasis on my personal life."

Kind of like him.

"It's interesting that we both appear to be in the same place at the same time."

"Very." She met his gaze.

So the lady was as interested as he was in seeing where the sparks between them might lead.

Mixing business and pleasure wasn't wise, however. From day one of his professional life, he'd kept the two separate—and he wasn't changing course now.

But as long as Lisa had given him this opening, he needed to lay some groundwork for down the road . . . and put his cards on the table.

"Once this case is over and we aren't working together anymore, what do you say we investigate this odd coincidence in timing?"

A hint of pleasure danced across her face. "I could be persuaded."

That was the best news he'd had all day.

"On that high note, I think I'll exit. If the mayor is paying calls, you must have some hot potatoes on your plate." He rose.

She stood too, wrinkling her nose. "I got pulled into mediating a dispute between him and one of the city council members this morning. As I'm discovering, politics is rampant even in small municipalities."

"Amen to that. So what's next on the agenda?"

"Calls to the FBI and the Columbia PD."

"How can County help—me, specifically? I know you can handle this on your own, but I'd like to stay in the loop." For personal as well as professional reasons.

Folding her arms, she cocked her head as she considered his question. "You know . . . since the County lab will do the DNA analysis on the sample we get from the Czech Republic, would you want to work with the FBI to make those arrangements? That would save me a few steps."

"I'd be happy to."

"I'll try to nail down some contact information over there ASAP. In the meantime, enjoy the rest of your visit with your brothers. Any special plans?"

"No. They're content to eat, sleep, and play couch potato."

"Hard to blame them, after what they deal with on a daily basis."

"Yeah." And they'd be heading back into the thick of it way too soon. His stomach clenched, and he took a slow, deep breath.

Tally's ears perked up, and he circled the desk to nose against his hand.

"See what I mean about his sixth sense?" At Lisa's soft comment, he looked over at her. "He knows when people are worried and need comforting. If it's any consolation, you have my empathy too. It can't be easy having loved ones in combat zones."

"No. It's not." He patted Tally. The dog's ministrations were welcome—but far better would be a hug from the woman on the other side of the desk.

Not on the agenda today, unfortunately.

With one final scratch behind the dog's ear, he picked up his file and crossed to the door.

"I'll keep them in my prayers, Mac."

At her gentle comment, he turned.

She was watching him from behind her desk, slender fingers resting on the polished surface, a beam of sun setting off those fiery sparks in her hair.

Funny.

True McGregor that he was, he'd noticed her considerable physical attributes immediately, just as his brothers had.

Yet there was so much more to Lisa.

While he still appreciated her beauty, these days he also saw the compassion in her features. Heard the warmth in her voice. Felt the caring in her heart.

She was the whole package.

And once again, he wished he could seek comfort in her arms.

Instead, with a husky thank-you, he beat a hasty retreat before he did anything rash.

But he consoled himself with one parting thought.

Maybe someday.

9

Tapping her foot on the tile floor, Jessica checked her watch and did another three-sixty of the mall from her seat at the Starbucks kiosk.

Erika had two more minutes. Max.

Jessica took a sip of her iced green tea, pulled out her phone, and scrolled through her schedule. Fridays were always busy, but tomorrow would be crazy—a staff meeting, a working lunch with the strategic planning committee, and a full afternoon of presentations for their newest client, Gram's Table restaurant chain.

She cringed. Couldn't they have chosen a less folksy—and tacky—name?

Still, she couldn't fault the company's success. Frank Nelson's winning formula of home cooking, coupled with a family-friendly environment and family-style service, was giving established chains serious competition. Who'd have thought, when he started the business fifteen years ago, that a concept built on hearth, home, and traditional values would ever be anything more than a niche market? Especially with his insistence that the restaurants close on Sunday—a big family out-to-eat day—and that every table feature a framed blessing for the meal.

Not very PC—but customers nationwide loved it, and the chain was experiencing exponential growth.

The very reason she'd gone after the account. Hard.

And all the homework, all the schmoozing, had paid off. She'd wooed Frank Nelson away from his previous PR firm, and the CEO had signed on the dotted line with Peterson-Bradshaw four weeks ago. Tomorrow they'd be presenting their ideas for a brand-new publicity campaign aimed directly at target consumers, designed to ratchet up the chain's visibility, standing, and sales.

It was an amazing coup—and Robert Bradshaw was pleased with her work.

Very pleased.

The corners of her mouth rose. Impressing the boss was always a smart move, even for the heir apparent.

But there was still a lot of work to do before tomorrow's meeting with Nelson and his team.

She checked her watch again, her smile fading. Five-forty. Erika was ten minutes late. If she hadn't intended to keep this appointment, why had she made it? Then again, she'd sounded tipsier than usual when she'd called to set it up Tuesday night. She'd probably forgotten about it, or written down the wrong time.

Her problem.

Jessica slid the phone back into her purse and reached for her briefcase. She was out of here. Erika had overblown the whole thing, anyway. There hadn't been a word in the media about that discovery in the field since her return from London. It was a dead issue.

Lips twitching at the unintended pun, she started to stand—only to spot the other woman bearing down on her.

She muttered a curse. So much for making a fast escape.

"Sorry I'm late." Erika huffed to a stop beside her. Her fake blonde hair needed combing and a root touch-up, her mascara was smudged, and her eyes were red-rimmed.

The woman was a mess.

Jessica swallowed past her disgust as she adjusted the lapel of her Armani suit. No doubt Erika had spent big bucks on that dress—a Gucci, perhaps?—but she looked like a floozy. That low neckline was more appropriate for a cocktail party than a courtroom, and the silk clung to her like a second skin, highlighting the roll of fat at her waist.

The woman had never had one ounce of taste or class, despite her silver-plated upbringing.

"I got here as fast as I could." Erika cast a nervous glance over her shoulder. "It took me a while to ditch the reporters. They were on my heels like a pack of dogs, shoving their cameras in my face, asking for a statement."

Jessica's breath hitched.

Cameras? Reporters?

She scanned the mall again. The last thing she needed was to be linked with Erika and her slimeball husband. That was why she'd chosen a busy mall for their meeting. Why she planned to relocate to one of the benches off to the side, away from prying eyes and ears, once they both had their drinks. There was always anonymity in crowds. No one would pay any attention to them in this madhouse—unless a reporter was on Erika's trail.

"What are you talking about?"

"Didn't you hear the news?" Erika swiped at her nose and collapsed into the chair on the other side of the café table.

"I don't have time to keep up with the news during the day."

"Jack was convicted a little while ago. His lawyer said his sentence could be as much as ten years! I didn't even get to say good-bye before they hauled him off." As her pitch rose, several passersby looked their way.

Jessica leaned close. "Take a deep breath, Erika. And keep your voice down." Her words came out in a hiss. "What do you want to drink?"

"Scotch would be good."

"We're at a coffee shop. You'll have to make do with a latte. Stay put and try to get yourself under control."

While Erika dug through her purse for a tissue, Jessica pitched the dregs of her own drink and moved to the counter. After placing the order, she surveyed the milling crowds. No sign of anyone who looked like a reporter, nor of a news camera.

That was one plus, at least.

As soon as the barista handed her the drink, she rejoined Erika.

"Let's find a less busy spot. There's a bench over there that will give us some privacy." She gestured to one tucked in among some large potted plants, half hidden from view.

Erika struggled to her feet and trudged along beside her. Once they sat, she handed over the drink.

The woman took a noisy slurp, and Jessica eased away, suppressing her revulsion.

"I can't believe this actually happened." As Erika choked out the words, a fat tear formed at the corner of her eye and spilled out, leaving a streak of mascara as it tracked down her cheek.

"Crying isn't going to change anything. You had to know this was coming."

"I guess I didn't want to believe it."

Typical Erika, hiding her head in the sand.

"At least it's over."

"No, it's not. I have to meet with the lawyer tomorrow. He wanted to meet today, but I told him I had another commitment."

"You didn't mention my name, did you?"

"No." Erika sniffled and glared at her. "I'm not stupid."

She let that pass. "Let's focus on the reason for this meeting. No names, no specifics, okay?"

"I told you . . . I'm not stupid!" Sparks flared in her eyes.

Hmm. Not typical mousey Erika behavior. But life wasn't exactly typical for her at the moment.

Time to pull out the conciliatory, understanding tone that had served her so well in her PR career.

"I didn't mean to imply that. I know you're upset, and people don't always behave rationally while under stress."

Erika's anger deflated, her shoulders slumping. "I know. You're right. I wish I could be more like you. You never lose your cool—even when bad things happen."

"Speaking of that . . ." Jessica did a casual survey of the mall. Everyone was hurrying along, intent on their next purchase or their conversation. "I've been keeping tabs on the media. Nothing else has been reported—which is what I expected. As I told you last weekend, there's no reason to worry. You haven't been in touch with anyone to the south, have you?"

"No. I've been too busy with the trial to worry much about the . . . other . . . thing."

"Well, you don't have to. This will fade away, like it did the first time."

Erika chewed on her lip. "It took a while back then, though. All those questions . . ." A shudder rippled through her. "It was hard. I don't want to do that again."

"Like I said, it's old news. I doubt we'll hear another word about it."

"I hope not."

"You want my advice? Go home and forget about this. Focus on getting your life back."

She let out a shuddering sigh. "I'm not sure how I'll manage alone."

You'll manage better than you did with your loser of a husband.

But no need to stir the waters. The calmer Erika was, the fewer ripples she'd create.

"I have confidence in you. You're a lot stronger than you think." The glib lie fell off her tongue. Whatever it took to get the job done.

"Thanks." The woman dabbed at her eyes. "I always feel better after I talk to you."

That made one of them.

Jessica picked up her briefcase and stood. "Let me know if anything else comes up regarding the reason for today's get-together. Otherwise, we need to go back to our infrequent contact mode. Agreed?"

"Yeah."

Erika started to rise, but Jessica pressed her back with a hand on her shoulder. "Stay here and finish your latte. You'll feel better if you take a few minutes alone to chill."

"I don't do alone very well."

"You have other girlfriends you can call, though, right? Set up some lunches or shopping trips. That will perk you up."

"I guess. Maybe I'll plan a lunch with Lauren from the country club. We bum around once in a while."

"Great idea. And we'll touch base in a few weeks."

Without waiting for a reply, Jessica walked away.

If only walking out of Erika's life could be so easy.

But Erika needed hand-holding—and watching. Especially with Jack out of the picture.

Jessica picked up her pace, putting distance between them. What had Erika seen in that jerk, anyway? And why had her father ever let her marry such a lowlife?

There could be only one explanation—her husband had known how to turn on the charm. How else would he have been able to talk all those retirees out of their hard-earned money?

Clamping her fingers around the handle of her briefcase, she shouldered her way through the throng of shoppers. People like Jack deserved to rot in prison. No one who took the fruit of someone else's hard labor should go unpunished.

She pushed through the door into the evening light. Inhaled. Strode toward her BMW coupe.

Better.

Today she'd dealt with Erika. Tomorrow the Peterson-Bradshaw team would knock the socks off Frank Nelson and his team.

Life was good.

And she intended to keep it that way.

Mac twisted the knob on the door to his apartment, passed through the living room, stuck his head into the kitchen.

"Hey, where is everybody? It's chow time."

No response.

Weird.

His brothers were never late for meals—and with a gourmet Italian splurge in the offing for their last night in town, why weren't they spit-polished and ready to go?

A movement on the balcony caught his eye, and he leaned sideways. Lance was sitting in one of the folding chairs the previous tenants had left, dressed for the evening.

He crossed to the slider and pulled it open. "You ready to go?"

"Yeah. But Finn's not back from his run yet."

Meaning his youngest brother still had to shower and change.

Mac frowned. Finn might not be the most organized guy, but he was usually more considerate than that.

"I thought we decided to leave at six?"

Lance shrugged. "He'll be here any minute. I doubt they'll run out of food at that fancy place you're taking us to. Want to join me for a drink while we wait?" He lifted the can in his hand.

The question was casual; the undertone wasn't.

Was his brother finally ready to spill whatever had been eating him all week?

Since none of his attempts to ferret it out had worked, Mac wasn't about to pass up this opportunity.

"Yeah. I'll be right with you."

As he retrieved a can from the fridge, he took a moment to psyche himself up. Mental preparedness was as important as physical readiness for any challenge, as one of his instructors had repeated ad nauseam during SEAL training.

And he had a feeling he'd better be prepared for whatever bombshell Lance was about to drop.

Back on the balcony, he claimed the empty chair, the fizzy release of carbonation the only sound. Tempted as he was to prod, he swigged his drink and waited for his brother to take the lead.

When the silence lengthened, however, he slid a glance to the left.

Lance had a death grip on his can. Every muscle in his body seemed taut. His Adam's apple bobbed.

What in the world was so difficult to spit out?

Maybe it was up to him to start the conversation after all.

"What time are you guys heading out tomorrow?" Innocuous, but it might get the dialogue flowing.

"Early. We're confirmed on Space A flights out of Scott. Finn is wheels up at seven-thirty. I'm out at ten."

"I'm surprised one of you didn't get bumped. Those Air Force space-available flights sound great in theory, but they're not all that reliable."

"I guess we got lucky."

"Might be worth trying again on your next leave. Your luck might hold. Like I said when you called last week, you're always welcome. I might even have a real bed in the extra bedroom by then."

Lance's can crinkled. "I won't be having any more leaves."

Brow knitted, Mac turned toward him. "You want to explain that?"

Lance finished off his drink in several gulps and crushed the aluminum can in his fingers. "I'm not re-upping."

What?!

His brother was leaving Delta Force?

No way.

Since their days of backyard pretend war games, Lance had always been the brother most gung ho on military service. Without constant exposure to his enthusiasm, Mac wasn't sure either he or Finn would have considered enlisting. And while Delta Force, with its unrelenting physical demands, wasn't a lifetime gig, he'd always assumed Lance would move into a command or training position at some point and stay until he retired.

"You're surprised, aren't you?"

Surprise didn't come close to describing his reaction.

"I don't know if I'd use that term." He spoke slowly, choosing his words with care. "Blindsided, maybe. Do the others know?"

"Yeah. I told Mom and Dad last weekend, and I laid it on Finn during the flight here."

"Why was I the last to hear?"

Lance swallowed. When he spoke, his voice was subdued. "Telling the others was easier."

His eyebrows rose. "Why?"

"Because I know you expected me to be career Army. And I did too. But after a lot of soul-searching, I realized it's not where I want to spend my life." He fingered the crumpled can. "The thing is, I wasn't even a Delta Force operator as long as you were a SEAL. You kind of set the bar, you know?"

As his admission echoed in the quiet air, Mac stopped breathing.

Lance was afraid he'd failed to measure up in his big brother's eyes. That was why he'd put off telling him.

Yet nothing could be further from the truth.

"Lance." He waited until the other man looked over at him. "First of all, no one's keeping score or setting bars. But if they were, you saw a lot more active combat than I did and you gave a hundred-plus percent every day. Trust me, we're even. As for thinking less of you for your choice—how could I, when I made the same one? And you want the truth? I'm relieved. Worrying about you two guys being in the line of fire day in and day out is giving me gray hair. I found a new one just last week. If that had kept up, I'd be stocking my shelves with Grecian Formula."

He didn't flinch as Lance scrutinized his face. Every word he'd spoken had been true—though the gray hair might have been a slight exaggeration—and he wanted his brother to understand that.

Finally, Lance responded. "You'd probably look distinguished with gray hair."

"I'm in no hurry to find out."

"So you're okay with this?"

"More than okay. How did the others react?"

"Mom was happy. Dad was surprised. Finn was . . . hard to tell. He didn't say much, but I think it threw him."

"I wonder if that's why he's been on edge this week?"

"That would be my guess."

Despite the logic, that conclusion still didn't feel right.

"Aren't you going to ask me about my plans?" Lance set the mangled can on the tiny patio table between them.

He refocused. "My next question. What are your plans?"

"FBI."

Talk about a day for surprises

"You're gonna be a Fed?"

"Yep. I started the application process fourteen months ago. With my background, I thought I might be able to skip a few steps, but no dice. I had to go the full nine yards. It paid off, though. After I get out next month, I'll be going directly to the academy."

"My brother, the FBI agent." Mac shook his head. "That'll take me a while to process."

The slider behind them rattled, and Lance looked over his shoulder. "The runt just banged the front door. Guess it's time to go eat." He rose.

Mac followed his lead, but as his brother reached for the door, he grasped his shoulder. "In case there's any doubt in your mind . . . I've always been proud of you. I still am—and that will never change."

Spots of color appeared on Lance's cheeks. The kind that had always popped up when the middle McGregor brother was trying not to cry.

"Thanks." The word came out scratchy, and a sheen filmed his eyes.

"You're welcome." Mac gave him a shove toward the door. No reason to embarrass him further. "Now let's tell Finn to make his shower quick so we can go celebrate."

◆

She shouldn't have called Mac last night.

Lisa pricked her finger with the lancet, squeezed a drop of blood on the test strip, and fed it into the glucometer. So what if she'd been working late on the bones case and needed a pick-me-up? If she'd thought it through instead of acting on impulse, she'd have realized the man would be in the middle of a going-away dinner with his brothers. What else would he be doing on their last night in town?

Not that he'd seemed to mind the interruption, however—and the outcome had been better than expected. Who'd have guessed he'd offer to accompany her to Columbia today to talk to the retired detective who'd handled the Alena Komisky case?

"You can come out now, Tally. The grinding's all over." She flipped off the blender, and he poked his head into the room to verify the coast was clear before venturing in.

As she poured her fruit smoothie into a glass, he trotted over.

"Want a doggie treat?"

His ears perked up.

"I'll take that as a yes."

She pulled one out of the bag she kept in the cupboard. Instead of snatching it from her fingers as usual, though, he sniffed. Paused. Looked at her as if to say, *Where's the good stuff that nice detective brought?* Finally he took it.

"Sorry, buddy. This is all my budget will allow. You'll have to go to Mac for the gourmet fare."

Smoothie in one hand, a slice of whole wheat toast in the other, she stepped out onto the patio and inhaled the fresh air. Bliss. Especially after spending ten years in a cramped apartment with nary a tree in sight. In fact, the five-acre wooded lot filled with birds, deer, foliage, and privacy was the best part of her new home. Tally loved it too.

She watched her canine friend chase a squirrel, investigate a new mole mound—drat—and shake off a bee that had taken a liking to his ear. As she finished off her breakfast, the sound of crunching gravel added some background percussion to the chirp of the cardinals.

Mac was here.

Snapping her fingers for Tally, she grabbed his collar and towed him to the spacious run she'd had built.

"Sorry, buddy. I know this isn't your favorite place, but I'll be gone too long to leave you in the house, and you've proven much too adept at scaling the fence. You could end up under the wheels of a car on the road. We'll have a game of catch when I get back, okay?"

He gave her a doleful look while she locked the gate.

"Hey. It's a beautiful day. You'll be fine."

He turned his back.

Hmph. Hopefully she'd get a warmer greeting from the driver of the car pulling up her driveway.

After depositing her glass in the sink, she grabbed her purse and touched up her lipstick. As she dropped the tube back into her purse, the bell rang.

The man was punctual—one more virtue to add to his growing list.

Stopping in the foyer, she tugged at the hem of her linen jacket and smoothed a hand down her slacks.

Ready.

She opened the door to find Mac smiling at her, and her heart skipped a beat.

Not so ready after all.

"Reporting for duty." He gave her a jaunty salute.

She did her best to match his light tone as she ushered him in. "I feel guilty about usurping your Saturday."

"You didn't usurp it. I volunteered." He gave the room a quick inspection. "Nice. Much homier than my place."

She studied the cozy living room, trying to see it through his eyes. An off-white couch with a soft, teal throw. A wing chair upholstered in teal and beige stripes. An old trunk for a card table. Brass lamps. Family photos on the mantel. Impressionist prints on the walls. Yeah. It *was* nice. And restful.

"Thanks. But you've only been in your place a few weeks. It'll come together."

"Not according to Lance. He thinks I should hire an interior decorator. If my what-do-I-need-with-a-kitchen-table-when-a-card-table-will-do brother noticed it's bare bones, trust me—it's bare bones. Maybe you could give me a few tips."

"I'd have to see it first."

"That could be arranged."

At his husky tone, she tilted her head. "I thought you wanted to put the personal stuff on ice until we finished this case."

"Are decorating tips personal?"

"No. But visiting a man's apartment is."

"I'm in your house."

"For business reasons." She was tempted to add the word *unfortunately*—but resisted. Instead, she tapped her watch. "And speaking of business . . ."

"We need to hit the road. Got it. Would you like me to drive?"

"Why don't we take turns?" She picked up her briefcase and purse. "The Columbia PD faxed the case report to my office this morning, but I haven't had a chance to read it. We could switch places halfway there. That would give us both a chance to get up to speed before we meet with Detective Breton."

"You've already been to your office?"

"I'm used to getting up early. I'll join you by the garage after I activate the alarm system."

She waited until he exited, then locked and bolted the front door. Once in the kitchen, she tapped the activation code into the keypad beside the back door and slipped through, double-checking the knob to make certain it was locked.

Yep. She was good to go.

Better than good, actually, as she headed toward the detached garage and Mac came into sight.

Maybe this had ended up being another working Saturday, even though she'd vowed to break that habit. If she wanted to create the life she'd promised herself as she lay in the hospital in Chicago during the days following her close encounter with death, she needed to start carving out some personal time.

But for once she didn't mind putting in weekend hours.

Because Mac would be with her.

And if all went well after she got to the bottom of the buried bones case, perhaps he'd become a regular part of her weekends—for personal rather than business reasons.

Now there was a thought to brighten a woman's day!

10

Mac turned the final page of the material the Columbia PD had faxed to Lisa and read the last few lines. He sensed her gaze, but she didn't speak. In fact, they'd had little conversation during the entire drive. She'd read the file for the first hour while he took the wheel and drove in silence, and she'd given him the same courtesy.

But they were approaching the outskirts of the college town, and it was time to talk.

He closed the file and looked over at her. "The Columbia PD did a thorough job."

"I agree. But they got nowhere."

"Not for lack of trying."

"Did any particular interviews stand out for you?"

"Yeah." He opened the file again and riffled through the pages. "Alena's roommate—Erika. The roommate's boyfriend—Joe. And the girl who joined them on their trip to St. Louis the night Alena went missing—Jessica. Their stories were exactly the same."

"Almost verbatim, in some cases."

She'd come to the same conclusion he had.

"You're thinking they sounded too perfect. Too practiced. Like they'd been rehearsed."

"Yes." Lisa skirted past a slow-moving driver, as impatient behind the wheel as he was. One more thing they had in common. "Did you notice the follow-up interviews with Erika? She used a lot of the same phrases again, word for word."

"I noticed. Yet their story checked out. They were in St. Louis the weekend Alena went missing, at Erika's parents' house. A neighbor saw them. They did go to a concert Saturday night. And Erika did report Alena missing on Monday after the girl didn't show in their dorm room."

Lisa veered off onto the exit ramp. "But there are holes in that story."

He hadn't figured she'd missed them. "True. The neighbor didn't see them until Saturday morning, so their only alibi for Friday night is each other. But there's an issue with motive. The Columbia PD couldn't find one."

"I know." She skimmed the directions in her lap and hung a right. "We should see the retirement center on the left . . . there it is, up ahead."

As she swung into the parking area, Mac examined the three connected buildings clustered around a central courtyard. "How long has Stan Breton been here?"

"Two years. He moved in after his wife died because his children are scattered around the country. They all invited him to live with them, but he feels more at home in Columbia. This is where he met his wife and spent most of his adult life." She angled into an empty spot and set the brake.

"Sounds like you got his life story."

"I told you—I have a tendency to slip into interrogation mode even in casual conversations. Shall we?"

Before he could respond, let alone circle the car to open her door, she slid from behind the wheel and led the way toward the entrance.

Definitely a take-charge kind of woman.

His kind of woman.

A spare older man with a shock of white hair and keen blue eyes limped toward them the instant they stepped through the main door.

"Chief Grant, I assume. And Detective McGregor." The man stuck his hand out to Lisa.

Smiling, she took it. "Detective Breton, I presume. Good thing we weren't trying to sneak in."

Mac returned the man's firm grip.

"These old eyes aren't what they used to be, but after thirty-three years in the business, I can pick law enforcement out of any crowd. And in this place?" He waved a hand around the spacious lobby, populated on this Saturday morning by the geriatric set. "It's a no-brainer. I've staked out a quiet corner over there for us, if that's okay." He indicated a settee and chair facing a fountain.

"Perfect." Lisa gave an approving nod.

Stan led the way, taking the single chair and leaving the small settee for his visitors.

Mac stifled a grin. Perfect, indeed—and not just because the splashing water would provide cover for their conversation.

Although Lisa gave the cozy setup an uncertain look, she sat without comment, scooting over to allow him as much room as possible.

He sat next to her, keeping to his side.

But it was still cozy.

"Where are my manners? May I offer you coffee or a soft drink before we begin?" The older man started to rise.

"I'm fine," Lisa assured him.

"Me too."

While the man sank back into his seat, she opened the file they'd reviewed en route. "Mac—Detective McGregor—and I were impressed with the thoroughness of your investigation, Detective Breton."

146

"Make it Stan. My detective days are long past. Thanks for those kind words, but it wasn't thorough enough. Someone was responsible for that young girl's disappearance, and while I had a few other cold cases in my career, this one always haunted me."

"Why?" Lisa reached for her pen at the same moment Mac extracted his notebook from his pocket.

"You read the case report. She was all alone here, thrust into a foreign world as part of what educators and politicians assumed, I suppose, was a benevolent gesture. Taking a poor young girl from a small university in the Czech Republic and offering her a chance to experience a taste of American life." He shook his head. "Can you imagine the culture shock, after two decades living under a communist regime, often in impoverished circumstances?"

"It had to be very hard." Lisa finished jotting a note and looked up. "Based on your interviews with her acquaintances, it sounded as if she had difficulty making friends."

"Yes. Her English skills weren't strong, so communicating—and connecting—were a challenge. She was smart, according to her teachers, but she was out of her element and overwhelmed. If pressure hadn't been put on her from various sources to stick out the academic year, she'd have bailed." He leaned forward. "How certain are you the bones you discovered belong to her?"

While Lisa filled the retired detective in on their findings and theories, Mac took the Columbia PD file from her and flipped through it again, scribbling down the most recent contact information for Alena's parents, last updated more than a decade ago. First thing Monday, he'd place a call to the St. Louis FBI office and get things moving to obtain a DNA sample from a relative.

"Even though a lot of the clues suggest this could be Alena, to be honest, it's the red stone that's most convincing," Lisa concluded.

"I agree." Stan tapped the arm of his chair. "Based on the

severed finger, it would appear someone went to a lot of effort to get rid of incriminating evidence. From what I could gather, the ring was unique—a cluster of small red stones with a larger one in the middle. A family heirloom, as I recall. No one I interviewed had ever seen Alena without it." His expression grew thoughtful. "Strange how despite the effort made to get rid of it, one small, possibly incriminating, stone fell out."

"Providential more than strange, I'm thinking," Lisa said.

"I hope so. Providence sure wasn't smiling on me twenty-four years ago when I was trying to crack the case. I'd like to think that young woman's disappearance will finally be solved, though. Her parents were shattered."

"Speaking of her parents . . ." Mac indicated the file. "I assume this is the most recent contact information?"

"As far as I know. I kept in touch with them for a long while. I didn't want them to think we'd forgotten about their daughter. But after her father died ten years ago, I communicated less often. The last time I contacted her mother, right before I retired, I simply wished her well and told her if there was ever any news to report, someone would let her know. We both assumed that was the end of it. Now this." He exhaled. "It's amazing."

"It's also possible this will end up being a dead end." Mac slipped his pen back in his pocket.

"That's not what my gut is telling me."

"Ours, either." Lisa jumped back in. "Mac is going to have the FBI arrange for its legal attaché in Prague to coordinate with the local authorities to get a DNA sample. It might not be a bad idea to give Alena's mother a heads-up. Would you like to do that?"

As Stan's face softened, Mac glanced at Lisa. She didn't have to do that. In truth, she probably shouldn't. This was an official police matter, in her jurisdiction now, and Stan was retired.

But Stan had worked Alena's case hard—and being the one

to bring this news to a grieving parent would close the circle for him.

The choice said a lot about Lisa.

She might be a total pro. She might be cool, composed, and thick-skinned, as Mitch had noted based on the exchange he'd witnessed between her and a meth tweaker. She might be tough enough to withstand any harassment thrown her way in a male-dominated field.

Yet beneath that tough exterior beat a kind, tender, caring heart. She was a cop, yes. And a good one. But she was also a woman who rescued stray dogs and bent the rules to give a retired detective a sense of closure.

All of which reinforced his determination to get to know her a whole lot better once this thing was over.

"I'd appreciate that very much." Stan's voice rasped.

"It's my pleasure. This was your case long before it was ours. We're just getting our feet wet. I'd ask you to wait until Monday, when we contact the FBI, and request her discretion until we're certain we have a match."

"Of course." He knitted his fingers together. "So what happens next? Even if this is Alena, aren't we back to square one? The players have scattered, and it doesn't appear there are any new leads."

"Yet." Mac added the caveat. This was Lisa's investigation, and while he had no intention of dominating it—or this conversation—he wanted to be part of it . . . to the end. "It would be interesting to chat again with some of the people closest to Alena. See if their script has changed."

A spark of—approval?—flickered in the man's eyes. "Script. Interesting word choice. I take it you noticed the similarity in their interviews too."

"Yes. Any thoughts or conjectures you'd like to share that couldn't be put in the report? Off the record." Mac shifted on the settee, resisting the temptation to loosen his tie. Was the air-conditioning in this place on the blink?

Or perhaps Lisa's leg brushing against his was the culprit for his temperature uptick.

He did his best to focus on problem solving instead of proximity.

The man considered the question before he responded. "I don't know what happened the night Alena disappeared, but every instinct I honed over a lifetime in law enforcement tells me those three have that answer. Hard as I tried, though, I couldn't find any motive for foul play. The daughter of a state senator. A Rhodes Scholar. A woman who aced almost every class she took and had an excellent job waiting for her when she graduated. Why would they get involved in anything dark or dirty?"

Lisa tapped her pen against her notebook, creases scoring her forehead. "We talked about motive on the way here too, after reviewing the case files. And I agree—there doesn't seem to be one. So I'm wondering if a cover-up might have been involved. Not a malicious or planned killing, but an accident none of them wanted to be linked to. They all had a lot to lose if they were involved in any sort of scandal."

"That occurred to me too, but I couldn't find any evidence to support that theory—and I worked the roommate over several times. Of the three, she struck me as the most likely to crack. On the ditzy side, and very emotional. The tears were flowing, let me tell you. She claimed she was just upset about her roommate's disappearance, but I always thought it was more than that. I had the feeling she was scared out of her mind."

"Interesting." Lisa made a note.

"On the other hand, it's possible our suspicions are wrong, that it was a random killing. Maybe Alena crossed paths with someone looking for trouble, who had no connection to the university." Stan sighed. "In the end, I had to let it go. You might have to do the same. It's a very cold case. But if the DNA matches, at least her mother will be able to bring her daughter's remains home."

Mac might not have known Lisa for long, but the puckers on her brow told him she wasn't going to be satisfied with that.

She wanted to solve this case.

"You could be right, but I'm going to do some serious digging before I put it back on ice." She closed the file in her lap and tapped the sheets until everything was in place, no loose ends hanging out. Then she pulled a card from her pocket and handed it to the man. "I'd appreciate it if you'd let me know once you make contact with Alena's mother. And if any other helpful thoughts come to mind, don't hesitate to call."

"After thinking about this for twenty-four years, I doubt that will happen."

The man stood, and Mac handed over one of his cards too. "This is Lisa's case, but if for any reason you can't reach her, consider me backup."

Stan tucked both cards in his pocket as he walked them to the door. "I wish you both good luck." He shook their hands, his grip firm.

"Thanks." Lisa hoisted her shoulder purse into position. "We'll let you know how things progress— and thank you for your time."

"Time is one commodity I have plenty of these days. Have a safe drive back."

They walked to the car in silence, and Lisa circled around to the driver's side.

"I'd be happy to take a shift driving back." He slid into the passenger seat.

"Let me see how it goes. I'm feeling pretty energized after that meeting."

He buckled his seat belt as she eased out of the parking spot and accelerated toward the highway. "How so? We didn't learn anything new."

"No, but Stan worked that case for a long time, and it was helpful to have him reinforce our conclusions about the similarity in the interviews among Alena's three friends—and to hear he'd also considered the accident theory, which could explain the absence of a motive."

"But as he also pointed out, Alena might simply have crossed paths with the wrong person."

She gave a firm shake of her head. "That doesn't feel right."

"Proving otherwise could be tough."

Her chin rose a fraction. "I'm not afraid of tough. I want justice for that girl. I also want an explanation for how she ended up in a shallow grave on wooded property with a fatal head trauma. And I'm going to start with the roommate—assuming she's still in the area."

"That would be my choice too."

"You want to come along? If it fits with your schedule?"

"I'll make it fit. This may be your case, but I've got a vested interest in it now too."

"Personal or professional?"

"Both."

Humor glinted in her eyes. "An honest man."

"Always." A yawn snuck up on him. "Sorry."

"Late night?"

"Very. It was a combination farewell and celebration. Lance told me last night he's leaving Delta Force to join the FBI."

"Wow. That's a big change. Were you surprised?"

"*Stunned* would be a better word."

"I have a lot of respect for the FBI. All the agents I've worked with have been very sharp. Besides, I've seen the organization from the inside—sort of. I attended the FBI National Academy. A great program."

"Also rigorous, from what I've heard." The FBI course for law enforcement personnel wasn't for sissies.

"Worthwhile, though. So how do you feel about your brother's decision?"

"I'm not sorry he'll be leaving combat zones behind." He yawned again.

She gave a soft chuckle. "Why don't you take a quick nap? It's a long drive."

Much as he hated to give up a single minute of Lisa's company, his two-thirty turn-in last night was taking a toll. "You sure you don't mind?"

"Nope. I have a lot to think about."

"In that case, I accept your offer."

Settling into the corner, he let the sound of tires against road lull him. Five or ten minutes of rest, max. That was all he needed.

Except the next time he opened his eyes, it was to the crunch of gravel.

It took a moment for him to orient himself—but his head snapped up when Lisa's house came into sight through the trees.

He'd slept for two hours?

"Have a nice rest?"

She grinned over at him as she maneuvered the car over a small pothole and aimed for the detached garage.

"I think I owe you an apology." He straightened his tie and ran his fingers through his hair.

"Not necessary. You needed the shut-eye, and I needed to think about the case. We were in perfect sync." She pressed the garage door opener, then nosed the car in and killed the motor.

Before he could respond, she slid from behind the wheel, grabbed her briefcase off the backseat, and moved outside to wait for him.

He fumbled the door handle, trying to chase the last vestiges of sleep from his brain, and joined her in the midday sun, shading his eyes as he emerged from the dim garage.

"Thanks for coming with me today." She hit the garage door opener attached to her keychain, and as the door slid down, an excited bark sounded from the rear of her house. She smiled. "My homecoming committee."

He let a beat pass. Would she mention lunch? It was well past noon.

She didn't.

Tally barked again.

His cue to exit.

"I guess I'll be off. Are you working the rest of the day?"

"Not much." A hedge if he'd ever heard one. "I want to do a little checking on Alena's roommate and the others. I'll let you know what I find out. If they're local, we should be able to get to them next week. I don't want to wait for confirmation on a DNA match."

"Probably smart. It shouldn't take long to get and process the sample from Alena's mother—assuming she's still at our contact number—but Texas could take a while."

"I might make a few calls, see if I can speed things up a bit."

He cocked his head. "You have some pull?"

"A former colleague in Chicago used them a lot and built a strong network of connections there. It's possible he can get me moved up in the queue."

"Might be worth a try. It would be nice to have answers on this sooner rather than later."

"I agree. When you contact the FBI, could you see if they can ask Alena's mother a few things while they're at it?"

"About the bone breaks and scurvy? Already on the list. Dental health too." Tally yipped again, and he dug his keys out of his pocket. "Why don't we touch base early in the week?"

"Sounds like a plan. In the meantime, I hope you have a relaxing rest of the weekend."

Too bad it didn't include some socializing with the woman standing in front of him. A candlelit dinner, maybe, in a quiet restaurant with . . .

Get out of here, McGregor.

Right.

He backed off. Lifted a hand. "Take care." And then he high-tailed it to his car, the gravel crunching beneath his shoes, before he pushed too hard and made a mistake he might regret.

Not until he was behind the wheel did he look back. Lisa was still standing there, watching him. Was she, too, thinking about the long, lonely weekend that stretched ahead?

At least she had Tally for company.

He started the engine. Maneuvered the car so he was facing down the woodsy drive. Accelerated.

As he followed the curve of the driveway, he lost sight of her in the rearview mirror.

But the image of her standing there, watching him, lingered in his mind.

A relaxing weekend?

Not likely.

It would take a heavy-duty workout session and a long, strenuous run to quiet the relentless buzz in his nerve endings put there by a certain gorgeous police chief.

In fact, it might take two.

He sighed.

Monday was going to be a long time coming.

11

Erika slammed the door on her Audi, jabbed the key into the door that led from the garage to the mudroom, and twisted the knob. A high-pitched *beep, beep, beep* pierced the air, and she punched in the code to deactivate the security system.

Not that she'd need protection for her worldly goods much longer—if her lawyer was right.

Could the court really seize all her property for restitution?

Of course, as the esteemed Warren Mitchell of Mitchell, Trent & Lawrence had pointed out in his fancy office an hour ago, it wasn't her property. Jack had put everything in his name.

The louse.

Head throbbing, she shoved her hair back from her face. Dumped her purse on the kitchen table. Dug out a pack of cigarettes.

Not only did she have to face the humiliation of being married to a felon, she was also broke.

The whole thing stunk.

Fingers fumbling, she lit a cigarette. Took a long drag.

She needed a drink.

The stronger the better.

Instead of sneaking a quick pick-me-up from the bottle of

156

scotch stashed under the sink, she went straight to Jack's bar in the paneled office where he'd conducted his estate-planning business.

No, scratch that.

It hadn't been a business; it had been a Ponzi scheme, according to the judge.

She poured herself a full glass of scotch, added ice, and took a long gulp. How had the man described it exactly? A nefarious plan to defraud seniors of their retirement savings through a bond-trading program, using bonds that didn't exist.

All those seminars Jack had held at hotels and banquet halls hadn't been about financial planning; they'd been about bilking old folks out of their lifetime savings to support the lavish lifestyle he craved.

And now it was all gone—including Jack.

She took another long gulp. Kicked off her spike heels. Loosened the belt on her dress.

Could life get any worse?

By the time the glass was empty and the cigarette half-smoked, however, she was feeling more upbeat. There had to be a way out of this. There were always options, as Jack used to say. And she'd think of some. Maybe not today, but after a full night's sleep, when her mind wasn't so foggy.

She poured herself another drink.

Sipping it, she wandered into the living room. It would be nice to get out tonight, go to the club for dinner, forget about everything.

But Lauren's cold shoulder when she'd called on Saturday to arrange a lunch date wasn't a positive omen. Apparently no one wanted to associate with the wife of a felon.

And they sure wouldn't want to associate with her once all the trappings of wealth were stripped away.

Despite the numbing effect of the liquor, panic bubbled up

inside her again. She downed another gulp of scotch. Took another drag on the cigarette.

Neither helped.

Her hand began to shake, rattling the ice in the glass.

She had to talk to someone.

Jess?

No. She'd said not to call.

Joe?

Not a great idea. Jess would be mad if she contacted him.

But who else did she have? Mom and Dad were gone, and she had no siblings. Her friends at the club weren't likely to remain her friends after this scandal.

That left Joe. And he would understand. He always had. Too bad she hadn't married him instead of falling for smooth-talking Jack with his big, empty dreams.

Well, that was water under the bridge. But at least she could talk to him.

She started toward the phone. Froze as the chime of the doorbell echoed in the empty house. Who would be dropping by unannounced on a Tuesday morning? The cleaning people had a key. Besides, it was the wrong day for them.

The bell rang again.

She frowned.

A salesman or evangelist, maybe? Except they didn't usually work upscale neighborhoods like this.

She crossed the foyer, bare feet slapping against the cold marble, and peered through the peephole. A nice-looking man in a sport coat and a woman in a crisp cabernet-colored jacket and tan slacks stood on the other side.

She straightened up. They seemed respectable—and she wouldn't mind hearing a friendly voice. Having a pleasant chat about inconsequential matters might take her mind off her problems for a few minutes.

After fluffing her hair, she unlocked the door and pulled it open. "May I help you?"

Even though they smiled, Erika didn't miss their swift, subtle perusal.

She should have taken the time to put her shoes back on, tighten her belt, and ditch the drink and cigarette.

Still, what did it matter what these strangers thought of her? It wasn't as if—

". . . and Detective McGregor with St. Louis County. We'd like to talk to you for a few minutes."

Her attention snapped back to the woman. "Detective?"

"Yes. May we come in?"

She gripped the edge of the door. "Why?"

"It might be better if we discuss that inside."

"Is this about my husband?" *Please, let it be about Jack!*

"No. This is a different matter."

Erika's stomach bottomed out.

There could only be one other matter they'd want to talk to her about.

Lungs stalling, she looked at the detective. He hadn't said a word, but he had sharp eyes. The kind that didn't miss a thing.

Talking to these two people would be dangerous.

Jess wouldn't like it.

She started to shut the door. "This isn't the best time. If you'd call—"

The detective put his hand on the door, holding it in place. When he spoke, his tone was pleasant—but firm. "This won't take long. And since we're already here, why not give us a few minutes?"

Her heart began to pound, and her mouth went dry.

She couldn't talk to these people.

Yet if she refused, wouldn't that make them suspicious?

A length of glowing ash dropped off the end of her cigarette, close to her fingers. She released her grip on the door and stumbled toward the ashtray on the table in the foyer to stub it out before she got burned.

But as she turned back toward the two cops framed in the doorway, she had a feeling she was about to get burned anyway.

"Ms. Butler, we do need to talk with you. I'm certain you can spare ten minutes." The woman studied her with those analytical eyes.

There was no way out of this.

"Yes. I . . . I can do that." The ice in her glass rattled.

The cops glanced at it.

She grasped it with both hands, then set it down beside the extinguished cigarette. "We can talk in there." She fluttered her fingers toward the living room.

As she led the way, her feet once again smacked against the marble. Too late to retrieve her shoes now—but all at once she felt naked.

Choosing a French provincial chair, she perched on the edge, tucking her bare toes under the seat. The police chief and detective split up, the woman sitting across from her on the couch while the detective took a seat out of her line of vision, just inside the door.

She felt like a bug under a microscope.

Squirming, she gripped the arms of the chair.

The woman smiled and opened her notebook. "We appreciate your cooperation. As I said, I'm the police chief in Carson. We're investigating remains that were recently discovered on a construction site in my municipality." She stopped.

Erika licked her parched lips and tried to think. What was she supposed to say? What would Jess *want* her to say?

From twenty-four years ago, through the haze of scotch, Jess's voice echoed in her mind.

"Don't offer anything that's not asked."

Erika swallowed. "I don't know why you're telling me this."
That was good. Cool. Composed. A hint of puzzlement.

"Because we believe the remains belong to Alena Komisky."

Her lungs froze.

Oh, God!

They'd identified the body!

But how? Hadn't Jess said they'd never be able to figure out
who it was? That the whole thing would blow—

"Ms. Butler? Are you all right?" The woman leaned forward,
eyes assessing. Probing.

"Yes. Fine. Just . . . shocked. Are you sure it's . . . her? I mean
. . . how can you tell from bones?"

The woman's gaze drilled into her. "I don't believe I mentioned the condition of the remains."

Mistake, mistake, mistake!

"Well . . ." She tried to think past the buzzing in her head. "I
mean, what else would be left after all these years?"

The chief didn't comment on that. "Forensic science has come
a long way in the past couple of decades. We'd like to talk with
you about the night she disappeared."

Erika tried to take a deep breath. Couldn't. "It's been a long
time. My memory's . . . not that clear anymore. Maybe you
could get the report . . . from the Columbia police. I talked to
them . . . several times."

"We already did that." The cop tapped a file folder in her
lap. "But it never hurts to revisit the events. Sometimes time and
distance clarify memories. People recall small details that are
forgotten in the midst of trauma. I understand you and Alena
were close."

Erika stared at the file folder. What had she said back then?
What had Jess coached her to say? It was all so fuzzy . . .

"I wouldn't call us close." Best to hedge if she couldn't remember.

"No?" The woman raised an eyebrow. "You were roommates, weren't you?"

"Yes. But I didn't know her before that. She was here on a cultural exchange program. My father . . . he was a state senator . . . was involved in it. He asked me to be her roommate."

Coerced was more like it. He'd made that high-and-mighty speech about how it would be broadening for her to be exposed to someone who'd grown up in a country where freedom was nothing more than a word, then offered that Mercedes convertible as a bribe.

Too bad she'd succumbed. Without those wheels, the whole tragedy might—

". . . during the year?"

She blinked, trying to refocus on the cop. "What?"

"I said, didn't you become close during the year? Hang out together?"

"Some." She scoured her brain, trying to remember what she'd told that detective in Columbia. "She didn't have a lot of friends, and I felt sorry for her. Sometimes we did stuff together."

"But not on the night she disappeared."

Erika twisted her hands together in her lap. "No."

"You came to St. Louis that night, correct? With two friends?"

"Yes."

"When did you last see Alena?"

What had she told that Columbia detective?

"At dinner . . . I think. In the dorm dining room."

The chief checked her notes. "According to another student interviewed at the time, Alena ate alone in the dining room."

Heat stole up her neck. "I didn't eat with her. I just . . . saw her there."

"You mean you ate there and saw her across the room?"

"Yes."

"Was she alone?"

"Yes."

"You didn't ask her to join you?"

Sweat broke out on her upper lip, and she swiped it away with a fingertip. "She was . . . uh . . . finishing as I came in." That's what she'd told the police twenty-four years ago, wasn't it?

"Was that the last time you saw her?"

"Yes."

"Are you certain of that?"

At the detective's question, she turned toward him, away from the woman. His eyes were as razor sharp as the police chief's. "Yes."

"You came back to Columbia from St. Louis on Sunday night, correct?"

"Yes."

"Yet you waited until Monday to report Alena missing."

"Yes."

"Why?"

Had anyone asked her that question twenty-four years ago? She couldn't remember.

"It was . . . uh . . . late when we got back. I went straight to bed."

"But Alena wasn't there."

"No."

"Weren't you worried about her?"

"Not too much." She crossed her legs and tried to call up her flirty smile. The one men always responded to. "People hook up, you know?"

This guy's expression didn't change. "Had she ever hooked up before?"

"No. But hey . . . there's always a first time, right?" She smiled again.

He didn't.

"I thought you said she didn't have any friends."

Her smile faded. "None that I knew of, but she didn't tell me everything."

"Tell us about your weekend in St. Louis." The woman cop spoke again, flipping over a page in her notebook.

Erika swiveled back toward her. What was she writing down, anyway?

"We came to town for a concert."

"Who?"

"Me and Joe Andrews and Jess . . . Jessica Lee."

"When did you arrive?"

"Late Friday night. We stayed at my parents' house. They were in Jeff City for the end of the legislative session. We bummed around on Saturday, went to the concert, met up with some friends on Sunday for brunch in the Central West End, and drove back."

The woman looked up from her jotting. "We appreciate your willingness to answer questions. I expect this has been a trying time for you, given the outcome of your husband's trial."

So they knew about Jack.

What else did they know?

"I've had better days."

"Before we leave, is there anything else you can think of that might be helpful?"

So they didn't have all the answers.

Yet.

But the chief's tone made it clear she intended to find them.

"No. I'm sorry."

The woman closed her notebook and stood. So did the man. Both of them withdrew cards and handed them to her. The cardboard stock stuck to her clammy fingers like glue.

"We'd like to give some closure to Alena's mother." The detective guy—McGregor?—edged in on her. She had to tip her head back to see his face. "It has to be difficult for her, wondering what happened to her only daughter for all these years."

Erika crumpled the cards in her fist. "Yeah." She'd tried not to think a lot about that. Jess had told her to put it from her mind. What happened hadn't been their fault. Not directly. Who knew Alena would get high so fast and act stupid?

"Was she a nice girl, Erika?"

At the police chief's soft question, moisture clouded her vision. It was easier to hold on to her emotions when the woman was more brusque and businesslike. "Yes, in a sweet kind of way. But she was out of her element, you know? She didn't fit into American life, and she missed her family. She was counting the days until she could leave, and she was kind of depressed because she didn't think she'd done a very good job representing her country. I tried to cheer her up by including her in stuff, like taking her with me when I went out with my friends."

"Was she depressed on that Friday night?"

"Yeah."

"Did you think about inviting her to go with you for the weekend?"

A warning light began to strobe in her brain.

"No!"

The woman's eyebrows rose. "Why not?" Her inflection was casual, but the question wasn't.

She was digging.

Setting a trap.

And Erika wasn't about to get caught in it.

She tried for a careless shrug. "I already had one girlfriend along. I didn't need two chaperones—or more competition."

"Hmm." With that noncommittal comment, the woman slipped the strap of her purse over her shoulder, her expression neutral. "Thank you again for your time. We may be in touch if we need any additional information." She walked toward the front door, and the tall detective fell in beside her.

Erika trailed along behind them, stopping in the middle of

the foyer as they let themselves out. The cold from the marble seeped into her toes—and her heart.

A shiver rippled through her.

Those cops suspected something—and that woman police chief didn't seem like the type who gave up.

Neither did the detective.

They both had relentless eyes.

Legs shaky, Erika crept to the window and steadied herself on the solid grandfather clock beside the front door. She lifted the drape slightly and peered out.

Her two visitors were talking at the end of the walkway, but as she watched, they drew apart and headed toward separate cars.

They were leaving.

But unlike her felon husband, they'd be back.

It was time to call Jess.

◆

Mac pulled into the Starbucks lot, Lisa on his tail. Considering how quickly she'd agreed to his suggestion about regrouping here, she must be as anxious to get his take on their meeting with Erika as he was to get hers.

She swung into the spot next to him and was already waiting, files and notes in hand, as he slid out of his car and set the locks. She looked great today, with the sun setting off those fiery sparks in her hair and her fitted, dark jacket hinting at the curves beneath.

Could he stall for a few more seconds and just enjoy the view?

"Ready?"

Apparently not.

"Yes."

As they entered the shop, he homed in on the solitary unoccupied table in the far corner. "If you grab that, I'll get the drinks. What would you like?"

"I can get my own . . ."

A man toting a computer case pushed through the door behind them, eying the table.

"A bottled water is fine." She called her order over her shoulder as she made a beeline for the table, cutting off the other guy. He flung her a disgruntled look.

Grinning, Mac got in line and placed their orders.

By the time he joined her, she was tapping her finger against the tabletop.

"I'm getting the distinct impression patience isn't your strong suit." Smiling, he took the seat opposite her and sipped his Americano.

"Guilty as charged—especially when I'm on a case." She leaned forward, her eyes intent. "So what did you think?"

"I think Stan Breton is right. She knows more than she's telling. And her body language spelled fear in capital letters."

Lisa twisted the cap off her water. "I agree. Her flustered reaction when I called her on the bones comment was revealing. And based on several other missteps it was clear she's forgotten the details of her original script for the events of that night."

"I expect she'll alert the other two about our visit."

"That would be my guess." Lisa took a swig of water. "And that's okay. Keeping people off balance, wondering what's coming next, can work to our advantage." She opened the file folder on the table. "Since I didn't have a chance before our meeting with Erika to bring you up to date on her companions that night, do you want the quick and dirty now?"

"I'm all ears."

"Let's start with Joe Andrews, the Rhodes Scholar. He majored in economics at Mizzou and went to Oxford to study mathematical modeling. One year into the program, he dropped out and relocated to Paducah, Kentucky, where he now works for a small accounting firm as an auditor."

"Not the kind of career you'd expect from a Rhodes Scholar. Does he have a family?"

"No. He never married."

"And Erika smokes and drinks too much."

"I know what you're thinking—two people haunted by their pasts . . . and perhaps by guilt. But that model doesn't hold for Jessica Lee."

Mac sipped his coffee as Lisa gave him a rundown on the woman's accomplishments.

When she finished, he set his cup down. "You're right. She's at the other end of the spectrum—a high achiever with a successful career at a prestigious company. Should I assume, since she has the same name she had in college, that she never married?"

"No. That's where things get more interesting." Lisa flipped to the next page in her file. "She was married to Dr. Charles Turner, a widower, for three years. He died five years ago of a heart attack. Going back further than that, Jessica's father was an alcoholic with a DWI, according to St. Louis police records. The family lived in a South City flat—not a great area, if you haven't already discovered that during your short tenure in our fair city. Her mother died young, and her father lost his sales job. From what I could piece together, Jessica spent her teen years working a fast-food job to try and keep a roof over her and her younger brother's head."

"That's a lot of intel. You've been busy since I last saw you."

"I like a case I can sink my teeth into."

"This one qualifies. So Jessica Lee had a tough youth."

"Yeah. I'm sure it got tougher after her kid brother, Jason, died of a drug overdose and her father disappeared, leaving her to fend for herself at age seventeen."

"A history like that could lead a person down a very rocky road."

"Or provide the motivation to create a smoother one." She

took another sip of water. "It might also harden a person. Make them pragmatic about dealing with harsher realities."

"Like disposing of a body?"

She lifted one shoulder. "I'm just throwing out theories here."

"And they all make sense. The problem is, we're still in the same boat as Stan—shy of hard evidence."

"So far." She set the bottle down and once more leaned toward him. A fresh scent wafted his way, and he had to forcibly restrain himself from bending closer for a better whiff. "But I found something else interesting. Ron and Marjorie Wright, who owned the property where the bones were discovered? They were next-door neighbors of Erika's parents twenty-four years ago."

This lady was good.

"I'm impressed."

She brushed off his compliment with a flick of her hand. "Don't be. It's the same neighbors who told Stan about seeing the three students in St. Louis the day after Alena disappeared."

He squinted. "I read Stan's interviews. How did I miss that connection?"

"I missed it the first time too. Marjorie Wright's first husband was Ed Kraus. Stan's interview was with Marjorie Kraus. She changed the title on the property when she remarried after Ed died. The first name didn't register until my third reading. I figured it was coincidence, but went ahead and checked it out. Surprise, surprise."

"That puts a different spin on things."

"Yep. Erika could have known about their property."

"Why didn't you bring that up with her earlier?"

She tapped her empty water bottle on the table. "I never play all my cards at once."

"Meaning you intend to talk to her again?"

"Oh yeah. But Jessica's next on my list."

He finished off his coffee. "Can I join that party?"

"You sure you have time?"

No, he didn't. He and Mitch had some follow-up to do on the home burglary case, and the list of people he had to track down and interview from last week's homicide continued to grow.

But he wasn't about to miss this.

"I'll make time. Are you planning to show up unannounced, like we did at Erika's?"

"I don't know. It won't be as easy. Erika's probably already tipped her off, so we've lost the element of surprise. Besides, she lives in a high-rise with a secured lobby."

"If you set up an appointment, she's going to want it at a time and place of her choosing. It might not be bad to just drop by her office. The pressure of having to explain to co-workers why police are talking with her could throw her off balance, put her on the defensive. People trying to cover their tracks on the fly often make mistakes."

She gave him a speculative look. "I like the way you think. You want to pay her a visit tomorrow?"

"Sure."

"Why don't we touch base first thing, see how our schedules match up?" She closed the file.

"Works for me." He reached for her empty bottle.

"I can get that." She reached for it too—and her fingers connected with his.

She didn't pull back.

He didn't, either.

"This electricity thing . . . it's potent." His words came out hoarse as he locked gazes with her. No sense dancing around the obvious.

"Yeah." Her voice was ragged too.

After a few moments, she retracted her fingers.

He closed his around her water bottle.

"I'll get rid of these." He stood and crossed to the trash container, grabbing a few napkins from the dispenser to wipe his perfectly clean hands—and buy himself a few moments to regain his equilibrium.

Potent didn't even begin to describe the electrifying connection between the two of them. It almost had a life of its own.

He looked back at Lisa. She was angled away from him, attempting to zip her purse.

It took her three tries.

At least he wasn't alone.

And while personal matters were on hold until this case was solved, he was looking forward to seeing what happened afterward.

Because the way sparks were already flying, this thing was likely to heat up.

Fast.

12

Jessica advanced the PowerPoint presentation to the next image and surveyed the group assembled in the conference room. Every single member of the strategic planning committee was focused on her, as they had been throughout her presentation—including Robert Bradshaw.

And why not?

She was smart, savvy, professional, and polished—and this was where she belonged. Up front. Leading the group.

Her power outfit didn't hurt, either. The Italian-made silk gabardine Ralph Lauren jacket and slacks were class personified, especially when paired with a black cashmere tank and Hermes scarf. The combination of elegance and subtle sexiness made it a perfect presentation outfit. The women admired the clothes, the men admired the body . . . and all of them envied her status as the chosen one.

Life didn't get much better than this.

She aimed her laser pointer at the screen. "As you can see from this chart, in the past five years, new-client revenue has grown steadily, accounting for 28 percent of our total corporate revenue and increasing profits by 15 percent. Our outreach to clients in Europe has been very successful, and we've also broadened our base in the US. The plans I'm outlining today will ensure new-client growth continues."

As she pointed the remote to click to the next image, the chief financial officer spoke.

"Those numbers are impressive, Jessica—but we've also been racking up some serious expenses."

"Wooing customers does cost money, Gary."

He consulted a paper in front of him. "I realize that. But the first-class flights, high-end hotels, expensive meals, and lavish client entertainment are cutting into the revenues you've highlighted. The bottom line could be as much as 10 or 12 percent higher if we curtailed some of those expenses."

She held on to her pleasant expression despite the surge in her blood pressure. "Of course we don't want to be ostentatious, but we have to remember that the kinds of clients we're pursuing are major players in industry." She used her well-practiced conciliatory tone. The one that usually defused dissent. "They're used to first-class treatment. If we want to play with the big boys, we have to act like the big boys and spend like the big boys."

"I understand the need to invest in new business." Gary adjusted his glasses but didn't break eye contact. "I'm just suggesting we cut some expenses that aren't related to client entertainment. For example, a business-class ticket is less expensive than first class."

What a penny-pinching jerk.

But Robert liked him.

Be nice, Jessica.

She set the remote control down at the end of the long conference table, adopting a serious demeanor. "I have the utmost respect for your opinion, Gary—and I think we all appreciate the effort you make to ensure we keep our focus on the bottom line. Your suggestion about travel certainly has merit, though I must say, the excellent night's sleep Robert and I had in first class on our recent flight to London was a great advantage. It allowed us to hit the ground running when we landed." She addressed her next comment to the senior partner—her ally—and smiled. "And run we did, as I'm sure Robert will attest."

"Very true. And I, for one, was happy to have a decent night's sleep on the flight over. However, your point is well taken, Gary. We don't want to overextend. At the same time, we *have* moved into a different league in recent years, and we have to pay to play at this new level. Why don't we monitor expenses, cut where we can, and revisit this in six months?"

"An excellent suggestion, Robert." Jessica picked up the remote control again. "Frugality is commendable—in moderation. As long as we don't cut corners with our clients, I'm happy to do my part to help control expenses."

And the first thing she'd do once she took over the reins of this company would be to push Gary out the door and hire a less highly compensated CFO. That would save a few bucks—and a boatload of aggravation.

She advanced to the next screen shot. "Our US customer base at present is still heavily concentrated in the Midwest, but we're making inroads in other parts of the country. I've developed a list of prospective clients headquartered on both coasts who would be an excellent fit for Peterson-Bradshaw."

The door at the back of the room silently cracked open, and her secretary peeked in.

Jessica's blood pressure edged up again. Had the woman not understood her instruction that she wasn't to be disturbed under any circumstances?

She angled away from her, sending what she hoped was a clear message. "As you can see, there are quite a few major . . ."

A cough sounded in the back of the room.

Everyone looked that direction.

Jessica gripped the remote tighter. No way to ignore the woman now.

"What did you need, Cathy?" With an effort, she managed to maintain a cordial expression and inflection.

The woman's complexion reddened. "I'm sorry to interrupt, but could I have a word with you? A situation has come up that . . . requires your attention."

Robert glanced at the clock on the wall. "Why don't we take a break and regroup in ten minutes?"

Before Jessica could instruct Cathy to delay whoever needed her until she was finished, the committee members were shuffling papers, pulling out their phones to check email, or heading to the credenza where coffee and Danish had been set out.

She stifled a curse.

All her hours of practice were toast. The momentum she'd worked so hard to build was gone.

Thanks to a secretary hovering at the back of the room.

Despite the fury nipping at her composure, she managed a polite tone as she addressed the woman. "I'll be there in a minute, Cathy."

With a quick nod, she slipped out.

"Take your time, Jessica." Robert rose as she approached him. "Clients always come first. If you get tied up, we'll move on to Matt's presentation and come back to yours later."

Not if she could help it.

"I'm sure whatever has come up won't take more than a few minutes to handle." She called up the deferential smile she reserved for the CEO.

As Matt claimed Robert's attention, Jessica crossed the room and exited into the quiet hallway, the thick carpet muting the tap of her three-inch heels.

With each step, her anger grew.

Cathy might only have been with the firm for six months,

but at this rate she'd be gone before the year was up. Like her predecessors.

Secretaries who didn't follow instructions were expendable.

The woman was waiting in the anteroom of the office, standing beside her desk, wringing her hands. Even without the gray streaks in her nondescript brown hair, she'd look older than her forty-nine years.

Jessica entered, glared at her, and closed the door. "Didn't I tell you not to disturb me?"

"Yes. I'm sorry. But I didn't know what to do. The receptionist says a police chief and a detective are in the lobby. They want to talk to you."

As the words hung in the air between them, the world around Jessica went blank.

There was no sound. No movement. No color.

Nothing.

Her brain was focused on one thing, and one thing only.

She was on police radar.

So that was why Erika had been calling her incessantly since yesterday. For once, her college acquaintance hadn't needed a shoulder to cry on. She'd been trying to pass on a warning—the cops had paid her a visit.

That could mean just one thing.

They'd identified Alena.

Jessica's stomach twisted, the same way it had twenty-four years ago as they'd huddled on that dark roadside beside the dead Czech student while the future she'd planned tottered on the edge of a precipice.

Yet she'd thought her way out of that.

And she'd think her way out of this.

There'd be explanations to make later to the Peterson-Bradshaw staff, but she could handle that. She'd had plenty of experience doing damage control during her PR career.

But first she had to find out what the cops had said to Erika—and what she'd said to them.

Slowly the world began to click back into focus—including Cathy, who was staring at her with a mixture of curiosity and fear.

"Did you tell them I was in a meeting?"

"Yes. They said they'd wait."

"Fine. I'll talk to them in a minute."

Turning her back, she strode into her office. Closed the door. Exhaled.

You can manage this, Jessica. Remember . . . it's been twenty-four years. So what if they've identified her? There's nothing to link you to what happened that night. You were careful. You covered your tracks. You left no clues.

But if that was true, how had the police identified Alena?

They'd missed something.

But what?

Fingers tingling, she yanked her phone out of her pocket and tapped in Erika's cell number.

It rolled to voice mail.

Of all times for the woman not to answer her phone.

Scrolling through her directory, she found Erika's home number and tried again.

Once more, the phone kicked into voice mail.

Jessica opened her bottom drawer, fumbled for a tissue, and dabbed at her brow.

Just as she started to hang up, Erika answered, speaking over the recorded message.

She swiveled away from the door. The glass walls of her office were thick, but why take chances? "What's going on, Erika?"

"I've been trying to reesh you since yesterday!" Hysteria raised the pitch of her voice.

Jessica gritted her teeth. How could she have a coherent

conversation with a drunk? "I've been busy. Did the police contact you?"

"Yes. Thash why I called. They came to the house yesterday. A 'tective and pleesh chief."

The same people now waiting in the lobby to talk to her.

"What did they say?"

"They found her!"

"We already knew that."

"No . . . I mean, they know who she is!"

"I figured that out. How did they know it was her?"

"I asked that. They mentioned forensic science. And they had a lot of questions. Jess . . . I think they'll be back!"

The woman was having a meltdown.

And meltdowns were dangerous.

"Erika, calm down—and knock off the booze until this is over. Your visitors are waiting in my lobby right now. After I meet with them, I'll be in touch. Don't talk to anyone else . . . or have you already called our mutual friend?"

"I had to talk to somebody, and you didn't call me back." Erika sounded peevish—and more than a little defiant.

She muttered a curse.

More damage control to do.

"I'm hanging up. Stay home and don't talk to anyone else until you hear from me. Got it?"

"Yeah. But—"

She broke the connection before Erika could start whining again.

Leaning forward, she pressed the intercom button. "Show them back." Then she reached for another tissue and blotted her forehead again.

She needed a makeup retouch.

As she dug in her purse for her cosmetics, she took several slow, steady breaths. No matter what the police had found to help them identify Alena, there was nothing to link the three of them to her demise. They had alibis. No one had seen what they'd done, or they'd have been fingered long ago. The cops were just following up on a dead-end cold case.

She should be safe.

She *would* be safe.

Whatever it took.

◆

The door from the lobby to the inner sanctum of Peterson-Bradshaw opened, and Mac looked over as a middle-aged woman spoke from the threshold.

"Ms. Lee will see you now."

Beside him, Lisa picked up her briefcase and rose. He followed her through the door, down a silent hallway lined with awards the firm had won on behalf of its clients, and into a swanky office with a brass plate bearing the name Jessica Lee.

Nice digs.

He exchanged a look with Lisa. The slight lift of her eyebrows told him she'd sized up the posh setup too.

The woman who'd retrieved them gave a timid knock on the door to the glass-walled inner office.

No response from the figure seated at the desk, whose back was to them.

Turning, the secretary twisted her fingers, "Ms. Lee may be . . . uh . . . on the phone. If you'd like to take a seat, I'm sure she'll be with you in a moment."

As if on cue, the desk chair inside the office swiveled to reveal a slender, attractive woman with blonde, perfectly styled hair. She rose, crossed to the door, and pulled it open with a smile as her secretary took a quick step back. She might be in her mid-forties, but she could pass for early thirties. Botox—or genes?

No matter.

This was a woman who took very good care of herself.

"Jessica Lee." She moved toward them and extended her manicured fingers first to Lisa, then to him. "I hope you'll accept my apologies for keeping you waiting. I was in the middle of a presentation."

After Lisa did the introductions, Jessica gestured toward her office. "Please . . . come in. May I offer you a beverage?"

They both demurred, and Mac let Lisa precede him. They waited as the executive followed them in, closed the door, and motioned toward a sleek glass conference table off to the side. A notebook and pen rested at the head.

Jessica had already staked out her spot.

She was also a woman who liked to be in control.

"Make yourselves comfortable."

Lisa slid into one of the modern upholstered chairs at the table. He sat across from her.

Jessica took her seat, her movements graceful, her demeanor open and friendly. If she was nervous, she was doing a stellar job hiding it.

She folded her hands in a loose clasp on the table. No sign of tension there, either. "I understand from Erika Butler that you may have found her roommate's remains. I assume that's what this is about?"

"Yes." Lisa opened her notebook. "The remains were found in a construction site in Carson—my jurisdiction. St. Louis County is providing assistance, which is why Detective McGregor is here. We'd like to ask you a few questions."

"Certainly." The woman's expression grew pained, and she shook her head. "It was a horrible tragedy when Alena disappeared. Erika was distraught for weeks. She kept blaming herself for not inviting Alena to go with us to St. Louis. But hindsight is always twenty-twenty, as they say. I saw the news story about the discovery of bones west of the city. Was that . . . her?"

"That's our assumption." Lisa linked her own fingers. "We're waiting for DNA confirmation, but that's more of a formality."

"I don't know a thing about police work, but I have to say I'm impressed by your investigative skills. After all these years, it must be difficult to identify someone." The woman tipped her head, her eyes curious—and innocent. "However did you manage it?"

Mac kept his focus on Jessica as Lisa answered.

"There are a lot of ways to make an ID. Sometimes we use dental records. Sometimes clothing. Sometimes jewelry—like a ring."

If he hadn't been homed in on her eyes, Mac would have missed their infinitesimal widening—and the sudden dilation in her pupils that signaled surprise . . . and fear? The reaction was well-masked—and she recovered quickly—but it was there. He'd seen it many times during his SEAL career.

"Alena did have a very striking ring." As Jessica spoke, Mac checked out her fingers. Still loosely clasped. "A cluster of red stones. I don't recall what they were, but the piece was quite distinctive. I suppose if you found an item like that, it would help a great deal."

"Jewelry can be very useful." With that noncommittal response, Lisa looked his way, passing the baton—just as they'd planned. She wanted a chance to study the woman unobserved too.

He ran through the same questions they'd asked Erika. Unlike her friend, who'd groped for answers, Jessica's responses were smooth. Though she apologized for any lapses in memory, there were none. She repeated the same story she'd told Stan Breton more than two decades ago.

The woman either had a phenomenal recall or had done some serious prepping.

"Were you good friends with Alena?" Mac tapped his pen against his notepad, watching her.

181

"No, not at all. To be honest, none of us were—even Erika. They had little in common. I saw her now and then when I stopped in to visit Erika, but she was the quiet sort. I can't say I ever got to know her very well. Still . . . we all felt terrible about her disappearance. Perhaps you'll finally be able to bring closure to the mystery. Though I have to think after all these years, clues would be few and far between."

It wasn't a question, but she was digging again.

Before he could respond, Lisa stepped back in. "You'd be surprised. Technology today is amazing." She closed her notebook. "We do appreciate your time. Is there anything else you've remembered through the years that could prove helpful?"

She shook her head. "I wish I could say yes, but it all feels like ancient history now. I'll certainly give it some more thought in light of this new development."

Lisa slid a card across the table, and he did the same. "Feel free to call either of us if something comes to mind."

"Of course. I'll be happy to assist in any way I can." She pushed her chair back and rose. "I don't mean to rush you, but if we're finished, I do need to get back to my meeting. Although I suspect the other members of the committee aren't waiting with bated breath for more of my data dump." She gave a self-deprecating laugh.

Lisa looked at him and reached for her shoulder tote. "That's all we need for today."

As she stood, the strap caught on the back of the chair and she lost her grip. It fell to the floor, her wallet and glucometer spilling out along with a tube of lipstick that rolled toward Jessica's feet.

Jessica bent to retrieve the lipstick while Lisa stuffed the rest back in her tote. "The most important item in any woman's purse." She smiled as she handed it over.

"Thanks."

After another round of handshakes, Jessica led them to the door and spoke to the woman behind the polished desk in the anteroom. "Cathy, would you be kind enough to show Chief Grant and Detective McGregor to the front? I need to get back to the meeting."

The woman leaped to her feet. "Of course."

"Good luck with your case." With one more smile, Jessica Lee disappeared back into her office, closing the door behind her.

The walk back down the hall was silent once again as they followed Jessica's stiff-backed secretary to the lobby. Was she unfriendly—or nervous?

Might not hurt to find out.

"It's Cathy, right?"

At his question, the woman's step faltered. "Yes." She looked back, casting a nervous glance over his shoulder . . . as if she was afraid the hall monitor would catch her talking between classes and send her to detention.

Interesting.

"Have you worked here long?"

She started forward again. "No. Just six months."

"Seems like a nice environment."

A couple of beats ticked by.

"The offices are . . . very nice."

Mac's gaze connected with Lisa's. Did Cathy's careful remark suggest that while the physical environment was agreeable, the people were a different story—Jessica in particular?

Yet the PR executive had been the epitome of graciousness with them.

The secretary opened the door to the lobby. "I hope you both have a nice day." Her rote send-off came out stiff and stilted.

Man, there was some serious stress happening here.

Why?

"Thank you." Lisa led the way out.

They didn't talk until they were alone in the elevator and descending to the ground floor.

"Well, that was a very smooth performance." Lisa resettled the strap of her tote on her shoulder.

So she was suspicious of the woman's poised demeanor too.

Nice to know they were again on the same page.

"I agree. Did you notice her eyes when you mentioned the ring?"

"Yes. She seemed surprised. But why would she be? Everyone who was acquainted with Alena said she always wore that ring."

"Unless Jessica knew it was supposed to be missing."

"Exactly." Lisa's eyes glinted with excitement—like Tally's did when he'd sniffed out a treat. "I think we're rattling some cages."

The elevator door opened, and he followed her out, pausing beside the lobby coffee bar. "Would you like to discuss this some more over a drink?"

"I wish I could, but I'm scheduled to do a school program this afternoon. And before that, I have a meeting with the mayor. I'm already running late, thanks to the delay while we cooled our heels."

He throttled back his disappointment. "Not a problem. What's next on the agenda?"

"I'm thinking I'll let things ride until we get DNA confirmation. If Jessica and her friends are as neck-deep in this thing as I think they are, it won't hurt to keep them off balance, let them wonder what's going on behind the scenes. Joe's a wild card, but we have two very different personalities in Erika and Jessica. There might be some interesting dynamics between them that could work to our advantage."

"I agree. By the way, my FBI contact said they were collecting the DNA sample from Alena's mother today. They'll also ask her the questions I sent. I'm thinking we'll have the DNA in hand by the end of the week. Did you have any luck accelerating the process in Texas?"

"Yes. I heard from my former colleague in Chicago this morning. He pulled a few strings. I'm hoping to have their analysis early next week."

He arched an eyebrow. "You have powerful friends."

She chuckled. "Persuasive, anyway. You'll let me know what Alena's mother says about our questions?"

"The minute I hear anything."

"Good enough. See you later."

She was off at a brisk pace, pushing through the revolving door that led to the street, disappearing outside the plate-glass window among the other pedestrians on the busy Clayton sidewalk.

As he lost sight of her, his phone began to vibrate and he pulled it off his belt. Mitch.

"What's up?" He pointed to the tallest cup and mouthed *Americano* to the woman behind the counter at the lobby coffee bar.

"You have a few minutes to talk about the latest on the burglary case?"

"Yeah." He fished some bills out of his pocket and laid them on the counter, listening to his fellow detective as he paid for the drink and carried it to a table half hidden behind one of the containers spilling over with tropical flowers. Might as well sit for a minute.

Because based on the growing list of people he had to track down for the homicide investigation, he wasn't going to be doing a whole lot of sitting for the rest of the day.

13

Joe wasn't answering.

Phone to ear, Jessica tapped a nail on the polished cherry surface. He was probably at work, in that dead-end job he'd settled for after throwing away the Rhodes Scholarship.

What a loser.

Just like Erika.

When the phone rolled to voice mail, she muttered a profanity and stabbed the end button without leaving a message. She needed to get back to the strategic planning committee meeting, finish her presentation.

But she also needed to talk to Joe. Try to figure out how the cops had connected those bones to the ring they'd gone to such effort to remove.

She swiveled toward the expansive window in her office, but for once she didn't savor the view from her executive suite. Instead, the gruesome scene from twenty-four years ago played out in her mind. The struggle to remove the ring. The realization that it wasn't going to budge. Joe, at her prompt, digging out the pocketknife he'd always carried. The crack of bone, loud in the quiet woods, as Alena's finger finally broke under the backward pressure she'd exerted. Erika barfing beside her. Joe going white as the full moon and looking away as she cut the finger free and removed the ring. The blood on her hands as she passed the ring to him for disposal.

The ring had *not* been in that grave. Joe had gotten rid of it.

At least that's what he'd claimed.

But had he instead dropped it somewhere on the site—perhaps even in the grave—and not discovered his mistake until the next day when they all went their separate ways to dump the incriminating clothing they'd shredded?

If so, why hadn't he told them? He had to know a missing ring was a major loose end.

No, that scenario didn't hold up. Erika might make a fumble like that, but Joe was a lot more precise and buttoned up.

Yet what other explanation could there be?

A soft knock sounded on her door, and her heart stuttered as she checked the Waterford crystal clock on her credenza. She'd been gone from the meeting for twenty-five minutes. No doubt someone had been sent in search of her—and with the light-speed of gossip in this place, every member of the staff had likely already heard about her visit from the cops.

Better to kill any rumors before they got out of hand.

She'd worry about Joe later.

Replacing her scowl with the pleasant corporate face she'd perfected, she rested her hands on the arms of her chair and swiveled back toward the door of her glass-enclosed office.

Cathy stood on the other side.

Her scowl was back in an instant as she motioned her in. "What is it?"

The woman wiped her palms down her off-the-rack discount-store slacks, and Jessica's nose twitched. They were better than her own bad-old-days Goodwill wardrobe as a child, but not by much. "I know this isn't the best time, but I-I have a family emergency. My son's coach called while you were talking to the police officers. Chris isn't feeling well, and they want me to pick him up."

"Get someone else to do it. I need you to finish making the changes to my PowerPoint presentation for the meeting tomorrow with Frank Nelson." Jessica rose and strode toward the door. "I'll be in the conference room."

"But there's only my mother, and she's not in the best of health. It's hard for her to—"

"That's your problem." She cut the woman off as she brushed past. "If you hadn't made so many mistakes on the first draft, you wouldn't have to worry about corrections. Have a clean version in my in-box by three o'clock."

She exited without looking back.

Once outside the conference room door, she straightened her jacket, summoned up a smile, and slipped inside.

Gary was presenting, but fifteen heads swiveled toward her when he stopped, curiosity etched on every face.

So the rumor mill had, indeed, been active during their break.

"Go ahead, Gary. I want to keep this moving." Robert rose and joined her in the back of the room. "Everything all right?" His expression was benevolent—but at odds with his undertone of concern.

No surprise there. Scandal was anathema to the CEO. Peterson-Bradshaw had a sterling reputation, and as he'd said on many occasions, if you lose your reputation, you lose everything. Hadn't he let both an account executive and secretary go after they'd violated the company's non-fraternizing rule by indulging in a fling? As he'd told the employees in a full-company meeting after their departure, there was zero tolerance for anything that could tarnish the company or bring its high moral standing into question. Their conservative clients wouldn't stand for it—and neither would he.

She had to play this just right.

"Yes. Everything's fine. I'm sorry Cathy interrupted the meeting." She gave him a topline of the police discovery, glossing over her association with the dead girl, her tone calm and reassuring. "They're talking again to everyone who knew her. I wish I could have been more helpful, but as I told the police at the time, I was only acquainted with her because she was the roommate of a friend of mine. My memory of her is even less clear after all these years. But you have to commend the authorities for following up on such an old case."

"Well . . ." The parallel creases above his nose smoothed out. "I'm glad it wasn't anything serious—from your perspective, anyway. As soon as Gary wraps up, we'll get back to your presentation." He motioned for her to retake her seat at the table.

She slid into her place, casting a surreptitious glance toward Robert as Gary resumed. His full attention was once again focused on the presenter. As usual, the head of the firm had addressed a prickly issue, dealt with it, and moved on. She'd convinced him there was no need to worry. That nothing connected with her would hurt Peterson-Bradshaw's reputation or undermine his plans for his heir apparent.

And nothing would.

She'd make sure of it.

Mac drained the dregs of his coffee and stood. Time to get back to work.

As he tossed the empty cup into the trash container next to the coffee bar in the lobby of the Peterson-Bradshaw building, the elevator door opened. Out of the corner of his eye he spotted a figure in dark glasses making a beeline toward the front door.

Jessica Lee's secretary.

Why was she in such a hurry?

Heeding his gut, he followed her.

By the time he exited through the revolving door, she was halfway down the block. A dozen seconds later, she made a sharp right and disappeared.

Picking up his pace, he kept his gaze on the spot where he'd lost sight of her.

As he approached the edge of the building, he slowed. A collection of shrubs and small trees came into view between the two tall, adjacent structures, marking the entrance to one of the tiny pocket parks scattered around the business district. A nice concept—no more than a bench or two, with lush plantings that disguised the concrete jungle, but they offered businesspeople privacy and a moment of respite from their busy lives.

Not that he'd ever had a spare minute to linger in one.

But the way Cathy had headed straight here, it wasn't her first visit.

He stepped into the narrow opening between the shrubs, zeroing in on her at once. In the leafy privacy, she'd claimed the only bench. Shoulders shaking, she was bent forward, her head in her hands.

A study in misery.

Because of something that had happened at work—or might her distress have a bearing on Alena's case?

Whatever the cause, he couldn't walk away at this point. His SEAL buddies had nailed his personality with that Uncle Sam moniker they'd sometimes used for him, which had no connection to the U.S. of A.; he'd been born with the Good Samaritan gene.

Moving toward her, he made no attempt to hide his approach. In fact, he was careful to create enough noise to alert someone who was half deaf to his presence.

As he drew closer, she jerked upright, uttered a small gasp, and sprang to her feet. Tension radiated off her in waves.

He stopped. One step closer, she might bolt.

"I'm sorry. I didn't mean to startle you. I stopped to have some coffee in the lobby and saw you run out." He shoved his hands in his pockets and smiled, doing his best to appear as nonthreatening as possible. "Blame it on my mom, but I was brought up to come to the aid of women in distress—even if that's not too PC these days. At the risk of being called a chauvinist or getting clobbered . . . is everything okay?"

He couldn't read her eyes behind the dark glasses, but her stiff shoulders relaxed a hair. "Yes. I—I'm fine. I just needed a . . . a breath of fresh air."

The tremor in her hands, clearly visible from several yards away as she pushed her hair back, belied her words.

But unless he could detain her, she was going to flee before he had a chance to find out why she was upset—and to dig a bit deeper into the dynamics of her office.

"By the way, the name is Mac McGregor. We were never properly introduced." Taking a chance, he extended his hand and closed the gap between them.

She gave it a wary look, then reached out. "Cathy Ryan."

Her fingers were ice cold—and quivering.

When he released them, she clutched her purse to her chest. "I appreciate your concern. Today's been a little . . . rocky."

"Are you sure there isn't anything I can do to help?"

"Not unless you can conjure up a new job for me."

The perfect opening.

Keeping his tone and stance casual, he slipped off his jacket and hooked it over his shoulder with a finger. "Peterson-Bradshaw isn't such a great place to work?"

She hesitated. "The place is fine."

Almost the same thing she'd said as she'd walked them out.

But this time he could follow up on the enigmatic comment. Fortunately, he'd done his homework on the firm.

"I know the company has a stellar reputation, but I guess politics can be an issue everywhere. I get the impression Robert Bradshaw is a by-the-book kind of guy. I suppose he can be a hard taskmaster."

"Oh no. Mr. Bradshaw is super. He expects a lot, but he's fair." She looked down. Fiddled with the clasp on her purse. "My problems are closer to my desk."

Careful, careful. Don't scare her off.

"With Jessica Lee?"

She hesitated again.

"I don't mean to undercut your loyalty to your boss, of course."

The woman snorted. "I have no loyalty to her." She whipped off her sunglasses to reveal puffy, red-rimmed eyes now flashing with anger. "She's nice to the people who matter, but she treats me—and every other underling—like dirt. You want the truth? I don't have any idea why you needed to talk to her today, but I hope she's in big trouble!"

Whoa.

Not the kind of reaction he'd expected.

Before he could respond to her bitter words, she sucked in a sharp breath. "I'm sorry. That sounds terrible." Her shoulders slumped again, and she groped in her purse for a tissue. "I'm not usually vindictive."

"It sounds as if you have legitimate reasons for the way you feel."

"I do. But it's still wrong." She swiped at her nose. "I just reached the breaking point today, I guess."

"May I ask what happened?"

She let out a quiet, resigned sigh. "It's a long story. More than you'd want to know, trust me."

"I wouldn't ask if I wasn't interested."

She assessed him for a moment, then launched into an explanation about her son's injury, her mother's poor health, and her husband's struggle with ALS. "I'd quit, but this job has great pay and benefits. I was very blessed to get it, with only a junior-college education. But I'm afraid Jessica will fire me eventually, anyway. Nothing I do seems to please her. And it's not like she's going anywhere. Rumor has it she'll step into Robert Bradshaw's shoes whenever he retires." As Cathy's eyes teared up, she slipped her glasses back on.

Mac searched for some words of comfort but came up with only the pat response. "I'm sorry things are so difficult."

"Me too." She checked her watch and hoisted her purse onto her shoulder. "I have to get back. The meeting she's in could wind down anytime. I just needed five minutes alone."

"Instead, you had to put up with me."

She swallowed. "Believe me, I appreciate the friendly ear. But I hope . . . that is, I wouldn't want anything I said here to get back to Jessica." An anxious note crept into her voice.

"Don't worry. She won't hear a word about our conversation from me."

Some of the strain in the woman's features eased. "Thank you. I hope the rest of your day will be better than mine."

With that, she hurried toward the entrance and exited onto the sidewalk.

Mac gave her a head start, then followed.

As he emerged from the green oasis, he looked down the street. She was already pushing through the door of the office building. Heading back to face the woman who'd so graciously greeted him and Lisa.

Mac surveyed the building that housed the offices of Peterson-Bradshaw. He still might not have a handle on what Jessica Lee knew about Alena's death or the role she'd played in it, but he did know one thing.

There was a whole lot more to the PR executive than met the

eye—and there were some very dark places under her veneer of civility.

◆

Erika closed the door behind her departing attorney, flipped the lock with shaky fingers, and leaned her forehead against the wood.

She was going to lose everything.

Not today or tomorrow—but soon.

All because Jack was a crook.

A tear leaked out of her eye, and she stumbled toward the study. She needed a scotch.

Straight up.

No ice.

Halfway there, she stopped.

No. Jess had said to lay off the booze—and she was right. If the police were going to be nosing around, she needed to keep her wits about her.

But Jess hadn't said anything about cigarettes.

She changed direction and hurried toward her stash in the kitchen.

Once there, she rooted through the drawer until her fingers closed over a new pack. Using her fingernail, she ripped off the cellophane and shook out a cigarette—or a coffin nail, as her father used to say. But who cared? If the courts took everything she had, what was the point of living? Jack had long ago plowed through the trust fund her parents had left her. She'd be penniless, with no means of support.

And no one gave a rip about her sorry state—even her so-called friends.

After flicking the lighter on the end of the cigarette, she took a long drag, sat on the stool at the counter, and eyed the phone. Speaking of friends . . . Jess had said she'd call, but the phone had been silent all afternoon.

Surprise, surprise.

Not.

Miss High-and-Mighty had always done things her way, pushed everyone else around, acted like she was the only one who ever had an intelligent thought.

Well, she wasn't.

Joe was smart too.

And while no one had ever praised Erika Butler's great intellect, she wasn't dumb, either—except when it came to Jack, maybe. Allowing him to sweet-talk her with his grandiose dreams had been dumb.

Real dumb.

But she was smart about other things.

A lot smarter than Jess thought.

She took another puff. Blew the smoke toward the ceiling.

In fact, if she put her mind to it, she could surely think of some way out of her financial mess. Not that she'd ever be able to make a fortune the way Jess had, with her high-paying, perk-filled, jet-setting job. There were no plush offices or stock options or a CEO spot in her future.

Tapping the ash into her orange juice glass from this morning, she studied the pulp congealed against the sides. No, she wasn't smart enough or focused enough to achieve that kind of success. Jessica Lee had been well on the road to independent wealth and status long before she'd married that doctor who died. Erika Butler's designer clothes and fancy car, on the other hand, were courtesy of other people's money.

She sucked in another lungful of nicotine.

Other people's money.

Hmm.

She toed off the high-heeled pump that was pinching her foot, letting the seed of a plan take root.

Now that was an interesting idea.

She blew out the smoke. Tapped off the ash.

There was some risk, but if it worked, she wouldn't have to worry about money anymore. She could start over. Move somewhere else and create a new life for herself.

And hadn't her father always said anything worth doing required some risk? That the reward was, in fact, often proportionate to the degree of risk?

Besides, what did she really have to lose? If it didn't work, she'd be no worse off than she was now—broke and facing a dismal future. Jess might dump her, but so what? She hadn't been the best of friends, anyway.

Erika straightened her shoulders, stubbed out her cigarette, and stood.

For once in her life, she was going to take the initiative. Go for the gold. Do what *she* wanted to do instead of what someone else told her to do.

But she wasn't going to act on impulse. She'd think this through before she took any action. Analyze all the pros and cons, then make careful plans, like Jess always did.

And if all went well, maybe her financial problems would soon be history.

How was your day?"

As her mother handed her a raspberry-flavored water, Lisa swirled a piece of celery in the low-fat dip. "Busy."

Stephanie Grant rolled her eyes. "Why do I even ask?"

"How are the preemies?"

Her mother's expression softened. "Precious."

Lisa grinned. "Why do I even ask?"

"Touché." Her mom turned the chicken breasts she was sautéing. "How is the bones case coming along?"

"That's one of the reasons I had a busy Wednesday." Lisa opened the cabinet and removed two plates. "Are we eating in or out?"

"In. It's too hot for the patio. Maybe we'll go out for dessert."

"Works for me." She moved to the table, grabbing cutlery on the way. "I interviewed another one of the girl's classmates today."

"Find out anything interesting?"

Lisa lined up a spoon and knife next to a plate on the table. "She was very cool and professional. But there were a couple of subtle slips that made us think she was giving a very polished performance."

"Us?"

Whoops.

"Um . . . the County detective who's been assigned to help with the case went with me. It's never a bad idea to have two heads processing info during an interview."

"Especially when one of those heads is handsome."

The very thing Florence had said.

"It was strictly business, Mom." She fumbled the container of paper napkins, and several wafted to the floor before she could grab them.

Her mother watched her, eyes assessing, as she scrambled to collect the wayward squares.

Time for a change of topic.

"What's new with Sherry?"

"I talked to her a little while ago. For their tenth anniversary, they're going back to the hotel on Maui where they spent their honeymoon. Isn't that romantic?"

So much for a change of topic.

"Yeah. How are the kids?"

Her second diversionary attempt worked. Once her mother got started on the subject of her grandchildren, everything else faded into the background.

But later, as Lisa was collecting her things to leave, her mom circled back to the original subject.

"When will you be seeing that detective again?"

"I don't know." She searched through her purse for her keys. "He's busy with his own cases."

"Not too busy to make time for you, I bet."

She was out of here.

"He's assigned to help me. It's part of his job." She grabbed the doorknob.

Her mother folded her arms and propped a shoulder against the wall. "I thought you preferred to handle investigations on your own?"

She *would* remember that.

"I prefer to be *in charge* of investigations. There's a difference. I don't have to worry about turf battles with Mac, like I did with some of my colleagues in Chicago."

"Hmm."

She wasn't about to ask for clarification of that ambiguous comment.

Slinging her purse over her shoulder, she opened the door. "Thanks again for dinner, Mom. I'll call you later in the week."

"I'll look forward to it. I'm following this case with great interest."

I'll just bet.

After dispensing a quick hug and kiss, Lisa stepped into the heat and walked toward her car.

Sheesh.

Her mother was as tenacious as Tally trying to sniff out the latest hiding place of those fancy treats Mac had bought for him.

In general, her pooch was successful.

But her mom wouldn't be. No way was she going to admit to any interest in Mac. Too many things could go wrong, despite the mutual attraction. Better to wait until they had a date or two under their belts before she got her mom's hopes up.

Besides, hers were high enough for both of them.

Still, anxious as she was to move into personal territory with Mac, until she solved this case, those hopes had to be put on hold

They were getting close, though. She could sense it. Something big was about to break.

And she had a feeling Jessica Lee was going to be right in the middle of it.

◆

Answer the phone, Joe!

Daily glass of chardonnay in hand, the prepaid phone she'd

purchased on her way home from the office pressed to her ear, Jessica paced the length of her living room. Turned. Paced back again. He should be home from work by now. His wasn't the sort of job that—

"Hello."

As the voice from the past came over the line, she stopped. He sounded exactly as he had twenty-four years ago.

"Joe, it's Jessica."

"I figured I'd hear from you. Erika called to tell me what was going on."

Jessica took a tiny sip of wine. "Not with any specifics, I hope."

"No. I'm fine, by the way. Thanks for asking. How are you?"

Her mouth tightened. "This isn't a social call."

"I didn't think it was. Sorry to waste your time with a touch of humanity."

She ignored that.

"There's been a new development. I had a visit from the same people who stopped at Erika's. It appears a ring was instrumental in the ID."

Several seconds of silence ticked by.

"That's impossible."

"Are you certain?"

"Yes." There was no hesitation in his response.

Jessica crossed to the sliding door that overlooked the terrace. Muted orange and rose hues still tinted the western horizon, but the sky overhead was black. "Then why would they mention it?"

"I haven't a clue. Could it be a red herring? A bluff?"

"Maybe. But if the ring didn't tip them off to the ID, what did?"

Several more beats passed.

"I'm drawing a blank. We were very . . . thorough."

"Erika didn't have any involvement with the ring, did she?"

"No. But speaking of Erika . . . she's seriously worried."

"There's no need to be. As long as we stick to our story, we're fine. That detective in Columbia was tenacious, and he came up with nothing. These people won't, either. Panic is our biggest enemy, and we can control that. You haven't been contacted by anyone, have you?"

"No."

"Okay. Let's hang tight and see what happens next. This could all blow over. Just because they made an ID doesn't mean they'll find anything else."

"I'm not the one you need to reassure. Erika's a basket case. She's called me twice."

Anger bubbled up inside her. "You two shouldn't be talking."

"She doesn't have anyone else—and she's had some tough breaks."

"All of which she brought on herself."

He blew out a breath. "Nothing changes with you, does it? You always were a . . ."

She angled the phone away from her ear, the final word only a faint echo. Charles had called her that too, shortly before he'd died—with equal disgust.

But she didn't deserve their disdain.

Some men just couldn't deal with strong women.

"I didn't call you up to be insulted. Whatever you think of me, I saved our butts twenty-four years ago. Don't ever forget that."

"I'm not sure you did us any favors." Resignation deadened his words.

"Is it my fault you two made bad choices afterward?"

"Is it?"

Of all the idiotic questions.

"Look, people are responsible for their own actions. You can let bad stuff defeat you, or you can conquer it and move on. I chose to conquer." She took another swig of wine. "If anything else comes up, I'll call you. If you need to reach me, use this cell." She recited the number for the non-traceable phone she'd activated two hours ago. "And if Erika calls, I'd suggest you confine your discussion to the weather."

"Yes, sir."

Jerk.

"Good night, Joe."

Without waiting for him to reply, she ended the call with a jab of her finger. Erika's mild-mannered former boyfriend might have allowed his intellect to dull through the years in that eye-glazing nine-to-five job of his, but his tongue had certainly sharpened.

She took a long sip of wine and tapped in Erika's number.

The other woman answered on the third ring, her voice tentative.

"It's Jessica."

"This isn't your number."

"It is now." A few calls to her college friends she could explain. But there might end up being more than a few . . . and she didn't intend to leave phone records for the cops to find in case they checked. "Use this number—and only this number—if you need to call me. Write it down so you don't forget it."

"What did your . . . visitors today say? And why did you wait so long to call me?"

"I have more on my plate than this, Erika." She turned her back on the sky, which had gone completely dark. "They suggested they'd made the ID from the ring."

"What! That can't be. You . . . we . . . Joe got rid of it."

If Erika was faking shock, she was doing a great acting job—and she'd always been a lousy actress. Otherwise, it wouldn't have taken a whole weekend to coach her in words, body language, and facial expressions all those years ago.

Meaning she hadn't messed anything up with the ring—and Joe had disposed of it, as planned.

This was weird.

How *had* the police IDed the bones?

"Jess?"

"I don't have an explanation—but no matter how they figured out it was her, the fact is, there's no connection to us. We need to stay cool and let this play out—and fade out. Which it will, as long as we keep doing what we've been doing. I talked to Joe, and he's on board too. Are you staying off the booze?"

"Yes. That's the smart thing to do, and I'm not stupid."

She did sound coherent. That was good—but the edge in her voice wasn't. They all needed to remain calm. Panicked people made mistakes.

"I know that, Erika. Hang in, and we'll get through this."

Silence.

"Erika?"

"Yeah. I'm here. Look . . . I need to talk to you about something."

Jessica rolled her eyes and took another sip of wine. Sounded like a hand-holding session was in the offing. "Fine. I'm listening." She sat in the closest chair.

"No. Not on the phone. In person."

Oh, for pity's sake.

"Erika, I'm busy. I don't have time to socialize."

"This isn't a social visit."

"Then what is it?"

"Just meet me, okay? It's important."

What on earth was the woman up to?

"I don't think it's smart for us to be seen together right now."

"We could meet at the mall, like we did before. It's crowded there. No one will notice us. And considering how shorthanded most police departments are these days, it's not like they're going to be watching us 24/7. Unless you're more worried about all this than you're letting on."

Jessica squinted into the dregs of her chardonnay. When was the last time Erika had sounded so lucid—and analytical?

Maybe never.

She'd even called her bluff.

That, too, was a first.

Nor could she dispute the comment about the police. The chances they were under surveillance were slim to none.

"Fine." If a quick meeting kept her happy—and in line—she could spare forty-five minutes. "When?"

"Tomorrow afternoon?"

"I have a busy schedule tomorrow. What about Friday?"

"Does six work?"

"Yes. I'll see you then at the same Starbucks."

"Okay. Good night."

The line went dead.

Huh.

Erika had hung up first.

Another anomaly.

Jessica set the phone on the table beside her and drained the last of her wine.

What could Erika want to talk about?

She leaned back, twirling the slender stem of the goblet, drawing a blank. Who knew how the woman thought? At least she was sober. That was a plus.

All they had to do was chill and everything would be fine.

Jessica stood, wandered into the kitchen to set the empty glass beside the sink—and tried to ignore the sudden prickle of unease that slithered down her spine.

Now what was that all about?

She'd told Erika and Joe the truth. There wasn't anything to worry about. There had been nothing to tie the three of them to Alena twenty-four years ago, and there was even less now. However the police had IDed those bones was unrelated to them.

Nevertheless, a snake of fear coiled in the pit of her stomach.

And for the first time in her adult life, a tremor rippled through her carefully controlled world.

———◆———

"Here's that equipment list you wanted." Florence followed Lisa into her office and put several clipped pages in her in-box. "I asked my contact to email it, but I don't think she wanted an electronic trace. Like the list of standard patrol officer equipment in their municipality is top secret."

Lisa leaned down to pat Tally, who trotted over to greet her as she circled her desk and sat.

"Were you watching for me?" Lisa turned her attention to the office manager.

"I caught a glimpse of you as you turned the corner in the hall. I was restocking the supply cabinet. Speaking of which . . ." She set a battery on the desk. "You need to change the one in your phone. I charged this for you."

Lisa pulled her cell off her belt. Dead again—sometime in the past twenty minutes. It had been working fine when Craig had called to report on his interview with a suspect in his first solo detective case. She'd juiced it up before she left for her meeting, but the thing wasn't holding a charge anymore.

"Thanks for reminding me." She pried off the back and reached for the replacement battery.

"How did the mayor react to your neighborhood watch proposal?"

"Very favorably. He's going to bring the idea up at the next city council meeting. He was especially receptive to the notion that volunteer assistance like this can help reduce the need for additional officers and keep the police department budget under control."

"I'll bet he was . . . more so with elections looming. You plan to be in the office this afternoon?"

"Unless some crisis comes up." As the new battery slipped in, the phone began to vibrate in her hand. "Guess I missed a few messages."

"I'll let you attend to them, then."

On her way out, Florence bent to give Tally a quick pat as he trotted toward his corner.

Smiling, Lisa scrolled through her texts. Florence was such a softie.

There were three new messages in the past ten minutes—including one from Mac. She opened it first.

Tried to call, but phone rolled. Out of pocket rest of afternoon and knew you'd want update ASAP. DNA sample arrived in County lab this pm, + answers to our ?s. Alena did have scurvy as child & broke arm & leg in a fall at age 6. Garnet ring was family heirloom. Looking more & more like she's our victim. Lab's giving this priority. Talk to u soon.

Exactly what she'd expected to hear.

Now it was just a matter of waiting for Texas to come through and the County lab to do its DNA analysis on the Czech sample.

She leaned back in her chair, set her elbows on the arms, and steepled her fingers. Until she had confirmation of a DNA match, she'd lay low . . . although a follow-up visit with Erika Butler wouldn't hurt. But the longer she waited—within reason—to push hard, the more nervous the three concertgoers from that long-ago weekend would get . . . assuming they had secrets to hide.

In the meantime, it would be interesting to see what might grow from the seeds of doubt she'd planted.

15

"Y"ou wanted to see me, Robert?" Jessica stopped in the doorway of the CEO's office, deferential as always, waiting for a personal invitation to cross the threshold.

He looked up from the document he was reading and gave her a brief, distracted smile. "Yes. Come in. I'll join you in a moment." He waved her to the small seating area off to the side. "Make yourself comfortable."

She chose her usual chair, faced slightly away from the window, protecting her face from the harsh afternoon light that spilled through the expansive windows. No sense calling attention to the fine lines at the corners of her eyes. She'd have to schedule an appointment with Dr. Chandler again soon. Image was everything in this business.

Keeping one eye on Robert, she surveyed the executive office. It was spacious but dated—and bland. Still, it had potential. Arlene could do wonders with it, as she had with the condo. The woman had amazing skill with color and design. No doubt she'd suggest a striking piece of art for the far wall that now held nothing but a large photograph Robert had taken on some family vacation.

Of course, none of the changes would be ostentatious. Understated elegance was the key. Not that it would be inexpensive—but by then, Gary would be history. And the transformation would be gradual. New carpet one month. New furniture the next. Artwork added a piece at a time. All part of the multistage master plan she'd develop with Arlene. As for the color palette, with the western exposure it might—

"Sorry to keep you waiting." Robert edged around the plain wooden coffee table and claimed his usual chair.

"No problem. I was wrapping things up for the day, anyway."

"Any special weekend plans?"

"A lot of errands—and church on Sunday." Better attend services this week, as long as he'd asked. It had been at least a month since she'd shown her face there. "What about you?"

"Grandkids." The man fairly glowed. "We have them for the whole weekend. That's why I'm cutting out early today. They grow up too fast to miss a minute of fun with them. They're also one of the reasons I asked you to stop in. After much consideration and a great deal of discussion with my wife, I've decided it's time to pass the baton. I'll be stepping down at the end of the year."

Jessica's pulse surged.

This was it!

After years of laying groundwork and working her way up the corporate ladder, the payoff was at last in sight.

It took every ounce of her self-control to contain her excitement. "That's big news, Robert. I know you'll have a wonderful retirement, but the firm won't be the same without you."

"I appreciate that. And I'll stay involved to some extent, especially during the transition. Drake and I built this place from the ground up. It's hard to let go."

"Almost like turning a child loose into the world."

"Exactly. But I'll remain as chairman of the board so I can keep a discreet eye on things."

Not optimal. She'd hoped he'd offer to sell out—and she had the funds to buy his majority share, thanks to a sound investment strategy and her late husband's money. Charles had been a rich man.

One of the few benefits of that marriage.

"I won't be an intrusive presence to the new CEO, however."

She smiled at Robert's caveat. No, he wouldn't. She'd earned his trust. He'd let her run the show. "I wouldn't expect that to be an issue. You've always been an excellent delegator."

"Thank you. Delegation is a critical skill in any business. Which brings me to the reason I'm sharing all this with you today." He rested his elbows on the arms of his chair and linked his fingers. "I'm sure this won't come as a surprise, but I intend to recommend you to the board as my successor."

The magic words.

Yet in truth there was no magic about this accomplishment. She'd planned for it. Worked hard for it. Done every single thing that was expected of her.

And the payoff was sweet.

So sweet.

"Robert . . . what can I say? Thank you doesn't seem adequate for all the confidence you've placed in me, and for offering this wonderful opportunity."

"You deserve it. From the day you made that brilliant presentation years ago about demographic shifts and the potential impact on our business, I've kept my eye on you—and never once have you disappointed me. Thanks in large part to your contributions, this firm has grown bigger and more successful than I ever imagined. There's no one I'd rather see lead this company."

A discreet knock sounded on his door.

"Yes?"

His secretary opened it a few inches. "You said to let you know when your wife called. She's on the phone now."

"Thank you. Tell her I'll be right with her." He rose, and Jessica stood as well. "I'd ask you to keep this confidential for a few weeks, but I wanted you to have some advance notice to mentally prepare for the transition."

"I appreciate that—and all you've done for me." She held out her hand.

He took it and gave her fingers a firm squeeze. "It was my pleasure. Talent should be recognized and rewarded. I hope you celebrate this weekend."

"I intend to."

She slipped through his door, closing it behind her. As she exited his office suite, she paused to admire the embossed brass nameplate in the hall.

Someday soon it would bear her name.

Jessica Lee, CEO of one of the fastest-growing PR firms in America.

Victory was sweet.

And tonight she would celebrate, as Robert had suggested—as soon as she dealt with Erika's crisis.

A surge of annoyance swept over her, but she quashed it at once. She was not going to let anyone mar this moment. And once they got past this thing with Alena, she was cutting all ties with the other woman once and for all.

Erika was a complication she didn't need.

◆

She needed a smoke—but the mall was smoke-free.

Erika drummed her fingers on the table. Jess still had five minutes . . . but what if she didn't show?

And even if she did, what if she didn't go for her proposition? What if she called her bluff, laughed, and walked away?

Why did the plan that had sounded so perfect for the past two days suddenly feel shaky? Like it was a mistake?

"Because you don't have enough self-confidence, Erika. You never have."

From the recesses of her memory, Jess's words from that nightmare weekend echoed in her mind.

They'd been true back then, when she'd quaked at the thought of being interrogated—and they were true now. Chalk it up to living with a father who'd wanted a smart, ambitious son and ended up with a daughter who preferred partying to politics and ballet to balance sheets.

Still, she'd done okay twenty-four years ago once Jess drilled her about what to say and how to act. After hours of practice, she'd learned the script, learned the gestures, learned the tone of voice.

And that's what she'd done for these past two days too. It was lucky, really, that Jess had delayed their meeting a day. She'd had a lot more time to prepare and practice.

As for her sudden case of nerves . . . so what? She'd been nervous when they'd gone back to Columbia too, but she'd fooled those cops—and they'd been a tough sell.

She spotted Jess in the distance. Her college chum was scanning the tables clustered around the Starbucks kiosk.

Once again, for a brief second, her courage faltered.

Then, as Jess's gaze connected with hers, she straightened her shoulders. Lifted her chin. Took a deep breath.

She could do this.

She *had* to do this.

It was her only hope of preserving some semblance of the life she was accustomed to.

Failure wasn't an option.

◆

As Jessica approached Starbucks, she studied Erika. The woman looked . . . different.

It wasn't her physical appearance, though. The dark roots

remained in desperate need of a touch-up. The clothes were still too tight. The mascara was smudged, as usual.

But there was a subtle change in her demeanor.

Erika rose as she drew close. "Do you want anything to drink?"

"No."

"Then why don't we talk over there?" She indicated the same spot they'd occupied a few days ago.

"Fine." At least the woman seemed to be coherent today.

Jessica led the way. The sooner she could get this over with, the sooner she could begin her private celebration. After Robert's news, dinner at one of St. Louis's top-tier restaurants would be the perfect end to a perfect day. She wasn't going to let this slight detour to meet with Erika dampen her upbeat mood.

As they sat on the bench, she angled toward the other woman. "What was so important that we had to talk in person? I gave you a secure number."

"I heard from our lawyer on Wednesday. He confirmed that the court is going to seize all our property for restitution—what they can find of it."

That's what this was about? She wanted a shoulder to cry on about her financial woes?

"Maybe the judge will take pity on you."

"It won't matter. None of the big stuff is in my name. Jack put it all—including our house and cars—into some sort of corporation he created, and only he can access it. I'm going to need to provide for myself."

Good luck with that. The woman had no marketable skills.

"That could be . . . challenging."

"Not necessarily."

"What do you mean?" Jessica glanced at her watch. She needed to get out of here so she could go home and change into the new Valentino lace sheath she'd been saving for a special—

". . . have to rely on you."

Her head jerked up. "What did you say?"

Erika wiped a palm down the fabric covering her thigh. She looked nervous . . . but determined. That little jut in her chin was new.

"I said that since my options for generating enough cash to live even a modest lifestyle are limited, I'm going to have to rely on you."

Jessica frowned. "I have no idea what you're talking about." Was the woman tipsy after all?

She leaned closer and lowered her voice. "It's simple. You have a whole lot more to lose than Joe or I do if the cops find out what happened that night. It might be worth an investment on your part to guarantee they don't."

Jessica blinked.

Surely Erika wasn't suggesting . . .

She narrowed her eyes. "That sounds like a threat."

"I prefer to think of it as a business proposition."

"It's blackmail."

Erika's gaze didn't waver. "So report me to the police."

Checkmate.

Jessica regarded her one-time classmate. The meek little lamb had teeth—and more brainpower than she'd given her credit for.

This would require some finessing.

"Let's be logical, Erika." She kept her tone pleasant and reasonable. "Things might be tough for you right now, but going to prison would be worse."

"Don't try that scare tactic on me. I did some checking on the internet. The statute of limitations on involuntary manslaughter ran out long ago—and that only affected Joe, since he was the driver. Even if he'd been charged, a good lawyer could have proven it was all an accident. You and I would have been fine. We could have dumped the joints before the police arrived, and they can't prosecute you for being high."

Erika had done her homework.

Underestimating her had been a mistake.

"You're looking at the best-case scenario. Even if we'd all walked away, we'd have carried a taint. Joe's scholarship could have been revoked, I might not have been offered the job that launched my career, and you'd have had to deal with your father's wrath."

"I'd have lived. And Joe lost his scholarship anyway."

"He didn't lose it. He gave it up—by choice."

"Because he couldn't live with the guilt."

"Guilt is a sign of weakness."

"No, it isn't." Erika glared at her, eyes leaking venom. "Guilt is a sign of compassion and caring. Not that you'd know anything about those things."

This conversation was veering way off grid.

And she was fast losing control of it.

Time to regroup—and placate.

"Look, insults aren't going to solve anything. Maybe I've always been a practical person, but that doesn't mean I don't have feelings. Why don't we forget about the past for a minute and think about the future. Even if there's no legal liability at this stage, why would you want to air all that dirty laundry and drag our names through the mud?"

"My name's already being dragged through the mud, thanks to Jack. I doubt the Paducah news media will care much about something that happened twenty-four years ago in Missouri, so Joe's safe. In fact, he told me he doesn't really care at this point if the truth comes out. That maybe it would be for the best to come clean. You're the one who has the most to lose if the cops find out what happened that night. The involvement of a high-profile PR executive in a case like this will make national headlines, even if no charges are involved."

An icy chill settled in the pit of her stomach, and a tentacle of panic wrapped itself around her windpipe.

But she fought it off, just as she had on that long-ago night.

This was simply another problem to solve. A challenge to overcome. A knot in need of untangling.

Her forte.

"Headlines would be bad for you, Jess." The other woman leaned closer and whispered the words.

As if she didn't know that.

Too bad Erika had figured it out too.

The question was, how to deal with it?

She needed to buy herself some time. Think this through. She could strategize on the fly if necessary, but that wasn't optimal—especially when so much was at stake.

"You've given me a lot to think about." She kept her expression neutral, her voice steady.

"I need you to think fast."

"What kind of dollar amount are you talking about?"

When Erika named the figure, Jessica's eyes widened. "You've got to be kidding."

Erika stared her down. "No. I'm not. You have a great job and your husband was wealthy. A few years' worth of bonuses alone ought to cover that amount. You wouldn't even miss it."

Fury began to build deep inside her.

"I worked hard for every penny I made, Erika. This is stealing."

The other woman shrugged. "I like the term *insurance* better."

Jessica's stomach curdled. She had the money, but paying off Erika would make a huge dent in her Peterson-Bradshaw buyout fund. All the rest of her cash went to support her lifestyle.

No way was she going to agree to this.

But Erika didn't need to know that.

Yet.

"I'll have to sleep on it." She picked up her bag. "I'll call you tomorrow."

Erika tucked her purse under her arm. "I'll be waiting to hear from you. Have a nice evening."

She rose and walked away without a backward glance.

Jessica watched her until she disappeared from view in the Friday night throng at the mall.

So the kitten had developed claws.

Slowly she stood and walked toward the exit, still trying to assimilate this bizarre turn of events.

Erika, a blackmailer.

It was surreal.

How in the world had she morphed from docile to defiant overnight?

Then again, desperate people did desperate things.

But some of them put a lot more thought into it.

She pushed through the door, the early evening heat blasting her in the face. It was too hot for the first day of summer.

And she didn't need any extra heat from Erika.

As she started toward her car, she caught sight of the other woman heading toward the exit in her Audi. Thinking she had the upper hand.

But she didn't.

A kitten might have claws—but it was no match for a lion.

Jessica pressed the auto unlock on her keychain, slipped behind the wheel of the BMW, and cranked up the air.

There were a few things Erika didn't know about her new adversary.

Things no one knew.

If her college chum wanted to go against type and play rough, she'd picked the wrong person for her trial run.

The air conditioner began to kick in, and Jessica aimed all the vents toward her. But the chilly air didn't cool her temper. What should have been the happiest evening of her life, the culmination of all her years of hard work, had been ruined. There would be no celebratory dinner tonight.

Instead, she had plans to make.

And already an idea was coalescing in her mind.

She put the car in gear and backed out of her parking space, brain firing on all cylinders as it always did when things got dicey.

Of course she wasn't going to give in to Erika's demands. Her request to sleep on the ultimatum had been nothing more than a stall tactic while she assessed the situation.

As for the idea she was playing with . . . it had serious potential.

Flipping on her turn signal, she edged into the exit lane from the mall, then accelerated toward the highway while she mulled it over.

It could work. Careful execution would be necessary, but she could pull it off. Logistics were her specialty.

So she'd spend her evening thinking through all the contingencies. Refining her plan. Nailing down the details.

And when she launched her attack, Erika would wish she'd never tangled with Jessica Lee.

16

Sweat dripping off his temples, Mac jogged up the steps to his front door, retrieved the key from the back pocket of his shorts, and inserted it in the lock. Getting in his daily run early to miss the heat had sounded smart in theory—but who knew the mercury would climb to eighty-five by nine o'clock?

He pushed into his apartment, closed the door behind him, and stood with arms outstretched, letting the cool air wash over him.

Better—but a cold shower would get the job done faster.

His cell began to vibrate as he moved down the hall, and he unzipped his running belt to pull it out. Caller ID was blocked.

Hmm.

Delay the shower and take the call, or take the shower and return the call later? It wasn't Lisa—she wouldn't block her number—and who else was worth getting overheated about?

Except one of his clandestine sources on the homicide investigation.

Better take it. The way that case was going, he needed every lead he could get.

"McGregor."

"Back at you."

He squinted and cocked his head. "Lance?"

"Give the man a gold star."

Mac positioned himself under the cold-air vent in the bathroom. "Where are you?"

"Stateside. That's why I called. I wanted to let you know that in light of my short remaining tenure, the powers that be decided it wasn't worth sending me back overseas. I get to coast for the next month."

One less brother in the line of fire.

That was the best news he'd had all day.

"Lucky you. You'll have a chance to rest up before you have to report to the academy. You heard anything from Finn?"

"One quick call two days ago. He got pulled back to the Middle East early. Very hush-hush."

Mac's gut clenched. So much for his temporary reprieve from worry. "You ever nail down what was bugging him while you guys were here?"

"No. You know how he can clam up. He's never been the most communicative guy. I think he's just bummed because we both bailed from the service."

"I don't know . . ."

"Hey, you don't have to play big brother anymore, you know? We're all grown up. If Finn has some issue, he'll deal with it. Let's talk about you. Got a date for tonight?"

He shifted position until the cool air hit the back of his soggy T-shirt. "I told you—I'm too new here to know anyone."

"There are plenty of places in St. Louis to meet women."

"Are you speaking from experience?"

"Finn and I scoped out a few."

Naturally.

"I've spent what little free time I've had in my short tenure here trying to settle in."

"You aren't making much progress on that front, either. You hire a decorator yet?"

"Not on my priority list."

"Say . . . I bet that police chief could offer some advice about how to warm the place up."

The very thing he'd suggested. But Lisa hadn't bitten. Which was probably prudent if they wanted to keep things professional.

He leaned into the shower and flipped it on.

Lance's chuckle came over the line. "A cold shower, huh? Yeah, I can see how thinking about Chief Grant might drive a man to that."

"For your information, I just got back from a run."

"Sure, sure."

"So was there another purpose for your call besides harassing the senior McGregor sibling?"

"Isn't that a good enough reason?"

Mac smiled. With his quick wit and humorous banter, Lance had always been able to lighten up his day. "I'm getting in the shower."

"Fine. I can take a hint. But do yourself a favor. If you're going to sit home alone tonight, at least call the lady."

"She might have a date." He adjusted the water temperature.

"Nah. Not with all that electricity pinging between you two. She'll be going solo too."

"Since when did you develop psychic powers?"

"Doesn't take a psychic to detect flying bolts of electricity. I was almost afraid to stand between the two of you. Even Finn noticed, and you know how oblivious he can be to that kind of stuff."

"I'm hanging up now."

"Touchy, touchy. Fine, I'll let you go."

Mac propped a shoulder against the cool tile. "Listen . . . now that you're home, don't be a stranger, okay?"

"I'll keep in touch."

"You better. And I'm really glad you're back on US soil."
His voice rasped.

"You want the truth? It's nice to be back. Delta was a great
gig, but it's time to move on. Speaking of that, how long did it
take you to decompress?"

"You mean before I stopped waking up with an adrenaline
rush and scrambling for my weapon whenever a car backfired
at night?"

"Yeah."

"A year, maybe. Still happens once in a while, in fact—but
less often. You okay on that front?" His hand tightened on the
phone as he asked the question. One of his best SEAL buddies
had been slammed with PTSD, and it hadn't been pretty.

"Yeah, I'm fine. Just the normal stuff all soldiers deal with
after a few tours. I'm planning on sleeping real fine sooner rather
than later."

"You'll get help if you need it, right?" That had been the
trouble with his buddy. He'd never admitted he had a problem.
SEALs were too strong to get PTSD.

Not.

"Hey, bro, chill. I'm perfectly sane—or as sane as I've ever
been. It was a simple question. You need to get that worry gene
of yours under control."

"Hard to do when you have kid brothers who tried to rappel
from a third-floor apartment and almost broke their necks."

"That was more than twenty years ago. But you're never
going to let us forget it, are you?"

He grinned. "Probably not. As I recall, Dad had to do some
fast-talking to keep us from being evicted. At least you tried that
stunt while he was assigned to London. Authorities in Qatar
might have shot first and asked questions later."

"Very funny. In any case, you can stop worrying about me
now. If you need a distraction, call the hottie."

"Good-bye, Lance."

Once again, his brother chuckled. "See ya."

The line went dead, and Mac set the cell on the vanity. Lance was a piece of work—but he had great intuition. A handy professional asset, even if it could be annoying on a personal level.

He pulled off his watch. Not yet nine-thirty, and no real plans for the day—or evening.

Maybe he'd follow his brother's advice and give Lisa a call later. It wouldn't be as satisfying as a date, but it was better than spending a mindless evening watching TV. He could use the case as an excuse, then work his way into more personal territory. It couldn't hurt to lay some more groundwork for their less-official relationship.

A relationship he intended to pursue the instant the Alena Komisky case was put to rest.

◆

Jessica slid open the door to her terrace and stepped out.

Still hot, even with the sun dipping low in the west. But after being shuttered all day in the condo making plans, she needed a break before she placed the call that would set everything in motion.

In the dusky light, she strolled over to the railing. What she was about to undertake was ambitious—and there'd be no turning back once she started down this road.

But what choice did she have? Everything she'd worked for all these years was a whisper away. As long as there were no glitches, the board would rubber-stamp Robert's recommendation—and in a few months she'd be sitting in the corner office, running the show. Filling the role she'd been born to play.

Jessica Lee—CEO.

See, Dad. I did amount to something after all.

She wrapped her fingers around the railing, frowning.

Where had *that* come from?

Who cared about Ned Lee's opinion, wherever he was . . . if he was even still alive. His liver had probably given out long ago. A father who drank his family into ruin, heaped verbal abuse on his wife and children, then abandoned his daughter when things got too tough, didn't deserve a millisecond of thought. Good riddance to him. She'd done fine on her own. Far better than he had, despite his grandiose dreams and plans.

Streetlights began to blink on far below, and the muted sound of traffic filtered up to her terrace, close enough for her to feel part of the city, but far enough away to give her absolute privacy and solitude.

Just the way she liked it.

People were messy.

But she was about to clean up one particular mess.

She moved over to the lounge chair, sat on the edge, and pulled the disposable cell out of her pocket.

Strange that Erika hadn't called all day. Patience had never been her strong suit. But perhaps she'd had second thoughts about her blackmail plan. Recognized she'd made a mistake.

Too late.

If she'd done it once, she could do it again—and that kind of hovering threat wasn't tolerable. Erika had started this game, and they were going to play it out to the finish.

Finger poised over her number, she paused.

Last chance to change her mind.

But her plan was sound. She could pull it off. Her talent for damage control was one of the reasons she excelled at PR. That, and her ability to read people, to know which buttons to push to win their trust without ever tipping them off they'd been manipulated. Her excellent research and planning skills had also helped propel her to the top. All those abilities would serve her well as she implemented her plan.

There was no reason to hesitate. This was the best solution to the problem. The risk was minimal.

To her, anyway.

Smiling, she swung her legs onto the lounge chair, leaned back, and tapped in Erika's number.

◆

"One, two, three, awesome! Keep going . . . arms—one, two, three, four . . . again—one, two, three, four . . . skip, skip, skip, skip . . . shoulders—push, push, push, push . . . Repeat . . . jazz square—one, two, three, four. Repeat. Keep it moving . . . one, two . . ."

Without missing a beat of her routine, Lisa cocked her ear. Was that her cell ringing?

She ran over to it, staying in rhythm.

Yep. It was ringing.

She paused the DVD and read the digital display. Mac.

All at once her day got brighter.

She snagged her towel from the back of the chair in her exercise room and mopped her forehead. "Hi, Mac. What's up?"

"Nothing much, but I haven't talked to you in a couple of days and thought I'd check in."

"Nothing new on my end, either." Tally poked his nose in the door, as if to reassure himself the loud music had been extinguished, and trotted over. "Thanks again for being the FBI liaison with Alena's mother. They got the job done fast."

"The FBI is nothing if not efficient. They're experts at maneuvering through protocols and red tape. With the lab backlog here, things will be a bit slower on our end, I'm afraid. It usually takes about two weeks to get DNA results, but I'm going to ask one of my colleagues with longer tenure to lean on them. So how come you're out of breath?"

"You interrupted my jazzercise routine."

"Sounds like an exciting Saturday night."

"Not—but I didn't have any better offers." Her eyes widened at her flirty response. That wasn't her usual style.

But a lot of things were different with Mac.

"Hmm. Lonesome?"

Yeah, strangely enough she was. In general, Tally provided plenty of companionship.

Admitting that, though, might prompt an offer she wouldn't be able to refuse—and they needed to stay the course until Alena's case was put to rest.

"I have Tally." She ruffled his ears, evading the question.

"Nice to know who the competition is."

"Cute. What are *you* doing tonight?"

"Thinking about you."

Her eyebrows rose. "You don't beat around the bush, do you?"

"Not when I'm on a mission."

She fanned herself with her free hand. "Are all SEALs so . . . focused?"

"I can't vouch for all SEALs—but it's a definitive McGregor trait."

She could buy that . . . at least socially. Lance and Finn hadn't made any secret of their interest in her the day they'd met.

"You make it sound like a tactical exercise."

He chuckled. "There are some similarities. And I'll let you in on my next tactic. The minute this case wraps, I'm inviting you to dinner."

A quiver of anticipation thrummed through her. "I'll pencil it in."

"Use indelible ink. So what can we do to speed things along . . . other than light a fire under the County lab people to get the DNA sample tested?"

She wiped her face again and draped the towel around her neck. "I want to pay Erika another visit later next week. She's a lot less smooth and in control than Jessica. If we keep rattling her cage, we might shake a few pieces of information loose."

"Want some company?"

"That would be great, if you can fit it in."

"I can fit it in." No hesitation.

"He's not too busy to make time for you, I bet."

As her mother's words echoed in her mind, she grinned. Chalk one up for Mom.

"I'm also thinking there are some interesting dynamics in her relationship with Jessica that could work to our advantage." She walked back and forth, keeping her muscles warmed up. "Those two don't seem at all simpatico."

"I agree. Crime can create strange bedfellows. If nothing pans out here, though, it might be worth a trip to Paducah to talk with Joe Andrews."

"You're reading my mind." She patted Tally's head as he trotted along beside her. "But if none of them slip, we're sunk. Stan Breton did a thorough job twenty-four years ago. Despite his suspicions and diligent digging, he didn't find one piece of hard evidence to tie the three of them to Alena's disappearance. I agree with him that they know a whole lot more than they're telling, but to move this along, one of them has to make a mistake."

"I have a feeling Erika's our best hope on that score."

"Me too. Any time work best for you later next week to pay her a visit?"

"No. I have no idea what will be on my schedule. I'll try to shift things around if they conflict with your interview."

"Are you this accommodating with everybody?"

"No."

His firm, single-word response sent a rush of warmth to her heart. "I'll call you."

"I'll look forward to it. Now I guess I better let you get back to your jazzercise."

"Somehow it's lost its allure. Talking to you is a whole lot more fun."

A chuckle came over the line. "If you think this was fun, wait for the dinner date I have planned."

"That's a big promise to live up to."

"Worried I'll fall short?"

"Nope. I have every confidence you'll deliver."

"Count on it."

The conversational ball was back in her court, and she tried to think of something—anything—to extend their banter. "So have you heard anything from your brothers?"

She listened as he recounted his phone conversation with Lance earlier in the day and mentioned Finn's redeployment.

"You know, you all have interesting names—but I assume Mac is a nickname, right? Your parents didn't actually name you Mac McGregor."

There was a long pause before he responded. "No."

She waited.

Nothing.

"That's it? You're not going to tell me your real name?"

"I've gone by Mac for as long as I can remember. My given name is very . . . Scottish."

"It's not Angus, is it?"

"Worse." He sighed. "Promise you won't laugh?"

"Cross my heart."

"Okay. I've shared this with only a few people. Consider it a sacred trust. Brace yourself—it's Archibald."

A giggle bubbled up, but she managed to contain it. Thank goodness they were on the phone and not talking in person. Mac was so *not* an Archibald.

"You still there, or did I scare you off?"

"Still here." She swallowed past her chortle. "I have to say I prefer Mac."

"You and me both. And now I'll hang up so you can let out that laugh you're holding in."

"Why do you think I'm trying not to laugh?"

"Because if I were you, that's what I'd be trying to do. Have fun with your jazzercise, and give Tally a pat for me."

She reached down. "Doing the latter as we speak. Talk to you soon."

"Can't be soon enough for me. Sleep well."

The line disconnected, and she slowly set the phone down. Not much chance of a restful night with Mac—and his mission—occupying her thoughts.

Maybe she could wear herself out with a double dose of exercise.

After dispensing one final pat to Tally, she aimed the DVD remote toward the TV. Her canine companion took one look and galloped away.

Two seconds later, the instructional video reappeared on the screen. She cranked up the sound and dove back in.

But no matter how many jazz squares or stretches or grape-vines or kick-ball-changes she did, she couldn't stop thinking about what role a handsome—and determined—ex-SEAL might play in her future.

17

"Sorry again about having to ask you to come to my rescue." Jessica balanced the tote bag on her lap and adjusted her sunglasses. "I just had the BMW checked out. You'd think the mechanics would have been more thorough."

"I don't mind. That shopping center isn't far from the house." Erika swung her car into the entrance of the upscale residential area she called home—for now. "I like your hair in that upswept do, by the way. It gives you a different look."

Exactly the reason she'd chosen this style.

Plus, with all the spray she'd used to cement it in place, there wasn't much chance she'd lose any stray—and potentially incriminating—hairs.

"Thanks." As Erika turned down her street, Jessica tipped her bag, spilling some of the contents onto the floor.

"Oops. Sorry about that." Erika eased back on the accelerator. "Jack always said I drove too fast."

"No problem." Jessica bent down and began gathering up the items that had fallen out, keeping her face hidden from anyone who might happen to be out and about on this warm Tuesday evening walking a dog . . . watering a planter . . . keeping an eye on the neighbors. The light was growing dim—as she'd planned—but it never hurt to take extra precautions.

She didn't finish collecting the items and straighten up until Erika swung into her driveway and rolled toward the attached rear-entry garage.

Once the car was hidden from view and the engine went silent, Jessica opened her door, keeping a mental inventory of everything she touched. So far, just the outer and inner door handles of the Audi.

She followed Erika into the house, through the mudroom, across a kitchen filled with high-end appliances and expensive finishes. Jack had spent some big bucks on this place.

Other people's bucks.

She tightened her grip on the tote bag. Stealing was despicable—and deserved to be punished.

"Do you want to talk in the living room or the study?" Erika paused on the far side of the kitchen.

"You choose."

"The bar's in the study, if you'd like a drink. It's fully stocked—soft drinks too, if that's your preference."

"Fine by me."

Jessica continued to catalogue Jack's trappings of success as she crossed the polished marble floor and passed a glass case displaying what appeared to be a Boehm sculpture. And was that a Schonbek chandelier above her head? Only Swarovski crystal had that kind of sparkle. Too fussy and ostentatious for her taste, but a piece like that could easily have set him back twenty-five grand.

Maybe some of those people he'd bilked out of their hard-earned cash would get a chunk of their money back after all, once the court swooped in and cleaned the place out.

As she entered the study, Erika motioned toward two burgundy, brass-studded leather chairs angled in front of the fireplace. "What would you like?"

"Chardonnay, if you have it."

"Jack has everything."

Not for long.

"I brought you a present." She chose a chair and pulled a gift bag out of her tote. "This is what I was buying when my car died. I'm not an aficionado, but the clerk told me it's an excellent brand."

Erika finished pouring the wine and circled around the bar to join her. "You bought me a present?"

"Consider it a peace offering." She held up the bag with both hands, forcing Erika to set the wine on the table between the chairs. The other woman's eyes were actually misty.

Sentiment was such a pathetic emotion.

"I was afraid you'd be mad at me after my . . . proposal." She took the bag.

"I'll admit I was taken aback, but I understand your motivations. And what point is there in getting angry?"

"Does this mean you're going to give me the money?"

"Why else would I be bringing you a present?"

Relief washed over Erika's face—but it morphed to puzzlement when she pulled out the bottle of Glenfiddich. "You got me scotch? I thought you didn't want me to touch alcohol until this thing was over?"

"Sharing a few drinks with an old friend won't hurt. I doubt those detectives are going to bother you tonight."

Or ever again.

"That's true. But they haven't given up. That lady police chief called and left a message yesterday. She wants to come talk to me again. I haven't responded, because I wanted to see if our . . . business deal . . . was a go or not. I'm glad you came through."

So the cops were still poking around, trying to solve the twenty-four-year-old mystery. That meant they hadn't found anything more than the detective in Columbia had. Nor would they. The only way ancient history would become an issue was if one of them talked.

And that wasn't going to happen.

Erika grabbed a cut-crystal tumbler—Waterford, perhaps?—from the bar and plopped into the chair on the other side of the small table. Once she had the bottle open, she poured herself a generous drink, straight up.

While the other woman began to sip her scotch, Jessica crossed her legs and folded her hands in her lap. No need to waste a lot of time on conversation . . . but she'd chitchat until Erika had one drink under her belt. This would be easier if she was starting to feel the buzz.

It didn't take her college chum long to toss back the first drink—or refill her glass.

As Erika set the bottle on the table, she inspected the untouched wine glass. "You're not drinking your chardonnay."

Jessica picked up the glass by the stem and took a sip. "Very nice."

"Only the best for Jack." Her mouth twisted, and she swirled the amber liquid in her tumbler. "So we're good on the money thing?"

"That's why I'm here." She set her wine down again and reached into her bag to withdraw an inch-thick packet of fifty-dollar bills encased in plastic wrap. "Arranging the transfer of that much money will take a few days, but I brought some cash from home to tide you over in the meantime." She set it on the table between them.

Erika perused the stack. "How much is that?"

"Twelve thousand dollars."

She blinked. "You keep that kind of money in your condo?"

"I like to have cash on hand." Pocket money now, but since the day her father had cleaned out her bank account and taken off after Jason died, she'd always kept an emergency stash.

Who knew it would ever be used for an emergency like this, though?

Erika picked it up. "I've never seen this much cash in real life—but it's kind of a small stack. Is there really twelve thousand dollars here?"

"Yes. Trust me, I've counted it. I'll have to make arrangements for the rest."

"No rush. This will last me a few weeks." She set the money back on the table, picked up her glass again, and raised it. "To peace of mind."

Jessica retrieved her own glass and tapped it against Erika's. "The perfect toast."

She continued to chat until Erika was halfway through her second glass, then tipped a small splash of wine onto her slacks. "Oh no!" She set the glass down and used a cocktail napkin to blot at the stain. "These are brand new too. Do you have any liquid laundry detergent?"

"I don't know. Our maid takes care of that kind of stuff. Let me check the laundry room."

The instant Erika disappeared out the door, Jessica reached into her tote bag, removed the plastic-wrapped packet of hot-pink pills, and set them on the table. Reaching deeper still, her fingers closed over the steel barrel of the compact Beretta Charles had always carried when he'd volunteered at that free clinic in the worst part of North St. Louis.

He'd never needed to use it.

But it would serve a purpose tonight.

She felt around until her fingers found the grip, then pulled the weapon out, weighing it in her hand. So small—yet so deadly.

Slipping her finger in front of the trigger, she lowered her hand to her lap, pointed it at the fireplace . . . and waited.

Thirty seconds later, the *tap-tap-tap* of Erika's heels sounded as she crossed the marble foyer.

It was time.

Absolute calm settled over her. No blip in her pulse. No change in respiration. No quiver in her fingers.

Most people would be nervous about taking a life.

But she wasn't most people.

Erika circled in front of the chairs, bottles of laundry detergent and stain remover in hand. "I wasn't sure exactly what you needed, so I brought . . ."

Jessica lifted the gun and aimed it at the other woman's heart.

The sudden widening of Erika's eyes was almost comical. "What . . . what are you doing?"

"I'm not paying you any money, Erika."

Some of the color drained from the other woman's complexion. "Look, it's not . . . we can . . . you know . . . talk about it, okay?" One of the plastic bottles slipped from her fingers and tumbled to the floor. She didn't seem to notice.

"I'm done talking. Put down the other bottle and sit in your chair."

She hesitated.

"Now." Jessica flicked off the safety.

"Okay, okay." She sat quickly, setting the container beside her, never taking her gaze off the gun. "Why don't we forget about the money. I'll . . . I'll figure something else out."

"The money isn't the only issue. You're a loose end, Erika—and a potential impediment. I don't like either."

Beads of sweat broke out on Erika's forehead, and she twisted her hands in her lap. "I'm sorry, okay? I did a dumb thing. I should never have threatened you. I promise I won't talk to the cops."

"Like I said, too late. You might change your mind down the road."

"I won't—I promise!" A flash of panic ricocheted through her eyes.

"Sorry. I can't take that chance."

"So you're going to . . . to shoot me?" Hysteria raised the pitch of her voice. She was breathing faster now. Hyperventilating, like she had all those years ago on that rural roadside.

"If it comes to that. I hope it doesn't." And it wouldn't. Erika was too chicken to call her bluff. She motioned toward the packet of pills. "Pop out two of those and take them."

Erika looked at them, and her skin lost the last of its color. "W-what are they?"

"Benadryl."

"Benadryl?" Her face went blank. "I don't get it."

Of course she didn't. Erika never had been able to put two and two together until too late.

"You don't have to get it. Just take them."

She picked up the card of pills and fumbled with the plastic wrap. By the time she'd removed it, her fingers were shaking so badly it took her several attempts to pop two out.

"Wash them down with that." Jessica tapped the bottle of scotch with the barrel of the gun.

"Alcohol and p-pills don't mix."

"It's only two pills, Erika. Take them."

She chewed on her lip but followed the instruction. As she started to set the glass down again, Jessica motioned to it.

"Finish the scotch."

Holding the glass with both hands, Erika did as she was told.

"Very good. Now fill it up again. All the way."

Erika's eyes grew round. "I can't drink that much!"

"Do it."

Flicking a terrified glance at the gun, she complied, spilling some of the alcohol on the table as she poured.

"Now we're going to play a little game." Jessica leaned toward her. "Like college kids do. You're going to drink that whole glass. In five minutes."

A bead of sweat trickled down from her temple. "That's too much—even for me! I'll get sick!"

The woman really was a moron.

"I wouldn't worry about that if I were you. But if you'd rather . . ." She raised the gun.

"No!" She picked up the glass, sloshing out more of the liquid, her gaze darting around the room, as if she was seeking a way out.

There wasn't one.

Jessica looked at her watch. "The clock is ticking."

The room went silent as Erika coughed down the liquor.

As she drank, Jessica calculated. Factoring in spillage, Erika would probably ingest about seven ounces in this round. She'd already had two generous drinks, bringing the total to eleven or twelve ounces. That should do the trick for most people—but considering how much her one-time classmate drank, her tolerance could be higher than average. Better too much than not enough.

Erika finished the glass in four minutes flat.

"Excellent. Now have one more for the road."

Tears began to trickle down Erika's cheeks. "Why are you doing this? I thought we were friends."

She gave a derisive snort. "I was never your friend, Erika. You were a means to an end. I needed your father's connections. It was his influence that got me the internships I wanted and the job I needed to launch my career. Back in the day, he'd do anything for his daughter's best friend." She gestured to the bottle. "Pour."

Hand shaking, Erika picked up the bottle again. "I guess Joe was right about you."

Her fingers tightened around the gun. "Joe is a nobody. His opinion means nothing. Fill it up more than halfway and drink it fast."

Jessica waited until Erika downed the last of the liquor, then leaned back in her chair.

It was done.

Erika stared at her. "Now what?"

"We wait."

"For what?"

"For the problem to go away."

"What are you talking about?"

She picked up her glass of wine. Took a sip. It really was a very good vintage. Jack might be a jerk, but he had excellent taste in wine.

"It's simple, Erika. I've worked for years to get where I am. Whenever something—or someone—got in the way of my plans, I dealt with the problem. You've become a problem . . . like Charles did."

Erika blinked, as if she was having trouble focusing. "Charles, your hushban?"

"Yes." Why not admit it? Erika wouldn't be telling any tales.

"He had a heart attack."

"Yes, he did. Amazing what a few too many whiffs of amyl nitrite can do to a man with coronary artery disease." She swirled her glass but kept the gun aimed at Erika.

"You . . . you killed Charles?" Horror filled Erika's eyes as she whispered the words.

Jessica shrugged. "Let's just say I facilitated his demise. Some powdered Ambien in his salad dressing, plus a jigger of tasteless vodka in his iced tea, put him to sleep. After that, all I had to do was break a few capsules of his amyl nitrite and hold them under his nose. Can I help it if his blood pressure dropped and his cardiac rhythm went berserk?"

Erika blinked again. Her eyes were beginning to glaze. "I thought you . . . loved him?"

"Love?" She gave a disparaging sniff. "Love is a highly overrated

237

emotion. Peterson-Bradshaw is a family-oriented company that holds traditional relationships in high esteem. Having a husband was desirable for career purposes. So I did my research and found the perfect candidate—a wealthy, lonely, childless widower in desperate need of female companionship."

"Then why . . . why did you k-kill him?" Erika was struggling to form words now.

She took a sip of wine and inspected the clear, golden liquid. "Unfortunately, after three years he decided he wanted a divorce. That was unacceptable. It would have derailed my career. What choice did I have?"

Erika slumped in her chair but managed to cling to lucidity. "Joe always said you were coldhearted, but you're worse than that. You're . . . you're evil."

"Evil." She twirled the stem of her glass. "An interesting concept. One we might debate if your brain was fully operational. But I prefer to think of myself as practical."

"Don't . . . you have any . . . conshience?"

Jessica leaned toward her, anger nipping at her composure. "Yes, I have a conscience. I think it's wrong for anyone to take what someone else has worked hard to earn. Your husband stole money from retirees. My husband was going to steal my career—just as you were. That's wrong."

"At leasht I . . . never killed anybody." Her eyelids flickered. Drifted closed. A moment later, her head fell forward, chin resting on her chest.

Jessica glared at her. Who did Erika think she was, making judgments? What did a privileged little rich girl who'd always had everything handed to her know about life? Had she ever lain in bed at night, too afraid to sleep for fear the rats that came out in the dark would bite her? Had she ever been called filthy names by her father and made to feel like a worthless piece of trash? Had she ever been betrayed and abandoned? Had she ever had to claw her way out of the gutter and painstakingly create her own destiny, earning every single thing she'd acquired through her own sweat and wits?

No.

And who was she to point fingers and talk about conscience, when she'd resorted to blackmail herself?

Jessica took another sip of wine, letting the alcohol relax the tight muscles in her shoulders.

Erika was nothing.

And she'd soon be history.

As she finished her wine, she watched the other woman's breathing slow, just the way Charles had described early in their relationship when he'd lost a college-age patient to alcohol poisoning after the kid spent a night binge drinking. The alcohol would continue to enter Erika's bloodstream faster than it could be metabolized by her liver, depressing the central nervous system. She'd go into a coma. Soon, her heart would slow and her breathing would stop . . . unless she died first by drowning in her own vomit.

Jessica wrinkled her nose.

Not the most pleasant way to go.

On the other hand, Erika was out of it. She'd never know what caused her death.

Only the coroner would.

And it would be ruled accidental. A distraught wife, her husband sent to prison, her fortune ruined, a heavy drinker and smoker, who'd decided to drown her sorrows . . . and ended up dead.

Those two cops who'd visited her might wonder about the death, but there would be nothing to tie Jessica Lee to it.

Just as there was nothing to tie her to Alena.

Leaning down, she opened her tote bag and set the gun inside. Then she withdrew a pair of latex gloves and the novel she was reading. It was hard to say how long it would take for the alcohol to finish the job, and sitting around doing nothing was boring.

As she opened the book to the marked page, she took a mental inventory of the tasks to be accomplished before she left.

Put on the gloves.

Wipe the door handles on the car with the soft cloth she'd brought.

Wash the wine glass and wipe the stem.

Collect the plastic wrap for later disposal.

Return the bottles of cleaning solution to the laundry room.

Tuck the gift bag back in her tote to ditch in a trash container on the way home. No need to worry about her fingerprints being on the scotch; the clerk had put it in the bag for her.

Finally, let herself out the back door, skirt around front in the shadows, and walk back to her car, half a mile away in the parking lot where it had "broken down."

Piece of cake.

She picked up her book, sparing Erika no more than a quick glance before she got back to her story.

One down.

One to go.

Mac pulled in behind the Carson police cruiser parked in front of Erika's house. As he braked, Lisa slid out from the driver's seat and slipped on her uniform jacket.

Adjusting his tie, he joined her at the end of the flagstone walk that led to the columned entry of the two-story house.

"Going the official-looking route for round two, I see." He nodded toward her uniform and the car.

"Yeah." She flipped her hair out from under the collar of the jacket. "Police accoutrements have a certain intimidation effect."

"You might want to use the same strategy if we revisit Jessica. I doubt our polished PR executive would appreciate having a uniformed law enforcement officer come calling at her swanky office—especially one who's next in line for the CEO spot."

"That thought did cross my mind. I don't see her being intimidated, but the embarrassment factor would be huge. If today's visit doesn't pan out, I may give it a try. Joe's an untapped resource too. I'd have paid him a visit already if he was local." She motioned toward the curving walk. "Shall we?"

"After you."

He followed as she walked toward the door, passing first

one newspaper, then another, both encased in plastic wrappers. When a third came into view, he stopped.

"Lisa."

She paused and turned. "You noticed the papers too?"

"Yeah."

"I'm thinking she might have skipped town after I called and left the message about wanting to talk with her again. That will complicate things—or slow them down, at the very least."

"Maybe she just hasn't bothered to pick them up. She's had a lot on her mind lately."

"Possible. Let's find out."

He drew up beside her as she ascended the porch steps and pressed the bell.

After fifteen seconds, she tried again.

Still no response.

"I guess tipping her off to my visit wasn't the best idea." Lisa huffed out a breath. "For all we know, she took off for Tahiti."

"Maybe Jessica can shed some light on her whereabouts."

Lisa cocked her head. "Are you thinking we should drop in and pay her an unannounced visit today?"

He shrugged. "Your call—but you're in uniform, I cleared my schedule, and there isn't any reason to wait."

"Good point. We could talk about the DNA sample, bring up the ring again, have her run through the events of that night once more. Let's do it."

As they started back down the walk, a slightly stooped man with thinning gray hair came out of the front door of the house across the street and headed their direction.

Lisa leaned closer. Close enough for him to catch a faint whiff of the fresh, sweet fragrance he'd come to associate with her. "Wanna bet that's the neighborhood busybody?"

"I don't bet when the odds are against me. He looks the type."

"They can be a font of information."

"True."

They waited at the end of the walk for the man to approach.

"Hi, folks. Tom Cooper." He stuck out his hand and gave them each a hearty shake as they introduced themselves. "I couldn't help but notice the police car. Everything okay here? I'd hate for Erika to have any more trouble, what with her husband's problems and all. Such a nice woman."

"We were hoping to catch her, but it appears she might be out of town." Lisa sidestepped his question and gestured to the newspapers on the lawn.

"Far as I know she's here. They've been staying real close to home with the trial in progress." He studied the papers. "Strange thing about those newspapers, though. Since I moved in with my daughter and son-in-law two years ago, she always comes out first thing every morning—'bout the same time I get our paper. Told me once she likes to read the comic section and the society page while she eats breakfast."

"When did you last see her?" Mac asked.

"Tuesday evening. These eighty-four-year-old eyes don't have great night vision, but I did notice her car pull out. She wasn't gone long." He scratched his head. "You know, she gave us her cell number a while back when she and her husband were going on a trip, in case there was any kind of emergency. Would you like me to get it for you?"

Mac deferred to Lisa. She could get it herself if she wanted to, but this would save a step or two.

"If you don't mind, that would be very helpful."

"Glad to do it. I'll be back in a jiffy."

As Erika's neighbor retraced his steps, Mac surveyed the house. "While we're waiting, I'm going to see if there are any windows in the garage."

"Wondering if her car is in there?"

"Yeah. The paper thing bothers me. Based on what Mr. Cooper said, it's out-of-pattern behavior."

"I agree. I'll wait for him here while you take a look."

Mac returned to his car, retrieved a flashlight, and followed the driveway to the back of the house.

No windows in the garage itself—but there was a row of small, paned rectangular windows along the top of each of the four doors.

Standing on tiptoe, he could just see into the bottom of the lower panes.

Too dark to make out the interior.

He flipped on the light and flashed it inside.

Each of the four bays held a car.

Dropping back onto his heels, he clicked off the light and frowned. There could be several logical reasons why Erika hadn't answered their ring. A friend had picked her up and she was out for the day. She was taking a shower. She'd spotted them and decided to ignore their presence. She was sleeping off some booze.

Or something was wrong.

His gut said it was the latter.

"What did you find?" Lisa rounded the garage.

"Her car's here. So are three other vehicles."

"I don't have good vibes about this."

"Me, neither. Want to trespass a little more?" He tipped his head toward the back of the house.

"I'm game."

He led the way to the shrub-shrouded backyard, which featured a large pool, slate terrace, groupings of patio furniture, and lush landscaping. Sort of like the house he and Mitch had been to for that robbery earlier in the month.

"No expense spared here." Lisa surveyed the posh layout.

"Ponzi schemes pay—until you get caught."

"Apparently so." She wandered over to the French doors that

led into the house. The shades were drawn tight on every one. "Not much chance we're going to find anything helpful back here." She pulled out her cell and extracted a slip of paper from her pocket. "Let me try the number her neighbor provided. Then we'll pay Jessica a visit."

While she wandered a few feet away and tapped in the digits, Mac took her place at the shuttered doors. It was a shame there wasn't a small opening somewhere that . . .

He froze. Cocked his ear toward the house. Was that . . . music?

No. It was gone now. He must have . . .

Wait.

There it was again. The exact same melody.

It was a ringtone.

He looked toward Lisa, who still had her cell to her ear. The music in the house played a third time. Stopped.

She sighed and closed her phone. "No answer."

"Try it again . . . over here."

She sent him a quizzical look but walked toward him. "Why?"

"I think her phone's ringing on the other side of this door."

In silence, she pressed redial, angled the phone so they could both hear it, and put her ear to the glass.

The music started again as the ring sounded on her phone.

After three times through, the ringtone stopped and voice mail kicked in on her cell.

She tapped the end button. "This is weird. I can see why her car would be in the garage if she went out with a friend, but why leave her cell behind?"

"Maybe she forgot it. Or she's taking a shower or sleeping off a bender."

"Given her condition on our initial visit, your last theory is very possible." She slid the phone back on her belt. "It's also possible there's a problem inside."

Mac folded his arms. "I wonder if she has any local relatives who might have a key?"

"I don't know about that—but her friendly neighbor does . . . for emergencies. He offered that piece of information when he gave me the phone number. He said she'd given him carte blanche to go in the house anytime if there was a problem."

"Do you think we could convince him there might be?"

"I do—but let me try the doorbell once more."

They circled the house again. Tom Cooper was sitting on his terrace, watching the proceedings as Lisa returned to the front door and rang the bell again.

Still no response.

As she descended the porch steps, Mac crossed the street.

Tom rose as he approached, face alight with interest. "What can I do for you now, young man?"

"To be honest, we're concerned. While we were checking out the back of the house, Chief Grant called the cell number you gave her. We could hear it ringing through the French doors. And Ms. Butler's car is in the garage."

"Hmm. Could be she just doesn't want to talk to the police, what with all the problems she's had."

The guy might be eighty-four, but he was sharp.

"Could be—but we're thinking there might be a problem inside."

"You want me to try ringing her from this house? She knows our number, and she wouldn't have any reason to ignore a call from us."

Yep. Sharp as a tack.

"That's not a bad idea. But give us a chance to drive around the block first. If she is inside and happens to be watching, she might assume we put you up to making the call. If you wait until we drive away, she'd be more inclined to think you were calling to tell her what you've learned."

The man squinted at him. "You have a good head on your shoulders, young man. You aren't going to make any trouble for Erika, are you?"

"At this point, we just want to verify she's okay."

"All right. I'll wait until you get to the end of the street before I call."

"Thanks."

Mac rejoined Lisa, told her the plan, and sixty seconds later they were both pulling away from the curb.

When they returned less than five minutes later, Tom Cooper was waiting for them on the sidewalk, two parallel wrinkles engraved on his forehead. Lisa was on her phone as she slid out from behind the wheel, so he walked over to the older man.

"No answer for me, either. I'm starting to worry about that little lady too."

"Chief Grant tells me you have a key for emergency access. Do you think it might be prudent to take a quick look inside, make certain everything's okay? We'll wait on the porch."

"Well, now . . . I hate to invade anyone's privacy. Could be she's sleeping."

"We'll pound on the door first." That would wake her—unless she was passed out from booze.

No need to mention that, however.

"Then I expect it'd be all right. Let me get the key."

"We'll meet you on her porch."

As the man disappeared inside and Lisa ended her call, Mac gave her a thumbs-up. "I promised him we'd pound on the door before he opens it, in case she's sleeping, and that we'd wait outside while he does a quick walk-through."

"Works for me."

Tom reappeared, his gait spry as he closed the distance between them.

Once he was on the porch, Mac pounded on the door with his fist.

The man flinched. "My word. That's loud enough to wake the dead. You keep that up, you won't need the key at all; the door will fall in."

Mac grinned. "Let's give it thirty seconds."

Half a minute later, he stepped back. "Your turn."

Tom moved into position and inserted the key. "You want me to walk around and call her name?"

"Yes. We'll wait here."

Pocketing the key, he twisted the knob and entered, leaving the door open behind him.

From their position, he and Lisa could follow some of Tom's progress. He went right first, into the living room where Erika had talked with them on their first visit. He continued to the back of the house, his voice echoing in the distance as he called her name. Then he reappeared in the foyer and crossed to the room on the left.

Fifteen seconds later, he spoke again.

"Erika?"

At his questioning tone, Mac looked at Lisa.

"Erika? Oh my . . ." His voice faded out.

Moments later, he stumbled back into the foyer, his complexion pasty.

Mac stepped over the threshold and strode over to him, Lisa on his heels.

"She's . . ." His hand fluttered toward the room behind him. "She's in there. I don't think . . . I think she's . . . dead."

Mac took his arm and guided him to the closest chair. "Sit here and take a few deep breaths. We'll check it out."

Pulling out his Sig Sauer, he followed Lisa into the room. She was headed for a chair faced toward the fireplace, where a woman's limp, hanging arm was visible. Her weapon, too, was at the ready, her gaze roaming the room.

248

But it was empty except for Erika.

And she was dead.

It took no more than one quick glance for Mac to confirm that.

And she'd been dead a while, based on the lividity in her hanging hand.

He holstered his weapon and pulled out his phone.

While he tapped in his boss's number, Lisa did a three-sixty turn, Glock still in hand. But by the time he'd reported the death, asked if Mitch was available, and requested the medical examiner's assistance, she, too, had holstered her weapon.

She nodded to the bottle of scotch, the empty tumbler, the packet of pink pills. "I think I know how this is going to play out."

"Yeah. And there are plenty of obvious reasons why she might overindulge, given all her problems—even without adding in Alena."

"How convenient . . . for Jessica."

"I don't like the coincidence, either, but proving it's anything more could be difficult."

"I know." She tucked her hair behind her ear. Exhaled. "We better deal with Mr. Cooper."

The older man was sitting where they'd left him, eyes wide with shock. "I can't believe this. I know she drank too much, but . . . this is terrible."

Even he was jumping to the obvious conclusion.

"Let's wait outside, Mr. Cooper." Mac moved beside the man. "Some of my colleagues will be here shortly."

He assisted him up, holding his arm as they crossed the foyer, exited, and walked down the stone path to the street.

"Will you be okay going the rest of the way home by yourself?"

"Yes. Thank you, young man." He shook his head. "Funny. I was just thinking this morning how quiet my life is these days and wishing there'd be a little more excitement. Guess I better be more careful what I wish for in the future."

As he trudged back across the street under the blazing sun, Lisa slipped off her jacket, brow puckered. "I know how this looks—but Jessica had motive. Given her high-profile job and the nature of their clientele, she has a lot to lose if she's connected with a scandal, even if no crime was involved. If she and Erika and Joe had any part in Alena's death, she might be worried Erika would crack. And based on what you told me about your encounter with her secretary, she has a callous side."

"I agree with your reasoning. However, I also think she's very smart. We'll go over this place with a fine-tooth comb, and I'm going to see if my colleague can talk the ME into getting us the BAC from Erika's tox panel as soon as possible, but if Jessica had anything to do with this, my guess is she covered her tracks."

"I have a feeling you're right." She blew out a breath. "There's not a whole lot here for me to do except wait for your results. This is local and County jurisdiction."

"I'll let you know as soon as we have anything. You still plan to pay a visit to Jessica?"

"Not today. I'd rather wait until you and your colleague check the place out and we hear from the ME. In the meantime, I'll tackle the pile of reports waiting for me at my office." She eyed the stately home. "You never know what's behind the walls of a house, do you? Who'd have guessed this mansion harbored alcohol abuse, death, crime, deception . . ."

"And maybe answers."

She swiveled back to him, flashing a quick smile. "Let's hope so." With a flip-of-the-hand farewell, she returned to her cruiser and drove away.

Mac checked on Tom Cooper. He was back on the terrace. Waiting for the next act, no doubt.

His phone began to vibrate, and he pulled it off his belt. Mitch.

"You on the way?"

"Yeah. What's the deal?"

He gave him a fast briefing.

"What's your take?"

He perused the house again. "I didn't see anything at first glance to suggest foul play. But we're now down a player in the Carson old bones case."

"Suspicious."

"Tell me about it."

"Look for me in fifteen. If there's anything there to be found, we'll find it."

As the line went dead, Mac slid behind the wheel of his car and cranked up the air. It was too hot to stand around in the sun waiting for his colleague to show.

Once Mitch got here, though, they'd do a thorough search in Erika's house.

But while his instincts told him her death was more than accidental, he had a bad feeling they'd find nothing to support that theory.

And if Jessica was involved, if she'd managed to pull this off without leaving a trace, the ambitious PR executive wasn't just smart.

She was a dangerous, cold-blooded murderer who would stop at nothing to eliminate anyone she regarded as a threat.

19

Jessica double-checked the directions Joe had given her. She'd exited I-64 after one of the most boring three-hour drives of her life. Headed west on 358. Clocked five miles since leaving the highway. Seen the sign for West Kentucky State Wildlife Management Area.

She was getting close.

Rolling her shoulders, she surveyed the mixture of fields and woods. The man was in the middle of nowhere—which about summed up his life.

Still, he could have rotted in his rural hideaway for all she cared if Erika hadn't told her his resolution to keep quiet about what had happened was wavering. And it might waver even more after he found out about his one-time girlfriend's demise.

She couldn't risk that.

Her gaze flicked to the rearview mirror. Meeting him on his own turf hadn't been her first choice . . . until he'd told her he didn't live in town but on ten secluded acres abutting the wildlife area. As long as no one saw her turn in to his drive, she'd be safe. If she spotted a car as she approached, she'd drive past and circle back. As for leaving afterward, she'd wait until the light faded . . . even though that would mean a long, dark drive back to St. Louis.

Not how she'd have chosen to spend her Saturday evening . . . but necessary.

A mailbox came into view, and she slowed to read the numbers.

This was it.

A long gravel drive led to a small brick bungalow tucked among the trees, barely visible from the road. A trip through a carwash would be a must after traversing such a gritty road. She grimaced. One final chore on her to-do list for the day.

With one more scan of the empty road, she swung in and started down the drive, a cloud of dust billowing behind her. When she reached his house, she circled around to the back, as Joe had instructed. The modest dwelling opened to a large field in the rear and on one side, and she parked between a storage shed and a detached garage. From here, her car would be completely hidden from the road, as he'd promised.

Picking up the two small containers from the seat beside her, she verified the contents were still in good shape, then nestled them in the top of her shoulder bag. She also gave her upswept do one more quick spray. Extra precautions never hurt. Her meticulous attention to detail was why she could pull off feats the average person would fumble. Dealing with Erika and Joe in such a short time frame wasn't ideal, but she'd planned every facet of both jobs with scrupulous thoroughness. Even if the timing raised eyebrows, there was no way anyone could pin either of the "accidents" on her.

Just like the authorities had never been able to link Alena's disappearance to any of them.

This would be no different.

Tote bag over her shoulder, she slid out of the car. As she retrieved a plastic grocery bag and the Styrofoam cooler the gourmet shop had packed for her, the back door of the house opened.

A rail-thin, round-shouldered man wearing glasses stepped out, and she froze, lungs locked.

Had she misread the number and turned in at the wrong house?

The man shoved his hands in the pockets of his jeans and sent her a mirthless grin. "Hello, Jessica. I guess the years have been kinder to some of us than others."

She stared at him. The voice hadn't changed—but Joe Andrews, his thinning hair more salt than pepper, looked a decade or more older than his forty-six years.

Closing the car door with her hip, she summoned up a smile. "Good genes, I guess. I brought dinner, like I promised." She lifted the disposable Styrofoam cooler.

For a long moment he stood unmoving, as if he was having second thoughts about her visit.

Not the most gracious welcome she'd ever received.

Finally he angled toward the door. "Come in."

He let her precede him into the small kitchen, where a mammoth dog waited.

Her heart skipped a beat, and she took a hasty step back, holding the small cooler in front of her.

"Lucky won't bother you. He's more bark than bite."

She eyed the enormous dog. "What breed is he? Pony?"

"A mastiff." He crossed to the dog and patted its head. "Living alone in the country, a dog's a necessity for both safety and companionship. But you don't like dogs, do you? I forgot."

"I had a bad experience with one as a child." More than bad. The fabric of her slacks might cover the scars, but the memory of the night her drunk father had kicked a mutt out of the way on the stoop of their apartment building—and the dog taking its anger out on her—had never faded.

"I'll put him outside. That's where he'd rather be, anyway."

Joe returned to the door, opened it, and snapped his fingers.

Instead of trotting out, the dog kept watching her, its tongue hanging out.

"That's weird. He usually bolts the minute I open the door. Come on, Lucky."

The dog spared his owner no more than a quick glance before padding toward her instead. She backed up until she hit the counter, angling away, protecting the cooler. But the mammoth canine stretched its neck to sniff the tote, not the food.

"Lucky." Joe walked over and took him by the collar. "Come." He had to almost drag the dog outside.

As the screen door slapped shut behind the two of them, Jessica forced herself to take a deep breath. Strange how she could be so calm in life-and-death situations, but put her within twenty feet of a dog and her heart stuttered.

Chalk it up to the power of childhood memories.

"Sorry about that." Joe reentered the kitchen and closed the door. "You want a drink?"

"Thanks." A quiver lurked in her voice, and she quashed it before continuing. "A diet cola will be fine. We're having poached salmon." She tapped a finger against the cooler.

"Fancier than my usual fare. You mind if I have a beer?"

"Not at all."

He withdrew a Bud and a Diet Coke. "You want a glass?"

"No, thanks."

He popped both tops. "You don't strike me as a drink-from-the-can kind of woman."

She was tonight.

"You know what they say about judging a book by its cover."

"Yeah? I think I always read you pretty well." He took a sip of his beer. "But I have to admit, I can't figure out why you drove all the way down here to talk to me when a phone call would

255

have sufficed. Besides, I thought you didn't want us to have any contact right now."

She shrugged. "Erika and I have met. It seemed only fair to keep you in the loop, and I feel more secure doing it in person rather than by phone. Not that anyone will ever find out about my trip down here, but even if they did, they couldn't make a lot out of a visit between old friends."

"Hardly friends, Jessica."

"Whatever." Why dispute the truth? "Where would you like to eat?"

"Here." He rested a hand on the kitchen table. "Or we could go out on the screen porch. It's not too hot tonight, and it's private."

"I like the porch idea." That would dovetail nicely with her plan.

"You want to leave your purse in here?"

She smiled. "A lady never parts with her purse."

"Suit yourself." He crossed the kitchen and led her through a living room furnished in modified-bachelor style. It was neat and clean, but nothing matched. Brown leather recliner, old crate for a coffee table, a couch draped with a checkered throw, shades but no curtains, green carpet.

She tried not to wrinkle her nose.

Joe had never had much taste.

On the far end of the room he opened a door, holding it as she stepped through.

The screen porch was elevated and looked out over the field. Neither the road nor any other sign of civilization was visible.

Perfect.

She set the cooler on a small side table and pulled out an extra-spicy salsa dip.

"So what's going on with Alena's case?" Joe sat at a glass-topped café table for two.

"Why don't we talk about it while we have an appetizer?" She handed him the plastic grocery bag. "Tortilla chips—your favorite brand, as I recall. Would you open them?"

"Sure." He took another swig of beer. "Erika's been keeping me up to speed from her end, by the way."

So the two of them had been talking, as she'd suspected.

A spurt of annoyance shot through her—but she modulated her tone as she set the dip on the table. "Have you two always kept in touch?"

"On and off. She said she was going to call me this week, but I never heard from her. Any idea why?"

"Who knows? Erika's never been the most reliable person. I saw her Tuesday, but I haven't talked with her since."

"Of course not. The high-and-mighty Jessica Lee doesn't waste time on people she considers beneath her—unless she needs them."

She arched an eyebrow. "You've certainly gotten cynical with age."

"No. I've just learned to see things as they are, both the good and the bad." He maintained eye contact as he bit into a loaded chip.

The man had become a complete boor.

"Look . . . why don't we focus on the reason for my visit?" He was halfway through his beer—no reason to delay things.

"Fine." He scooped up another generous portion of dip.

While she recounted the sequence of events, beginning with the find on the construction site, she picked up her can of soda. No reason the same distraction technique wouldn't work again.

The instant he reached for his beer, she sloshed the can, spilling it on her slacks and the floor.

She jumped up, and he stood too.

"Wouldn't you know it? These are brand-new." She scrubbed

at the fabric with a paper napkin. "Do you by chance have any liquid laundry detergent? Or even dish detergent and a cloth dipped in hot water?"

"Sure. I'll be right back."

Once he disappeared inside, she went into action. Given the small size of Joe's house, she'd have less time than she'd had at Erika's—and more to do.

Moving quickly, she withdrew one of the small, clear containers from her tote. All three yellow jackets were moving about, anxious to escape the prison she'd consigned them to earlier in the day after attracting them in a roadside park en route with apple juice and a strip of bacon.

She shook the container until they were all at the bottom, then positioned it over the opened tab on Joe's beer. After removing the lid, she inverted it and tapped them into the opening.

One . . . two . . . three.

Done.

Grasping the can with a paper napkin, she swirled the beer in case any of the bees were clinging to the side. As she dropped the empty container back in her tote, Joe opened the door to the screen porch.

Very close, as she'd expected.

"No liquid laundry detergent, but here's a wet cloth and some dish soap."

"Thanks. Set them on the table for a minute, please." She pretended to inspect the stain. "Go ahead and enjoy your beer. It's going to get hot if you let it sit there."

After all those tortilla chips and spicy dip, he didn't need a second invitation.

She watched out of the corner of her eye as he lifted the can and took a long gulp.

Nothing happened.

Hmm.

Were the bees still floating in the liquid? Surely one of them would have—

All at once, Joe gasped. His eyes bulged and his body went rigid. Excellent. They were back on script.

She tipped her head, feigning innocence. "Joe? Is something wrong?"

He dropped the can and grasped his throat. "I don't . . . know. Can't . . . breathe." He looked down at the can as it rolled across the floor. One of the yellow jackets crawled out.

All the color drained from his face, and he vaulted to his feet. Swayed.

Jessica stood. "What can I do?"

"EpiPen . . . injector . . . kitchen drawer . . . by sink. Hurry."

"Sit down. I'll get it." She pressed him back into his chair and pushed through the door into the house.

Once inside, she stepped out of his line of sight, put on the latex gloves she'd tucked in her pocket before leaving home . . . and waited.

When he started to rise, she opened the door. Already his lips were puffy, and red splotches were appearing on his cheeks. Amazing how quickly anaphylactic shock could kick in when you had a severe allergy to bee venom. He was reacting even faster than he had the time they'd all gone to a backyard barbecue at Erika's parents' house in their college days.

Of course, stings to the mouth—or throat—accelerated the process. An injection of epinephrine wouldn't help a whole lot in a case like this . . . not that he'd be getting one, anyway.

"I'm not finding it, Joe."

His mouth opened, like a freshly caught fish gasping for air.

He jolted forward, knocking over his chair in the process. She shifted aside as he staggered past her, then weaving like a drunk, trailed behind him while he lurched through the living room and headed for the kitchen.

The EpiPen was in the drawer by the sink, just as he'd said.

He grabbed for it, but his fingers fumbled. They, too, must be swelling already—like his throat.

"Why don't you let me help you?" She moved toward him and pulled the pen from his clumsy fingers.

Then she backed away, smacked it hard against the ninety-degree edge of the counter, and handed it back to him.

Through the panic in his eyes, she saw shock morph to understanding as the lifesaving liquid leaked onto his fingers.

With a strangled sound, he dropped the pen to the floor and stumbled toward the hall.

Of course he had another pen stashed somewhere. Joe was a numbers guy, meticulous about details. That's why she'd trusted him with Alena's ring—though if it turned out that steely-eyed police chief wasn't bluffing, he'd blown that assignment.

She followed him down the hall. Adrenaline and desperation could keep people on their feet past normal limits . . . but they couldn't send air to your lungs.

And his airway was swelling closed.

Fast.

All at once he staggered. Fell to one knee. Listed against the wall.

When he blinked up at her, there was a faint blue tinge to his lips and he was sweating.

"Still have that bad bee allergy, I see." She folded her arms and propped her shoulder against the wall. "I hear that can be deadly."

He tried to speak, but no sound came out. His eyes were puffing up now too, and in slow motion he tilted sideways, onto the floor, his labored gasps the only sound in the silent house.

For five minutes, she remained in place. He was still breathing, but he wouldn't be for long. And there wasn't much chance he was going to budge from where he lay.

Leaving him in the hall, she returned to the screen porch. Their dinner remained in the cooler, since things had progressed faster than expected. But she picked up the dip. Before putting the lid back on, she helped herself to a couple of chips. It was going to be a long, hungry drive back. At least she could enjoy the gourmet dinner in the cooler once she arrived. Maybe she'd open that bottle of champagne she'd been saving for a special occasion. Celebrate the resolution of all her problems.

By the time she'd packed up her things and finished off her soda, ten minutes had elapsed.

Better check on Joe.

She wrapped her soda can in the plastic grocery bag and fitted it into her purse, next to the second container of bees. The backup team. If they were alive once she got back to St. Louis, she might even let them go.

Innocent creatures didn't deserve to die.

At the door to the house, she stopped and gave the screen porch a final scrutiny. Overturned chair. Bag of chips on the table. Beer can on the floor.

It looked exactly the way she'd planned: Joe had come out to enjoy the pleasant weather, a bee had somehow infiltrated the screen porch and been attracted by the beer—and he'd made a fast exit in search of the EpiPen.

Very plausible.

She moved on to the kitchen. The drawer was open, the pen on the floor. In his panic, he'd dropped it. The medication had leaked. He'd gone for his spare pen.

Shifting the cooler in her hands, she crossed into the hall.

Joe was right where she'd left him.

She eased closer and leaned down. The wheezing had stopped, and his chest wasn't rising and falling. If there was any respiration, it was very shallow.

And it wouldn't last much longer.

No reason to wait around.

Except it wasn't dark yet, and the risk someone would witness her departure was too high.

Who'd have thought the whole thing would be over so fast?

She sighed. Hanging around the house wasn't smart. The less time she spent inside, the less chance of leaving any evidence of her visit, even with latex gloves on and her hair cemented in place.

Best to wait for nightfall outside in the car.

After retracing her steps to the kitchen, she opened the back door—and found the monster dog waiting for her on the other side of the screen door.

He peered at her, emitting a low, ominous growl.

Her heart stumbled.

Calm down, Jessica. It's only a dog. Joe said he wasn't aggressive. Just let him in, walk out, and pull the door closed behind you. You can do this.

The little pep talk didn't calm her much—but what choice did she have?

Taking a deep breath, she pushed the door open, prepared to skirt around the dog as he trotted inside.

But the gargantuan canine stopped halfway in. Still growling, he bared his teeth.

Big teeth.

Her heart lurched, and she made a quick move to escape.

Not quick enough, however.

He nipped at her fingers, and she lost her grip on the cooler.

It fell, half in, half out of the doorway, tipping sideways. The lid flew off, and she watched in horror as the container of salsa dip rolled across the floor.

The dog bounded after it, batting at it with his paw as he skidded over the tile. Like it was some kind of game.

For a fleeting instant she considered leaving it. But that would be stupid. Her fingerprints were all over the container. She had to retrieve it.

Lucky continued to pounce and paw at the plastic tub. Then he grabbed it with his teeth and shook it.

Any second the contents were going to spew all over the floor. She had to get it back.

Now.

Leaving her tote and the cooler on the back stoop, she rubbed her palms down her thighs. Maybe there was some dog food in the closet and she could distract him.

One eye locked on the canine, she sidled in and opened the pantry door.

Yes!

A giant bag of dog food rested on the floor.

She opened the top, pulled out a handful of the dried food, and tossed it on the floor on the opposite side of the room.

That got the dog's attention.

Abandoning his new toy, he bounded over and began scarfing it up.

Jessica crossed the kitchen in three long strides, snatched up the dip, and ran out the back door, pulling it closed behind her.

Heart pounding, she shoved the dog-slobbered dip container into the plastic bag with her soda can, grabbed her stuff, and hightailed it to the car.

Only after everything was stowed, the latex gloves stripped off, and she was behind the wheel did her respiration slow. But her fingers continued to tremble.

All because of a stupid dog.

No matter. She was done here, and as soon as the light faded, she'd be on her way home—finally free of the past, with no impediments to the shining future that lay ahead of her.

She rolled down her window, nerves beginning to calm . . . until the scent of fresh-cut hay wafted toward her.

The same scent scorched into her memory from that long-ago night.

Doing her best to ignore the smell, she drummed her finger against the wheel. How annoying, after all these years, to have to deal with reminders of that incident. The whole thing should be dead and buried—just as Alena had been.

And if that lady cop hadn't been so determined to get to the bottom of the mystery, it still would be.

The wind picked up, and a faint rumble of thunder sounded in the distance. A moment later, a few splatters of rain plopped on the windshield.

She inspected the sky. The storm clouds she'd seen earlier massing on the horizon were moving closer.

But that was okay. Rain would wash away tire tracks on the gravel, if someone should happen to look for any.

Not likely, though. Once again, there would be no sign of her presence at the scene of this tragic, accidental death.

The rain intensified, and as she started to roll up her window, she detected the faint sound of barking from within Joe's house.

Lucky.

She snorted. That dog was the only lucky thing in Joe's life.

Sinking back in her seat, Jessica left the window cracked. The way the heavy clouds were rolling in, it would soon be dark enough for her to leave.

And once she was back home in her condo, she was definitely going to break open that bottle of champagne.

The irritating Alena interlude was over at last.

20

Joe Andrews was dead.

As Lisa gaped at the news headline her Google search had pulled up, a boom of thunder rattled the window in her office. Tally whimpered and crept closer, cowering at her feet while the rain lashed against the glass.

She gave him a distracted pat. "It's okay, boy. You're safe."

Too bad the same couldn't be said about Joe.

She clicked on the headline and read the short article. The coroner still had to weigh in, but evidence at the scene suggested he'd died of anaphylactic shock.

Another accident.

Another one of the trio from the night of Alena's disappearance dead.

Another voice silenced.

She leaned back in her chair.

What a dramatic start for a Monday—and all she'd been trying to do was supplement her meager background file on the man in advance of a trip down to visit him.

So much for that plan.

Wait until Mac heard about this.

She grabbed her phone and punched in his cell number.

Three rings in, he picked up. "McGregor."

She frowned at his groggy, slurred greeting. "Mac? It's Lisa. Are you all right?"

A soft grunt came over the line. "I've been better. Give me a minute."

In the background, a squeak sounded.

Silence.

A few seconds later, she picked up the muffled sound of running water.

More silence.

Then he was back. "Sorry. I worked a double homicide over the weekend. I think I've logged a total of six hours of shut-eye since Friday night. The sun was coming up this morning when I finally crashed."

She cringed. "And I interrupted your sleep. Sorry about that."

"It's okay. I have stuff to do, anyway. Consider yourself my wake-up call. What's up?"

"Get ready for this—Joe Andrews is dead."

Silence.

"Say that again."

"You heard me right. Joe Andrews is dead."

"What happened?" He sounded wide awake now.

She filled him in on the little she knew. "According to the article, he was discovered by the pastor of his church, who stopped by the house when Joe didn't show up at services for his assigned Sunday as a greeter."

"Have you talked to the local police?"

"Not yet. They're next on my list."

He expelled a breath. "If this wasn't an accident—and given the timing, I'm having a hard time believing it was—I suspect we'll be looking at a scenario similar to Erika's."

"Unfortunately, I agree." Even though Mac and his ex-SEAL buddy had gone over that scene inch by inch, they'd come up with zilch. No trace evidence other than fingerprints, which all belonged to Erika, her husband, or their cleaning woman, who'd provided elimination prints. "Jessica Lee is starting to get very scary."

"No kidding."

"Once I finish talking to the police in Kentucky, I think I'll pay her a visit—armed with several much more pointed questions than I had last round."

"Want me to meet you there?"

Her spirits took an uptick. "Are you certain you're up for that?"

"I will be once I swing through a Starbucks drive-through and guzzle down a triple espresso."

"If you're sure, that would be great."

"I'll also give the ME a call and see if he's got a BAC on Erika yet . . . or any other useful information."

"Why don't we meet in the lobby of Jessica's building at eleven?"

"You in uniform?"

"Uh-huh."

"That should liven things up. See you there."

Florence appeared in the doorway as another crash of thunder shook the windows and Tally let out a pitiful whine.

"You want to let Tally hang out by your desk till the storm passes?" Lisa patted the pooch. "He's freaking."

The older woman dropped some files in her in-box. "He's such a wimp."

"You might be too if you'd been mistreated." Lisa ran her hand over his side, feeling for the raised scars she'd discovered under his fur not long after she'd found him curled into a quivering ball under her car one stormy evening.

"True enough." The older woman's voice softened. "Come on, Tally. You and me will sit out the storm away from the windows. I might even find a dog biscuit or two for you."

Lisa stifled her grin. From the quick glimpse she'd gotten a week ago while Florence was rummaging around for a couple of binder clips in her desk, a whole new box of those high-end treats Mac had brought was stashed in her bottom drawer.

"Go on, Tally. Florence will take good care of you." She gave the dog a gentle nudge.

As another boom of thunder shook the building, he took off for the door, careened around the corner, and disappeared in the direction of their office manager's desk.

Florence winced as the rumble continued to reverberate. "I can't say I'm partial to all that noise, either."

"Sad to say, I'm about to plunge into it—as soon as I talk to the Ballard County, Kentucky, Sheriff's Office. Could you get them on the phone while I grab a bottle of water from the break room?"

"Sure thing. And be careful out there. The roads will be slippery."

"I will."

But as she hustled down the hall for her water, it wasn't the storm that concerned her. Weather, she could deal with.

Clever criminals—that was more dicey.

If Jessica Lee had masterminded the cover-up of Alena Komisky's death twenty-four years ago, she'd done a superb job. Had the forensic anthropologist not unearthed that small, stray garnet, the bones might never have been identified.

She grabbed a bottle of water from the fridge and twisted off the top while she retraced her steps to her office. Back then, Jessica had been young and no doubt operating on the fly. Yet she'd pulled off the deception masterfully.

Now, with years of maturity on her side, plus time to develop a detailed plan, she would be a formidable adversary. Pinning Erika's and Joe's demises on her was going to pose a serious challenge.

But no one was going to get away with murder on Lisa Grant's watch.

The light was blinking on her phone as she circled her desk, meaning Florence had the sheriff's office on hold. Taking a long swig of water, she sat and picked up the receiver. Hopefully, the local cops had done a thorough search of Joe's house.

Nevertheless, she intended to convince them to take a second look after she passed on one piece of critical information.

A possible motive for murder.

From his spot in the lobby of the Peterson-Bradshaw office building, Mac watched Lisa push through the revolving door, pummeled by a gust of wind and rain.

Eleven o'clock on the dot. The lady was a pro through and through. Conscientious, thorough, dedicated—and punctual, as always.

He rose as she approached, a stream of water trailing behind her.

"Have you been waiting long?" She held her umbrella at arm's length while it continued to drip.

"Long enough to get a chaser for my Starbucks espresso." He held up his twelve-ounce cup of brew. "Want to sit for a minute before we go up? I have some news."

"I was going to suggest the same thing. I have news too."

He motioned toward the table he'd claimed and followed her over. "Would you like a drink? They have herbal tea—iced and hot. That's safe for you, isn't it?"

She flashed him a smile and slid into a chair. "It is, but I'm fine. Thanks for offering, though. What do you have?"

"I heard from the ME. Erika's BAC was .41."

Her eyes widened. "Wow. Five times the legal limit."

"Right. So alcohol poisoning is the obvious cause of death, which the ME estimates occurred on Tuesday night. And since

269

Mitch and I didn't find anything to suggest foul play, it's going to be ruled accidental."

"Bad news."

"On the flip side, the DNA from Alena's mother matched the DNA analysis you got from Texas for the bones."

"That's what I expected, but I'm glad we have official confirmation. I can use that piece of info when we talk to Jessica."

"What's your news?"

"I talked to the sheriff in Kentucky." She filled him in on the findings—and the man's original freak accident theory. "The scene is still locked up, so based on our conversation, he had his people do another pass. Take a look at this." She pulled a glossy printout of a photograph from her portfolio and handed it to him. "They found it on the kitchen floor on their second time through, not far from the damaged epinephrine injector."

He studied the image. It appeared to be some sort of graphic design . . . parts of two letters of the alphabet, perhaps? The blue squiggles were laid over a sheaf of blue-green leaves on a gray background.

The significance eluded him.

"I give up. What is it?"

"Part of a logo. I wouldn't have made the connection, either, if a thankful Carson resident hadn't sent me a gift box from this place last Christmas. As it was, even though the design seemed vaguely familiar, it took me several minutes to place it."

She reached back in her portfolio and handed him another printout that displayed a full logo.

Gourmet to Go.

The partial o from "to" and the first half of the G from "Go" were a perfect match for the fragment of a label the sheriff's office had found in Joe's kitchen. As was the sheaf of leaves.

"Tell me why this is important."

She leaned closer, excitement sparking in her eyes. "Because

Gourmet to Go is a high-end St. Louis shop with only two locations, both here in town—one of which is very close to Jessica Lee's condo."

A spurt of adrenaline pinged in his nerve endings.

"Was there a fingerprint on it?"

"That would be nice—but no. It's clean. Jessica fits the client profile, though . . . personally and professionally. In addition to individual customers, the shop does takeout trays for in-office client entertaining and meetings."

"Cathy might be able to confirm if Peterson-Bradshaw orders from the place."

"Since you have an in with her, maybe you can find an opportunity to ask about that while we're here."

"Consider it done." Tipping his cup back, he finished his coffee. "Ready?"

"More than. I want this baby solved." She stood and marched toward the elevators, shoulders back, chin set, her body language spelling determination in capital letters.

He tossed his empty cup in the trash and fell in behind her.

Jessica Lee might be smart. She might be single-minded. She might be tough.

But she'd met her match in Chief Lisa Grant.

And if it came to a contest of wills, his money was on Lisa.

◆

A movement at the conference room door caught her eye, and Jessica glanced over as Robert answered a question from a member of the Gram's Table marketing team.

Cathy motioned to her.

With a murmured "Excuse me for just a minute," she pushed back from the table and moved to the door, closing it behind her as she joined Cathy in the hall.

"This better be important."

The secretary swallowed. "The police chief and detective are back."

Jessica didn't attempt to hide her irritation. This was beginning to border on harassment—and she might very well tell them that. "I'm in the middle of a meeting. They'll have to wait."

As she turned back toward the conference room, the door opened.

"We decided to break early for lunch. Everyone's hungry. Hi, Cathy." Robert nodded at the woman, then looked back at her. "If you need to attend to some business, feel free. I want to give Frank a tour of the offices and introduce him to a few more people before we go to lunch. Can you be ready in fifteen minutes?"

She hesitated. Could she ditch the cops that fast?

Yes. She'd tell them upfront she was in the middle of a meeting and hurry things along.

"No problem."

"Great. See you in a few minutes." Robert returned to the conference room, where Frank Nelson and his team were now milling about.

"Let's get this over with." Jessica strode toward her office, leaving Cathy to trail along behind her. "Show them back."

Once behind her desk, she smoothed a hand over her hair, touched up her lipstick, and adjusted her earrings.

This was going to be short and not-so-sweet.

She was still scrolling through voice mail as Cathy came into view in the hall through the large glass panels that dominated the interior walls—and her fingers froze on the keyboard.

Unlike her last visit, when she'd been wearing some off-the-rack civilian ensemble, the police chief was in full dress uniform today.

Gary's secretary stopped in the hall to ogle her as she passed, and Jessica spat out a muted curse. Word would spread like wildfire about this second visit from law enforcement.

She had to get them out of here as fast as possible. The longer they stayed, the more people would talk.

Cathy was smiling and chatting with the tall, good-looking detective, but once she realized her boss was watching, her face went blank and she dropped her gaze.

Why?

But there was no time to ponder that question. The three of them were on her doorstep.

She rose as the two cops entered and Cathy shut the door, but she stayed behind her desk, offering a polite yet put-upon smile. "I'm surprised to see you both again."

"There have been a few new developments we'd like to discuss with you." The chief's tone was pleasant, but there was steel underneath.

Jessica made a show of checking her watch. "Well, we need to do this quickly. I'm on a break from a client meeting and I have to be back in a few minutes. Have a seat." She gestured to the two chairs across from her desk, retook her own seat—and waited.

The lady cop sat and rested her hands in her lap, on top of a small portfolio. "First, I wanted to offer my condolences on the deaths of your two college friends."

Had Erika's death notice been in the paper? If so, she'd missed it. And even if Joe had been found, there would be no reason for her to know about his death.

The cop was testing her.

Play it cool, Jessica.

She adopted a puzzled air. "Excuse me?"

"You haven't heard that both Erika Butler and Joe Andrews were found dead in the past few days?"

Widening her eyes, she gave a slight gasp. "Oh my word! What happened?"

"We were hoping you might be able to shed some light on that."

"Me?" She arranged her features to express confusion. "Why would I know anything about this?"

For a long moment, the two of them watched her in silence. She didn't so much as blink.

Finally, the detective spoke. "Would you mind telling us your whereabouts on Tuesday evening?"

"Why?"

"According to the County medical examiner, that's when Erika died."

She parted her lips ever so slightly. "Are you suggesting that . . . ? Surely you don't suspect *me* of anything! I mean, accidents do happen—and Erika and I go back a long way."

The man's gaze never wavered. "I don't believe I mentioned it was an accident."

Mistake, mistake, mistake!

Stupid, stupid, stupid.

She had to backtrack.

Fast.

"What else could it be? If there'd been a crime, I'd have heard about it in the news." *Good save, Jessica.* She opened a drawer in her desk, pulled out a tissue, and dabbed at the corner of her dry eye. "I'm sorry. This is such a shock. I know you're just doing your job. Let's see . . . on Tuesday night I was home packing for a trip to the East Coast. I was in New York Wednesday through Friday night."

"Can anyone verify that?" The detective opened his notebook and extracted a pen from his pocket.

"I live alone." And if they somehow managed to come up with grounds for a subpoena or court order to gain access to the security tapes in the condo's parking garage, her lie would hold. Management was still using archaic tape instead of digital, and they only kept a week's worth before taping over them. The day guard in the lobby had been happy to share that information with her after she'd commented last week on the screens behind his desk and asked a couple of questions.

"Convenient."

She lifted her chin. "I don't think I care for your inference. Are you suggesting Erika's death *wasn't* an accident?"

The icy glare that intimidated most people didn't seem to faze the detective. Nor did he respond to her question. "Why don't you tell us where you were on Saturday night?"

"I was running some errands. Alone."

"Where?" It was the chief's turn again.

She shifted her attention to the woman and responded with a query of her own. "May I assume from your question that Joe died on Saturday?"

"You may."

She leaned forward. "Look . . . Joe and I were never friends. He and Erika were the ones who kept in touch. Now I'm happy to cooperate with the police, but I have nothing helpful to tell you. So if you'll excuse me . . ."

As she started to rise, the woman cop opened her portfolio, extracted a glossy eight-by-ten sheet of paper, and held it out. "Maybe you know something about this."

Jessica stared at the picture. It was only a fragment of a label, but she knew that logo. It had been on all the containers she'd taken to Joe's house.

Including the dip that stupid dog had used as a toy.

Had part of it fallen off?

No way to know, since she'd ditched the plastic bag during the drive back to St. Louis.

She took the photo and sat back down, pretending to examine it. "It seems familiar."

"It should. Peterson-Bradshaw does a lot of business with the firm." This from the detective.

How did he know that?

She glanced at the back of Cathy's head as the woman typed on the other side of the glass wall.

Was that what the two of them had been talking about while they walked toward her office from the lobby?

No matter. There was no reason to pretend she didn't recognize it.

She examined it again. "It's from Gourmet to Go, I believe."

"That's right." The chief crossed her legs, her posture relaxed . . . but her eyes were sharp as nails. "The police found it in Joe Andrews's house. I wonder how it got there?"

Stay cool. You might have made one small slip with the accident assumption, but you covered it well. This label fragment proves nothing.

"I have no idea. Perhaps he had . . ." She looked up just as Robert stepped into her outer office, Frank Nelson in tow.

He came to an abrupt halt outside her closed door when he spotted the police uniform.

Beside him, Nelson stiffened.

Silently she cursed the fishbowl environment Robert believed engendered openness and communication.

That would change under her leadership. People deserved some privacy.

Before she could rise and join them to smooth things out, the two men turned and left.

Wonderful.

More explanations to make—all thanks to the woman sitting across from her. Chief Grant should have let the dead rest in peace.

She stood. "I think we're finished here. And I need to return to my meeting."

The two cops looked at each other and rose.

"By the way, we did get a DNA confirmation on the bones.

276

They're Alena's." The woman tucked her portfolio under her arm but didn't extend her hand.

Just as well. Jessica wasn't in the mood to play nice anymore.

"We'll be in touch." The detective didn't offer his hand, either.

"I can't imagine why you'd waste your time with me. I won't be of any help to your investigation. But if you do need to contact me again, please do so at my home. I don't have time for these kinds of interruptions during business hours."

"Even in the cause of justice?" The lady cop studied her.

"I've told you everything I know." She crossed to the door and opened it. "Cathy will walk you to the lobby."

Her secretary jumped up, circled her desk, and waited.

In silence, the two cops moved past her and followed the woman down the hall.

As they disappeared, Jessica let out a long, slow breath. Everything was fine. She was okay. The cops were still fishing. Still working a hunch. They had no hard evidence, other than that piece of label from the salsa. The clerk at Gourmet to Go who'd been on duty Saturday could confirm her order, but that didn't prove anything. She was a regular customer who often ordered takeout dinners on weekends.

The label itself was suspicious, but not incriminating.

Unless her fingerprint was on it.

Her heart skipped a beat, and she steadied herself on the edge of the desk. Might she have touched that part of the label?

Yet even if she had, they didn't have her prints to check for a match.

Or did they?

She'd held the photo the lady cop handed her.

Her heart stuttered again.

Had the woman done that on purpose, to get her prints—or was she being paranoid?

Surely the latter.

Besides, what were the chances a legible print would be on such a tiny piece of the label? As near as she could remember, she'd only touched the edges of the lid.

Yes. The odds were in her favor. They might suspect she was involved—she would, in their place—but they'd find no proof.

Better to focus on damage control with Robert and Frank than worry about her visitors. She'd covered her tracks.

The police would never be able to touch her.

21

That was interesting." Mac aimed for a bench in the lobby as they exited the elevator from the Peterson-Bradshaw offices.

"Very." Lisa sat and angled toward him. "She did her best to recover, but the accident reference was a big slip."

"That wasn't her only one. Early on she asked what happened to Erika and Joe but never followed up when we didn't respond."

"No need to if she already knew."

"Bingo. And I'm not certain she caught that lapse."

"Maybe she was distracted by the accident misstep. The label threw her too."

He rested his arm along the back of the bench. "It also planted some doubt. She has to be wondering if there are prints on it."

"There aren't. I asked the sheriff. As a matter of fact, the only prints they found in the house were Joe's and his pastor's."

"Jessica doesn't know that, though. Despite her calm, cool façade, my guess is she's rattled—and rattled people make mistakes, especially if the pressure intensifies."

She squinted at him. "You have something in mind?"

His gaze flicked to her hair, inches from his fingers, its soft-ness calling out to be touched. Oh yeah. He had something in mind. One of these days he was going to—

"Mac?"

He blinked. "What?"

Amusement glinted in her eyes. "Do you need another shot of caffeine?"

"No. My adrenaline is already juiced." *And how.* "I just got distracted for a moment."

"You mentioned exerting pressure. Did you have a specific idea about how to do that?"

He forced his mind back to the subject at hand. "Yes. Is your reporter friend Rick still hanging around?"

"He calls every few days asking for an update on the bones case. So does a writer from the *Post-Dispatch*. I've been putting them off."

"Maybe it's time to fill them in on the latest—the official ID on the bones, the recent deaths of two of Alena's college friends . . . one of whom we questioned. Then there's the third friend, who's alive and kicking and definitely qualifies as a person of interest. I doubt she'd welcome a lot of media attention."

Lisa's expression grew pensive. "Using the press to our benefit. That's an interesting strategy."

"I've seen it work."

"I have too—though never in a case quite like this. But I'm willing to try almost anything that might give us a break. We're running out of options."

A sudden, strong urge to reach over and smooth away the creases in her brow swept over him, and he tightened his grip on the back of the bench, fisting his other hand in his lap. "You want to talk through some ideas?"

"Yes. You go first." She turned even more toward him, her

knee brushing his. He could feel the warmth of her skin through both layers of fabric.

Focus, McGregor.

He shifted his leg a hair away. "What do you know about these reporters?"

"Rick strikes me as smart, ambitious, and searching for a story that will help him break out of the pack. Look how fast he showed up at the construction site. I don't know the woman—not much worthy of *Post* coverage happens in Carson. She called as soon as Rick broke the bones story and did a small article."

"It would be advantageous to have both print and broadcast media on this. Wider coverage will ratchet up the pressure."

She tipped her head. "Are you thinking publicity that ties her to a police investigation might make Jessica crack?"

"Honestly? I'm not certain what it will do. But she's in line for the top slot in a firm known for its integrity. Peterson-Bradshaw boasts a roster of ethical, conservative clients who wouldn't look kindly on a company led by a scandal-plagued executive. Media coverage will add one more layer of pressure, and we can capitalize on that by paying her another visit at her office. Every time we show up there, every time we talk to her, is another opportunity for her to slip—like she did today. Sooner or later she might make an incriminating comment."

She raised an eyebrow. "Remind me always to stay on your good side."

He unlocked his hold on the back of the bench and brushed his fingers over her shoulder. "I don't think you need to worry about that."

He was rewarded with the hint of a smile. "Nice to know. So . . . I think I'll add a small press conference to tomorrow morning's agenda. Special invitation only."

"Sounds like a plan." He shifted around to survey the tempest outside. "I'd suggest waiting for a break in the weather before we leave, but that could be a while."

"I'm prepared for the storm." She lifted her collapsible umbrella. "We could share."

Tempting.

Very tempting.

But after all the caffeine he'd ingested, his heart was beating plenty fast already. Getting that up close and personal with the lovely police chief might vault it into the danger zone.

"I'll be fine. I can run fast."

She inspected the street scene through the windows in the two-story atrium, her expression skeptical. "If you say so." She rose, and he stood too. "I'll let you know how the mini press conference goes. Once I share the news, I'll sit tight until the stories break, then drop in again on Jessica."

"Count me in for that visit. Now that Erika's dead, I have a vested interest in shaking some clues loose too."

"You got it. Stay dry." With a wave of her umbrella, she strode toward the door.

Mac followed more slowly. He hadn't lied about being able to run fast—but even he couldn't outpace this relentless rain. His jacket would be soaked by the time he got to his car.

Still . . . getting a little waterlogged was a small price to pay if today's visit with Jessica Lee helped solve the mystery.

Trouble was, they weren't a whole lot closer than they'd been before talking with her again. The truth about that fateful day remained as buried as Alena's bones had been.

And for all they knew, that truth might not be as unsavory as they suspected. Maybe the whole thing had been nothing more than a dumb, innocent college prank gone very wrong.

But the latest deaths weren't innocent. He knew that as surely as he knew Lisa wouldn't rest until she got to the bottom of this thing. They were far too coincidental to be accidents. Jessica had something to hide, a connection to Alena's death she didn't want revealed, and Erika and Joe knew about it . . . making them a threat she'd needed to eliminate.

Every instinct he'd developed over the past dozen years told him that.

Lisa wasn't giving up, and neither was he. Like her, he'd been born with the justice gene—along with a sixth sense that had served him well as both a SEAL and a cop.

And right now, that sixth sense was telling him they were getting very close to discovering the truth—whatever that turned out to be.

◆

"Thank you both for coming out so early. At least the rain stopped overnight." Lisa ushered the two reporters into her office and toward the chairs across from her desk.

They eyed each other, their rivalry clear despite their different mediums.

Good. She wanted them both to hustle on this. To aggressively pursue the story. To dig deep.

To annoy Jessica Lee.

She took her seat and positioned a sheet of paper in front of her. "I know you've both been interested in the bones that were unearthed four weeks ago. Since that day, an active investigation has been under way by this police department, with assistance from the St. Louis County Police Bureau of Crimes Against Persons. We've been following leads and talking to people of interest. I can now report, based on DNA matching, that the bones belonged to Alena Komisky, a Czech Republic national who was in the US as part of a student exchange program. She was reported missing from Mizzou twenty-four years ago."

"Can I get some on-camera comments after we're finished here?" Rick continued scribbling.

"A few."

Diane from the *Post* scowled at him. "Are you going to scoop me with this on the noon news?"

He grinned at her. "That's my plan."

"But there's more to the story, which might lend itself to the kind of in-depth coverage best provided in print," Lisa said.

That seemed to mollify the woman. "Can you tell us how you identified her?"

"Sure." She explained how the botanist had helped them date the grave, how the small garnet found by the forensic anthropologist had been instrumental in helping her pick Alena out from the missing persons reports, and how they'd visited with the original case detective in Columbia.

"This is a great human interest story. It could be worthy of a feature. Missing student turns up after twenty-four years . . ." Diane's eyes glittered like a bloodhound's hot on a trail.

They were reacting exactly as she and Mac had hoped.

"But what happened to her after she disappeared? How did she die?" Rick asked.

"Blunt force trauma to the head."

"So this was murder?" Diane jotted some notes in the notebook on her lap.

Lisa leaned forward and folded her hands on her desk. "We're continuing to investigate that—and here's where the story gets even more interesting. We tracked down her roommate and the two friends who were with the roommate the night Alena disappeared. That roommate and one of her friends both died in the past week."

The two reporters stared at her.

"Were they . . . killed?" Diane's pen was poised above her notebook.

"Both deaths appear to be accidental." She gave them a few details—and the names of the deceased.

"What about the third friend?" Rick asked.

"We've talked with her twice. She lives in the area."

"Is she a suspect?"

Lisa hesitated—purposely. "Let's just say we're interested in continuing our conversation with her."

"Who is she?"

"At this point, I'd prefer not to reveal her name." She stood. They had more than enough to get started—and if they were as eager to dig into this as they seemed, it wouldn't take them long to uncover the identity of the third friend. "Rick, I'll be glad to answer a few questions on camera now. And Diane, if you need anything else, let me know." She handed over one of her cards.

The woman wasted no time heading out while Rick summoned his waiting cameraman.

They filmed in her office, where she confined her answers to fact rather than supposition, again avoiding any mention of Jessica by name. She wouldn't put it past the woman to sue for libel.

Seconds after Rick and his colleague packed up and left, Florence strolled in, Tally on her heels. "Things are hopping around here today."

Lisa slipped off her uniform jacket and hung it on the hanger behind her door. "I hope they start hopping even more. All we have so far with Jessica Lee is speculation."

"Near as I can tell, you're doing your best to smoke her out."

"I just hope it's enough." Lisa gave Tally a pat on the way back to her desk. "I'm running out of strategies."

"Well, I'll bend the good Lord's ear on this one. If that woman was involved in all those deaths, she needs to be brought to justice."

"I agree—and I think I'll join you in that prayer campaign."

Because truth be told, it might very well take the intervention of a higher power to bring a just resolution to this case.

◆

285

At the discreet knock on her office door, Jessica looked up from the consumer demographic report she was reading.

Robert was standing on the threshold, parallel creases denting his forehead.

She set the report aside. Despite a flicker of unease, she managed to maintain a pleasant expression. "Come in."

He entered, closing the door behind him.

Not a positive sign.

Robert was an open-door, up-front kind of guy.

She studied him as he sat in one of the chairs across from her desk. Was this more fallout from the impromptu visit he and Frank Nelson had paid to her office while the police were here?

No. Not likely. She'd passed the visit off as investigative protocol, a final follow-up with one of the few people who'd known Alena. He'd seemed to buy that explanation yesterday—though it was clear he'd have preferred no client witness the incident. Especially a new—and huge—client like Gram's Table.

So what was this about?

She leaned forward, fingers linked, matching his concerned demeanor. "Is everything all right?"

He adjusted his tie. No casual attire for this guy on the job. He understood the importance of image in their business—just as she did. "I'm not certain. My wife called a few minutes ago. She said there was a story on the noon news about that young student you knew who disappeared. I thought we should watch it together. Apparently there's more to the story now. Could you pull it up on your computer?"

TV coverage?

That police chief had to be behind this. If she hadn't passed more info to the press, they wouldn't still be on the story.

Fighting down a surge of anger, she modulated her voice and swung toward her computer. "Of course."

Don't say anything more until you see the coverage. Silent is always better than sorry.

She googled the noon news and found the story immediately. It had been the lead item—and that relentless police chief was front and center on the screen.

Another swell of anger rolled through her. That woman had done nothing but cause problems since the day those bones were uncovered.

Positioning her chair so she could keep one eye on Robert and one on the screen, she tuned in to the reporter.

The man didn't say a thing she hadn't already heard, but the deaths of Erika and Joe were news to Robert. His frown deepened as the reporter noted that the investigation was ongoing, then mentioned that the police were continuing to talk with a local resident who'd also been an acquaintance of the deceased student.

The reporter didn't mention her by name—but if he dug into the original story, it was only a matter of time before he figured it out. All he had to do was pull some of the articles from the *Missourian* that had come out after Alena disappeared. It had been a huge deal in Columbia, and though she'd tried to evade the press, her name had been mentioned a few times as an acquaintance of the roommate.

But maybe he wouldn't dig.

Maybe the story would just go away.

When the reporter finished, she leaned forward and closed the window.

"I didn't know about the other two people." Robert rested his elbows on the arms of his chair, linked his fingers, and locked gazes with her.

"I didn't either, until the police visited yesterday. It's very sad—and such a strange coincidence."

"Yes. A very strange coincidence." For the first time, a flicker of doubt clouded his eyes.

Her stomach knotted.

Play this smart, Jessica. You know his biggest concern is the reputation of the company. Acknowledge that—apologize—and alleviate it.

"I realize this isn't the kind of press we like to generate—for ourselves or our clients." She chose each word with care. "I'm very sorry such an old incident is causing problems. But you know how news stories are, especially ones that are more sensational than substantive—they die out very fast. This will be old news in a day or two."

"I hope so. You know as well as I do that the majority of our clients would find this sort of thing off-putting. Any hint of scandal could send them running to a competitor. Plus, with us wooing Brendan Blake Ministries, the timing couldn't be worse."

Stay calm. Stay cool.

"They're based in Nashville, though." She kept her tone serious but reassuring. "I doubt local news like this will travel far. And since many of our larger clients are in other parts of the country, I don't anticipate any problems. I got the impression yesterday from the police that they're at an impasse and about ready to reclassify this as a cold case, so the story should fade very fast."

"Perhaps . . . but the reporter inferred they're still looking into the other two deaths."

Yes, he had—unfortunately.

"I suppose they have to, given the timing and the connection to the original case." *Build your argument with logic and reason, Jessica.* "I assume they want to dot all the i's and cross all the t's. But from what they said yesterday, both deaths appeared accidental."

Wait.

Had the police chief or detective actually said that?

Maybe not.

Making that assumption was what had gotten her into trouble with them for a moment, in fact.

But it was true nonetheless—to the eyes of the world, anyway. She'd been careful. The only glitch had been that piece of label, thanks to Joe's stupid dog. If they'd found a fingerprint, however, they'd have been back to visit her by now.

She was safe.

"Well . . . let's hope that's true. I had to do some hand-holding with Frank Nelson yesterday after we spotted the police in here. I don't want to have to do that again."

"Of course not. Averting problems is always better than damage control—although we're certainly experts at that." She gave him a smile.

He didn't return it.

"I'll see you in the Campbell meeting tomorrow morning." With that, he stood and walked out.

In her peripheral vision, Jessica caught Cathy watching her. She swiveled back to her computer, away from prying eyes in this glass house of an office, and pretended to work on her presentation for tomorrow's meeting.

But while her fingers moved over the keys, her mind was fixed on personal matters.

Through the years, no matter what, Robert had always been solidly in her corner, deferring to her judgment over that of the other senior executives more times than she could count. She'd proven her worth to the company, and he'd rewarded that with steady advancement and trust.

Today was the first time she'd ever sensed a blip in his support.

Nevertheless, his doubt was manageable at this stage, assuming the scenario played out as she'd suggested and everything died down in a day or two.

If it didn't . . .

A quiver ran through her fingers and they slipped on the keys, throwing off her typing.

That, too, was a first.

She was always cool and clear-thinking under pressure. Always in control.

That, however, was the problem with this situation. Now that the press was involved, her control was slipping. Who knew what tangent that reporter might go off on next, what other sorts of insinuations he might make? Those media types were always hungry, always trying to sensationalize stories that were—

Her phone rang, and she jerked toward it. The name on the digital readout was unfamiliar; Cathy could answer it.

She yanked a tissue from her desk drawer and dabbed at her forehead. Was the air-conditioning working in here? The temperature seemed to—

A knock sounded at her door. She looked over to find her secretary hovering on the threshold.

"Sorry to interrupt . . . but this is a reporter from the *Post-Dispatch*. She says it's urgent. When I asked if I could take a message, she said it was personal."

Jessica wadded the tissue into a tight ball in her fingers.

The vultures were descending.

"Tell her I'm tied up." No way was she talking to a reporter about Alena or Erika or Joe. That's what this had to be about. She'd sent no news releases to the *Post* recently on behalf of any clients.

As Cathy retreated to pass on the message, she watched the display on her phone. A few moments later, the name disappeared.

But she had a feeling this whole mess wasn't going to disappear as quickly. Not if the print media was taking an interest too.

And if the story lingered, Robert's trust level could crumble further. In light of his imminent retirement, the timing stunk. Someone else could worm his way into the man's favor.

Like that tightwad Gary. Robert liked the man, with his fixation on controlling costs and nose-to-the-grindstone mentality.

Her eye twitched.

After all the groundwork she'd laid for this job, after working her butt off for years to reach the top, she wasn't going to stand aside and let anyone steal the position she'd earned with her blood, sweat, and tears.

Yet that persistent police chief was undermining the foundation she'd built and setting it up for someone to do just that.

Why couldn't the woman have let old secrets stay where they belonged—buried?

Jessica swung toward the window, fingers gripping the arms of her chair, and forced herself to face reality.

There could be serious negative consequences if this situation escalated.

But if it did, she wasn't the only one who was going to pay a steep price.

22

Plastic-wrapped newspaper tucked under his arm, cup of java in his hand, Mac pushed through to the balcony of his apartment and took a slow, deep breath. A Fourth of July spent in relative peace and quiet instead of dodging bullets.

What a change from his SEAL years.

Best of all, Lance was on home turf too, looking forward to a barbecue at Mom and Dad's. Too bad he hadn't been able to join them instead of spending the day alone.

Better here than wherever Finn was, though.

Frowning, he sat and propped his bare feet on the railing. No doubt his youngest brother was in the thick of things.

If only worry could keep him safe.

But since it couldn't, why not try to follow Lance's advice and give his worry gene a rest for the holiday?

Tipping his head back, he closed his eyes, let the sun warm his face, and focused on the small pleasures of the day—the chirp of the birds, the laughter of the children who'd already invaded the pool, the unaccustomed luxury of sleeping late.

His respiration modulated.

Better.

As for being alone, maybe he wouldn't be taking in his fireworks solo next Fourth of July. In fact, if a certain dark-haired, hazel-eyed police chief was in the picture, they might be sharing a whole different kind of fireworks.

Grinning, he took a sip of coffee. Interesting to be thinking long term about a woman. And a first. The notion of making that kind of commitment had always been more than a little intimidating.

Yet the thought of long term with this particular lady didn't scare him in the least.

Chalk another one up for Mom. She'd always said it just took the right woman to make a man grasp the joy of settling down.

Still smiling, he slid the paper out of the plastic sleeve, opened it to the front page—and blinked as the missing-person photo of Alena stared back at him.

The reporter from the *Post* had wrangled a cover spot for her story?

Even better than they'd expected.

He skimmed the lead, then flipped to the jump on page ten. The feature that took up two-thirds of the page included photos of Erika, Joe—and Jessica.

Yes!

He sped-read the article. The reporter had included a few quotes from Lisa, but mostly she seemed to have cobbled the piece together from various reference sources, including stories from the *Columbia Missourian* archives. She'd also tracked down Stan Breton at the retirement center and added a few insights from him. According to the story, Jessica had declined to comment.

No matter. Her name was out there now, smack in the middle of this mess.

If this didn't add some pressure, he didn't know what would.

He set down his coffee, pulled his phone off his belt, and tapped in Lisa's speed dial number. She must not have seen this yet, or she'd have called.

Three rings in, she answered, her voice clipped and distracted.

"Sounds like I caught you at a bad time." He pulled his sunglasses out of his pocket and slid them over his nose.

"You might say that. Hold a minute."

Muffled words came over the line as she barked out orders in a tone he'd never heard her use. "See if Dave's free. If he isn't, pull in Scott. Deal with the ambulance. Start calling the parents. We'll transport as soon as I get off this call." There was a rustle, the sound of a siren in the background, then she was back. "Sorry."

"We can talk later."

"Is it important?"

"It can wait till you clear up whatever trouble you've got."

"I'll get back to you as soon as I can." The line went dead.

He set the phone on the side table next to him. She'd warned him there was a strong possibility she'd be called in today. No surprise, given the small size of her department and the fact that the Fourth of July was the second most deadly holiday of the year behind New Year's Eve for drunk driving. Violent crime often spiked too—not to mention all the prankster stuff that went on.

He hoped she was dealing with the latter—though the ambulance would suggest a more serious incident.

While he waited, he read the article again. This reporter had done an even more thorough job than the TV guy—and left a lot more questions unanswered.

If Jessica had seen this, she had to be seriously concerned.

By the time Lisa called him back an hour later, he'd finished the paper, scrambled some eggs, and was back on the deck with his third cup of coffee.

"Sorry I had to hang up before." She sounded winded.

"No problem. You okay?"

"Yeah. We had a scuffle with a group of teenage boys who started their day with three six-packs and then thought it would be hysterical to toss fireworks into the pavilion in the park where a senior group was having a picnic. One of the older women was so startled she tripped and broke her arm."

He homed in on her first comment. "What do you mean by scuffle?"

"Let's just say the boys did not react well to being rounded up and hauled in."

His grip on the mug tightened. "Did one of those punks hit you?"

"I got clipped on the jaw. No big deal—for me, that is. For the kid . . . different story. Assaulting a police officer, even if beer has short-circuited your brain, is a big problem. The ice pack is helping, though. So what did you need?"

He tried to shift gears, but the notion of Lisa getting socked wasn't sitting well. Yeah, she'd been injured a lot worse in Chicago. But this was Carson, Missouri—small-town America. That should be far lower on the danger scale.

A cop job was never risk-free, though, no matter the location.

He had a feeling his worry gene better gear up for a serious, long-term workout.

"Mac?"

He picked up the newspaper. "Yeah, I'm here. I take it you haven't seen the *Post* today."

"Are you kidding? I've been on the run since six this morning. Did our reporter come through with a story?"

"I'll say. A front-page feature that includes photos of all the victims—plus Jessica."

"Whoa! That's way more than I expected."

"I'd say we've rattled her cage big time."

"Your idea was inspired."

"I have my moments. Shall we put her on our agenda for next week?"

"Absolutely. I'd like to let this percolate, allow for some fallout on her end. How does Wednesday sound?"

"Works for me." He took a sip of coffee. "You on duty all day?"

"It's looking that way. I'm just hoping I get to my mom's in time to sample her barbecue and watch a few fireworks. What's your day like?"

"I'm almost ashamed to say I'm free as a bird. As we speak, I'm sitting on my deck and deciding whether to join the kids in the pool or go to a movie."

"Both options sound great."

"I can think of an even better one—a drive to the country, a picnic for two, fireworks."

A beat of silence ticked by. "Are you flirting with me?"

"Yep. But I mean every word."

She sighed. "It sounds like the perfect Fourth."

"Maybe next year." Why not clue her in to his long-term plans?

"Be careful. I may hold you to that."

"You may."

Somewhere in the background a door opened, and her words grew indistinct as she spoke with someone else.

"Sorry. I need to go. The parents are beginning to descend. Let's regroup next week and set up a time to drop in on Jessica."

"I'll be at your disposal. Don't work too hard—and be careful."

"The boys have been subdued. I'm safe. Talk to you soon."

As the line went dead, he slowly slid the cell back onto his belt. She might be safe at the moment, but that could change in an hour . . . or tomorrow . . . or next week . . . or anytime.

It was tough enough having brothers in the line of fire.

Could he handle falling for someone who would activate his worry gene as easily as they did?

He took a sip of coffee and admitted the truth.

Based on the way his protective instincts had kicked in after hearing she'd been hurt, the question was rhetorical.

He was already falling for Lisa Grant.

Hard.

So he'd have to figure out how to make peace with her profession. To be protective without being smothering. To give her the space to do the job she loved while keeping his blood pressure under control.

All challenges he'd need to address soon.

Because their bag of tricks on the Alena Komisky case was empty, and this case was about to wrap.

If anything was going to break, it was going to break soon.

No!

Jessica reread the front-page headline in the *Post*, scanned the story, and flipped to the jump.

No! No! No!

The photo they'd sent to the business editor with her last promotion announcement stared back at her.

Robert was going to have a stroke.

She grabbed her latte, rolled up the paper, and wove through her favorite Starbucks, past the good-humored holiday crowd.

They might be in a festive mood, but her Fourth of July had just gone down the tubes.

Once on the sidewalk, she slipped on her dark sunglasses and continued toward her condo half a block away, trying to sort through the turmoil in her mind.

"Ms. Lee?"

At the summons from a male voice, she stopped a few yards from the entrance to her high-rise.

A man with a microphone stepped out of the shadow of a bush. The guy from the news report. Another man appeared beside him, a mini-cam propped on his shoulder.

It was aimed at her.

The reporter rattled off his name and station. "I understand you've been talking with the police about the deaths of Erika

Butler and Joe Andrews. Would you like to comment on that, or on the mysterious disappearance of Alena Komisky twenty-four years ago?"

Instead of responding, she turned her back and stalked toward the lobby. Once inside, she punched the button beside the double doors and forced herself to keep breathing as the elevator whisked her to the eighteenth floor.

Only after she was safely ensconced in her private domain did she let herself absorb the impact of the front-page story and the reporter lying in wait.

No question about it—this was getting dangerously out of hand.

On the plus side, Robert was out of town for the holiday weekend. That would buy her some time to develop a strategy.

But what could she do to contain the damage? The local press was all over the story, like vultures swooping in at the smell of death.

She threw her glasses on the kitchen counter, tossed the paper beside them, and began to pace, forcing the left side of her brain to engage.

First, she would not talk to the press. That would just add to their feeding frenzy.

Second, if no additional information came forward—and it wouldn't—neither the *Post* reporter nor the TV guy would have anything new to relate. Nothing new equaled no news coverage. The story would die.

Third, these people were making a whole lot of noise about nothing.

She snatched up the paper again and reread the article with more care. Lots of insinuations, none of them provable, and one new piece of information.

The police hadn't found Alena's ring. They'd found a stone from her ring.

That, she could buy. The thing had been a bear to get off, and it had been covered with blood. A stone could have fallen out, and the empty spot could have been camouflaged by blood.

One mystery solved, anyway.

But how ironic that a simple little stone could lead to such a big, complicated mess.

As for the woman reporter, she'd pretty much shot her wad with this story. It was a detailed overview of the entire scenario, but while it made for intriguing copy, it was a one-off.

Same for the TV guy.

Exhaling, she set the paper down.

The thing to do now was convince Robert the story had gotten far more publicity than it deserved, courtesy of two overeager reporters and a slow news day. That while it was unfortunate they'd linked her to the whole sordid mess, it spoke more to their lack of ethics than any culpability on her part.

Then she'd offer to speak personally to any client who happened to see the coverage and who expressed a concern—and she was skilled at smoothing things over, as Robert knew. She'd saved the hide of more than one client whose company had been embroiled in a controversy far more serious than this.

She picked up her latte and took a sip. It was growing cool—just as this story soon would. All she had to do was tread water and stay afloat until it blew over. Once it was consigned to the archives, she'd be back on track in her trek to the CEO spot.

And one year from now, barring any other glitches, she'd be exactly where she'd always planned to be—running the show at Peterson-Bradshaw. This whole incident would be nothing but a bad memory.

Because Chief Lisa Grant would lose and Jessica Lee would win. Guaranteed.

"I'm glad you could meet me for the fireworks." Stephanie Grant opened her folding chair and set it on the grass in the park. "But I'm sorry you missed dinner."

"I grabbed some food when I swung by the house to change out of uniform." Lisa popped open her chair and set it next to her mother's in the empty spot they'd found among the family groups waiting for the show.

"Sounds like you had a busy day."

"More than. What about you?"

"Quiet. Not like the old days, when you and Sherry were little and your father was here." There was a touch of melancholy in her words.

"I'm sorry I had to cancel out on dinner, Mom."

In typical fashion, her mother moved on to a more upbeat topic. "Not a problem. I had a nice day overall. I ended up filling in for four hours at the hospital after one of the other nurses got sick. Being with those newborns always brightens my spirits. After that, I treated myself to a frappuccino and read the paper cover to cover. Speaking of the paper . . . I saw that your story made the front page. Or were you too busy to notice?"

"Too busy—but someone told me about it, and I read it before I came to meet you."

"Who might that have been? The handsome detective, perhaps?"

The darkness camouflaged her mother's features, but there was no missing the curiosity in her inflection.

"Good guess."

"Hardly a guess. You two stay in regular touch."

"We're working a case—more than one, as a matter of fact."

"I think he's working more than a case."

Oh, mercy!

"And I don't think he's having to work too hard." Now her mom's tone was amused.

No sense evading the subject. Things were going to be heating up between them soon, anyway—she hoped. "He isn't. The lady's willing to be wooed. He seems like a great guy."

Someone lit the ground display of an American flag.

"So what are you waiting for?"

"This case to end—which will be very soon if nothing breaks in the next few days. We've put as much pressure as we can on a certain PR executive. If she doesn't slip, we're at a dead end." A loud bang announced the launch of a single rocket that was more noise than color. Beside her, Lisa could feel her mother flinch. "You're as bad as Tally."

"Where is he tonight?"

"When I left, he was hiding under my bed. You know, we don't have to do fireworks every year if you don't like them."

"I love the sparkle. The noise, not so much. As for that PR executive—watch yourself around her. She doesn't strike me as a woman who appreciates being crossed. I have a feeling people who tangle with her get burned."

"You got all that from a picture?"

"I've nailed people before from photos."

That was true.

The fireworks began in earnest, lighting the sky with color, and Lisa tilted her head back to enjoy the display.

But though she didn't respond to her mom's comment, her advice was sound.

If Jessica had done what she and Mac suspected, the woman had a very ugly side. She liked things to go her way, and when they didn't, felt no compunction about removing obstacles that impeded her plans.

Since things weren't going her way at the moment, it would be very interesting to see how she tried to get herself out of her current mess.

And Lisa intended to watch her back while she watched the PR executive's maneuvers.

23

By the time the summons came from Robert's office at ten o'clock Monday morning, Jessica's stomach was as queasy as it had been on her one and only sea voyage, in the Greek islands four years ago. Who knew she'd succumb to motion sickness—a malady compounded by ferocious waves as the ship rode out a major squall?

She'd never again experienced that kind of out-of-control nausea on any moving conveyance . . . nor on dry land.

Until now.

After taking a cautious sip of white soda, she pulled her mirror out of her desk drawer and examined her reflection.

Not good.

No amount of makeup had been able to erase the dark shadows under her eyes after three nights of restless slumber. Nor had she been able to disguise the fine lines of tension at their corners.

She wasn't used to Robert ignoring her calls. He knew she respected his position that family holidays were sacrosanct, that he was only to be disturbed for emergencies. So on the few occasions when she'd broken that rule, he'd always responded.

Yet he'd disregarded the messages she'd left on Saturday and Sunday.

Why?

This *was* an emergency—in her mind, anyway. He needed to hear about the *Post* article from her, not secondhand from one of her colleagues.

Shoving the drawer closed, she stood and smoothed a hand down her silk sheath, adjusted the coordinated patterned jacket. She'd prepared for this meeting just as she prepared for any public appearance, rehearsing her lines out loud in the privacy of her condo, trying out different tones of voice and expressions in the mirror, until the words and emotions flowed so naturally no one would suspect she'd orchestrated both.

There might be knots in her stomach, but she was as ready for this meeting as she'd been for the dicey press conference when one of their clients was being hammered for using materials supplied by a country that employed child labor at subsistence wages.

She pushed through the door of her office and strode past Cathy. "I'll be with Robert."

The walk down the long hall seemed interminable, but the man's assistant waved her in as she approached. "He's waiting for you."

She offered a stiff nod and moved to the door.

For once it was closed.

Steeling herself, she gave a quick rap with her knuckles and twisted the knob.

Robert looked up from his desk. "Come in—and close the door behind you."

He'd said that the last time the two of them had a tête-à-tête . . . but based on his solemn demeanor, he wasn't getting ready to impart happy news today.

She entered, waiting for him to suggest they talk in his sitting area, as usual.

He didn't.

"Have a seat." He gestured to a chair across his desk.

The man was strictly business today.

As she crossed the room, the coil of knots in her stomach tightened.

"I tried to reach you over the weekend to discuss the story that appeared in the *Post*." She sat, posture alert but relaxed. It never paid to display nerves.

"Yes, I know. I got your messages. I also got messages from several clients. The story was picked up by the wire service on Sunday. So far, it's appeared in newspapers in Chicago, Atlanta, Denver, Kansas City, Cincinnati, Houston, and Nashville."

All cities where they had clients—or potential clients.

Including Brendan Blake Ministries.

This was a disaster.

But who'd have expected a decades-old story about some dead foreign exchange student to generate more than local interest?

Then again . . . spun right and sensationalized, it might have appeal to the masses, who seemed to relish anything with a hint of scandal.

She should have checked the net, prepped differently. Because the script she'd carefully prepared, laced with reassurances, was now toast.

But she could wing it. Shooting from the hip was one of her fortes. In fact, she excelled under pressure.

Resting her elbows on the arms of the chair, she twined her fingers and spaced out her breaths. "This has gotten way out of hand, Robert. I'm very distressed the so-called news has spread outside of St. Louis. Yet the fact remains there's no substance, and the story will die once the media realize there's nothing else to report."

"Maybe there is."

Her fingers tightened. "What do you mean?"

"According to all the reports, the police are continuing to

investigate. If there was no question the deaths of that Czech student's friends were accidental, there'd be no point in that. Plus, it's clear the authorities still hope to piece together what happened to that young girl all those years ago. This could drag on for weeks."

She couldn't argue with that.

Robert took off his glasses and massaged the bridge of his nose. "I've been fielding calls from concerned clients—and potential clients—all weekend, including Brendan Blake himself. That was not how I'd planned to spend my holiday. I assured them all I would deal with the issue first thing this morning." He folded his hands on his desk and locked gazes with her. "When was the last time you took a vacation?"

At the left-field question, she blinked. "I go on a spa week every year, as you know. And I always fly down to the Caribbean for a few days in the winter."

"I'm talking longer than a week."

Her throat constricted. "How long?"

"However long it takes for this to blow over."

Possibly weeks, as he'd just pointed out.

Long enough for someone else to curry Robert's favor and edge her out of her favored position.

"Do you think perhaps this is an overreaction?" She tried to keep her voice steady, but a slight quiver ran through her words.

"Maybe. But I can't take any chances, Jessica. I've spent my life building up this business, and I won't put it in jeopardy."

Anger began to churn in her gut.

You've *built up this business? Who do you think brought in the majority of your top-tier clients? The ones that put you on the map? Before I came, you were content to play in the local league. I'm as much responsible for the success of this company as you are!*

Exerting supreme effort, she reined in her fury and managed

to speak in a civil, reasonable tone. "I understand the need to protect the business, and I want what's best for Peterson-Bradshaw too. I just think this may be an extreme response. Perhaps we could—"

A discreet tap sounded on the door, and Robert directed an annoyed look toward it. "Yes?"

His secretary opened the door halfway but stayed on the threshold, casting a curious glance toward Jessica. "Excuse me, Mr. Bradshaw. I know you didn't want to be disturbed, but Cathy stopped in to say 20/20 is trying to reach Ms. Lee. I thought you might want to know ASAP. She took a message."

Robert's face grew even more grim. "Thank you."

As the door closed, displeasure tightened his features. "I don't think we have a choice here, Jessica. I'm going to position your time away as a personal leave. You will, of course, be fully compensated during your absence. Once things quiet down and all of the issues are resolved to the satisfaction of the police, we'll alert our clients of the outcome and resume business as usual."

She clenched her fingers in her lap. "There's a great deal on my agenda for the next few weeks—including presentations to several potential West Coast clients I've been wooing. I'm already on their calendars for later this month."

"Brief Adam. I'll assign him to cover for you while you're gone."

Adam?

The wet-behind-the-ears MBA grad with a degree so new the ink probably hadn't dried yet?

Robert couldn't be serious.

She steepled her fingers, pressing the tips firmly against each other to disguise their tremble. "Don't you think he may be a bit too inexperienced to handle these types of clients?" If Robert hadn't asked each of his senior staff members to mentor the new hire for a few weeks after he'd joined the firm in January, she'd never have wasted any time on such a green kid.

"I'm not suggesting he make the presentations, just assist with the prep. If necessary, I can do them. But he's smart and eager and a go-getter. In a lot of ways, he reminds me of you when you first joined the firm. With adequate coaching and some finessing, I expect he'll do great things here—and I like nurturing young talent." He rose and extended his hand. "Help him get up to speed and stay in touch. But use the break for some fun too. You deserve it after all the long hours you've put in over the years. Consider it a sabbatical . . . effective today."

She took his hand. What choice did she have?

His grip was firm . . . and final. And the warmth she'd grown accustomed to in his eyes had chilled.

There was no escaping the truth.

His confidence in her had been gravely undermined. Once this thing blew over, she'd have to claw her way back into his favor.

She turned and walked out the door, ignoring his secretary. Continued down the plush carpet in the hall. Stalked past Cathy without a look. Closed her office door behind her, keeping her back to the glass wall as she gripped the top of her desk chair.

No matter how Robert positioned her extended vacation, everyone would know she'd been asked to leave.

Jessica Lee didn't take long vacations.

Jessica Lee was the hardest-working member of the Peterson-Bradshaw team.

Jessica Lee had no patience for people who put their personal lives above their professional commitments.

Everyone would assume she was in trouble with the police who'd paid her more than one visit.

Yet the truth was, the police had nothing. Her life was in shambles due to evidence that didn't exist.

If it wasn't so tragic, the whole thing would be funny.

And this sorry state of affairs was all due to Chief Lisa Grant, who'd managed to upend her world and unravel everything she'd worked tirelessly to attain.

Jessica lowered herself into the desk chair, her back to the outer office, and took a slow, shaky breath. She'd give herself a few moments to calm down. To let reason supersede emotion. To wait for her mind to clear so she could make plans.

And she had a lot of plans to make.

Because her enforced vacation wasn't going to be about re-laxation.

It was going to be about revenge.

◆

"I'm sorry . . . Ms. Lee is on a leave of absence."

As the receptionist in the main lobby of Peterson-Bradshaw shared that news on Wednesday morning, Mac looked over at Lisa.

She slanted an eyebrow at him before refocusing on the woman. "As of when?"

"Yesterday."

"For how long?"

The woman lifted a shoulder. "I don't know. It was very . . . sudden. None of us have any details."

"Thank you." Mac smiled at her, took Lisa's arm, and urged her toward the door.

She sent him a silent *"What gives?"* query but followed his lead.

Only after they were in the hall, out of sight of the PR firm's offices, did she speak. "Why such a hurry to leave?"

He pressed the elevator button. "The receptionist isn't going to tell us anything. Neither is the head of the firm. I think we both know what happened—but I have an inside source

308

who can probably confirm it . . . and maybe pass on some scuttlebutt."

"Cathy."

"Right." He let her precede him into the elevator. "Why don't I call her from the lobby and see what she has to say? Then we can discuss next steps."

"Sounds reasonable. While you chat with her I'll have one of those herbal iced teas you mentioned the day of the monsoon."

As they exited into the lobby and headed toward the coffee bar, he started to dig for his wallet.

"No." She stopped him with a touch. "I'll get the drinks while you focus on more important things. You want coffee?"

"That'd be great."

"Black?"

"Always."

"How come I knew that?"

Without waiting for a response, she walked over to the counter while he claimed an empty café table.

He tapped in the main number for Peterson-Bradshaw, masking caller ID with *67 and opting for the automated phone directory rather than live routing by the receptionist.

The mechanical voice said Cathy's name as Lisa slid into the chair across from him and slipped off her uniform jacket. The light coming in from the expansive windows highlighted the blue tinge on her jaw that a heavy application of makeup hadn't been able to disguise.

His blood pressure shot up. If he'd been there when that punk hurt her, the kid would—

"What's wrong?" She cocked her head as she eyed him.

"Nothing." *Liar, liar.* Better to keep his proprietary, protective instincts to himself for now. A strong, independent woman like Lisa might not appreciate them at this stage of their relationship. "I'm just ringing through to her now."

She nodded and took a sip of her tea.

"Cathy Ryan."

"Cathy, it's Detective Mac McGregor from St. Louis County Police. Is this a convenient time to talk?"

"Um . . . I guess so."

"My colleague, Chief Lisa Grant, and I were up in your main lobby a few minutes ago and heard the news about Jessica Lee. We understand she's on a leave."

"That's right."

"I hope your job is secure, though."

"Yes. Mr. Bradshaw was clear about that. I'm very relieved."

"I'm sure you are—and I'm happy to hear that. Chief Grant and I were wondering if you might know what happened with Ms. Lee? The main receptionist didn't seem to have a clue."

When she spoke again, Cathy's voice was hushed. "I don't know a lot. Mr. Bradshaw called the whole staff in late Monday and said she was taking a leave for personal reasons. But we all think it's connected to that news coverage about all those people who died. I heard the *Post* story was picked up all over the country, and that Mr. Bradshaw was getting a lot of calls from clients. Plus, while she was in his office on Monday morning, a call came in for her from *20/20*."

"*20/20*." He cocked an eyebrow at Lisa. "Interesting. Any idea what she planned to do with her time off?"

"No. She didn't even say good-bye to me." The woman blew out a disparaging breath. "So what else is new?"

"Maybe she'll have a change of heart while she's gone."

"That would take a miracle."

"Well, hang in there and thanks for all your help."

As he signed off and slipped the phone back on his belt, Mac relayed the information to Lisa. "What do you say we drop by her condo and see if we can catch her in?"

"I'm all for that." She handed him his coffee. "We might as

well make one last attempt to exert some pressure before we deep-six this."

He stood. "Want to take my car? It's only a few blocks. I can bring you back here when we're done."

"Sure." She took a swig of her iced tea, grabbed her jacket, and fell in beside him as he started toward the door. "I'm crossing my fingers."

"Me too."

As it turned out, though, the gesture was wasted.

"I'm sorry, folks." The uniformed guard in the lobby of her condo shook his head when they asked for her. "Ms. Lee left yesterday afternoon. Told us to hold her mail, that she'd be gone for a while. A few minutes later I saw her car pull out of the garage." He motioned to an oversized monitor showing feed from four security cameras that covered the main entrance, lobby, and parking garage.

"Did she say where she was going?" Lisa asked.

The fortysomething, slightly overweight guard flashed a gleam of white teeth. "That wouldn't be her style. She doesn't chat with the riffraff. The only time she ever said more than two words to me was a couple of weeks ago, when she asked about the security cameras."

"I wonder why she was curious about that?" Mac rested his forearm on the tall desk in a casual, shoot-the-breeze pose.

"You got me. She seemed interested in the quad splitter we use to display the feed from all four cameras at once, and that we tape over the footage after a week." He grinned. "We don't exactly have high drama around here. I've worked at this condo for six years, and we've never had to reference any security tapes. But they help the residents feel more protected, so hey . . . they fork out big bucks to live here. Whatever makes 'em happy."

Mac chuckled. "A man who knows his customers."

"What can I say? The rich folks lead a different kind of life. As long as this job pays my bills, I aim to please."

After thanking him, they returned to Mac's car.

"Interesting that she asked about the security equipment not long before Erika and Joe died." Lisa buckled her seat belt.

"Very. She knew that within a week there'd be no record of her activities on the days they died. No one could dispute her claim about her whereabouts." Mac pulled into traffic.

"I'm more convinced than ever that getting her to crack is the only way we're ever going to piece this puzzle together."

"That won't be easy if she's gone incommunicado. And if she stays away two or three weeks, the story will be very old—and dead—by then. Unless *20/20* actually follows up on it."

"I'm classifying that as a long shot."

"Me too."

They fell silent until he eased in next to Lisa's car. "Any other ideas?"

Frustration sharpened her features. "Sad to say, no. But potentially letting someone get away with murder—or murders—is driving me crazy."

"There is one positive side to our current situation, though."

"What's that?"

"If the case ends, we can shift our relationship from professional to personal." He winked.

That coaxed a smile out of her. "There is that."

"But we'd both rather have a better resolution."

"Yeah." She massaged her temple. "I'll tell you what. Let's give this ten days. We'll pay her one more visit then. If she's still out of town and there haven't been any other developments, we'll close the file. Sound reasonable?"

"Ten days, huh?"

"We can talk by phone in the meantime."

He gave an exaggerated sigh. "Better than nothing—but not by much. I guess I can live with that."

"I'll call you tomorrow. Promise."

She reached for the door handle, but when he grabbed her other hand, she turned back. "Can we throw one lunch in there somewhere? Just to make certain you don't forget about me?"

Smiling, she leaned close. So close he caught the fresh fragrance that never failed to trigger an adrenaline rush. So close her soft hair brushed his hand resting on the wheel. "I think that could be arranged. But trust me, you are not a forgettable man."

Then, before he could follow his instincts and claim the kiss he'd been hankering for almost since the day they'd met, she slipped out of the car, closed the door, and walked toward her Impala.

A horn behind him honked, and he had no choice but to drive off, leaving her behind.

But not for long.

In ten days, no matter what happened with the Alena Komisky mystery, he and Lisa could move forward with their own future.

Yet as he sent her one final glance in his rearview mirror, he had a feeling her discouragement over this case was premature.

Because his gut told him they weren't yet finished with Jessica Lee.

24

Jessica pulled on the turtleneck, smoothed it over her hips, and inspected herself in the mirrored doors of the hotel room's closet.

Black top. Black slacks. Black shoes.

Check.

She picked up the black baseball cap and tugged it over the coil of hair on top of her head, then tucked in any loose strands.

The dark sunglasses came next.

Opening her black shoulder bag, she ticked off the critical items—driver's license, binoculars, latex gloves . . . and Charles's compact Beretta.

She was ready.

After eight days of tracking Lisa Grant's evening movements, after hours of strategizing, it was time to wrap up her "vacation," head home, and do her best to convince Robert to let her return to work. She needed to launch her repair-the-damage campaign ASAP.

If it wasn't too late.

An image of his doubt-filled eyes during their last meeting strobed across her brain, and a cold chill that had no connection to the hotel's overzealous air-conditioning swept over her.

No.

She snuffed out the image.

There was time to fix the damage.

There had to be.

And with Lisa Grant no longer dropping in unannounced, with the press silent on the Alena story since the holiday weekend, there was no reason for Robert to extend her leave.

First thing on Monday morning, she'd convince him of that.

In the meantime, she had a job to do.

Slinging her bag over her shoulder, she strode toward the door, shoulders back, chin up. She was ready for this. Had planned it down to the last detail.

And no one beat Jessica Lee when it came to planning.

After a glance through the fish-eye peephole revealed a deserted corridor, she slipped out and headed for the elevators.

A young couple was inside when the doors opened, but that was okay. With the glasses and her hair hidden under the cap, she wasn't recognizable. Besides, the two of them were intent on discussing their evening plans.

The instant they reached the first floor, she exited and wove through the clusters of people in the spacious lobby. Conference goers, no doubt. There were two groups meeting at the facility, and the activity level in the public spaces was high. The hotel had truly been an inspired choice for her close-to-home "spa" vacation. Not only was it convenient to her target site, but all the bustle provided anonymity.

She pushed through the main door and walked to the adjacent lot. Self-parking was also a plus. No one would notice one woman coming or going.

Pressing the lock-release button on her keychain, she hurried toward her car. Picking up a rental might not have been a bad idea—but why go overboard? No one was checking on her. Except for some reconnaissance outings, she'd been holed up in her hotel room for nine days, working on the West Coast client presentations, making a daily spa appointment in case anyone later checked on her activities during her "vacation," and formulating plans for tonight, and all had been quiet.

The story—and the case—were dead.

She slid behind the wheel, started the engine, and headed south on the route that had become all too familiar since she'd relocated to the hotel. The traffic was lighter tonight, so the trip should take fifteen minutes, max.

Then it would just be a matter of waiting for the right time—somewhere between eight-thirty and nine, if Lisa Grant's pattern of the past nine nights held.

The chief was nothing if not predictable in her leisure time.

As she accelerated toward her destination, Jessica ran through the woman's weekday evening routine. She came home from the office between six and seven. Let her dog run around for a few minutes in the backyard before calling him in. Cranked up her exercise tape sometime between eight and eight-thirty, based on the peeks she'd managed to get with her binoculars through blinds that weren't fully dropped in the workout room. On Thursday night, after thirty minutes of gyrations, she let her dog out in the backyard while she rolled her trash can to the curb.

The only night the woman had ventured out after arriving home from work was on Wednesday, when she'd gone to her parents' house—or some relative. According to a Google search, she shared the same last name as the owners of the modest home Jessica had trailed her to. Those visits had all the earmarks of a standing engagement.

For the most part, though, Lisa Grant lived a very quiet, solitary life off duty.

Tonight that was going to change.

Yawning, Lisa secured her hair at the nape of her neck with a stretchy band and gave Tally a pat. "Your favorite time of day, boy."

He eyed her yoga capris and tank top and backed away.

She chuckled. "Yep, the music's going to shake, rattle, and roll very soon. Take cover."

The pup was out the door and careening for the basement before she finished her warning. As he clattered down the steps, she chuckled and walked toward her workout room, angling her wrist. Eight forty-five—a little later than usual. Why was it always the end of the day when she got around to her exercise routine?

Her mother's response to that lament at dinner last night echoed in her mind.

Because you spend too many hours on the job.

That was true—and it was a habit she was finding difficult to break, despite her best intentions. Her goals for her move to St. Louis hadn't changed; she still wanted to carve out time for a personal life that would someday include a husband and family. Yet a year into her new job, she'd made zero progress toward that goal.

Until Mac appeared out of the blue.

A flush of pleasure warmed her. Apparently the old adage was true.

Sometimes good things did come to those who waited.

She paused beside her weights. Today was upper-body day, so bench presses first.

As she positioned herself on the bench, hefted the bar, and went through her reps, resting two minutes between sets before adding weights, the rote routine left her mind free to think about the tall detective who was poised to play a new role in her life starting Saturday—or D Day, as they'd termed it. As in Done Day. Jessica had never returned to her condo, the press coverage had died, and no new leads had surfaced. The investigations were ready to be closed, despite their diligent efforts.

She blew out a breath and hefted the weights again.

The professional outcome wasn't what she'd hoped . . . but as Mac had pointed out, the results in the personal column were positive.

And she was more than ready to move forward with *that* investigation—beginning with their Saturday dinner date. The quick lunch they'd shared on Tuesday had been pleasant, if rushed—but Saturday was going to be the real deal . . . assuming, of course, nothing else happened with their case.

As far as she could tell, that was a safe assumption.

She finished the bench presses, wiped her face on the towel slung over a nearby chair, and moved on to dumbbell shoulder presses.

After readjusting the weight bench to an upright position, she once more did the presses by rote, waiting for the physical exertion to ease any lingering tensions from the day.

But the energy purge wasn't working its usual magic tonight.

How could she relax when she knew in her heart a killer was going unpunished?

Maybe Jessica Lee hadn't actually killed Alena. That mystery might remain forever unsolved. But she'd orchestrated the deaths of Erika and Joe—and done it so masterfully they'd been unable to find one speck of admissible evidence. All they had were theories, coincidence, and supposition.

In other words, nothing on which to build a case.

The whole thing stunk.

As she proceeded to barbell curls, the injustice of it grated on her. Yes, they'd given Alena's family some closure—but it wasn't enough.

She still wanted answers.

Yet as a veteran detective in Chicago had told her in her long-ago rookie days, sometimes the bad guys won. Sometimes you just had to let things go.

That's where they were with this case—like it or not.

Not. Not. Not.

But letting the less-than-desirable outcome in her professional life cast a shadow on her personal life would do nothing to solve the case. She had to learn to draw a line between the two and move on, as the experienced cop had advised her.

Sound advice, even if she'd never been able to apply it.

With Mac in her life, though, she had more incentive. She didn't want anything to overshadow their budding relationship.

She finished her curls, mopped her brow again, and picked up the DVD remote. Lunging, stretching, flick kicking, and heel hopping to a loud, upbeat tune might perk up her spirits.

That and thinking about her Saturday night date.

She could hope, anyway.

After all, dwelling on the less-than-optimal outcome wasn't going to change anything. She and Mac had done everything humanly possible to solve this thing. It wasn't their fault that Jessica Lee remained free.

Much as it galled her, the case was a wrap.

◆

The lights went out in the exercise room.

Finally.

Jessica tightened her grip on the Beretta and tugged her cap further down on her head. Thank goodness the woman's house was in the country. This would be a lot more difficult to pull off if the police chief lived in the tiny town of Carson.

Out here, it had been easier than she'd expected during her daytime scouting expedition to find a spot to tuck her car. The empty for-sale property adjacent to Lisa Grant had been tailor-made. Once she'd chosen that location, she'd just followed the long, curving drive each evening, parked behind the house, and taken a short walk through the woods. From there, she'd had a perfect line of sight to the side, front, and back of Lisa Grant's house.

A mosquito buzzed in her ear, and she swatted it away, muttering a curse. Even the noxious-smelling bug spray she'd applied after the first night couldn't keep all the bloodsuckers at bay.

Still, this spot was ideal. Better than the small, little-traveled road along the back of Lisa's property. That wasn't as close, and it didn't have as many concealed parking spots. Also better than the small country church a hundred yards down the road across from Lisa's house. The shrub-rimmed lot had been deserted every evening, and from there she would have been able to see the front of the woman's house clearly.

This less-exposed spot, however, seemed almost heaven-sent . . . if she believed in such things—or in God. Having a view of three sides of the house had given her important information about the woman's evening activities . . . and her dog.

A shiver rippled through her, despite the oppressive humidity of the July night.

The last thing she needed was another dog complication.

But she'd worked out how to deal with that issue.

A door slammed, and Lisa's faint voice broke the stillness. "I'll be back in a couple of minutes, Tally. No . . . you can't come. Stay inside the gate. Good boy."

Metal clanked.

A few seconds later, the wheels of her trash can crunched on the gravel as she began to roll it down the drive.

Now.

Jessica removed the latex gloves from her pocket, snapped them on, and crept silently through the woods, into the position she'd selected. In the distance, a sonorous boom of thunder rumbled through the dark night.

The corners of her mouth tipped up.

It was, indeed, time to rumble.

"Relax, Tally. I said I'd be right back." Lisa tossed the remark over her shoulder as her pooch let out a yip. "There are no more car chases in your future, my friend."

Picking up her pace, she half jogged down the gravel driveway, hauling her trash can behind her.

Poor Tally. He hated to be left behind almost as much as he hated leashes.

But after she'd discovered his propensity to chase cars the one and only time she'd let him accompany her on her trash run, his whines fell on deaf ears. Better a disappointed dog than a dead one. Besides, she'd nearly had a heart attack as he'd loped after any passing car with gleeful oblivion to the danger, ignoring her frantic summonses.

She positioned the trash can at the end of her drive as a flash of lightning illuminated the western sky, followed by a low growl of thunder.

Tally let out a mournful wail.

Breaking into a full jog, she retraced her steps. He'd be making a beeline for his hiding place under her bed the instant she opened the back door. But if that made him feel safe, it was . . .

A dark form emerged from the shadows just ahead, to her left. Her step faltered as her hand automatically reached for her holster.

But who wore a gun when exercising?

The person before her, however, was far better equipped. Though the night was dark, she had no problem seeing the outlines of the pistol aimed at her heart.

"We meet again."

At the familiar female voice, Lisa's lungs locked.

What in the world . . .

"Nothing to say? Strange. You've had plenty of words for me—and the press—until now." She moved slightly aside. "Keep walking toward the house. And don't try anything. I know how to use this, and I won't hesitate to pull the trigger. In fact, I have a feeling I'd enjoy it very much."

Mind churning, Lisa forced her feet to carry her forward, any lingering doubt about Jessica Lee's culpability evaporating. The woman was guilty of everything they'd suspected. Perhaps more.

As for whether she'd carry out her threat to use the gun . . . hard to say. That would be obvious homicide, and she'd been careful up till now to ensure the deaths she'd orchestrated appeared accidental.

But what if the pressure they'd exerted had at last made the woman crack? If so, she might change her modus operandi, be more willing to take risks.

Better to play this out for a few minutes, wait for an opportunity where the odds were a bit more in her favor before attempting to gain the upper hand. If the woman's main objective was to shoot her, she'd have done so already.

Once they drew near the back gate, Tally's happy, welcoming yips ceased. Gaze fixed on Jessica, he ground out an ominous snarl as they approached.

"Grab the mutt's collar and put him in the kennel. Make one wrong move or let loose of him before he's restrained, he dies."

Would she shoot Tally? A gunshot would be heard for a long distance in the open country around them.

The woman spoke as if reading her mind. "The house on your right is vacant. Your neighbors on the left are out for the evening. No one's at the church. The next closest sign of civilization is a quarter of a mile away. Do you really think anyone's going to notice a gunshot over the rumble of thunder and air conditioners?"

Whatever had possessed her to take this extreme step, Jessica's mind was still lucid. She'd thought this whole thing through, just as she'd thought the other murders through.

Except this time, there was one big difference.

Lisa was on to her, while the others might not have realized they were targets until it was too late.

"Move!"

Easing open the gate, Lisa grasped Tally's collar.

The dog surged toward the other woman, but she held tight. "It's okay, boy. Come on. Let's go to the run."

She had to drag him the entire way as he growled and snarled at Jessica, who was following at a safe distance.

As she lifted the latch on the gate, she hesitated for one split second. If she let Tally go, he'd barrel straight toward Jessica, do his best to protect the human who'd rescued him and lavished him with love.

But he'd die in that attempt. There was no doubt in Lisa's mind that Jessica would carry out her threat—and in the end, it might not buy her enough of an opening to cover the distance between them and wrestle the gun away from her, anyway. They were too far apart.

She opened the gate, pulled Tally inside, and slipped out before he could squeeze past her legs.

"Now let's go inside."

Lisa wiped her palms down the stretch fabric of her capris and walked toward the back door.

After she twisted the knob and pushed through into the kitchen, Jessica spoke again. "Move to the middle of the room."

She did as instructed.

The woman entered and closed the door behind her.

In the light, Lisa got her first clear look at the PR executive.

Her attire was reminiscent of Catwoman—but it was the cold, hard, merciless hate glittering in the woman's eyes that sent her adrenaline surging.

Jessica Lee had killing on her mind—and she wouldn't waste a lot of time leading up to it. Whatever her plan, she was going to implement it and get out fast.

The clock was ticking.

Jessica gestured toward the hall with the gun. "Walk down to your exercise room."

She knew about the exercise room?

Had she gotten into the house?

No. Lisa never left home without activating the alarm system.

Could she have looked in from the outside?

Once in the room, Lisa inspected the windows. There. On the far wall. There was a gap at the bottom of the blinds. Someone outside could have seen in.

Is that what Jessica had been doing on her out-of-town vacation? Stalking her quarry?

Lisa suppressed a shudder. She and Mac had always known the PR executive was smart, but she was even smarter than they'd thought.

"Drop the blinds all the way to the windowsill."

As she complied, the woman surveyed the room, then motioned toward the stationary bike. "Why don't you take a ride?"

Lisa stared at her.

This was getting more bizarre by the minute.

Her nemesis sat on the single chair in the room. "Ride."

Getting on the bike would put more distance—and barriers—between them. That wasn't going to give her any opportunity to lunge for the gun.

"Stop thinking so hard, Lisa. Just do it. Now."

"Why?" She had to stall. Figure out a way to maneuver herself closer to the woman.

Jessica smiled, but only evil shone from her eyes. "Vigorous exercise never hurt anybody . . . unless they happen to be diabetic."

As the woman's intent suddenly became clear, the bottom dropped out of Lisa's stomach.

Jessica had seen the glucometer that day in the Peterson-Bradshaw office when it had fallen from her purse. She'd been married to a doctor . . . and she clearly knew enough about diabetes to use the condition as a lethal weapon.

Just as she'd used alcohol and a bee allergy against Erika and Joe.

A surge of anger—and adrenaline—stiffened Lisa's backbone as she locked gazes with the gun-toting woman.

That ploy might have worked in the past, but this time she'd picked the wrong target. If Police Chief Lisa Grant did die tonight—and that was a very credible possibility—it wasn't going to look like an accident.

No matter the outcome for her, she was taking Jessica Lee down.

25

Why wasn't Lisa answering?

Crossing to the sliding doors that led to his balcony, Mac took a swig of soda as a distant flash of lightning lit the night sky. The storm the meteorologists had predicted was approaching fast.

When the call rolled to voice mail, he disconnected. No need to leave a second message. The one from fifteen minutes ago said all he had to say.

He weighed the phone in his hand. It was possible she'd been called out to help handle some crisis and was too busy to deal with phone calls.

But that didn't feel right.

Even on the Fourth of July, in the midst of all the chaos with the underage drinkers, she'd answered her cell.

And if she'd been in the shower for his first call, she'd have gotten his message by now and called back.

Should he try her home phone? That number was tucked in his directory too—though he'd never used it.

He scrolled down to it. Hesitated. Were three calls within fifteen minutes overkill?

Yeah—under normal circumstances.

But this was out of pattern. He'd been checking in with her every night around nine-thirty since the day they'd visited Jessica Lee's office and condo and begun the ten-day case-closed countdown. She'd always answered by the second ring or returned his calls within minutes.

Always.

Without further debate, he tapped in her home number.

Three rings in, he got another answering machine.

His apprehension ratcheted up another notch.

Lisa was always home by nine-thirty, barring an emergency at work.

On a whim, he tried her office number. Not that there was much chance she'd be sitting behind her desk if she *had* been called in. On the contrary. She'd be in the field, in the thick of things. Maybe setting herself up for another sock in the jaw.

No answer.

When the aluminum crinkled beneath his fingers, he loosened his grip, finished off the soda, and set the can on the pass-through counter between his galley kitchen and eating area.

This wasn't making any sense.

He moved into the living room. Began to pace.

She had to know he'd worry if she didn't answer—and Lisa wasn't the type of woman who brought unnecessary worry to those she cared about. That list now included him. They might have kept things professional between them, but her eyes didn't lie. She was as eager as he was to shift their relationship into high gear.

Maybe he could call that young cop who'd been on the construction site the first day he'd met Lisa. He still had the man's card somewhere. If there was some action in Carson, he'd know about it.

In his bedroom, he rooted through the overflowing dish on his dresser that held all the stuff he pulled out of his pockets each night. One of these days he'd have to sort through it and pitch the nonessentials—but for once, procrastination was going to pay dividends.

He found Craig Shelton's card at the bottom, a half-melted peppermint stuck to it, but once he scraped off the candy, the man's cell number was legible.

Unlike his boss, Shelton answered on the first ring.

Mac reintroduced himself, then hesitated. Had Lisa mentioned to anyone at her office that the two of them were . . . friendly? Not likely. Better to keep this official.

"Officer Shelton, I've been trying to reach Chief Grant this evening to discuss the cases we've been investigating." Not quite a lie; the subject always came up during their conversations. "She's not answering her cell, and I wondered if there might be some trouble in Carson that required her attention."

In the background, a police radio cackled to life. "No. I'm on duty, and it's a quiet night. Maybe her battery is dead."

"The phone would have gone straight to voice mail if that was the case. It rang."

"Hmm. Would you like her home number?"

A gust of wind whipped the branches of the tree outside his window, and Mac squinted at the black sky. Should he admit he already had it?

Why not? Their relationship would be public knowledge soon enough.

"I've already tried that. No answer."

If the guy was surprised, he gave no indication. "I'm not that far from her place. If it's important, I could swing by and see if she's home."

"If you wouldn't mind, I'd appreciate that. If she's there, ask her to call me."

"Will do. You should hear back from one of us within ten minutes."

"Thanks. I'll stand by."

While he waited for the return call, Mac slipped a section of his belt out of the loops on his jeans and slid on his holstered Sig Sauer. He also pocketed his creds, dug out his personal binoculars from the guest room closet, and grabbed some extra batteries for the flashlight in his car.

He hoped he didn't need any of that equipment—but he intended to be ready.

Just in case.

♦

"This is taking too long." Jessica frowned and glanced at her watch. "Increase the resistance."

As sweat trickled down her temple, Lisa stopped pedaling to fiddle with the adjustments on the bike.

Her fingers were still steady. That was good.

But if this strenuous exercise continued, symptoms of hypoglycemia would soon set in.

Exactly what Jessica had planned.

She needed to buy herself a few resting minutes while she tried to figure out how to get from the bike to the gun without taking a bullet in the process.

"Look . . . what's going on here? Why are you targeting me?"

The woman's features hardened. "I don't like people who steal."

Lisa cocked her head. "What are you talking about?"

"You stole from me as surely as Erika tried to. I spent years building my place at Peterson-Bradshaw, then you swept in and did your best to rob me of my future." A muscle twitched beside her eye. "I don't have a lot of patience for thieves. I would think you'd understand that, in your line of work. Behavior like that deserves to be punished." The woman's voice was cold. Steady. Merciless.

A faint throb began to pound in Lisa's head, and her fingers started to tingle.

Bad sign.

She did her best to rein in her panic. "How did Erika steal from you?"

Jessica rose, but the gun never wavered. "She threatened to go to the police and tell the story about Alena if I didn't give her an exorbitant amount of money."

Blackmail.

Not an uncommon motive for murder.

Lisa tightened her grip on the handlebar as a wave of dizziness swept over her. *Steady, steady. Hold on.* "So you killed her."

The woman smiled. "It was an accident. She always did drink too much."

"What about Joe?"

She shrugged. "I got the distinct impression he was sorry we'd ever covered up Alena's death and wouldn't mind in the least if the truth came out. That was the last thing I needed."

"And what is the truth?"

"Start pedaling again."

She flexed her fingers on the handlebar and began cycling again. "Look . . . I've spent weeks trying to piece together this puzzle. At least tell me what happened that night."

Jessica watched her in silence for a few moments. "I don't suppose it can hurt. It's not like you're going to be sharing the information with anyone—and I did come up with a masterful plan."

As the woman recounted the tale of that long-ago night—of the marijuana; of Alena's reckless decision to sit on the top of the backseat of the convertible; of the sudden high-speed dip that sent her flying into a ditch; of their trek through the night to the wooded property Erika's neighbors owned to dispose of the body—Lisa's vision began to blur. Her rhythm faltered, and one foot slipped out of the strap on the bike pedal.

"Having a little trouble?" Jessica took a step toward her.

"You know I am." If she exaggerated the symptoms, she might be able to lull the woman into a false sense of security. Draw her closer.

Jessica tut-tutted. "You should monitor your blood sugar more carefully. Letting it drop too low can be very dangerous. Fatal, even."

"You do realize that three accidents are going to be a lot for the authorities to swallow."

The woman gave her a smug smile. "Ah, but I'm very good at making accidents happen. No one found a thing to suggest the deaths of Erika and Joe were anything more than tragic mishaps. Nor will they with you. Exploiting your enemy's weakness is a classic battle strategy—and every enemy has one. Combined with careful research and planning, the technique works every time. Great leaders have—"

Headlights swept across the front of the house.

Lisa stopped pedaling.

Keeping the gun aimed straight at her, Jessica backed up to the front window. Eased the blinds a whisper away. Muttered an oath.

"It's a Carson cop car. Why would one of your cops be coming here at this hour?"

"I have . . . no idea." She pretended to have difficulty forming her words—but they were true. There would be no reason for one of the Carson police cars to be in her driveway.

Unless . . .

Might Mac have gotten worried when she didn't answer his call? He'd been phoning every night around nine-thirty. The land line had rung too—a follow-up after he'd been unable to reach her by cell? Had he somehow contacted one of her guys, asked him to swing by?

Or was she grasping at straws?

God, please let this be more than desperate wishful thinking!

Jessica edged closer. Not close enough to risk a lunge, but close enough for Lisa to see the hate in her eyes. "Don't move a muscle." The directive came out in a whispered hiss.

As they waited in silence, a crack of thunder rattled the walls. On the heels of that came Tally's faint, mournful wail.

No other sound intruded on the room—until the doorbell rang.

Jessica extended her arm straight out, putting the gun less than four feet away from Lisa's face.

She remained motionless—but she had to get off this bike soon. Free her arms and legs so she could lunge the instant an opportunity presented itself.

The bell rang again.

Silence as the minutes ticked by.

One.

Two.

Three.

Jessica returned to the window, raised the edge of the blinds a hair, and flicked her attention back and forth between the stationary bike and the driveway.

She was too far away now to rush. That would be suicide.

Lisa remained frozen, using as little energy as possible. Her blood sugar was dropping into the danger zone quickly, thanks to all this exercise. She needed to get some glucose into her system.

Fast.

Meaning she had to make her move very soon, before she became too weak and disoriented.

And before Jessica got any more nervous.

A bead of sweat had formed on the woman's temple. As Lisa watched, it began to trickle down the side of her face.

The cop visit had spooked her.

Big time.

She wasn't going to want to hang around here much longer. She'd try to accelerate this process.

In silence, Lisa prayed for inspiration and strength . . . and added a plea for mercy and forgiveness in case this was the night God planned to call her home.

—◆—

At the vibration of his cell, Mac yanked the device off his belt. Shelton's name flashed on the screen instead of Lisa's.

Not what he'd hoped to see.

Pressing the phone to his ear, he got straight to the point. "What did you find?"

"She's not answering the door. There are lights on in the house, though, and Tally's in the backyard pen. It's not like her to leave him out in a storm. He hates loud noise."

Mac grabbed his keys off the counter and strode toward the door. "Is her car there?"

"I can't tell. There aren't any windows in the garage, and it's shut up tight."

He let himself out and took off at a jog for his car. "Did you do a perimeter check?"

"Yeah. Everything seems okay, except for Tally being outside."

"Where are you now?"

"Still in the driveway."

As he reached his car and slid behind the wheel, Mac did some fast thinking. Tally's noise aversion was news to him, but Lisa loved that dog. She'd never leave him outside with thunder rumbling and a storm approaching.

He was getting very bad vibes.

After switching the phone to hands-free, he started the engine and put the car in gear. "I'm on my way. My gut says this needs to be investigated."

"You think this has something to do with the bones case you and the chief have been working on?"

"I don't know." How could it, with Jessica Lee out of town? Unless she wasn't.

Was it possible their attempt to smoke her out had worked too well? Backfired, even?

If so, Lisa was in danger because of him; it had been his idea to ratchet up the pressure.

Stomach twisting, he pressed harder on the accelerator.

"Have you had any other cases in Carson serious enough to provoke violence or revenge?"

"No. The biggest thing we've had in months is the Fourth of July debacle with the underage drinkers, but I think the whole experience scared some sense into all of them. What's your ETA?"

"Best case, fifteen minutes." Thank goodness he lived in Ballwin and not some closer-in suburb.

"You want me to wait here, in the driveway?"

He tightened his grip on the wheel as he wove through the slower-moving vehicles. Wasn't anyone in a hurry tonight except him? "Do one more perimeter check. Leave the headlights on, but don't use a flashlight. No reason to make yourself a target. If someone's hanging around, I just want to distract them from whatever they're doing inside."

As he issued the clipped instructions, he pulled around another car. "I'll call you once I'm five minutes away and we can meet behind that church across the street. Pull out with your headlights on, but after you're on the street and driving away from the house, kill them. If anything happens in the meantime, call me."

"Got it. You want me to call in a couple of the other officers?"

"No. Let me get a read on the situation first in case we're overreacting."

Besides, he didn't want a bunch of unseasoned cops mucking up the situation. Lisa's officers might be as solid as she claimed, but if things got dicey, he'd rather have reinforcements from County.

Hopefully, it wouldn't come to that.

But as he sped through the night, he had a feeling *dicey* might be way too tame a word for whatever was going on at Lisa's house.

⬥

"Finally."

As the headlights from the car arced across the blinds, signaling the officer's departure, Jessica swiped her forehead with the sleeve of her black top.

"Sweat contains DNA, you know." Lisa's vision was going in and out of focus, and she gripped the handlebar tighter. But it was difficult to hang on. Her fingers were getting numb, and the steady pounding in her head had intensified.

"Shut up." Jessica Lee glared at her and motioned to the bike. "Start pedaling again. Faster than before."

Tightening her fingers on the handlebar, she took a deep breath. The only plan she'd been able to come up with to draw Jessica closer wasn't great, but she was out of time. She had to give it a try and hope for the best.

"I said pedal."

"I'm trying, but I think the . . . the mechanism . . . is stuck." Slurring her words and stumbling over her phrasing might help convince the woman she was in worse shape than she actually was.

"Try again."

"I can't . . . get it . . . to move." She let one foot slip out of the strap on the pedal.

Jessica edged closer. "Fine. We'll use the treadmill. Get off the bike. Hurry."

Her limbs felt weak and clumsy, but again she exaggerated the problem, listing to the side and grabbing hold of her weight bench as she staggered across the room. Thankfully it was in the upright position. She stopped and hung her head. One of her ten-pound dumbbells was within reach.

"Keep walking."

"I'm too . . . dizzy." She blinked, trying to maintain focus, keeping tabs on Jessica out of the corner of her eye.

The woman was close enough now to give this a shot.

Her adrenaline surged.

"Then we should be about done."

"Yeah. I think . . . we are." Pretending to lose her balance, she dropped her right shoulder in a half stagger.

Jessica lowered the gun.

Now!

Praying her strength would hold and her legs wouldn't fold, she grabbed the dumbbell, straightened up, and swung it hard to her left.

Though Jessica tried to shield herself from the blow, the dumbbell connected with her gun arm. As she howled in pain, the Beretta flew out of her hand and slid across the hardwood floor.

Face contorted, cradling her arm, Jessica rushed toward it.

Lisa tackled her at the knees.

The woman went down hard—and with another wail of pain. Still, she tried to writhe out of Lisa's grasp.

But Lisa didn't let go.

She needed to get to the gun first and subdue the woman.

And along the way, she needed to make certain there was clear evidence of Jessica's presence in this room—in case things went south. No way was the woman getting away with another murder.

Dragging herself up the woman's body, she clawed at her cheek, drawing blood.

Jessica shrieked and tried to protect herself with one arm.

The other one appeared to be useless. But she had a powerful kick, and it was connecting solidly with Lisa's legs.

Strength fading fast, she managed to yank off the woman's baseball cap. As they grappled on the floor, she wrapped her fist around a length of hair and yanked. Hard. The woman's head snapped back, and she twisted, trying to free herself.

By the time Jessica wrenched free, Lisa was fairly certain she'd tugged out enough hair follicles to give the crime scene technicians plenty to find.

As the other woman scrambled after the gun, Lisa grabbed her ankle and yanked. Jessica fell on her injured arm with a moan.

Somehow Lisa managed to crawl past her and reach the gun first. But her fingers refused to close around the grip. As she fumbled with the Beretta, waves of blackness washed over her, and the world began to fade.

Behind her, she heard Jessica moving again.

Toward her.

She tried to press the magazine release button. If her fingers wouldn't let her use the gun, maybe she could pull out the bullets and render it more difficult to fire—especially if Jessica's right arm wasn't functional.

Since there was no sensation in her fingers, she pressed everywhere on the handle, hoping to hit the button.

If the magazine released, however, she couldn't tell.

And she was out of time.

Jessica was behind her, left hand stretching toward the Beretta. Palming the compact gun, Lisa held it as tight as she could.

Then, rolling away, she twisted around. Jessica was already crawling toward her, supporting herself on her usable arm. That left her with no arm to defend herself.

Hand extended, Lisa rotated toward her, aiming the side of the gun at her head.

The metal connected with her temple. Hard.

Jessica's lashes fluttered, and she fell sideways.

But she didn't pass out. Though her eyes were unfocused, they were open. Meaning she could mount another attack.

Except there'd be no need.

Because the edges of Lisa's consciousness were blurring. The dark vortex of insulin shock was sucking her down, down, down. In seconds, she was going to pass out.

Her gaze strayed to the cabinet on the far wall. There were glucose pills in there. And hard candy. Either could save her life.

Yet they might as well be a continent away.

As the last glimmers of awareness faded, as her eyelids flickered closed, three emotions swept over her in quick succession.

Peace in the knowledge that, no matter what, God was with her.

Regret that she and Mac would never have a chance to explore the shining future she'd envisioned.

And satisfaction that Jessica Lee would at last be brought to justice.

26

Mac killed his headlights as he approached Lisa's driveway, cut his speed, and bypassed her house to pull into the church parking lot. The Carson cruiser was on the far side of the steepled building, and Craig Shelton slid out of the car when he braked.

The wind had picked up during his drive, the gusts bending the tops of the trees that lined the rural road. Shouldering the door open, he kept a firm grip on the handle as the wind tried to rip it from his fingers. Sporadic drops of rain were beginning to splatter the pavement, and a slash of lightning was quickly followed by a loud boom of thunder.

This storm was about to hit.

As he joined the other man, a mournful wail keened in the distance.

"Tally." Craig peered into the darkness. "He is one unhappy dog."

A serious red flag. Lisa loved that dog. No way would she abandon him in a storm like this—if she could help it.

"Anything else happen since we talked?"

"The neighbors on the right pulled in. They must have been out for the evening. The light's still on in the same room at the

339

chief's house. If you walk forward a few feet, you can get a glimpse of it through the trees."

Mac did as the man suggested. A glimmer was barely visible through the dense, midsummer foliage. "Any idea what room that is?"

"Her home gym. She hosted a department Christmas party last year, and I saw it on my way to the bathroom."

"Any other lights on in the house?"

"The kitchen's lit up."

"Could you see inside?"

"No. All the blinds are shut tight."

"Okay. Let's leave the cars here. I want to take a look around. I assume you tested the back door when you did your perimeter check?"

"Yeah. It's locked."

"While I do some scouting, see if the neighbors happen to have a key. She might have left one with them for emergencies. If they don't come through, I'll find another way in."

Like breaking a window.

Lisa might be miffed if it turned out he'd overreacted, but he was willing to risk her ire. In fact, he'd welcome it. Incurring her annoyance would mean everything was okay.

That *she* was okay.

"Where do you want to meet?" Craig rested his hand on his holster.

"Driveway side of her house in ten. Keep your phone handy."

"Roger." The man took off at a fast jog for the neighbor's house while Mac headed for Lisa's.

The rain intensified, dampening the earth, and he dodged a muddy patch—praying that the worst outcome this night would be a bad case of mud on the face.

This was all wrong.

Jessica blinked, trying to clear her vision. She attempted to lift her right arm, but it hung limp at her side. Moisture slid down her cheek, and when she swiped at it, her left hand came away crimson.

There was blood on the floor too.

Her blood.

Because as far as she could tell, the police chief wasn't bleeding.

But she wasn't moving, either. Meaning that part of her plan had worked.

The rest . . . not so much.

Still, she could fix this. Jessica Lee was a problem solver extraordinaire.

Mouth set, she struggled to stand. But the room tilted, and her legs collapsed as a wave of nausea swept over her.

Closing her eyes, she willed the bile to subside. Strained to clear the fuzziness from her brain. But no matter how hard she tried to get her body under control, vomit continued to claw at her throat and she couldn't organize her thoughts.

Her heart began to pound. Harder than it had the night Alena started this whole thing with her stupid stunt. That had been a mess—but this was a catastrophe. Back then, she'd had help. And she hadn't been hurt. Could she drive the car with one arm, even if she managed to get to it with the ground spongy as a trampoline beneath her?

Yet what choice did she have? Staying here wasn't an option. Nor could she leave any evidence of her visit.

She surveyed the room, swallowing past her queasiness, trying to focus. She had to clean up the blood that had dripped on the floor. She had to retrieve her gun, wherever it had skidded across the floor. She had to find some paper towels and floor cleaner.

The list of things to be done made her head hurt—and her arm was throbbing too.

Tears pricked her eyes.

Hand shaking, she dashed them away.

She hadn't come this far to end up a failure, like her father. She was Jessica Lee, vice president of one of the most prestigious PR firms in the country. She'd worked hard. Masterfully played the corporate game. Dispatched every obstacle that threatened her plan. Her smarts, grit, and drive had destined her for greatness.

Until Lisa Grant began poking into things better left alone.

She glowered at the motionless, prone form a few feet away. Once again, the woman had complicated things.

But she'd paid the price.

When Jessica Lee developed a plan, it didn't fail—and tonight wasn't going to change that record.

Resolve spurring her on, she struggled to her feet and staggered toward the kitchen in search of cleaning supplies.

◆

"The neighbors had a key for the back door." Craig held it up as he joined Mac at the side of the house.

"That will make things easier. Here's how I want to play this. Go back to your car and pull in here again. I want all the attention focused on the front of the house. Bang on the door, call out—but stay off to the side."

"You think someone in there has a weapon?" A hint of anxiety ran through the officer's voice as his hand moved to his holster.

"I don't know—but let's not take any chances. I'll let myself in the back. Keep up the diversion until I flip the light in the exercise room on and off. Then join me through the back door. Got it?"

"Yeah."

"I'll wait here until you pull in. The minute you start banging, I'll go in. Hurry."

The man took instructions well. He didn't just jog down the drive; he sprinted.

Nevertheless, it felt like an eon passed before the lights of his car appeared through the trees on the long, curving drive.

The instant they did, Mac circled to the back of the house, his Sig Sauer at the ready, as it had been since he'd begun his trek up the driveway. The rain was coming down steady now, but so far the deluge had held off. The lightning and thunder, however, were intensifying.

As he let himself through the gate, Tally's whimper beseeched through the darkness.

Thank goodness the dog didn't bark.

He moved to the back door. Fitted the key in the lock as quietly as he could. Waited.

A car door slammed, and ten seconds later Craig began banging on the door.

His cue.

Twisting the key, he eased the door open a crack. The kitchen light was still on, but the room was deserted.

Finger poised on the trigger, he stepped across the threshold and shut the door behind him.

From inside, Craig's banging was wall-shaking. It would cover the noise of his movements—but also those of anyone else.

He crossed the kitchen, pistol aimed at the doorway to the hall . . . but no one appeared.

The small foyer and living room were dark. Too bad he didn't have the night vision goggles that had saved his life on more than one occasion as a SEAL.

But the rooms didn't offer any sizeable hiding places, and they appeared to be deserted. The activity seemed to be centered in the exercise room, which provided the only light spilling into the hall.

Staying close to the wall, he covered the short distance to the doorway.

From inside, he could hear movement—and an odd sound. Like . . . someone using a spray bottle?

Furrowing his brow, he stole a look around the side of the door frame—and froze at the tableau.

Jessica Lee was on her knees, scrubbing blood off the hardwood floor, a gun lying within snatching distance.

And Lisa was crumpled on the floor, on her stomach, still as death.

No!

In the couple of seconds it took for him to complete his sweep, Jessica lifted her head. Blood had dripped down her face, past her glazed eyes. Her mascara was smeared, giving her a ghoulish appearance. And one arm hung limp.

Lisa hadn't gone down without a fight.

As his sudden appearance registered, Jessica scrambled for the Beretta.

But he was faster—and in better shape.

He covered the distance between them in two sprints and kicked the weapon out of her hand.

When she started to go after it again, he pointed his Sig at her. "Don't even think about it."

Keeping her in his sights, he backed up and flipped the light switch in the room.

She squinted at him, confusion twisting her features.

"Stay where you are." He dropped down beside Lisa, praying as he'd never prayed before while he pressed his fingers against her carotid artery.

A very faint pulse whispered against his fingertips.

Thank you, God!

Craig strode into the room, gun drawn.

"Secure her." Mac tipped his head toward Jessica and punched in 911 as Craig proned out the other woman and cuffed her. Once the dispatch operator answered, he gave clipped instructions for County police backup, two ambulances, and the Crime Scene Unit. When the operator asked for an assessment of the victims' condition, he turned his back on Jessica and focused on Lisa. He couldn't care less about the other woman's injuries. "Hang on while I look her over."

He set his cell on the ground and gave her a swift but thorough once-over. There was no sign of a wound on her back. He ran his hands over her scalp. No bumps or contusions.

Gently he rolled her over and inspected her body.

No blood.

But something was seriously wrong.

He swung toward Jessica. "What did you do to her?"

The woman was lying on her stomach, head turned toward him, eyes open. Her lips were moving, but her words were gibberish. She seemed to be in some weird trancelike state.

He wasn't going to get anything out of her.

Think, McGregor!

He gave the room a quick survey. It was a gym, just like Craig had said, and Lisa was in her exercise clothes.

His gaze caught on her slender medical alert ankle bracelet.

She was diabetic.

Jessica's modus operandi was to use existing conditions against her victims. Make murder seem like an accident.

She must have forced Lisa to do something that would put her in insulin shock—the very condition Lisa had once told him could be deadly.

His heart skipped a beat. While his SEAL medical training had been excellent for battlefield conditions, it hadn't covered this kind of emergency.

"Craig . . . do you know anything about treating insulin shock?"

"No. Is that what's wrong with the chief?"

"I think so. She needs sugar." He leaned down and gave her a gentle shake. "Lisa. Can you hear me?" If he could coax her to consciousness, the hard candy she'd told him she always had on hand might help her hold on until the paramedics arrived.

No response.

He picked up the phone again and relayed Lisa's condition to the operator. "Is there anything I can do to help her until the paramedics get here?"

"Can you rouse her enough to give her some sugar?"

"No. I tried."

"Is there any evidence of seizures? Thrashing movements or stiffening of the arms or legs?"

"No. But she's pale, and her skin is cool and clammy."

"Turn her on her side, angled slightly toward the floor. Keep checking her pulse and respiration. Are you CPR trained?"

"Yes."

"Monitor her and sit tight. The paramedics have been dispatched. Their ETA is less than ten minutes."

A lifetime.

For a man who'd taken out Taliban insurgents, directed underwater demolition crews through heavily mined areas, and crawled on his belly during high-risk reconnaissance missions in the mountains of Afghanistan, sitting tight wasn't in his DNA.

But this was one enemy he wasn't equipped to fight. He had to wait for the experts.

Mac folded Lisa's cold hand in his and leaned close to check her breathing. "Hang on, sweetheart. Help is coming."

While they waited, the room fell silent. Craig kept a close watch on Jessica, but the woman was zoned out, muttering and moaning. Except for the rumble of thunder and Tally's howls, no other sound intruded on the heavy stillness.

The minutes crawled by, until at last, in the far distance, sirens soared over the thunder.

It was the sweetest sound he'd ever heard.

"Why don't you go unlock the front door and direct them in? I've got her covered." Mac trained his Sig on Jessica.

"Roger." Craig skirted the woman, who appeared to be oblivious to the activity around her.

Hard to believe the disheveled, babbling figure on the floor was the same designer-dressed, high-powered, in-control PR executive they'd interviewed at Peterson-Bradshaw. The woman had totally crumbled.

The paramedics arrived first, and Mac gave them a quick briefing on Lisa. The County officers were on their heels, and he brought them up to speed so they could secure the scene for the Crime Scene Unit as the paramedics went to work.

By the time he dropped down beside Lisa again, they'd already pricked her finger, fed a strip into a glucometer, and started an IV.

"Any idea how long she's been unconscious?" One of the paramedics tossed the question over his shoulder as he applied a blood pressure cuff.

"No." But Jessica knew. "Let me see if I can find out."

Another paramedic team was working on the other woman, but he inserted himself into the group and leaned close. Right into her face.

"When did Lisa lose consciousness, Jessica?" He spoke slowly, enunciating each word.

No response.

He gripped her shoulder. Tight. She let out a small moan.

"Hey!" One of the paramedics grabbed his arm. "She's hurt, man."

He skewered the guy with an icy look and shook him off. "She's also a murderer—at least twice over. I'm trying to keep her from succeeding with number three." Without giving the man a chance to respond, he increased the pressure on her shoulder. It was amazing how a little pain could clarify thinking. "Jessica—when did Lisa lose consciousness?"

Some of the haze in her eyes dissipated. "Maybe . . . ten o'clock."

He released her shoulder and moved back to Lisa. "About half an hour ago."

The paramedic gave a curt nod but offered nothing more as he continued to swab Lisa's skin with alcohol and attach electrodes to her wrists, ankles, and chest.

Mac summoned up the courage to voice the question he didn't want to ask. "Could she die?"

"I hope not." The other technician began connecting the lead wires for the EKG as the first guy responded to him. "But her blood sugar is only nineteen, and insulin shock is dangerous. It can cause a bunch of problems."

"Like what?"

"Seizures, stroke, organ shutdown, cardiac arrest, brain damage."

As the man ticked off the list, every word was like a punch in the gut.

The guy spared him a quick once-over. "You're law enforcement, aren't you?" He homed in on the holster.

"Yeah. But also a friend."

The man's expression softened. "I gave you worst case. Those would be more likely with longer-term insulin shock. If she's been out less than an hour, my guess is she'll start to come to any minute, recover fast, and be none the worse for wear."

As the man refocused on his patient, Mac studied him. Was he telling the truth or just working on his bedside manner?

He wanted to believe it was the former, but as he examined the nasty scar marring Lisa's left shoulder, he also prayed.

Because this woman had suffered enough—and they had a future together to plan.

◆

"I think she's coming around."

The words registered deep in Lisa's subconscious, rising

above the background cacophony of unfamiliar voices and odd noises.

She'd know that rich baritone anywhere.

Mac was here.

Her hand was taken in a warm, tender clasp, and the undulating world around her steadied. Stabilized.

Definitely Mac.

Squeezing his fingers, she kept her eyes closed as she tried to quell the slight roiling in her stomach and convince her brain to engage.

"Lisa . . . sweetheart . . . can you hear me? Can you open your eyes?"

For him . . . anything.

She blinked herself awake.

Mac was there, but he wasn't alone. Paramedics were hovering over her. In the background, uniformed County police officers milled about. Craig was off to the side. Another tall, lean guy in jeans stood in the far corner, posture relaxed but eyes on full alert. He looked familiar . . . but she couldn't place him.

Yet all at once the events of the night snapped into sharp focus. "Where's Jessica?"

Mac stroked a thumb over the back of her hand. "Another set of paramedics is working on her. You put up quite a fight."

"Yeah—but I thought I'd lost." Her voice choked.

The pressure of his fingers tightened. "The only loser here tonight is going to spend a long, long time behind bars."

Over the noise in the room, she heard the back door open. A crash of thunder shook the house. Tally let out a desperate wail.

Tally!

"Mac." She clutched his fingers. "Please, would you get Tally? He hates storms. You can put him in the basement."

He hesitated, but after a moment he released her hand—with obvious reluctance. "I'll be right back."

He rose and disappeared out the door, while one of the paramedics picked up her other hand. "Quick prick."

"I'm used to it." She watched as he fed the test strip into a glucometer. "How low was it?"

"Nineteen."

She swallowed. "Ouch."

"More than ouch—but it's rising fast. You're already at fifty-five."

"Sugar direct to the vein works every time."

"You've shocked out before?"

"Once. In a similar traumatic situation, before I was diagnosed. I'm well versed these days on keeping the disease under control—under normal circumstances."

A happy yip sounded at the back of the house, and behind her a woman shrieked.

"No dog! No dog!"

Had those hysteria-laced words come from Jessica?

Sounds of thrashing followed, and she tried to look behind her. But her view was blocked as several officers converged on the source of the disturbance.

A pair of jeans-clad legs moved past her field of vision, and Mac dropped down beside her.

"Is Tally okay?"

"Wet but fine." He glanced over at Jessica. "Weird that a dog would freak out the woman of steel."

"I guess we all have our Achilles' heels—and she certainly knew how to take advantage of other people's."

Mac's face hardened. "She won't be doing that again for a lot of years . . . if ever."

"We're set. Let's transport."

Behind her, she heard rustling, and then the sounds diminished as the other team of paramedics exited, accompanied by a couple of the officers.

"We're about ready to move here too." One of the technicians who'd been working on her spoke to his partner.

Lisa shook her head. "I don't need to go to the hospital."

The technician sent her a dubious look, and Mac took her hand. "Yes, you do. You have insulin shock."

"Had. In another few minutes, my blood sugar will be out of the danger range." She shifted her attention to the technician monitoring her EKG and blood pressure. "Any problems with those?" She motioned toward the equipment.

"No. Your heart is fine. Blood pressure's within the normal range. But it wouldn't hurt to let the ER monitor you for a few hours."

"Other than a slight headache, I feel fine. I want to stay home."

"There's going to be a lot of activity here, Lisa. The Crime Scene Unit is on the way." Mac kept a firm grip on her hand. Like he had no intention of letting go anytime soon.

Which was fine with her.

"This is the only room we were in, except for cutting through the kitchen. My bedroom and office and bathroom are clean—in an evidence sense. I can't vouch for the dust."

At her touch of humor, the taut line of his shoulders relaxed a hair. "Not into housekeeping?"

She grimaced. "Not my favorite sport. There are much more interesting things to do in what little free time I have. And even more interesting things in the future, I hope." Her gaze locked with his. Fused.

His heated up. "Count on it."

The lead paramedic rejoined the conversation. "Um, I would still strongly recommend a trip to the ER. You should continue to monitor your blood sugar for the next few hours, and you can't do that if you're sleeping."

Mac's gaze never left hers. "She could if someone woke her up."

A man who was willing to give up a night's sleep to keep her safe and well.

A keeper, no question about it.

But he was tired. Asking him to do that would be selfish.

"No." Lisa shook her head. "I don't expect you to hang around all night." She tried to look stern, but it was hard with her heart singing a joyful song.

"Me or the ER. Take your pick."

Hmm. When he put it that way . . .

She let her frown morph into a smile. "No contest."

"Can you two hang around until we're certain she's out of danger?" Mac included both paramedics in his question.

"Sure. Once she hits eighty or eighty-five—probably in the next five or ten minutes—we should be good to go." He shifted his attention back to her. "While we wait, we'll clean you up a little."

The paramedic lifted her hand, and she noticed the blood. Not hers. "I guess we won't need the DNA under my fingernails for evidence, since I survived. I ruined my manicure for nothing."

Mac didn't respond, and she looked over at him.

He was *not* smiling.

So much for her attempt at humor.

"Do you feel up to giving a statement?" He continued to stroke his thumb over the back of her hand.

"Sure."

He motioned to the jeans-clad guy in the corner, who pushed off from the wall, crossed the room, and dropped down to their level beside the stretcher.

"Lisa, I think you've met Mitch Morgan."

Now his identity clicked into place.

"Yes. The other half of the M&Ms."

Mitch arched an eyebrow at Mac, as if to say, *"She knows about that?"*

For the first time in their acquaintance, Mac seemed embarrassed. "It, uh, just came up in conversation."

"Just came up in conversation. Right." The man turned back to her, pulled out a notebook and pen, and smiled. "I know you've done this a thousand times."

"From the other end of the pen. Do you want to record this?"

He extracted a small digital recorder from his other pocket. "I came prepared when Mac called—even if it is practically the middle of the night and he woke up my wife." He regarded Mac. "Alison will be sure to remind you of that next time your paths cross at the courthouse."

"I'll mollify her with a Ted Drewes."

"A frozen custard bribe, huh?" The other man flashed him a grin. "That'll work." He started the recorder, gave the date, location, and other pertinent details, then launched into the interview.

Lisa provided a detailed recounting of the evening's events, including Jessica's admission of culpability in the deaths of Erika and Joe.

After he finished jotting his notes, Mitch switched off the recorder. "Unfortunately, her confession won't be admissible until she's Mirandized."

"And the high-priced attorney she'll hire won't let her admit a thing. But tonight's murder attempt is a different story." Mac touched her cheek. "We have a witness."

Mitch looked between the two of them, closed the notebook, and stood. "I'll hang around until the CSU tech gets here."

Mac nodded. "Thanks."

The paramedics finished as the other detective disappeared from her line of sight, and she laced her fingers with Mac's. "Quite a night, huh?"

He blew out a breath. "Yeah. Quite a night."

"At least we have answers to all our questions now."

"There is that."

"And I'm counting the hours until Saturday night."

Some of the tension in his features melted away. "Are you sure you'll be up to that?"

"Are you looking for an excuse to cancel?"

His eyes darkened and he moved in close. A mere whisper away. "Not a chance, Chief. Saturday belongs to me. And then we'll talk about all the Saturdays after that . . . and the Sundays, and the weeknights, and the holidays."

"Are you trying to monopolize me, Detective McGregor?"

"Guilty as charged. Any objections?"

Chuckling, she squeezed his hand. "Not a one."

Epilogue

Five Months Later

As Bing Crosby crooned "White Christmas" and Mac torqued over an icy spot on the snow-covered rural road, his cell began to vibrate.

After taming the SUV, he pulled the phone out of his pocket. Peering at the dark road through the monster flakes of swirling snow battering his window, he felt for the talk button. "McGregor."

"Yo, bro. Special Agent Lance McGregor here."

One corner of Mac's mouth hitched up. "How'd the graduation go?"

"Like any graduation. A lot of boring speeches."

Despite Lance's dismissive tone, graduation from the FBI Academy was a big deal—and he'd hated to miss it. "Sorry I didn't get there. I waited at the airport for hours, hoping they'd reopen, but the place is shut down tight with this storm. Did Mom and Dad make it?"

"Front row center—or as close as they could get to the primo seats. Finn emailed a message too."

Grinning, Mac skirted another icy patch. "Lay it on me. I'm

in a laughing mood." Whatever Finn had come up with by way of best wishes, it was sure to be amusing and irreverent.

"He said congrats and good luck."

Mac squinted. "That's it? Nothing funny?"

"No. We need to have a talk with that boy on his next leave. I think he's lost his sense of humor."

Living in a war zone could do that to a person . . . yet Finn had held on to his penchant for puns and witty jests until the past few months. He might always have been less vocal than his older siblings—probably because they'd never given him a chance to get a word in edgewise—but his pithy zingers were legendary in the McGregor clan.

"Any idea when he's coming home again?"

"I haven't been able to pin him down. I take it you haven't, either."

"No."

"Well, if he's got something on his mind, we'll wrestle it out of him the next time we get together. So the storm's still going strong out there?"

"Yeah." He forced himself to put his worries aside. He wasn't going to let anything siphon one iota of joy from his evening. Not Finn, not the storm, not the latest homicide case he'd been handed. This Saturday night belonged to him—and Lisa.

"I better pack my snowshoes, then."

Mac refocused on the conversation as he flicked on the turn signal for Lisa's driveway. "What do you mean?"

"Guess which FBI field office will be graced with my presence for my first assignment?"

Mac mashed down the brake and brought the SUV to a dead stop. This deserved his full attention. "You're coming to St. Louis?"

"Yeah. And I need a place to crash until I find my own digs. Your couch available?"

"You're coming to St. Louis?" He couldn't quite wrap his mind around the unexpected news.

"You losing your hearing in your old age?" Lance chuckled. "Yes, you're going to be saddled with one of your younger brothers again—like when we were kids."

"No complaints on my end." Mac's throat tightened. "Man, what a Christmas present." Almost as good as the other one he hoped to receive before this day ended.

"For me too." Lance cleared the hoarseness out of his voice. "Anyway, I'll be arriving a few days after Christmas. I thought we could ring in the new year together . . . unless you already have plans."

"Lisa and I are going over to Mitch's. It'll be us, plus all of his wife's family. I know you'd be welcome."

"Any single women in the group?"

"Sorry."

"No sweat. I'll have plenty of time to scout out the territory once I get acclimated. Count me in."

"I'll let Mitch know. You're going to Mom and Dad's for Christmas, right?"

"Yeah. Too bad you couldn't get away."

"I'm too new to have much vacation accrued, and Christmas falling on a Wednesday doesn't help. Maybe next year." He moved his foot from the brake to the gas pedal and edged forward again, tires crunching on the snow.

"We'll call you during the day."

"I hope so. And congratulations again, Special Agent Mc-Gregor."

"Thanks. See you soon, bro."

As the call disconnected, Mac slid the phone back into his pocket. Then he felt the inside pocket of his sport coat, near his heart, where the small box wrapped in silver foil rested.

Tonight was the night.

And if all went as he hoped, his status would change from single to engaged before this evening was over.

◆

"Sit, Tally. He'll be here in a minute." Lisa peered through the back window as the Explorer's headlights swept across her garage. "Is it Mac you love, or those gourmet treats he always brings you?"

The dog parked his haunches, looked up at her, and cocked his head as if puzzling over the question.

She, on the other hand, had no doubt about the reason for *her* enthusiasm. Mac might be bringing dinner so they didn't have to brave the elements for their pre-Christmas feast, but it was the man, not the meal, that set her heart dancing.

When he appeared out of the night, head bent against the wind, she pulled the door open.

He entered in a blustery whorl of white flakes, and she shut the door fast. In just the short walk from his Explorer, he'd become a veritable snowman.

She took the large Art of Entertaining shopping bag from his hands as Tally nuzzled his fingers, the pup's vigorous tail-wagging making his whole body vibrate. "Someone's been waiting very eagerly for you."

Before she could move away to set the bag on the counter, he grabbed her hand and tugged her close. Snowflakes clung to his hair and eyelashes, glistening like stars. Or were the stars in *her* eyes? "Is he the only one?"

At his husky question, she snuggled closer. So what if she got a little cold and wet from the snow on his jacket? Mac would warm her up.

"I've been counting the hours. You did promise me a gourmet dinner."

He grinned. "That'll put me in my place."

She slid her arms around his neck. "Why don't we start with dessert?"

"Mmm." He pulled her close. "I like how you think."

He dipped his head; she closed her eyes. No question about it. Having dessert first was an inspired idea.

Much too soon, however, a wet nose wormed its way between them.

With obvious reluctance, Mac straightened up.

Lisa sighed but didn't relinquish her hold. "He's waiting for his treat."

"So was I."

Fluttering her eyelashes, she eased back. "The night is young."

"That sounds promising." He dug in his pocket and pulled out two biscuits for Tally, who scarfed them down with a happy woof.

"He's your friend for life, you know."

Mac slid his hand under her hair and cupped the back of her neck. "How about his owner?"

"More than." At the warmth in his eyes—and some other nuance that sent a trill of excitement through her—she tipped her head. "You seem especially happy tonight, despite what had to be a white-knuckled trek through the storm."

"I am." He shrugged out of his jacket and draped it on a kitchen chair by the heat register. "I just talked to Lance. He's been assigned to the St. Louis office."

"Oh, Mac! That's fabulous news!" Better than fabulous. Over these past few months, she'd come to appreciate how much Mac loved—and worried about—his brothers. Having one close by would alleviate some of that concern.

"I have to admit, it was a great Christmas present."

"So we have something special to celebrate tonight."

"Yeah. Celebrating is definitely on my agenda for the evening."

Unable to interpret his enigmatic look, she moved over to the bag on the counter. "What goodies did you bring us?"

"All safe stuff." He strolled over.

She read the labels as she pulled out the containers. "Lime and cilantro shrimp kabobs. Artichoke and sun-dried tomato salad. Chicken Florentine. Grilled asparagus. White and wild rice medley. Whole wheat rolls. And . . . is that chocolate cream pie?" She peered into the clear container at the bottom of the bag.

"Yep. The clerk assured me even the graham crackers in the crust are sugar-free."

"Wow." She surveyed the feast spread out on the counter. "You went to a lot of trouble—and in this storm too. I can't believe the place was open."

"They shut down at noon. I got there at eleven fifty-five. And for you, nothing is too much trouble." After a moment, he tempered the heat in his eyes with a wink. "Besides, since I met you, I'm learning to eat a lot healthier myself."

"I'm glad our relationship has been beneficial for your waistline."

"At the very least."

"Likewise." Smiling, she motioned toward the living room. "I set a table by the fire. Would you like to take the kabobs in there and relax for a few minutes after the drive, before we dive into dinner?"

"Sounds good. I'll get the drinks. Your usual?"

"Yes. Thanks."

While he filled the glasses with ice, Lisa crossed the room and picked up the newspaper she'd retrieved earlier at the base of the driveway. Not that she wanted to introduce unpleasant topics—but the story was on her mind. And it would stay there until they talked it through. "Did you see today's *Post*?"

"No. I was on the run all day. Why?"

"I dug it out of the snow an hour ago and paged through." She handed him the turned-back paper. "Jessica's still making the news."

He set the glasses aside and read the brief article. "I'm not surprised she's appealing—but if you ask me, she got off easy. She should have gotten life, not a mere twenty years."

"She obviously doesn't agree—and she's got a sharp attorney. I've run into Deb Shapiro on occasion. One tough cookie, let me tell you. If anyone can get Jessica off, it's her." She tried to mask her concern, but as usual Mac picked up on her mood.

He folded up the paper and set it aside. "Not going to happen. I was there during your testimony, and you told a compelling story. Plus, no one can refute the evidence. We might not have been able to get the charges for Erika and Joe to stick, but she's going to serve time for attempted murder." There wasn't one smidgeon of uncertainty in his tone.

"I hope you're right."

"I am."

Her anxiety dissipated. Mac didn't sugarcoat—and he had sound instincts. She'd take his word for it . . . and trust in God that justice would be done.

Shrimp skewers in hand, she retrieved some cocktail napkins. "You know, even after all these months, I find it hard to believe she tried to kill me." A muscle in Mac's jaw flicked at her blunt words, but she'd never been one to dance around reality. It was what it was. "I mean, if she'd simply backed off and played it cool, she'd have been home-free. We were ready to shut down the case."

"Except you turned her world upside down—and a thirst for revenge can short-circuit reason. Plus, her other plots succeeded. Maybe she figured she was invincible. Problem was, she didn't factor in the thing that set you apart from her other victims."

Lisa paused on her way to the living room and flashed him a grin. "You mean my superior intelligence and superwoman crime-fighting skills?"

"Absolutely." Then he grew more serious. "But you also have a close circle of family and friends who love you and check in on a daily basis. She was used to targeting people who were alone and vulnerable."

"Mmm." She continued toward the living room. "Too bad she and Erika and Joe didn't take their lumps twenty-four years ago. It's always better to face up to the consequences of your actions."

When he didn't respond, she set the shrimp down on the table and turned.

He'd stopped on the threshold. As the soft classical music she'd selected played in the background, he scanned the small, linen-draped table in front of the roaring fire and the candles flickering throughout the room.

"And you said I went to a lot of trouble."

"It's our holiday dinner, after all. Christmas will be great at my mom's, but this is our private celebration. I wanted it to be memorable."

But truth be told, simply being with Mac created all the romantic ambiance she needed—beginning with that dramatic night here in this house when he'd shifted from colleague to suitor. While she'd slept through the crime scene activity, he'd kept watch, waking her every hour or two to test her blood sugar. He'd followed that up with their first Saturday night date, which had exceeded all of her expectations. And the romance had continued nonstop ever since.

He set down their drinks and turned to her, his gaze warm and tender and everything she'd ever hoped to see in the eyes of the man she loved.

And she loved Mac, heart and soul.

"You know . . . I was going to wait until after dinner for this, but sometimes you have to go with the flow." He reached into the pocket of his sport jacket and withdrew a small, square box wrapped in shiny paper.

Her lungs locked.

"It's an early Christmas present—for me as well as for you . . . I hope." He held it out.

"Is that . . . ?" Her voice faltered.

He pressed it into her hand. "Open it and find out."

Her fingers were shaking as much as they did when her blood sugar got too low—but sugar wasn't the culprit for her reaction tonight.

Not that kind of sugar, anyway.

Once she had the paper off, she found a small white box. Inside that box was a velvet case. Slowly she lifted the lid. A marquise-shaped diamond on a platinum band twinkled back at her.

A big marquise-shaped diamond.

"Wow."

He took her hand, his own fingers none too steady, and she finally looked up.

"I'm not much on speeches. Lance is the one in our family with the silver tongue. But I'll do my best." He swallowed, and his Adam's apple bobbed. "I told you not long after we met that I'd come to St. Louis hoping for a new start. I wanted to settle down, find a wife, and create a family. I'd never told my plan to anyone before—which made me realize that even back then, I knew you were special. Every day since has proven that to me. There isn't anything about you I don't love, from your kind heart and great sense of humor to your dedication to justice and your independence."

He paused. Took a deep breath. "I may not be the best guy you'll ever find, but I promise no one will ever love or honor you more than I do. You are—and will be—the center of my world until the day I die. And with God's grace, that will be a long, long way down the road." He worked the ring out of the box and held it up. "Lisa, will you marry me and let me spend the rest of my life proving how much I love you?"

She could only manage one word—but it was enough. "Yes."

Exhaling, he slid the ring on her finger and pulled her close, the strong, staccato beat of his heart thumping against her chest. "Man. That was harder than my toughest SEAL mission."

"Were you really worried I'd say no?" She looped her arms around his neck and lifted her chin, watching the warm firelight dance across his skin.

"A guy never knows for sure until he hears the magic word."

"Can I add a few more?"

"Of course."

"I knew from the beginning you were special too. And even though I'd changed my life, hoping to find the same kind of relationship you were looking for, I hadn't made any effort to reach that goal. It was almost as if I was waiting for you. I think God intended us for each other all along. I love you, Mac McGregor, and I always will—through sunlight and shadows, through laughter and tears, through good times and bad." She traced her finger over the strong line of his jaw. "Feel more reassured now?"

"I will—after we seal this engagement with a kiss."

As she went up on tiptoe to meet him, a happy yip sounded from the doorway.

They turned in unison.

Tally was sitting on his haunches, watching the show, his tail sweeping back and forth over the floor.

Safe in the shelter of Mac's arm, Lisa smiled. "I bet he sees more gourmet dog biscuits in his future."

A chuckle rumbled deep in his chest. "A safe bet. Endless dog biscuits for Tally, endless love for the lady who rescued him—and who stole my heart. Sound appealing?"

"Sounds perfect."

"Then let's get this show on the road."

And without wasting another word, he did.

Read an excerpt from BOOK 2 in the

MEN OF VALOR

series

★ ★ ★

COMING

SPRING 2016

What was that odd shimmer in the night sky?

Christy Reed crested the hill on the undulating rural road and peered at the eerie dome of light above the trees in the distance. On a chilly, clear November evening, the heavens should be pitch black save for the stars strewn across the inky firmament, not tainted by unnatural illumination.

The road dived again, the woods snuffing out her view of the mysterious glow. But the twinge of unease that had compelled her to head to her sister's tonight instead of waiting until tomorrow intensified.

Pressing on the accelerator, she swooped through the dip in the road and shot up again.

At the peak of the next hill, her twinge of apprehension morphed to panic.

Flames were strafing the night sky—in the vicinity of her sister's house.

Please, God, no! Not again! We can't take any more trauma!

Smashing the accelerator to the floor, she plunged down the hill.

Only then did she notice the police cruiser at the bottom, angled sideways, blocking access to the narrow road that led to the Missouri farmhouse her sister called home.

She flinched as the harsh flashing lights strobed across her retinas. Lights that screamed emergency. Disaster. Trauma.

All the things that had changed her world forever six months ago.

Fingers clenched around the wheel, she sped toward the vehicle, screeching to a stop beside it.

As a uniformed officer emerged from the shadows and circled around to her side of the car, she fumbled for the auto window opener. Lowered the insulating sheet of glass. Inhaled the smoke-fouled air that leached into the car.

The coil of fear in the pit of her stomach tightened.

"Can I help you, ma'am?"

"I need to get down that road." Her last word hitched.

"Do you live that way?"

"No. My s-sister does."

Twin furrows dented the man's brow. "What's her name?"

"Ginny R-Reed."

"Hold on a minute." He pulled his radio off his belt and melted back into the shadows.

Christy closed her eyes and clung to the wheel, shudders coursing through her.

Please, Lord, let there be some simple reason Ginny wasn't answering her phones or returning calls all evening! A dead cell. An emergency at work. Anything that's not connected to this fire.

"Ma'am?"

She jerked her eyes open.

"There's a fire at your sister's house. I'll move my vehicle so you can get through. One of the officers at the scene will meet you."

Her knuckles whitened as she struggled to suck in air. "Is she okay?"

He shifted from one foot to the other, the leather of his belt squeaking as he rested one hand on his gun. "I don't know. But they're doing everything they can to contain the fire so they can get inside."

"You mean she's still in the house!" Hysteria raised the pitch of her voice.

"They aren't certain of that. Give me a minute."

Before she could respond, he jogged toward his car—putting as much distance between him and her questions as possible.

Because he didn't have the answers . . . or because he didn't want to deliver more bad news?

Please, God, let it be the former!

The instant the cruiser moved aside, she jerked her wheel to the right and accelerated down the woods-rimmed road. The glow grew brighter as she approached, and fingers of fire stabbed the night sky above parched leaves not yet willing to relinquish their tenuous hold on life.

Her lungs locked.

This was bad.

Really bad.

Though she tried to prepare for the worst, her first full look at Ginny's small, two-story clapboard farmhouse across a field of shriveled cornstalks destroyed the fragile hold she had on her composure.

The whole structure was engulfed in flames.

No, no, no, no, no!

Another uniformed officer appeared in her headlights, waving her to the shoulder before she could turn into her sister's driveway.

Swerving to the right, she bumped onto the uneven ground, then flung open her door and scrambled from the car. Despite the crisp chill of the late fall evening, the air was hot.

Too hot.

"Ma'am?"

She tore her gaze away from the fire to focus on the officer. Flashes of light darted across the woman's face, giving her a macabre appearance.

"Why don't you wait over there?" She gestured toward an ambulance parked halfway up Ginny's driveway, off to the side.

The paramedics were standing idle and silent at the rear door, watching the blaze.

Waiting for a victim to treat.

Meaning no one had yet rescued Ginny.

Unless . . .

Was it possible she wasn't here? Maybe she *had* been called in to work for an emergency.

Please!

Christy squinted toward the garage at the rear of the house . . . and her stomach bottomed out.

The door was open—and Ginny's car was inside.

Her sister was here.

But where?

Lifting her head, she homed in on Ginny's second-floor bedroom. The window was cracked open, as usual. Even on the coldest nights, her sister liked fresh air. There was no movement from inside, but maybe . . .

She grabbed the woman's arm and pointed. "That's my sister's bedroom! She might be in bed. Can't you get a ladder up there and—"

"Clear the collapse zone. Now!"

At the sudden, barked order, the firefighters who'd been struggling to quench the hungry flames dropped their hoses and scattered.

Seconds later, a shudder rippled through the house. The siding buckled. Then, spewing sparks high into the black sky, the second floor collapsed into the raging inferno below like an ancient Viking funeral pyre.

Christy stared in horror at the consuming flames, the world around her receding.

No!

This wasn't happening.

It couldn't be.

But the roar of the voracious blaze and the surge of scorching heat against her face mocked her denial, searing the ghastly truth across her mind.

No one could survive a fire like this.

Ginny was dead.

Despite the waves of heat rolling off the collapsed house, a numbing cold gripped her heart. Shudders rolled through her body. Blackness nipped at the edges of her consciousness.

And somewhere in the distance, screams ripped through the air.

Again.

And again.

And again.

Christy squeezed her eyes shut and wedged her hands against her ears, trying to shut them out.

But she couldn't.

Because they were her own.

Two Months Later

"You settling in okay?"

At the question, Lance McGregor swiveled in his desk chair. Mark Sanders stood on the threshold of the cubicle, holding two disposable cups of coffee. His new FBI colleague held one out.

"Thanks." Lance leaned forward and took it. "Still adjusting to St. Louis in the winter. When does the January thaw hit?"

"Don't hold your breath. I was referring to the job."

Lance took a sip of his brew and gestured to the warren of cubicles in the center of the St. Louis FBI office. "This bull pen arrangement will take some getting used to. Ditto for the suit and tie."

"You'll get there."

371

"I appreciate the encouragement—especially in light of the source." When Mark responded only with a raised eyebrow, Lance tipped his chair back and grinned. "As a former member of the Bureau's Hostage Rescue Team and the current leader of this office's SWAT team, I suspect you'd prefer to be in field dress chasing bad guys too."

"You've done some homework."

"I like to know the players."

"A skill that would have served you well as a Delta Force operator."

Touché.

"I see you've been checking me out too."

"SOP for new agents—especially ones fresh out of the academy. For the record, you came out rosy instead of green."

"Nice to know."

Mark took a sip of his own java. "If you're interested in the SWAT team, let me know. It's an ancillary duty, so don't expect any perks for volunteering, but we can always use members with your background. The Delta Force operators I've met were the kind of guys I'd want watching backs when lives are on the line."

Despite Lance's valiant attempt to hold on to his grin, it slipped a hair. "Thanks. But my first priority is to get the lay of the land."

"Makes sense." Though Mark's words were agreeable, the slight thinning of his eyes told Lance the man had picked up on his sudden discomfort. "If you want to consider it down the road, the door's open." Raising his cup in salute, he strolled off.

Lance waited until he disappeared, then pivoted back to his desk, mouth flattening. His new colleague's offer was flattering, but the SWAT team wasn't in his future. Sure, he'd handle trouble if any came his way as a special agent. But he was done seeking it out. Done having to watch people's backs 24/7. Done trying to be Superman.

Because even Superman had his Achilles' heel—and if you played the odds long enough, you were bound to lose. Mistakes happened.

And sometimes they were deadly.

A bead of sweat popped out on his forehead, and he scrubbed it away. Enough. He was past this. History couldn't be rewritten. It was over. Finished. He'd made his peace with that and moved on.

But if that was true, why had a simple invitation to join the SWAT team twisted his gut and short-circuited his lungs?

Blowing out a breath, he raked his fingers through his hair. This was *not* a complication he needed three days into his new career as a special agent.

The phone on his desk rang, and he grabbed for it, checking the digital display. A call from the receptionist might not provide much of a distraction, but it would do a better job redirecting his thoughts than attending insomnia-inducing meetings or reviewing eye-glazing case files—his lot since reporting for duty.

"Hi, Sharon. What's up?"

"Do you have anything urgent on your desk?"

"Not unless reviewing old 302s qualifies."

A chuckle came over the line. "I figured Steve would give you a pile of evidentiary interviews to read. I think it's his version of hazing for the new agents in the reactive squad. Kind of an endurance contest."

"If it is, I'm failing."

"Maybe I can rescue you. You ready for a real case?"

"More than."

"Don't be too anxious. I might be handing you a fruitcake."

"Better a fruitcake than files. What have you got?"

"I have no idea. She won't tell me. Won't give me her name, either. Just said she needs to talk to an agent."

"Okay. Go ahead and transfer her."

"I jotted down her number from caller ID in case you need it. The fourth digit is a nine."

Meaning there was a strong chance she was calling from a pay phone.

"Thanks."

"Good luck." The line clicked. "Ma'am, I'm putting you through to Agent McGregor." Another click as Sharon exited the call.

Lance leaned back in his chair. "This is Agent McGregor. Who am I speaking with?"

Silence.

"Ma'am?"

A beat of silence passed. Two. Three. He heard an indrawn breath. "A situation has come up that merits FBI involvement—but I can't discuss it by phone."

Still no name.

"Would you like to come to our office?"

"No! That would be too dangerous." She sounded agitated. Scared, even. But she was lucid. That was a plus. "I'd like to set up a meeting on neutral territory. I want it to look like friends getting together, in case anyone's watching."

He tapped the tip of his pen against the tablet in front of him. Paranoia—or valid caution? Too soon to tell. "Can you give me a clue what this is about?"

More silence.

He waited her out.

"I think it . . . it could be kidnapping."

He sat up straighter. "Have you called the police?"

"I can't do that. Please, I'll explain when I see you. Besides, this would fall under FBI jurisdiction."

"Is a child involved?"

"No."

He doodled a series of concentric circles on the blank sheet of paper in front of him. The woman was articulate, and she sounded intelligent. Yes, she could be a nut—but the mere mention of kidnapping warranted further investigation.

"All right. Where would you like us to meet you?"

"Us?" He could hear the frown in her voice.

"I'd like to bring another agent along." That was the usual protocol in a situation this filled with unknowns.

"No. Just you."

The tension in her words told him she was getting ready to hang up. Better to agree to her terms than lose her. He could always call for support if he needed it.

"Okay. Where?"

"I was thinking a Panera. They're busy, and the noise level should give us some privacy. But please wear casual clothes. A suit would draw too much attention."

The lady had thought this through.

He put a dot in the middle of his circles to complete the bull's-eye. "Which one?"

"It doesn't matter."

"Brentwood." The central corridor was a reasonable choice. Besides, it was the only Panera he'd visited to date. Why not make this easy on himself?

"Fine. I get off work at five. I'm available after that."

He'd have to bail on dinner with Mac, but his older sibling would understand. Police detectives didn't keep regular hours, either.

"Let's make it seven. I need to go home and change first. How will I recognize you?"

"I'll be wearing jeans and a dark green sweater. I have long-ish auburn hair."

"Got it."

"I'll see you at seven."

The instant the line went dead, he punched in Sharon's

extension and got the source number. A quick check of the crisscross directory confirmed what he'd suspected—the call had come from a pay phone.

The woman wasn't taking any chances.

A ping of adrenaline prickled his nerve endings. At least his first case was intriguing.

And even if the meeting led nowhere, a clandestine rendezvous was a whole lot more exciting than reading old case files.

Acknowledgments

O nce again, a number of people offered me gracious assistance with this book. I'd like to thank the following:

Lieutenant Tom Larkin, Commander of the St. Louis County Police Department's Bureau of Crimes Against Persons. Thank you for answering my questions promptly and thoroughly—and for giving me a great referral for forensic anthropology. I did accelerate the DNA extraction process and tox screen results, so please forgive me for taking some artistic license to keep the pace of the story moving!

Investigator Lindsay Trammell (PhD, D-ABMDI), St. Louis County Office of the Medical Examiner, for assisting with all things anthropological—and for the great idea about tree roots!

Glenn Kopp, Horticulture Information Manager at Missouri Botanical Garden, who helped me fine-tune the cedar-tree scenario that plays a key role in the case.

FBI veteran Tom Becker, now chief of police in Frontenac, Missouri, who weighed in on Bureau-related material and walked me through the coordination that would be done between an FBI legal attaché and a foreign law enforcement organization.

Captain Ed Nestor from the Chesterfield, Missouri, Police De-partment, my first law enforcement source when I branched into suspense, who continues to offer assistance whenever needed. Thanks for all the help with missing persons databases on this one!

The superb team at Revell. Thank you for going above and beyond to make my books the best they can be and to help them stand out in a crowded marketplace. You are a blessing.

My mom and dad. I feel so very lucky to have you as parents. Thank you for your unwavering support, constant encourage-ment, and unconditional love. Much of the credit for any success I've achieved belongs to you.

All the readers who buy my books—and allow me to give voice to all the characters who want their stories told.

And finally, my husband, Tom, who has been in my cheering section for more than twenty-five years. Thank you for taking such a keen interest in my career, for reading the drafts of my sus-pense novels and offering great insights, and for understanding—and respecting—that writing is very hard work.

Irene Hannon is a bestselling, award-winning author who took the publishing world by storm at the tender age of ten with a sparkling piece of fiction that received national attention.

Okay . . . maybe that's a slight exaggeration. But she *was* one of the honorees in a complete-the-story contest conducted by a national children's magazine. And she likes to think of that as her "official" fiction-writing debut!

Since then, she has written more than forty-five contemporary romance and romantic suspense novels. Irene has twice won the RITA award—the "Oscar" of romantic fiction—from Romance Writers of America, and her books have also been honored with a National Readers' Choice award, three HOLT medallions, a Daphne du Maurier award, a Retailers Choice award, a Booksellers' Best Award, and two Reviewers' Choice awards from *RT Book Reviews* magazine. In 2011, *Booklist* included one of her novels in its Top 10 Inspirational Fiction list for the year. She is also a two-time Christy award finalist.

Irene, who holds a BA in psychology and an MA in journalism, juggled two careers for many years until she gave up her executive corporate communications position with a Fortune 500 company to write full-time. She is happy to say she has no regrets! As she points out, leaving behind the rush-hour commute, corporate politics, and a relentless BlackBerry that never slept was no sacrifice.

A trained vocalist, Irene has sung the leading role in numerous community theater productions and is also a soloist at her church.

When not otherwise occupied, she and her husband enjoy traveling, Saturday mornings at their favorite coffee shop, and spending time with family. They make their home in Missouri.

To learn more about Irene and her books, visit www.irenehannon.com. She is also active on Facebook and Twitter.

Meet

IRENE HANNON

at www.IreneHannon.com

Learn news, sign up for her mailing list,
and more!

Find her on

"The Private Justice series . . . delivers on every level."

—CBA Retailers + Resources

"Whether it's a fast-paced suspense or a contemporary [romance], fans can't get enough of Hannon's uplifting stories."
—*RT Book Reviews*